CHAPTER 1

N erissa Khoury relaxed on the couch in the well-insulated room in Manassas, Virginia. Known in technical circles as a Faraday Cage, it had been constructed to filter out virtually all Radio Frequency, or RF, waves that permeated the atmosphere. Additionally, the temperature, humidity and air quality were precisely adjusted to the occupant's preference and were therefore near perfect, and there was no ambient noise in the room that the occupants did not generate themselves.

It had been warm in Washington and since she did not have to meet with anyone special that day, she had gone the route of comfort, and chosen blue gym shorts, a white t-shirt, and flip-flops. She had put her hair up under the hat she had picked up at the Mari Vineyards in Michigan a year earlier, which now rested on the table just a few feet away. Her cell phone, car keys and the intriguing oval opal ring, were in her desk down the hall. The key fob and cell phone had obvious RF transmission capabilities. The opal ring had a miniature passive circuit that, when waved over a hidden reader in the wall, retracted the steel bolts in the heavy door leading from the lobby to their suite. It sent an identification signal to a sophisticated video-analytic application that synced with her complete personnel and medical history. If anyone but her attempted to use it for entry to the mundane-looking office, alarms would go off and bad things would happen to the unfortunate malfeasant who tried to use it unlawfully.

She steadied her breathing and concentrated on the pleasant hemi-sync track that had been prepared for her by the technical consultants in *The Tank*; the unofficial title of the highly secret remote viewer team, comprised of unique professionals from a variety of government and private backgrounds, that basically served their country as psychic spies. When the CIA publicly proclaimed that they closed the Remote Viewing program in 1995, they merely changed the access classification and location from which these activities were conducted. Further, they took it away from the Army and DIA and outsourced it to private companies, to prevent researchers from filing under the Freedom of Information Act with the hope of obtaining information about it. While the program had become increasingly effective over the years, it still represented a career path that many of the more traditional public servants in official government channels wanted to avoid. Actually, they did not even refer to it as remote viewing any longer. Too many people had heard about the practice and were able to duplicate it in the privacy of their own homes with varying degrees of success.

Confidential requests for this sort of thing were now processed as Non-Traditional Information Analysis. Besides, as counter-espionage programs went, it was only a secret from the taxpayers who chose not to acknowledge it. Most of the world's spy agencies including the Russians, Chinese and everyone else that had a chip in the game, were not only familiar with its existence, but could be counted upon to try to remote view our own viewers on occasion. There was so much information available on the internet about psychic functioning, that millions of people were experimenting with it on their own. Some better than others. Thus, the number of true secrets extant in the universe was shrinking.

Nerissa was one of the best. Had she not grown up in the business, she probably would have felt isolated and abnormal by this point in her life. But from a young age, her mother, Yasmina, had urged her to be herself and confront her fears about the process. About how it was okay to be different from the other kids. Her mother had been there from the start at the Institute and was able to guide her competently, and lovingly, along as she explored her own psychic abilities. Her grandmother had held the gift of second

UNFINISHED CACOPHONY

Eric Lowans

TERRAPIN Group Publishing LLC

TERRAPIN Group Publishing LLC

ISBN: 978-0-578-27963-3

PRINTED IN THE UNITED STATES OF AMERICA

sight herself. Thus, one could suggest that she was merely carrying on the family business.

The Institute, as it was known then, was established by a team of physicists and engineers to study the phenomenon of Extra Sensory Perception back in the early 1970's after a report leaked out that the Soviets were using it, quite successfully, as another intelligence source. The CIA was curious to see if the reports were deliberate and calculated misinformation placed by our enemies, or if there was really something to it. The government initially outsourced the study to a west-coast university laboratory and were stunned by the reports they got back. Somewhat in disbelief, they sent an Army officer out to try to poke holes in their research, only to find that there were no holes. Further, to the consternation of the old-world brains that continued to run Washington at the time, the Army officer, a true skeptic, was taught how to do it in a couple of hours and produce extraordinary results.

Now, the United States government was left with a dilemma. Their reports indicated the Soviets were exploiting it, and their study demonstrated that it was quite possible to generate intelligence data remotely. No one knew how it worked. It just did. The scary part, for them, was that anyone could be taught how to do it. One did not have to be a military officer, or an intelligence operative. Anyone who had an interest could learn the protocol. And so it became necessary for the government to step down as hard as it could to create the narrative that anyone who believed in psychic functioning was simply a kook. It was not a huge reach. In years past, the Catholic church had burned people at the stake for just bringing the idea into the confessional.

At five foot four and just over a hundred thirty pounds, the stunning raven-haired beauty was still running marathons at the age of fifty-two. Her penetrating brown eyes had seen things that the rest of the world could not fathom. She had been to other times and unreachable places, including other planets and star systems. She could mentally interrupt electronic circuits and topple guidance systems anywhere in the world. She was an intelligence asset that the government could not allow to fall into the wrong hands. No matter what.

She had never known her father. In the physical world, anyway. A Major in the United States Marine Corps, he was killed in Da Nang, 9 February 1968, during the bloody Tet Offensive, after having been in-country for only six weeks. Neri was born that August and would know only stories of her father through the pictures shared by her mother.

It had all started early for her. Neri's mother had been one of the first US Government psychics assigned to a program that would know many code names over the years. Yasmina had seen the program go from the research phase to the operational phase and, after twenty years, she gradually emerged as the program's chief executive. With that promotion came not only exposure to more intriguing taskings, but the need to learn the back-channel ways to secure funding and manage a government contract budget. It was a crazy time. Most members of the political machine denied the existence and utility of psychic functioning, but at the same time felt no qualms about reaping the benefits of information that was otherwise unobtainable from any other intelligence source. But now, after years of evolution, Yasmina ran the privatized group of government spooks, while a tendentious and tenebrous gentleman named Paul ran the government side; a group often referred to as *The Tank*.

Her cool-down period complete, Neri drew a nonsensical ideo-gram in the top left corner of the blank page that she had pulled off the stack. She had done her best to quiet the earthly issues and problems that plague most of the people who think they have a good handle on the world. She had seen too much. She knew how the universe worked, how it started and where it would end, but she needed to escape all of that. She needed to be present, and she needed to be totally unbiased in the perceptions she was about to receive from that illusive database known to some as the Akashic Record. She needed to access it with a clean mind, a blank slate. She had to sweep all her earthly thoughts into a mental dustpan so that she could lock them away until she came back from her psychic journey.

What she was doing was not weird, by any stretch of the imagination. Millions of people meditated each day with the goal of getting to where she was right then. Some people relaxed through meditation, some through chemicals, and some through a toxic collection of artificial depressants and narcotics that got them to a place of peace. Unfortunately, drugs and alcohol impeded the ability of a person to connect with the spiritual realm. The ancients, especially the Hindus, used reverberating sound waves to achieve this mental plateau. The Buddhist monks chanted, "Auommmm."

It was resonance. Something that they had been doing for centuries that would not be confirmed in scientific laboratories for many years to come. Scientists who needed big words to explain simple concepts called it Non-linear Fractal Resonance. The ability or process to use frequencies, or musical tones, to achieve a variety of results. Surprising results. Some studies proved that one could use certain frequencies to relax. Or heal. Others proved that you could move or suspend objects, seemingly weightlessly, by forcing certain frequencies through transducers.

Frequency had a special meaning for her. She had worked her way through San Jose State as a singer in local bands and had a voice that was often compared to the late Doris Day. She could perform the icon's songs so flawlessly that with one's eyes closed; they could easily envision that they were in the same room with the international music phenom. Music helped establish a mood. Whichever mood she wanted to be in. It cheered her up when she was sad. It kept her awake on long drives.

Being raised in a Lebanese American household had also allowed Nerissa to easily learn Arabic and French, with native proficiency. Her language skills, her natural beauty and her unparalleled psychic functioning caused organizational salivation within the CIA. They called upon her often to help them wade through the unique political discord in the Middle East and provide them with solutions that were otherwise unavailable using traditional sources.

Because she was far too valuable to send abroad, her skills were often exploited in a room in Langley, even though her special type of intelligence could be collated from any place in the world, including the Institute's offices in Manassas. The US government could not risk sending her anywhere in the Middle East, even if she were provided the level of protection afforded a sitting US President. Presidents come and go, but she was a precious commodity, and there were too many people, as well as governments, who would want her if they knew who she was.

She gently touched the ideogram and waited for sensations to rise from the depths of her sub-conscious mind. She concentrated on the target coordinate; a simple reference number that drew her to something that was in an envelope on her tasker's desk in another part of the country. She focused on TR71788. The number itself meant nothing. It had probably been hastily written on an envelope by her tasker, who might or might not know what was in the envelope. For all the tasker knew, the envelope might have contained another coordinate, or a photograph. Or often a drawing of something that her clients wanted to know more about. Somewhere out there in the universe, the information was there. It was waiting for her to receive it and record it. Somehow.

Psychic information did not surface to the conscious brain in any logical form. Or language. Or sequence. It emerged in the form of gestalts. Forms, shapes, patterns. Even by the end of the session, it was highly likely that she would not know the thing that they wanted her to describe. At some point in the future, her sponsors might give her feedback and let her know she either attached to the target or did not. Sometimes, she saw events reported in the news a few days later and was able to discern their relevance to her assignment.

"A place." She wrote on the upper left-hand side of the page. Her target was a specific location of interest.

"Solid. Well-built." She noted.

"Relatively recent construction but considered old by some standards."

She took a couple of deep, even breaths and tried to relax. She was receiving input. She was comfortable that she had locked on to the target that had been assigned her.

"Respected." She wrote, and then added "A monument of sorts?"

"Constructed for a special purpose. By the government. By a leader?"

She tapped the ideogram lightly and traced along it as data began to surface. "Gray...or colorless. Hard."

"Secure."

Sensations ran through her body. "Valuable."

She thought for a moment and then drew a line through her entry and wrote "Was built to house valuables. Like a bank."

In her mind she could see wealth. Importance. Security.

It had financial significance, but it also had historical significance.

"A large plot of land. Surrounded by force. Human force. Secure."

"Not just wealth, but items of importance. Documents. Trappings of power and greatness. Historical documents."

"Pride of a people."

She heard a buzzing in her ears. As she attempted to shake it off, it gradually evolved into more of a hum. A harmonic. A piercing vibration that alternated between pleasant and discordant. A noise that somehow felt like movement. Work. Whatever was in the structure was being given to others. Lawfully, but quietly. Secretly. The tone seemed to modulate and then settled on a single perfect note, like a concert orchestra tuning their instruments before a performance.

The valuables contained therein were being traded; exchanged for something. For something important. There was agreement among everyone. The valuables had been given, donated. Under duress, perhaps from some government decree. But it was for the greater good. It's a secret. No one could know. Serious ramifications if it ever leaked out. Someone high in government has been killed to prevent his disclosure of it.

She traced her pencil lightly back and forth across the page waiting for some sort of image to emerge. Signals were being sent from her sub-conscious to her conscious mind through her hand. A layer cake. A square-sided layer cake made of concrete, steel, marble, granite. A structure that could withstand the ravages of time and weather. Of...of physical attack. Square? Squares stacked. Concrete layer cake, stacked. Protected. Can't get to it. Fences. Barricades.

The hum grew louder. She saw an entity. Several entities, certainly not of this world or dimension. They needed what was in this structure. We gave it to them.

Stan Marchand and his regular golf partner, a retired oilman named George Griffiths, were playing the back nine of the East Course at Bear Creek. They needed a pleasant change from their weekly ritual at their club in Plano, the famed Gleneagles Country Club. It was George's seventy-fifth birthday and Stan suggested doing something that neither of them had done in a while. Several options were advanced and discussed, but in the end, it came back to golf. Just, golf at a different course.

The Ted Robinson-designed course had been on Golf Digest's list of the top fifty resort courses in the country, beautiful and reasonably challenging for the bogey golfer. Though not a ball-eater like Pebble Beach, the course boasted a slope rating from the Championship tees of 138. The slope rating of a course was a complex mathematical process that did not indicate a course's difficulty so much as it was an admonition to bogey golfers, as to how they would fare against scratch shooters during the round. It was sometimes likened to the way that ski resorts defined their snow-covered hills according to a formula of green circles, being the easiest, blue squares of intermediate difficulty, and black diamonds, which were for the more advanced skiers. However, a black diamond in the Midwest, might likely be a green circle in a place like Stowe,

Vermont, where the mountains were taller and the trails more exacting. It offered an idea as to what one might be up against, but the rating was not transferable from location to location without some degree of understanding and personal deliberation.

Marchand himself had just turned sixty-three, but still maintained the muscular chest and shoulders atop a flat abdomen, which enabled him to fit into the same suits he had worn while protecting US Presidents and other key dignitaries for more than twenty years as an agent with the United States Secret Service. His dark skin, angular jaw, bright smile, and aquiline nose had served as a model for how agents were supposed to look while standing next to the most powerful man in the world, and endeared him to members of the opposite sex, regardless of their marital status. His appearance, intellect and conversational skills had supported his career goals, but had caused him problems on more than one occasion when he was off the clock. Men trusted him with their lives, but not their wives.

"It's my birthday." Griffiths said as he bent to shove his tee and ball into the ground with engineering precision. "Are you gonna spot me a stroke or two?" He had asked that morning on the number one tee.

Despite a bumpy start to their relationship, the two men had grown close over the years. Stan had been the agent in charge of a detail for then President George W. Bush as TRAILBLAZER, or simply *43,* as he was unofficially referred to by many agents, visited the oilman's sprawling home near Plano. Secret Service regulations required a safe space for their Protectees, which meant the large Texan had to lock his guns up for the duration of the visit. "You're taking my gun? In my own home?" Griffiths bellowed that night. "You don't never take a Texan's gun away from him son!"

Stan had done his best to diplomatically explain the process, and eventually Griffiths acquiesced. He knew Marchand was just doing his job, and the reality was that if someone had tried to attack his residence that night, there would have been more firepower on the ground than the Cubans had faced October 25, 1983, in Grenada, as Stan's group, the 2nd Battalion of the 8th Marine Regiment, landed south of Pearls Airport.

Coming in on CH-46 and CH-53 helicopters at five-thirty in the morning, the battalion captured Pearls Airport, after encountering only light resistance. It had not been much of a battle, but it was his first and last in the Marine Corps. He suppressed resentment of his Army counterparts who seemed to have been awarded medals for just about everything. However, the Navy and Marine Corps were still traditionally strict about issuing awards for just doing one's job. Something had to be truly meritorious to qualify. So, while the Army gave out medals with seemingly reckless abandon, the Marines gave out a simple Expeditionary Award.

Stan did not even qualify for the National Defense Service Medal that thousands of troops had been given for enlistment during Viet Nam and the Gulf wars since. Nevertheless, he had done his duty when called. He was a patriot at heart, and he had served his country when it was his time. Besides, people knew he had made his mark and demonstrated his professionalism many times in the years afterwards.

Stan shook off the memory and replied with a smile, "I'll give you a stroke on the front nine and one on the back nine. But at ten bucks a hole, that's about as far as I care to tread right now."

Now, two strokes behind, Griffiths eyed the hole and adjusted his stance a bit to the left. It wasn't the money. The large Texan could easily buy and sell the entire golf course if he had wanted. It was for honor. For bragging rights. He carefully drew his driver back and followed through flawlessly as the connection with the clubhead brought a distinctive *whoosh-tink*, indicating the shot had connected well and true. He watched with a smile as it sailed straight down the fairway, and with a suitable roll, landed him about two hundred sixty yards in the middle of the fairway.

Griffiths picked up his tee and grinned broadly. "I'll take it!"

The course was notorious for its deep roughs, large bunkers, and challenging water hazards. Well-manicured Bermuda fairways were outlined with mature oak trees that seemed to jump out at golf balls like an NBA player blocking a shot at the basket. Naturally, because they were playing from the championship tees, and it was already nearing ninety degrees, it was going to be a long course.

"Not bad." Marchand said as he flipped someone else's tee out of the way to make room for his. He needed to play his own game. He didn't want to compete with the Texan. He had to fight the urge to swing hard in an effort to outdrive his friend. The club would do the work. All he had to do was remember the fundamentals and swing slow and smooth.

"You're gonna really have to smash it to out drive me." The oil man said with an obvious hint of gamesmanship.

Marchand brought the huge clubhead back and focused on his technique. There was a slight wobble at the apex of his arc and then he brought the clubhead back through just as he had planned. Ignoring his competitor, it was slow and smooth. He forced himself to keep his head down until he knew the ball was airborne. When he allowed himself to look up, it was gaining altitude, straight down the fairway.

Together they watched as the ball carried two hundred fifty yards before bouncing haughtily past Griffith's ball by at least fifteen yards. "Yeaahh." Marchand said smugly. "That'll play too."

It was a tight competition for the remainder of the round and by the time they putted out on number eighteen, both men were physically drained. Miraculously, Griffiths sank a forty-foot put that gave him a birdie. But Marchand's par kept him two strokes ahead. With the two strokes he had offered up at the beginning of the round, that made them even. On paper, anyway. The truth was that both men were dehydrated and dragging and could not wait to get out of the hot and humid Texas afternoon, which was approaching one hundred degrees.

George Griffiths lifted his cap and ran his hand through his thinning silver hair, drenched with sweat. "Okay, this officially sucks. I think I could have had you on sixteen, but my game just went to shit. I can't take the heat like I used to. What do you say you buy me a nice eighteen-year-old...single malt, that is." He winked. "And we'll call it a day."

"Agreed." Marchand replied as he bent to retrieve his ball from the cup.

Marchand steered the cart into the parking lot and parked it halfway between his Cosmos Blue Audi Q3, and Griffiths' custom Chevy 2500 HD dually, parked next to him, which proudly flaunted the elaborate steel bumper system that could probably smash through most concrete block walls.

Owing to the heat that they had both tolerated for the past five hours, they broke with tradition and asked for their eighteen-year-old Glenmorangie to be served on the rocks. Most single-malt drinkers preferred to savor the distilled beverage neat, the way the Scots had intended it. But neither man was standing on historical preference when it was so wicked hot outside.

Halfway through the first drink, the suspense had gotten to Griffiths, and he felt compelled to ask as Marchand scrolled through the messages on his phone. "You never miss a chance to tell me about how *retired* you are, but you've been flipping through that thing every five minutes since we left number fifteen. What's going on? Are you working again? And don't tell me it's *nothing* because I know better."

Marchand looked at the tasking he had received from Grand Emperor Insurance and quickly exited, laying the phone face down on the table. "I'm still doing some consulting for the government." He said quietly as he sipped his drink.

"Consulting? Really? Is that government-speak for simple double-dipping or have you got something really exciting going on?"

Marchand exhaled through tight lips. "Seriously, it's nothing. I analyze reports."

"Uh huh. What kind of reports? You're still in the game, aren't you?"

"George, it's not like you think. Every once in a while Uncle Sam sends me something to review, and I review it. No big deal. I look at it and give them an opinion. Nuttin' more."

"You're full of shit. I know you. If that's all it was, it wouldn't bother you on the golf course. And I could tell, on the last few holes, you were bothered by something."

"George, you're a fucking genius at the oil business, but you're not a behavioral scientist. Believe me, it's nothing that you'd be interested in. Mundane threat reports about stuff that's not in the news." He recited, omitting the word *yet,* which probably should have followed the sentence.

Griffiths downed his scotch and signaled the waiter for another round. "Oh, come on. It's just you and me. You know I spent a couple years in the Army, right? Chemical Corps. Fort Leonard Wood. I had a clearance, so you can tell me...something."

Stan grinned. "It's got nothing to do with chemicals or biological stuff." Stan downed his glass as he surmised that a refill was close at hand. "Besides, until I read the report, I really don't know what it is."

"Anything that would affect oil prices?" Griffiths pressed.

Stan smiled slyly. "Hardly. But if I see something that might affect your portfolio, I'll be sure to let you know." It was the tiniest of lies, uttered with the best of intentions.

⎯⎯⎯►((◆))◄⎯⎯⎯

The man known only as Paul to an intimate microcosm of the intelligence community, was ready to call it a day and lock things up before leaving his eighth-floor office in the nondescript high-rise building off Richmond Highway in Crystal City Virginia. Though the building had been in the same place for years, it had undergone structural and cosmetic upgrades, as well as an address change, as attitudes towards racial equity drove communities to be more aware of the iniquities of the past. Originally having a Jefferson Davis Highway address, with little fanfare, it was converted to Richmond Highway on January 1, 2019. In 2021, other parts of US Route 1, that had not already been renamed through other political processes, became Emancipation Highway.

He looked at the monitor on the left side of his desk. He had three laptops; one for US government communications including JWICS, one for open communications, and a special one for communications among his team members that went through a ProtonMail encryption process.

ProtonMail had replaced the PGP product that public and private agencies had been using for the past twenty years. Based in Switzerland, the company offered public and private-key communications through their own servers with such confidence that they themselves could not decrypt messages without the private key that the intended recipient alone would have. Because data was encrypted in all the steps of the transmission process, the risk of unlawful interception was mathematically eliminated.

He examined the message from STARLET2 and compared the task reference number to his assignments list, before looking at her summary and the attached notes and sketches. While there were several highly placed members of the intelligence community who were familiar with her work product, Paul was one of only a handful of people in the world who knew that STARLET2 was Nerissa Khoury.

He went to the far side of his office and opened the second drawer down of the heavy-duty Fire King security cabinet. After plucking the eight-by-ten manilla envelope from a stack wrapped with a large green rubber band, he returned to his desk and sat down. He read over her narrative and tried to digest it before opening the envelope that had the task reference TR71788, printed in large bold type on a white slip of paper, taped to the front. He broke the transparent security seal and slid out the contents. The second he saw the large color photograph inside; he knew exactly what he was looking at. It was an aerial photograph of the iconic building that had been featured in several movies and many news stories through the years.

He looked for key words that would indicate that she had attached to the correct target. "A place, which was solid and well-built." She had written.

"Relatively recent construction but considered old by some standards." He whispered to himself.

The US Bullion Depository at Fort Knox, built by the Treasury Department in 1936, was said to be home to more than 4,500 metric tons of gold that had previously been stored in New York and Philadelphia. Popular thought at the time was that the gold would be more secure further inland, away from coastal cities that could fall victim to attack by foreign adversaries. From 1937 through 1941, it was rumored that nearly 13,000 metric tons of gold were shipped to the high-security building. And during World War II, important national documents such as the Constitution and the Declaration of Independence were also stored in one of the vaults.

"Respected. A monument of sorts?"

"Constructed for a special purpose. By the government. By a leader?"

"Gray...or colorless. Hard."

Paul was impressed. Neri had certainly locked on to the target and had received solid input. "Was built to house valuables. Like a bank."

"A large plot of land, surrounded by force. Human and mechanical force. Secure. A square layer cake made of dense concrete and steel."

Situated on 109,000 acres that crossed into three counties about fifty miles Southwest of Louisville, it was home to more than forty thousand troops armed with everything from rifles and bayonets to missiles and tanks.

"Not just wealth, but items of importance. Documents. Trappings of power and greatness. Historical documents representing the pride and conviction of a people."

The report seemed to be accurate regarding the physical attributes or *gestalts* about the target, but Paul frowned as he read the last section of her session comments.

"Viewing was distracted by discordant hum that seemed to inhibit perception. It became a buzzing sound that was not related to the task but seemed to mean something to the target."

"At some point in the past, there was significant movement. Work. Whatever was in the structure was being given to others. Lawfully, but quietly. Secretly.

"The valuables contained therein were being given, traded or donated. Exchanged for something. Under duress, perhaps from some government decree. But it was for the greater good. It's a secret. No one can know. Serious ramifications if it ever leaks out. A senior government official was killed to protect the secret."

"Non-terrestrial entities were involved and are watching now. They needed what was in this structure. We gave it to them."

Paul re-read the report and then checked his assignments list to see which agency had made the request and provided the photograph. Typically, operational taskings were requested by military intelligence units, at very high levels, or various civilian US intelligence agencies such as the CIA, DIA, NSA, or FBI. The alphabet soup of Washington. He unconsciously chewed the inside of his cheek as he scanned the intake form. "USSF?" He asked himself out loud.

The US Space Force was the newest branch of the Armed Forces. Established in December of 2019, it officially launched in Fiscal Year 2020 under the National Defense Authorization Act, reporting to the Secretary of the Air Force. A four-star general had been appointed to lead it and held a seat on the Joint Chiefs of Staff, co-equal with his Air Force counterpart. Comprised of 16,000 military and civilian personnel, the majority of whom moved over from Air Force jobs, its mission was to organize, train and equip forces to protect allied interests in space, and to provide so-called space capabilities to joint military forces.

It was strange. Paul's unit had never received a tasking from the latest addition to the Defense Department. He read through Neri's report one more time. "Why would the Space Force be interested in Fort Knox?" He muttered as he entered his password into the government computer, located in the center of his desk.

After stripping Neri's report of headers and any other identifying information, including abbreviating her code name from STARLET2 to a simple *S-2*, he cut and pasted the narrative and exhibits into an electronic form developed for supplying information to the organization's customers. He read through the finished product and then forwarded it from his internal secure computer to his slightly-less-secure government one. When he saw the report come into his in-basket, he went through the same process of stripping the information that would identify the sender, before forwarding it to his customer for the tasking, Lieutenant Colonel Jonathan Babic.

He powered down his internal department computer and replaced the picture in the manilla envelope before returning it to his secure filing cabinet. He gently pushed the heavy door shut and then spun the combination dial a few times to the left and flipped the cardboard tag that was inserted through the handle of the top drawer, from the green *open* side to the red side indicating *closed*. It was a way to quickly determine which file cabinets were unlocked and which needed to be secured prior to leaving the SCIF; the Sensitive Compartmented Information Facility in the area of the suite where his office was located.

He tossed the day's meeting notes and other printed correspondence into the paper bag with the red and white diagonal stripes. Known as a burn bag, the specially designated paper bag held sensitive materials for disposal in the team's disintegrator. Often used by government agencies and carefully vetted contractors to dispose of classified documents with confidence, the burn bag was filled with documents containing sensitive information, sealed shut, and then tossed into an expensive disintegrator to be destroyed. The person responsible for the transportation and destruction process was also carefully vetted by the United States Government, and armed to the teeth, with instructions to shoot anyone who tried to prevent him or her from destroying the bag and its contents. The Critical Documents Technicians, as they were known, were subject to random polygraph examinations several times a year to ensure that each bag given them was disposed of in accordance with policy, and that they had not seen any of the contents contained therein. It was clear that the government wanted to keep its secrets secret.

He powered down his public computer and was about to switch

off his government computer as well when he saw the message come through from his client for this most recent assignment, Lieutenant Colonel Jonathan Babic.

"Interesting. Need to meet with S-2 to discuss additional research. Most urgent."

Paul read Babic's succinct reply and instinctively glanced at his wristwatch; the stainless Omega Seamaster given him years before by his parents as a graduation present from Yale. Babic had not had the information for more than five minutes. Not nearly enough time to interpret and digest the material. Regardless, the *Tank's* protocol was straightforward.

"No." He typed on his keyboard. "All taskings must come through me." He was slightly miffed that this new customer would attempt to dodge the rules on the first tasking. Certainly, this officer must have known how the process worked. Otherwise, he never would have been directed to Paul's team in the first place.

He didn't have to wait long for Babic's reply. "Urgent request. Can get DOGHOUSE approval."

Paul winced as he read the latest code name for the NSA liaison to the White House, thoughtlessly used so lightly. The Secret Service and the White House Communications Agency assigned code names to locations and people who were active in the day-to-day operation of the government. Each President had a unique code name and each member of his or her family was assigned a code name that began with the same letter. In the Kennedy administration, for example, the White House was known as CROWN in radio communications. However, now that communications were encrypted, and the names changed with unpredictable frequency, one had to have a guide to know what the latest iteration was. Regardless, Paul didn't share information with the NSA, POTUS, or anyone else on Pennsylvania Avenue, unless it came through the secure communications conduit.

"Out of policy." He typed. "Contact me tomorrow." He was exhausted and wanted to go home.

His cursor hovered over the exit button as the response came back. "Your office 0900."

Paul shook his head as he exited his email application and powered the laptop down. "Cheeky bastard." He said as he folded all three laptops and slid them into their space in the small safe on the floor to the right of his desk. He spun the dial, and as he headed towards the door and reached for the light switch, he shook his head. "What a cheeky bastard."

———◦《◊》◦———

Two miles away, in the bowels of the Pentagon, Lieutenant Colonel Jonathan Babic reached for his STE desk phone and dialed an internal extension that rang on the other side of the building. With more than six million square feet of floor space, the Pentagon was the largest office building in the world, with a footprint exceeding eighty-five acres. Five ringed corridors, with five floors above ground and at least two below, gave it nearly eighteen miles of hallways. Two people could spend a career there and never meet each other.

Babic heard it ring twice before being answered by the authoritative voice that had been expecting his call. "Yes?"

Babic cleared his throat as quietly as he could. "Sir, we have a problem."

The deep voice that came back resounded the timbre of someone that had specialized in problems through the years. "You're sure it's her?"

"Yes, sir. It has to be. The report originated from viewer S-2. It's the same one that caused us to declassify the AATIP program two years ago." Babic said, referencing the Advanced Aerospace Threat Identification Program, as the government's UFO research department was known then. "The one we asked the agency to assign to PRODIGAL. She called herself Nerissa Fayad on that op, but I doubt that was her real name."

"Did you ask to meet her…to assign additional tasking?"

"I did, but…"

The Lieutenant General cut him off. "But he told you to fuck off."

"Yes, sir." Replied a demoralized Babic. "However, I have an appointment with Paul at 0900 tomorrow. I'll see what I can find out."

"Remember what those people do for a living. If you're thinking about bullshitting him, it won't work. Call him first thing tomorrow and cancel the meeting. I don't want to draw any more attention to this than we already have. This report she generated indicates that she simply locked on to our target. If we ask her for more information, then she'll likely discover the truth, and that won't be good for anyone." He was silent for a moment. "Cancel the meeting and apologize for violating protocol. Then give them another tasking. Something else."

"Something else, sir? Like what?"

"I don't care. Something that has real value. Remember, they're psychics. If you send them something bogus, they'll know. One way or the other. And, if it comes up in conversation, which I doubt it will, just tell him that we were trying to determine if our psychics could see more about the target than the new Russian and Chinese satellites can from space."

The General hung up and Babic replaced the handset in the cradle. "Something with value?" He asked out loud.

CHAPTER 2

The bright orange, size eleven, ASICS beat out a steady tap on the warm asphalt of the sleepy suburb of Plano as the sun rose with a reddish-pink hue in the east. Marchand knew that the day promised to be another scorcher, interspersed with thunderstorms, and he knew that he needed to run out the remnants of the Glenmorangie scotch from his evening with George Griffiths before he would be able to meet the demands of the day. He had a similar holistic cure for bouts with the common cold, which was to get out and run until he sweat-out or hacked-up any of the toxins remaining in his system.

The new Gel-Kayano shoes fit perfectly. For Marchand, it wasn't about what products the professionals used, but rather, what felt good to him. He had the same rule with golf clubs and every other product he used or consumed. The Kayano model gave him a stable stride with good heel and ankle support, and most of all, the company didn't waste time or effort making noxious political statements. They just made quality footwear, and their shoes gave him a comfortable, softer landing, without compromising speed. He didn't care about politics. He just wanted dependable products that helped him do what he wanted to do.

The meteorologists predicted that by the early afternoon it was going to be in the nineties again with humidity near sixty percent, and if Marchand was going to get out and run, he needed to do it before the sun creeped above the horizon. People were stirring in their homes, but traffic had not picked up, so he felt alone with his thoughts. As he made his way past the large homes in the upscale neighborhoods of *The Greens* and his own Willow Bend, he found his mind drifting to what each family might be facing today. The same problems that plagued the lower-middle-class urban areas were similarly prevalent in the large homes with expensive cars. Fears of job loss, concerns of spousal infidelity, trouble with the children.

He rounded Plantation Lane and headed east along West Park Boulevard. His breathing was steady, he felt good, and he was sweating just enough to know that he was getting exercise. But despite outward appearances, he was lost in thought. He was focused on the project that he knew awaited him when he returned home. The tasking from Grand Emperor Insurance. He knew it was something important because, as Griffiths had pointed out the day before, the multiple text messages had caused him to lose focus on his golf game from about hole number fifteen on. And, as everyone knew, he was supposed to be retired, and if it affected his golf game it had to be serious.

A few hundred yards from his driveway, he glanced at his watch. It had been just over thirty minutes, so he calculated that he had gotten in his three miles. Maybe three and a half. He punched in the code to raise his garage door and once inside the kitchen, disarmed the alarm panel, as the smell of coffee stimulated his olfactory senses. He poured a cup and strolled softly into the den to switch on his laptop. Out of habit, he grabbed some blank paper off his printer, and some pens and pencils from his desk drawer. He knew what he would require for the assignment but was not quite ready to start. He needed a shower and some food.

Thirty minutes later he was clean, rested and content with a half a grapefruit, an English muffin, and a bowl of oatmeal for breakfast. In the old days, it wasn't considered breakfast unless it had included a couple of eggs, and an ample amount of bacon or sausage. Nowadays though, he had to maintain a modicum of interest in nutrition just in case there was really something to all that health talk. And, if nothing more, a healthy diet kept him in good stead with Tricia, the former Air Force Tech Sergeant, almost twenty years his junior, who was now his semi-permanent houseguest. While he appreciated the wisdom of age, he truly missed his youth.

After shutting his cell phone off and turning the blinds to make the room darker, he put his feet up on his desk and leaned back in the leather office chair. The relaxing hemi sync recording began to play in his earphones as he read the email from Grand Emperor Insurance. Somewhere, presumably near Washington, someone had an envelope on his or her desk with the target reference of A6228I. And, in accordance with protocol, that particular someone might or might not know what was in the envelope. Nevertheless, his assignment was to lock onto it and tell them more about what it was or what it meant. He closed his eyes and began to push out all his earthly problems. The mortgage was paid, the utilities were paid, and the Audi was paid off. The air conditioner was working. There was no reason for concern. There was nothing in his physical existence that should distract him for the next hour or so.

Ten minutes later, his breathing had slowed and deepened, and a weightless sensation spontaneously overtook him. He was in a deep dark cavern where sound was almost nonexistent, save for a hollow echo of emptiness. The air was crisp and clean. He could feel himself drifting into a peaceful darkness of spiritual explication and comfort. All was well. He reached for the blue pen and quickly sketched a meaningless ideogram in the top left corner of the page and rested the tip of the pen on one end. To an onlooker, it might have resembled characters from a 1960's shorthand course pushed together. In reality, it meant nothing to a conscious observer. It was simply a mechanism to connect the subconscious with the conscious. Something to help him attach to the specific target that his tasker wanted to know about. The information was out there. All he had to do was let it find its way into his conscious brain, down his arm, into his hand and onto the page.

He slowly filled his lungs, inhaling through his nose, exhaling through his mouth, and began to drag the pen sideways across the page. In his mind, he saw a room. A room with human entities. Entities that were united for a common goal, but in disagreement about how to get there. There were quiet discussions and disputes between several of them. Using elementary stick figures, he sketched a table, with five or six people sitting across from each other. The gestalt he was searching for finally came to him. It was a person.

On the left side of the page, he wrote "Person", and circled it three times.

"Intelligent."

"Beautiful."

"Insightful."

"Psychic?"

"A friend. One of us?" He wrote the basic gestalts on the left side of the page. An image was trying to push through, but he wasn't getting it. "Truthful, honest, ethical."

He was distracted by an intermittent hum that seemed to be relevant to the tasking but served as more of a distraction than a facilitating input. "Someone who investigates. Someone who works for our government. For us."

Marchand sat upright as the input punched him like a fist. "Someone he had met in the physical plane." He made the notation, underlined it, and drew an asterisk to the side.

A collage of images faded in and out of the blank screen in the front of his mind. Faces. Faces he did not recognize. Men, women, young, old. Serious. Without emotion of any kind. For a fleeting moment, he saw faces that resembled Franklin D. Roosevelt and Harry Truman, but something told him that they were not the target. The target was a woman. A good woman. He tried to focus on her. Something she was doing had scared powerful people. Not angered necessarily, but things she knew were of extreme concern to them. They were sitting around a large conference table deciding what to do about her. He made the notations off on the side of his page and then tried to sketch the conference table. When he had finished his drawing, he pushed the sheet aside and reached for a blank sheet. He drew another ideogram and tapped it lightly. He tried to put himself in the conference room where the discussion was taking place. He could not make out voices, but perceived feelings. He frowned as he made a notation on the left side of the page. "Not something she did...something she might do in the future."

"She uncovered a secret." He whispered and wrote. "Something of significance. Very few people knew about it." An image was coming to him. He noted the basic gestalts: concrete or stone. Square or rectangular. A large square on the bottom, a smaller one atop that. Hard. Secure. His pen raced back and forth across the page as the image began to surface. A layer cake of stone.

Lieutenant Colonel Jonathan Babic glanced at the clock on the wall and picked up the handset from the secure telephone unit.

"Good morning." Paul answered flatly on the second ring. "I was under the impression that you were dropping by for a face-to-face meeting today."

Babic cleared his throat. "Yes. Initially, that was my plan, but after conferring with my boss we decided that a personal meeting wasn't necessary."

"I see. Then what can I do for you?" Paul asked with only mild impatience in his voice.

"We have another tasking. I'll be sending it over this morning via courier and I'd like to get your analysis as soon as possible."

"Very good." Paul looked at his assignment log and typed the request into the electronic file. When he hit the submit button, the randomizer generated the task reference number. "Please assign it Zulu Alpha seven one seven eight."

"ZA7178." Babic repeated back as he wrote the sequence on the envelope in front of him. "I'll have it there before lunch." There was a brief pause before he continued. "And...I apologize if yesterday's exchange seemed, you know, pushy. I'm new to this role."

A corner of Paul's mouth turned up into half a smile. "Not to worry. Most of our clients are new to this. Our agency is rather unorthodox and doesn't get much publicity."

"Thank you." Babic replied and hung up.

Paul replaced the handset in the cradle of his secure telephone set and frowned. Even though he commanded one of the top psychic espionage teams in the world, he hadn't any more personal psychic ability than the average person on the street. His own training and experiences into the discipline had been less than impressive, almost to the point of frustration. Nevertheless, through thirty-some years of experience he was quite adept at behavioral analysis and could tell when someone was not being completely forthcoming.

Babic's message from the day before had seemed both critical and time sensitive. But sometime after that, probably in the referenced meeting with his boss, he had been told to drop it. Paul had a nagging sensation that the new target was a diversion of sorts. But why? Nevertheless, as quickly as the thought struck him, he forced himself to get it out of his mind. He did not want to pollute the new target with any type of emotional front-loading. If there was something suspicious in the tasking, then someone in the Tank would eventually discover it.

"Jillian!" He yelled loud enough that the department's administrative assistant could hear above the usual din of a Washington DC office.

The fifty-year old matron appeared in his doorway. "You know, there's an intercom on your desk that you can use so that you don't have to bellow." She had run a marathon or two in her time and had raised three kids and had become a no-nonsense professional who was used to dishing it out when it was necessary. She had been with the department for twenty-two years at a level that insulated her from political pressures of any kind. Between her tenure, sex and her Native American ancestry, she was untouchable as they said in civil service circles. She was also indispensable. No one in the business could do what she did with the same level of proficiency.

"Sorry. Who's free right now?" Asked a sufficiently chided Paul.

She shrugged. "Everyone's got something going on. Well, except for the new guy, Hart."

Lenny Hart was the latest addition to the Tank. A retired police officer who had tried his hand in corporate security for a while, the six-foot-one, two-hundred-pound former Bando and Muay Thai kickboxer was the newest addition to the team. He had survived open heart surgery to repair a valve and was now on his third career and fourth wife. He was amiable and intuitive, and when their paths had crossed two years earlier on a missing person case, he and Paul had developed a bond of sorts.

Paul looked him up in the agency's scorecard application; the unofficial tabulation that recorded hits, misses and maybes. Thus far, Hart had been assigned as a trainee working with some of the more seasoned viewers to develop his skills. He had been a natural and seemed to take to the training rather well. On the research side, he had been ranked fairly high, but he had not yet been assigned an operational tasking.

Paul studied the results and then said, "Okay. Get him. I have a real-world op that I'd like to give him. But..." He paused. "Let's give it to two others just to hedge our bets."

Jillian Fairbanks nodded and left. A few minutes later, she returned with the sixty-year-old in tow. The sturdy lad-at-heart entered with excitement; his reading glasses perched atop his balding pate.

"You sent for me, boss?"

Paul shook his head with raised eyebrows. It was simply a term of deference, so he let the comment slide. "Yeah. Close the door and have a seat."

Hart pushed the door shut and then seated himself across the desk from his new superior. He was excited, engaged, and inquisitive, but he didn't want Paul to think that he was rushing the process. He was anxious to fit in to this unique group, if for no other reason than he'd never failed at anything before, other than marriage, and couldn't envision failing now.

Paul pulled a three-by-five index card out of his center desk drawer and wrote the task reference coordinates on it with a Sharpie marker. Theoretically speaking, he wouldn't have had to do it, but some of the newer viewers preferred to have something physical in their hands, on which they could focus. He slid it across the desk to Hart. "Here. This one is for real. I want you to take your time. Go out and walk around the block if you'd like. Get an ice-cream or something, but get your head straight, and when you come back, find one of the quiet rooms and relax. Tell me what you can about this target."

Hart looked at the coordinate, the task reference number. "Zebra Adam seven one seven eight?"

Paul winced. "You're not a cop anymore. We use the International Phonetic Alphabetic in the federal system."

Lenny smiled. "Right. Zulu Alpha?"

Paul nodded. "Relax. Get your head clear and let me know what you think. You have all day, so there's no rush."

"Thanks, boss." Hart said as he picked up the card and headed for the door. Remembering the process, he knew better than to ask any questions. He had to be totally blind to the target.

Paul rotated his chair around to look out the eighth-floor windows at the Pentagon, just beyond the Interstate 395 Beltway. The center of government, as most knew it. It was a beautiful day, even if it was a little warm. There was some haze in the air, but the planes taking off from nearby Reagan National airport would soon be above it. It was hazy near the earth, but it was always clearer when one was above the clouds, the haze, the pollution. It took a lot of energy to get there. Aircraft used the bulk of their fuel supply to get to cruising altitude. Once there, the cruising and descent stages of the flight cost them almost nothing. Psychic functioning was often the same.

For many years, he had thought that his agency was on top, where it needed to be. But now, he had the sudden feeling of vulnerability. Something he had not felt in years. More people in government and industry were using remote viewing to gain an edge on their competition. It followed then that more organizations and individuals were providing it. Almost as an afterthought, he entered his password into his agency computer and sent a note to STARLET2.

"Status check. Are you and SPINNAKER okay?"

He sat back and then began looking up references to the US Space Force on his public computer. As he read through their mission statement and congressional authorizations his mind drifted to SPINNAKER and how they had met years earlier.

She had been one of the original founding members of the Institute in the 1970's, the widow of a Marine officer killed in Da Nang in 1968. Born in Beirut in 1934, she had met then Captain Sheppard while he was serving in a quasi-intelligence capacity with the US Embassy in 1954. They emigrated to the United States the following year, two months after the birth of their first daughter, Aleyna.

Yasmina busied herself attending college classes and raising their new baby girl, while her husband was off doing Marine Corps things, defending his country against all enemies foreign and domestic. They had a good life, but in 1961, Aleyna developed scarlet fever and despite the best medical interventions, succumbed after experiencing one of the highest fevers the hospital had ever recorded. For a long time, Yasmina could not see herself as a candidate for motherhood, ever again. Then, in 1968, Major Sheppard received orders to Viet Nam. It was a day after she told him she was pregnant. Her second daughter, Nerissa would never get to meet her father.

Yasmina Sheppard had been one of the best marketing representatives that the Institute could have had. Not only was she extremely intuitive and gifted in her psychic abilities, but she was also able to teach it to others, and to talk about it publicly without the subject sounding like lunacy. She was respected in both the spiritual and scientific communities due to her medical background. She had received her MD degree from a well-respected school, but after meeting a laser physicist named Dr. Kravitz, the Institute's founder, she knew that her path was going to go a different direction. Together with the other members, they created a credible scientific program, in response to reports that the Russians were already ahead of us in the psychic battlefield. They developed laboratory protocols that facilitated the reception and interpretation of non-local communications, and eventually sold the program, first to the Army, and ultimately, to the CIA.

At the time, Paul was still a relatively new agent with the Office of Special Investigations, the Air Force's equivalent of the Army's CID unit. He was hot on the trail of some highly sensitive missing documents when he had been introduced to the special unit she represented. At first, he was skeptical of the capabilities of this unusual cadre but quickly became impressed with their results. Ultimately, he became a believer, even though his own forays were somewhat lackluster. He sat through numerous training experiences only to find that he didn't have any more psychic skill than the next guy. Nevertheless, he became comfortable with her team and grew confident in and appreciative of their contributions to a wide variety of intelligence operations.

Yasmina had been given the code name SPINNAKER for no other reason than the director at the time was a sailing aficionado and thought of her as the large sail that vessels used when running with the wind. In official reports, she had been labeled S1. And later, her daughter Nerissa had become S2. Yasmina's exploits and offerings had been phenomenal and would have made great copy for the news media and Hollywood in the seventies. If they could have been made public. In the wake of the Viet Nam war, the world was mistrustful of government, but ripe for something new. Something that didn't have anything to do with military intervention in far-off lands. Something that could be used for positive outcomes.

He looked through the day's news reports and shook his head as story after story seemed to be nothing, but history revisited. Politicians made the same mistakes year after year, decade after decade. Generation after generation. Why couldn't an intelligent nation learn? Almost ten minutes later, he saw Nerissa's reply. "All is well. What's up?"

There was no way to communicate the depth of his feelings in a brief electronic passage. He typed, "Nothing. Just checking." He clicked on the button to send the communication and knew in an instant after sending it that it had been a mistake. Anyone who knew him, knew that he didn't just *check* on his employees for no reason.

Thirty miles away, in her home on Saffron Hill Drive in Manassas, Neri studied the email with increasing curiosity. She had gone to dinner with her mother the previous evening and the two of them had chuckled at the video provided by Neri's twenty-four-year-old son, Hunter. It was silly. He had foregone the arts expressive of his Lebanese roots, and instead opted to learn the bagpipes as a stress-relieving diversion from his demanding electrical engineering career. Now, after a quick tutelage on his wooden chanter, he was attempting to deliver a refrain of *Amazing Grace* on his newly acquired set of thousand-dollar Gibson pipes. By most accounts, it would have been considered acoustically painful. But to a mother and grandmother, it was angelic. As far as she knew, life was good, and everyone was right where they needed to be in time and space.

"Okay, what's up?" She typed. Something was going on. Yet, for all her psychic wanderings and vision, she saw no threat of tumult on the horizon. She and Yasmina had celebrated Hunter's birthday, and his new job, just a week earlier. He had introduced them to his newest love. His supposed soulmate, Brittany. He had accepted a scholarship to Ohio State because that was where his high school girlfriend was going. But a year later, the girlfriend had moved on and Hunter began playing the part of the handsome upper classman with scholarship money and his own car. He had made friends quickly. Especially, female friends. Yasmina and Neri were delighted to see that graduate school and life-experience had finally settled him down and he was now thinking about a serious relationship. He was employed in some classified capacity with one of the many Beltway Bandits that built secret things for the government. It was lucrative and safe, and a proud mom was happy.

She busied herself cleaning up notes and drawings from her desk and somewhat impatiently awaited a reply that she knew would be less than quieting. It didn't take long.

"Take a couple of weeks off, on us."

She stared at the screen. She had known Paul for many years and recognized his suggestion as something that could be taken as anything from a simple offering of a bonus for work well done, to an admonition to stay away from the office for a while, for reasons known only to him. She thought about her recent taskings and tried to surmise if something had caused consternation in the Pentagon, or if the DC bureaucracy was growing temporarily wearisome of her trade.

She typed carefully. "I have been thinking about finding a beach somewhere. If you're sure you don't need me for a fortnight." She knew that he would recognize the proper old-English term for the two-week period he suggested, as a request for confirmation.

A moment later, she saw his reply. "Enjoy."

Her mother was now in her eighties, and even though Yasmina did not wish to acknowledge that she was in an assisted care facility, she still needed someone to look in on her from time to time to take care of things like cleaning and groceries. She had been out of the business for several years now. Neri quickly determined that her mother was not in any danger. Neither was Hunter in any immediate jeopardy. She didn't understand the situation to the degree she would have liked.

"Thanks." She typed and then closed out her e-mail. Something was not right. That was certain.

⸺ ⊙ ⸺

Stan Marchand looked out the bay window in the living room at the rain beating down on his custom LimeCoat driveway. In his hand, he held his cell phone like a waiter holding a sterling silver serving tray accommodating a bottle of the finest cognac. He frowned as he heard, through the tiny speaker, Tricia explaining that she would be a day late getting back to Dallas.

"I'm sorry baby. I need one more day to help mom get to her doctor's appointment and then I'll be back."

He missed her and wanted her with him. Especially to tag along for the event at Gleneagles that night. He hated going to country club functions. He really hated it when he had to attend without the appropriate eye candy on his arm. Tricia was gorgeous and he loved her. He loved her for who she was. Not just because she was attractive. Nevertheless, he had promised Griffiths he'd be there, and he didn't want to disappoint his favorite golf partner. It was a charity thing for some hospital that the big Texan was supporting. The five-hundred-dollar buy-in was only an afterthought.

"I know. You have to take care of family. I'll do the thing at Gleneagles tonight and just see you tomorrow when you get in."

"Thanks for understanding. I can't wait to see you." They exchanged some syrupy dialogue, which was normally outside of his limited diction, and then they rang off. He was sincere, but hoped that no one was eavesdropping on the conversation, for if they were, then he certainly would have lost his *cool-card*. He was supposed to be one of the toughest operators in the business, and if anyone heard him reciting such mawkish, saccharine raillery then he would have been taken to task at the next meeting of the man-club.

He wanted to cancel out of the affair, but there was no way. Griffiths and his wife were on the board, and they needed to see their friends supporting them. That meant he had to appear open and engaging, at least for a couple of hours. No more than two drinks. If he stayed for a third, it could mean trouble. Marchand lost his verbal filter on the third drink and was no longer able to abide the wealthy *erudites* who thought they knew everything. He enjoyed his home, neighbors, and the country club life, but he wasn't really one of them.

He had worked his way up through the ranks of the Secret Service beginning as a first-office agent in New York and gradually breaking some difficult cases that got him noticed and made him eligible for transfers and promotions to more coveted postings. Twice he was assigned to the White House, the first time on the Counter Assault Team. Then after two years as an Assistant to the Special Agent in Charge in Los Angeles, he returned to serve on the protection detail for George W. Bush. He had worked hard and enjoyed the trenches. People liked him.

But even though his wife and he had been frugal and smart with their investments, it was an inheritance from his paternal grandfather that had dumped some money into his lap a year after his divorce. Being a man of high ethics and flawless character, aside from some occasional philandering, he split the money with his ex-wife and their son. He still loved her. He just knew that he was no longer right for her.

He snapped his iPhone back into the Otter Box case that was clipped to the waistband of his shorts and returned to his office. He scrolled through the day's headlines and then switched over to check his email. Grand Emperor Insurance had sent him a reply to his report.

The request was brief, but not what he was expecting. "Tell us more about the hum."

The hum? Marchand went back through the pile of notes that he had made in the earlier session.

He flipped through the pages until he found the one that contained a reference to an intermittent hum that was, at the time, distracting. He recalled that it was there for only a moment and then he gradually worked around it. He paid it no further attention for the rest of the session.

The hum?

It seemed inconsequential, but if that was what they wanted, that was what he would give them. He repeated his earlier ritual of darkening the room and silencing his phone. He felt rested and reasonably carefree, so as he focused on his breathing, he began to relax and was able to clear the movie screen in his mind. It had to be blank before additional input could be brought in.

A few moments later, he reached for a blank sheet of paper and wrote the date and time of the session in the upper left-hand corner and then quickly drew another ideogram with one stroke of his pen. He opened his mind and concentrated on the humming sound from the previous session. In his mind he was entering the earth's atmosphere, descending in lazy circles into farmland. Lush woods with green trees, rolling fields, and the square concrete layer cake in the middle. He orbited around it a few times and then continued his descent through the roof and into the top floor. There were offices. People working. Some people wore uniforms. Some were there for administrative purposes. Others were there to guard something.

He moved around the top floor of the building and drew out general perceptions of activity. It had a financial tone about it. But it also seemed dry and stale, like government. There was the feeling of cigar and cigarette smoke in the air. People were used to it. He knew that he could not be in present day. He must have entered the facility in the past when smoking was still acceptable in the workplace. People worked at a slow pace. There was no hurry to get anything done. There were no productivity goals of any kind. The workers knew what the building was for but had never seen most of the interior. Even the men in uniform; guards of sorts, had never seen what it was they were guarding. Nevertheless, there was something in the building of great value.

Marchand allowed his mind to float to the ground floor. He pushed through a steel garage door and tasted the fresh air. There was more activity. People in uniforms, and some in suits waited for something. A delivery. Off in the distance he could sense a forceful presence. A group united for a common goal, trained for war. He was surrounded by an army unit of some kind. They weren't in the immediate area but were nevertheless close. Only a few people knew of the upcoming delivery. At the end of a long driveway, men opened the steel gates so that a truck could back in. The truck was clean, but old. Maybe something from the forties or fifties. It looked like a regular delivery truck but was unmarked.

Marchand sketched the rear of the truck, the driveway, and the open gates, and then reached for a fresh sheet of paper. Data began to emerge about the target. He sensed that the steel door that he had dissolved through was now open so that men could begin to offload the contents of the truck onto hand carts. There was not much. Only two boxes, each smaller than a case of beer, but much heavier. The dark cases had handles on the sides. It took two men to move the cases from the truck onto the hand cart.

Marchand's mind moved into the back of the now empty truck. There was a person in the back. Armed. He was assigned to escort the two cases to this building. He was not allowed out of the truck, so he waited for one of the others to close the rear doors, and then the truck departed.

Marchand followed the two men pulling the hand cart with the two dark cases on it. They moved through the lobby of the building to an elevator bank. The lobby was opulent compared to the upstairs offices. Granite and marble walls and floors. It felt cool and smooth to the touch. When the elevator doors opened, the men pulled the cart in and pushed a button that took them down.

The doors open to a hallway, which is less lavish, but offers strength. Concrete floors and walls. Heavy office doors. Doors are made of a heavy metal. Steel. Two men greet the other men with the cart and help pull it off the elevator. There is activity around the cart. They wheel the cart a few feet down the hall and the boxes are opened. One of the men hands a clipboard to another as he inspects the contents. Something of great value.

Marchand began to sketch a one-point perspective drawing of walls, floor, and ceiling narrowing and converging on a distant point. He sketched a cart in front of a door with four life-forms looking at the cart. He took a couple of deep breaths and tried to move closer to their activity. One of the men approached a large heavy door and did something to unlock it before he and his associate were dismissed and returned to the elevator. Once they were gone, the other two men each entered some type of code and opened the door. A heavy door. It took both men to open it.

The men move down a hallway past other doors and stop at one. There are two different keys to the door, and once unlocked, one man uses both hands to swing the door open. It is also heavy. Inside the room, they remove the contents of the boxes. Shiny. Heavy. Gold?

On the lower left side of the page, Marchand made the notation AO, and then circled it. Analytic Overlay. He was getting the impression of something like Fort Knox and wanted to indicate that his conscious mind was attempting to jump ahead and fill in the blanks. Maybe it was, and maybe it wasn't. An overlay occurred when the viewer was distracted by an assumption or analysis and wanted to return to the raw input.

Marchand deepened and slowed his breathing. He had to get past his momentary return to the physical, logical realm and concentrate on the gestalts. The sounds, smells, and the sensations. The two men secured their delivery and returned to the elevator. Their leather shoe soles clip-clopped on the hard floor and echoed off the walls. They returned to the main floor and completed their paperwork. Nothing. It was silent.

He knew his job. He had to find that annoying hum. He moved forward, mentally, in time. Days, weeks, months. It is now nighttime. There are still people present. Different people. They are joined by outsiders. People who don't work at the site from day to day. Strangers who have authority from someplace distant to the location. The regular workers have been dismissed. The new workers are officials in some capacity. They represent something powerful. Government. Or a part of government.

Marchand sensed sadness among them. They have lost one of their leaders, someone who saw them through an insidious economic crisis. Someone who saw them through global conflict. A major war. A war that resulted in the release of energy never seen by anyone on the planet. The creation of a weapon that attracted civilizations not of this world or this time and space. The new leader was doing his best but lacked experience in their minds.

It was cool, with a light breeze. Marchand focused his attention on sound. A high squeal began to emerge. It was natural. Maybe crickets in the nearby fields and woodlands. As his breathing continued to deepen he detected the presence of something else. He hovered over the concrete layer cake structure. Somewhere nearby, perhaps to the north of his target, he perceived aircraft. High speed propeller aircraft. Once considered advanced, they are now obsolete. He can make out constructed surfaces, like roads, but straight. They are like a V resting atop a straight line. Like airport runways. He made a quick notation off to the side, "AO, airport?"

They circled the area, looking for something. They are aware of the presence of the other craft and had been instructed to observe and keep unauthorized aircraft away from the area. On a previous visit, one of the older aircraft climbed too high in pursuit of one of the extra-worldly vehicles, the pilot became hypoxic and crashed. But, there was something else in the air. Something highly mechanized. More so than the other aircraft. It was capable of speeds that the other pilots cannot fathom. Marchand concentrated on the thing hovering over the layer cake and squinted his eyes tightly.

He forced himself to clear the movie screen in his conscious mind and allow the hum to gradually build. It was like bass violins and cellos trying to tune before a concert. The sound was accompanied by vibration that caused his head to ring. The sound crescendoed and the pitch climbed. Violas and violins, all out of tune. A loud painful orchestra that seemed in tune for only a moment before resonance began to pulsate at different speeds. Cacophonous. First slow as the sounds aligned, and then quicker as they seemed to fall out of tune and phase. The discordant hum began to intensify, and he perceived strange light reigning down from the unusual aircraft to the layer cake. The concrete structure was bathed in a special type of luminescence that persons within the immediate area could see, but someone who was outside the beam would not.

Marchand felt the hum flow from within his head down through the roof of his mouth and into his teeth, and he clenched as if to keep them from being pushed out of their sockets. He felt pressure in his head increase like a SCUBA diver diving deeper and deeper without equalizing. The hum grew louder and seemed to stabilize in pitch and intensity. It was doing something. It was causing something to move. Inside the concrete structure, the valuable commodity that had recently been offloaded was dissolving. Materializing into...not a gas, but some sort of molecular mist. It was moving from the structure through the beam into the craft.

The people watching are impressed. They do not understand what is happening but have been told to watch for this. It is the reason they are there.

The process continues for a brief period. Several minutes. The propeller aircraft continue to orbit the layer cake until the beam suddenly shuts off and the curious craft zips across the horizon. Whoever is driving it is gone almost instantaneously. They have what they came for.

Marchand listened for the hum, but it was gone as well. He tried to push for an explanation or answer but received nothing. The men on the ground returned to their normal duties. His mind orbited the concrete layer cake one last time as he felt his session was nearing its end. And then, as he was about to return to the present, he received an almost fleeting glimpse of a slowly spinning letter in the back of his mind. It was only there for a second. A slowly spinning Z. Like a sign on a pole for a gasoline station located just off a freeway. Lit from inside, the Z was spinning as if to provide drivers with the location of something down below. A large ornate Z. At the bottom of the imaginary pole, a line of people formed. The long line took the shape of a large S.

———— ((◉)) ————

Neri was as gracious as she could be. The man was attractive and educated. He was a successful CPA from Richmond who had been introduced to her by a college classmate. A classmate whom she hadn't seen in years but kept in touch with via social media. When her friend learned she was living in Manassas, she couldn't wait to pass along the name of a fellow she had known, who had recently gone through a divorce and would be *perfect* for her. Neri had grown skeptical of these so-called perfect matchups over the years and had avoided many of them. However, she was at a point in her life when she felt that she had to start letting others in emotionally or she would grow to be a cynical empty nester, like most of her friends and co-workers who were divorced or widowed. The man was a handsome specimen, just over six feet tall, and had a body that demonstrated that he took care of himself.

Like many men in their mid-fifties, he had attempted to conceal the premature balding and graying by shaving his head. With his athletic build, it worked for him. He was certainly a catch, as her friends would say, but he was just a bit pushy for her. After all, she was a successful professional, who literally had the keys to the universe. She didn't need to be corralled by a man who presented obvious control issues on the first date. He picked the restaurant. He told her what she should order for dinner. He picked the wine. He wanted to tell her what to do with her life.

He had asked her all the right first-date questions, and seemed genuinely interested in her, but there was something about him that made her think that his self-confidence was purely superficial. It wasn't psychic functioning, or *psi* as it was known in the business. She was just experienced at meeting men who wanted to date her and had learned to read behavior rather well. While he outwardly exuded confidence, he struck her as the type that would withdraw into submission or lash out in anger when something didn't go his way. It was, perhaps, an unfair character analysis, but it was how she made her living. She could not turn it off when she wasn't working.

She smiled at him through dinner and laughed at his jokes, but in the end, she knew there was nothing there. Perhaps because she was still a bit preoccupied by her earlier exchange with Paul, she was not in a receptive mood. In retrospect, she had only accepted the date to placate a former classmate and to be somewhat truthful when she told her mother that she was dating. Despite deteriorating health, Yasmina continued to remind her of the fact that her son was grown, her ex-husband was remarried, and she needed to find someone with whom to share her life. Through the years, she'd gone out with doctors, lawyers, scientists, and government employees. Even a stray politician from time to time. But none of them felt right to her. She was beautiful and educated and knew she didn't have to settle.

"How about a cup of coffee?" He asked innocently enough as he pulled into her driveway.

She dredged up her finest acting skills. "Not tonight. I have to work early tomorrow. Maybe another time?"

He seemed momentarily startled at her response. It was obvious that he had planned on the evening going a different way. "So, I should call you?"

"That would be nice." Her hand was on the door handle of the C-Class Mercedes sedan; the entry level model for people who wanted to drive a Mercedes but couldn't afford a real one. "I'm out of town next week. Maybe in a couple of weeks?"

He feigned a smile and leaned in to kiss her. She turned her head at the last second so that his buss landed on her left cheek. She smiled again. "Thanks for a great evening." She was out of the car and to her front door before he had backed into the quiet Manassas street. As she waved goodbye, she caught a quick glimpse of the white van that was parked across the street two driveways down. It had been there when she left, and now, two hours later, it was still there, and occupied by a man dressed in dark clothing.

She let herself in and locked the door behind her before disarming the alarm at the panel. Maybe out of practice, or an abundance of caution, she quickly looked around the first floor of the house. Nothing appeared out of place. The house looked as she had left it two hours earlier. She reactivated the alarm system and then tossed her keys into the bowl by the door. Just to be safe, she opened the drawer of the credenza in the hallway. Underneath the stack of home improvement magazines, she could feel the butt of the Glock 43, a flat little 9MM semi-automatic that one of her friends had talked her into buying two years earlier. Sensibly, they had also talked her into taking private lessons to learn how to shoot the noisy thing. It was there.

She wandered through the first floor of the house and checked the back door that led to the patio and then the garage door. Everything was as it should be. She turned the kitchen light off and headed upstairs as she tried to recall her most recent tasking. It seemed like nothing, but she had toppled governments, defunded billionaires, and changed the course of history. Was the feeling paranoia, or just good common sense based on years of experience? She kicked off her shoes and moved silently into the darkened guest room at the front of the house. She gently moved the venetian blinds back about an inch so that she could have another look at the white van. The occupant was talking on his cell phone. Seconds later, she saw the headlights come on and he drove slowly down the street past her house and into the night.

Maybe he was a service technician working late at a neighbor's house on an important project. Maybe he was a private investigator working for someone's spouse. Whoever he was, he wasn't CIA. They knew where she was every hour of the day. Coincidence? Maybe. But she had been told to take a couple of weeks leave. All of a sudden it seemed like a responsible thing to do.

CHAPTER 3

Paul quickly glanced at his watch as he waved his innocuous Platinum American Express card in front of the decorative plaque on the wall, next to the door leading into his suite. To the casual observer, the card looked like any other, but had been programmed into their access control system to admit him to the high-security office. It also worked as a charge card when used for that purpose. But then, everyone's American Express card did that.

Hearing the electronic latch click, he pulled open the door to the smell of freshly brewing coffee and the subtle sounds of fingers lightly tapping keyboards with subdued conversations coming from the various cubicles in the first row. "Good morning!" He said to Jillian with enough exuberance to let everyone know that the boss had arrived, and that they should now look busy whether they were or not. As he stopped at her desk to check his message basket, he caught the flash of Lenny Hart's bald head, peaking around the wall of his cube.

Jillian looked up from her monitor and noticed the two men catch each other's glance. "Good morning!" She lowered her voice to just above a whisper. "He's been here since seven. I think he'd like a minute of your time."

Paul nodded and quietly moved past her to the kitchenette beyond her desk. The coffee smelled good, and he needed a liquid jolt to get him used to the fact that he had to earn his pay for the next ten hours. He was a dedicated professional, but after thirty years, the daily ritual had become tedious. Once he had poured a cup he came back around the corner and nodded at Hart, who was approaching with a file folder in hand.

"Close the door." Paul said once he had found his way to his office, and carefully set the coffee on his desk.

Paul had not quite seated himself when Hart began. "I'm sorry, Boss. I'm not sure what I've got. I followed the protocol and did my best, but it doesn't make sense." Hart wanted desperately to please. He knew that he was the rookie on the team but needed his superiors to believe in him.

Paul suppressed a grin as he held out his hand. "It rarely does. Let's see what you've got."

Lenny handed him the folder and moved a side chair closer so that he could walk Paul through his notes. "It's like nothing I've worked on before. I couldn't tell what it was I was supposed to attach to, but the gestalts were wild."

Paul flipped through the folder and looked at the crude drawings and the notations off on the side of each page. He carefully placed each page on the desk, six pages in two rows of three. "No problem. This is your first operational tasking, so I didn't expect you to hit it out of the park on the first try. Tell me what you came up with."

Lenny Hart squinted and pursed his lips. "I couldn't tell if the target was a place or a thing. I kept getting something that was far off and cold. Thin air, maybe like a high desert somewhere. Really old. Something that was probably made in the past by a person or a group that was no longer around. I kept getting an overlay of something like Mt. Rushmore, but I know it isn't that. I've been there, and it isn't that cold, and the elevation didn't make the air seem that thin."

Paul looked from one page to the next at the crude drawings. It appeared that Lenny was trying to sketch something that seemed like a desert with a monument or carving of something that, at least to Hart, resembled the face of a Sphinx. He read through the notes again.

"People, life forms, working. Labor intense. Mechanical assistance. You have *mining* circled. Tell me more about that."

Hart exhaled loudly. "I don't know. I got the feeling they were mining gold or some other valuable metals. The site, or the operation, ran dry and they moved to a new location where it was found in more abundance. They needed it for something, but not for jewelry, or trade. Whatever it was, it was like they needed it for survival."

"Interesting." Paul continued to look at the notations and drawings. "What can you tell me about life at the target?"

Lenny shook his head. "Long gone. For years. It's like they were there, did as much as they could, and then moved on. It feels like the place has been vacant for a long time."

Paul looked at him. "How long?"

Lenny Hart usually kept eye contact with people when he spoke but broke from tradition and risked a glance out the window at the puffy white clouds in the cobalt blue sky. "You'll think this is weird, but when I say *a long time*, I mean centuries. Maybe, thousands of years. Maybe longer. That's why it doesn't make sense to me."

Paul thought quickly. He had seen similar reports before, and considering the organization that had submitted the request, had to pause. "Any idea what part of the world you were viewing?"

"No. As a matter of fact, I didn't catch any location at all. It could be anywhere." He paused. "Wherever it is, it's not near here."

"What else?" Paul asked as he tried to visualize some sort of logical encapsulation.

Hart looked at the floor and then back up. "That's it. I can do it over if you like. I really thought..."

Paul shook his head. "Don't think. I gave you a task and you did what you could with it. I could give this same task to a dozen different viewers and some of them might get the same thing, and some of them might get something totally different. If you wanted exacting perfection, you're in the wrong department. I'm asking you for your perceptions and that's what you gave me." Paul stacked the notes on top of each other and returned them to the folder. "This is good. I'm hanging onto it until I get other feedback, and then I'll send it to the client when I hear from the other viewers."

"That's it? I'm done?" Hart asked somewhat incredulously.

Paul snorted with a smile. "No. You're done with this tasking, but you're still in the training cycle. I'll have the Chief get with you in a few minutes and get you back in the cage for some additional work." His smile turned into a grin, referencing former Chief Warrant Officer John McMaster, one of the more senior, and certainly one of the most experienced viewers in the Tank. "Take a few minutes and get yourself some breakfast. Be ready for the cage in an hour."

Hart stood. "Thanks, Boss. I mean, Paul." He stood and left the corner office that offered the most spectacular view of the city that could be had on the floor.

As Hart closed the door, Paul took another look at the drawings and notes and then hit the intercom button on his phone. "Hey Jillian, who else did we give this target to?"

There was a moment of silence before the matriarch responded. "Hart's? Uhmmm...Phelps and Kumar."

"Have they turned anything in yet?" He asked.

"No." she said hesitantly. "But they're not in yet. They were still here when I left last night."

Paul found a blank manila folder in his desk drawer and slid Hart's notes and file folder into it. "Okay, thanks. As soon as they get in, ask them to forward their stuff to me."

"Of course." She said flatly.

Marchand awakened immediately when he heard the custom ring-tone unique to his occasional employer in Washington. As he reached for his phone he looked at the clock on his nightstand and saw that it was almost seven-thirty. On any given day he would have been up already, but the soiree at Gleneagles kept him out until almost one. Despite his commitment to himself to leave after two drinks, some engaging conversation with an attorney from Dallas had led to two more scotches, before they were joined by a prosthodontist who seemed quite knowledgeable about civilian firearms training, and a rancher from Cresson who offered up five hundred acres to him to create the ultimate civilian survival training facility. And, of course, in Stan Marchand, they felt they had found the perfect candidate to lead the project.

The former Secret Service agent kept them on the edges of their seats as he regaled them with tales of secret fitness and marksmanship programs taught at their academy in Beltsville. While much of what Stan commented on was public information, he welcomed the opportunity to invent spectacular exercises that left them thinking that each agent emerged from the seventeen-week program as a superhero. He even improvised and elaborated on an entirely fictitious *advanced* course that lasted six months. By the time the super-agents graduated, they were ten times as capable as any of the *Double-O's* in Bond's time.

At some point during the fifth drink, he ran out fables, and they realized that they'd been conned when he explained that the final course evaluation involved swinging by one's legs from the skids of one helicopter and grabbing the hands of another agent swinging from a different helicopter. It was most likely an image he had dredged up from a childhood visit to the circus featuring an amazing trapeze act. As he broke a smile the prosthodontist frowned. "Hey! Are you fucking with us?"

It was about then that everyone's wives showed up in the corner of the ballroom to collect their inebriated husbands and head for home. Luckily, George Griffiths' wife had hired a driver for the evening, and they offered Stan a lift. His Audi would have to stay behind in the parking lot at the club until he could rescue it the next morning. He knew it would be safer there than someone's front yard, or a police impound lot.

"Yeah." He answered, his detachment from reality readily apparent.

"Am I waking you?" Paul asked, a hint of sarcasm in his voice.

"No. I had to get up to answer the phone." He returned the sarcasm. "What's up?"

"We have a slight problem."

Marchand considered the introduction with trepidation. What might be considered *a slight problem* for most normal people could very well signal an extinction-level event, coming from this particular office in the affluent Washington suburb. "How slight?"

Paul trusted the retired agent implicitly. However, he didn't trust the department's communications network nearly as much. Paul ran an agency that his counterparts in State and Defense preferred not to officially recognize. His area of expertise included not only the psychic, or non-traditional intelligence mission, but also the means to deal with issues uncovered in the process of these investigations without requiring overt diplomacy or military action. If they uncovered a threat to national security, on advice of the President, they could eliminate it. "There is a new client that has operationally tasked us, and I feel that we might have told them exactly what they wanted to know."

"That's a problem?" Marchand sat up in bed and rubbed his bloodshot eyes.

"The nature of the request was such that the inadvertent release of the requested information, even in rumor form, could substantially impact the security and stability of our nation. Even though our team members are all heavily screened and completely reliable, I am afraid that this new agency might try to cover their tracks. To the point of taking an unauthorized action."

Marchand listened carefully to what was being said, but it wasn't adding up in his foggy head. "They asked us to find something. We found it, and now they're scared about how we'll handle the information?" He scratched the top of his bald head. "What can you tell me?"

"You entered the Secret Service well before *nine-eleven* if I am correct?" Referencing the event and period during which the US Department of Homeland Security was formed.

"Well before." He snorted, suppressing a retort about his age.

"So," Paul continued. "You reported in through Treasury prior to that."

"Uh huh." He confirmed while trying to guess where the conversation was leading.

"During your time with Treasury, did you ever have occasion to work with the Mint Police?"

Marchand thought about his career, recalling that he had worked with about every federal law enforcement agency at one time or another. "Probably. I think I must have had a counterfeiting case with some of them at one point or another." His mind jumped to his most recent tasking. The concrete layer cake in the field. Fort Knox. An acidic heat began to churn in his stomach.

Paul was quiet for a moment. "Do you remember one of your Gleneagles members a couple of years back? A former Marine major-turned-cop?"

Marchand rubbed the stubble of his beard. "Wait a minute. Reynolds? Mark Reynolds? He was one of yours? Ours?"

"Not him." Paul was satisfied that his agent's recollection had not been dulled by the effects of an evening out. "You were not a part of our team yet. I want you to think about the young lady, a striking brunette with whom he had an intense fascination. A woman both of you had seen at your club. She usually played tennis or golf with a tall slender fellow who was substantially older than her."

Marchand squinted his eyes as he recalled the stunning raven-haired goddess that Reynolds had approached after a round. The body of a college cheerleader, and a face that belied her years. "Yeah. She was hot. Mary something."

"Close enough. She was one of ours." Paul said without emotion.

"What? What happened with them? She left the Club about the same time that he found religion or something and left town. She was one of your people?"

"Yes. I can't get into it now but wanted you to have a visual reference. She is one of our viewers, and I have reason to believe that she is about to become endangered."

Marchand stood and adjusted his boxer shorts. He needed to use the bathroom, but he was captivated by the conversation. "So, she's a viewer? She's the one that found something that no one wanted her to find?"

"That is our belief. I think we are going to need someone with your protection skills to look out for her for a few days. Maybe a couple of weeks."

Marchand thought about Tricia's return that afternoon. He was retired. He was good at protecting others but wanted to relax and enjoy his retirement. That fact was not a secret to his government clients. He didn't mind viewing the occasional tasking. He found the work interesting, and it kept him in the game. However, baby-sitting was not a part of his latest fantasy. "You say that she might have upset the apple cart, so to speak? That she has pissed off a government agency?"

"Precisely." Paul commented.

"What have you told her to do so far?"

"She is preparing to leave on a much-deserved vacation. She will be leaving town and heading to a beach somewhere."

"Yeah? Which beach?"

"Her travel itinerary suggests at least one stop at a diving resort in Belize. Well, Ambergris Key. It's a small island off the coast of..."

"I know where it is." Marchand inserted. "I was there about five years ago."

"Yes." Paul replied. "I recall you mentioning it."

Marchand once again drifted back to his days as a protector, and all the work that went into any particular trip. The advance, as it was known. "I hear you, but I'm not sure that I'm the right guy for the job."

"What do you mean?"

"I mean, that this is off the grid, so to speak. I think you need someone on this who is used to dealing with those sorts of...uh... parameters."

"You have someone in mind?" Paul asked as if he already knew the answer.

"Yeah. As do you, probably. I'm thinking Karlsson."

The line was silent for the better part of a minute, before Paul responded. "Matt made it clear the last time that he was officially out of the game and didn't want back in. As you recall, he stuck his neck way out to finish another job for us and wanted to avoid any further associations, so as to stay out of the public eye."

"I know, but he's your guy." Marchand moved towards his bathroom. "He is the only one I can think of that specializes in...well, moving around off the grid."

There was another long silence. "I was afraid you would say that."

———((●))———

Nerissa Khoury entered her credit card information into the airline reservation system, exactly as it was listed in her US passport. Her authentic one, anyway. She selected a United flight that would depart Reagan national at 6:15 the next morning, arriving at 8:36 in plenty of time to catch her connection to Philip S. W. Goldson International Airport in Belize City, arriving at 11:50. On her last trip there ten years earlier, she had taken a Continental flight that required a carrier change in Houston to TACA; Transportes Aereos del Continente Americano. She was familiar with the route and the airports and did not want the flight to take her any place with which she was not. Times change. Continental had been acquired by United Airlines in 2010, and TACA had merged with Avianca in 2009. Nevertheless, she knew what to expect, and how to plan.

From Belize City she would take a short hop to the island of Ambergris Key in one of the local puddle-jumpers, Maya Island Air, for the fifteen-minute trip to the island airstrip, which was literally across the street from the SunBreeze Hotel. The hotel was reasonably priced, on the beach, and within walking distance to most of the restaurants on the island. And most of those restaurants had signs in their front windows that declared, "No shirt, no shoes, Better service." To call the island casual would be more than accurate.

She had enjoyed her previous excursion, a New Year's Eve SCUBA package that included four tank-boat dives and a New Year's Eve bash. On that trip, she was recently divorced, her work was caught-up at the Institute, and Yasmina had told her she would take care of Hunter if she would agree to go and have some fun. Yasmina, forever the quintessential mom, had determined that her daughter needed a change of scenery, and mom always knew best. Reluctantly Neri acquiesced and agreed to force herself to have a good time for a week. It worked. When she returned a week later, tanned, rested and content, she was able to dive back into her work with a renewed passion. The fact that her *ex* had already found someone new shouldn't have irritated her, but it did. The divorce had been amiable and amicable, but she had expected him to suffer longer. Like her.

She turned left on Hadley and headed north towards Wellington Road for the five-minute drive to the Arbors of Whispering Glen Assisted Care facility. Yasmina had put up only minimal resistance to the idea of moving into what she termed the *old-folks-home* but recognized that she could still retain her independence and come and go as she chose. If she felt like going out, she called a car, and they took her wherever she wanted to go. However, groceries and doctors' appointments were provided as a part of the five-thousand dollar a month service plan. It was a nice apartment. She had privacy when she wanted, and a grand piano in the lobby if she felt like playing. Her neighbors were of the same age group, and enjoyed the same music, so it came as no surprise that she quickly assimilated into her new surroundings and made new friends.

As Neri left her house on Saffron, she noted that the white van she had spotted the previous evening was nowhere to be seen, and she breathed a sigh of relief. She paid no attention to the highway survey crew that were busy trying to laser-measure the intersection at Wellington. Another traffic project, no doubt. She accelerated quickly Northeast, past the Exxon station on Grant Avenue, and looked over her shoulder to change lanes. She needed to turn left on Clark Street, but an idiot in a black pickup truck was racing past her at a ridiculous speed and she tromped her brake to keep from hitting him as he cut in front of her. It might have been what saved her. If it hadn't been for her quick reflexes and the substantial brakes on her Volvo XC40, she might have taken the full broadside impact of the ready-mix concrete truck that went through the light at Main Street and caught the left rear quarter of the offending pickup truck, spinning it violently across the eastbound lanes of Wellington, and leaving it to rest in the grass.

Instinctively, perhaps because of her training at the Vehicle Dynamics Institute course a few years earlier, she whipped the wheel a quarter turn to her left and then back to the right to swerve around the thundering obstacle. When she was several hundred yards past the scene, she gave herself permission to process what had just happened. Her heart rate was elevated, and her breathing was a bit frenzied, but she told herself these were simply stress reactions to a dangerous event. "Drive through the ambush." She told herself.

There were plenty of people on the highway that would call police and EMS services. They could do more for the victims of the crash than she could. Ambush? Why had she so quickly jumped to the conclusion that the scenario that had just played out was anything more than a tragic accident?

She had taken the three-day program on a lark after hearing some Secret Service agents talking about it. It was designed for professional security drivers, executive chauffeurs, and protection specialists looking to improve upon the knowledge, skills, and ability needed to provide secure transportation for people at risk of attack by others. She had needed a diversion from her now-mundane activities and when she told her mother about it that day, Yasmina had shrugged and said, "Why not. You'll have fun."

Now, as she steadied her breathing, and drove on towards her mother's apartment, she thought about what had happened, and why she felt like she had. She quickly looked in her rear-view mirror to see if anyone was following her. Just to be safe, she drove past her turn and went to the next street so that she could turn left, and then find a suitable place to turn around again. No one had followed her and after she passed a couple of streets in the residential area off Garden Street, did a sharp U-turn in the intersection and returned to her previous route. When she got to Wellington, she looked Southwest and could see that people were rushing towards the accident. In the distance, she could hear sirens. Someone had summoned help. She eased back into the street and drove cautiously and vigilantly back towards Clark and turned right onto the drive that would take her to Whispering Glen. Her hands were affixed to the steering wheel with such energy that she thought she would leave permanent prints in the leather. She had to relax. After all, it might have been nothing. Just an accident. They happened every day.

Still trembling, but confident that she was not being followed, she parked in the visitor lot in front of the building and locked the car before she made her way up the winding sidewalk to the facility. She waved briefly at Miranda, the receptionist, who recognized her with a smile, and then walked down the hallway toward suite 127. When she knocked, she was quickly greeted by the short-statured icon in her eighties who knew the secrets to the universe and was ready to take as many of them as necessary to her grave.

"Hi sweetie!" Yasmina exclaimed.

"Hi Mom." She said with a smile her mother immediately recognized as false.

"What's wrong?"

Neri sat her purse on the stand next to the door and gave her mother a firm hug. "Nothing. A truck ran through a light up the street and hit a car in front of me."

"What?" Yasmina asked. "Are you okay?"

Neri quickly shook her head but answered in the affirmative, belying her non-verbal cue. "Yes, I'm fine. How are you? What did you have for breakfast?" She wanted to change the subject so that her mother would not bombard her with a barrage of questions. Despite Yasmina's blanket of security clearances while on the job, now that she was retired, there were some things that daughter and mother could no longer discuss.

People had mostly forgotten about the diminutive matriarch who had brought psychic intelligence into the contested space it occupied today. She had combined her education as a medical doctor with the para-psychological functioning of a dedicated few who fought battles in the background. Way in the background. She was entitled to go into old age with the respect and gratitude of a grateful nation and not have to hide in the shadows any longer.

Yasmina frowned at her for a moment, the reality of their professional relationship evident. "How's Hunter?"

Neri smiled and nodded in appreciation. "He's fine. He sends his love and says to tell you that he will be down this weekend."

"Is he bringing Brittany?" Yasmina asked with a glimmer in her eye.

Neri nodded. "Of course. They've become inseparable. She's like his *weekend wife* now." Both women laughed.

"Have you got time for tea?" Yasmina asked as she headed to the small kitchen in her suite and began filling the well-used teapot that was permanently stationed on her stove.

Neri glanced at her watch, the Breitling Endurance with the blue rubber strap that had seen her through her last three marathons. She had errands to run, but they would wait. "Of course. I've never turned down a cup of tea in my life." She smiled, paraphrasing a line from an old James Garner western, *Support Your Local Sheriff*.

Yasmina turned the burner up to its highest setting. All of her life she had cooked with gas heat, but the *home*, correction, senior community didn't want open flames in any of the apartments. "This will take a couple of minutes." After an uneasy silence, she added, "Where to, and for how long?"

Neri looked at her like a child who had just been caught in a fib of sorts, and then smiled broadly. "What makes you think I'm going somewhere?"

Yasmina chuckled and moved past her into the living room. "I could tell you I was psychic, but it isn't that complicated. Whenever you answer a question with an old movie line, I know you're uneasy about something. I assume it's work, and therefore I can conclude that you're not going to tell me the truth, are you?"

Neri frowned, but then bobbed her head lightly indicating concession. "I'm going to Belize for a week or so. After that, maybe on to Costa Rica to meet up with a friend."

Yasmina straightened the magazines on the coffee table. "A friend? Male or female?"

"Mom, would you stop already? I'm dating. Okay?" She slid a housekeeping magazine over to where her mother was sitting, so that it could be added to the stack. "As a matter of fact, I had a date last night. Nice guy. We went to dinner."

"Uh huh." She smirked. "You had him drop you in the driveway and told him you'd be out of town for a couple of weeks."

"I *am* going to be out of town for a couple of weeks." Neri retorted.

"Look, sweetie, I just want you to be happy. You must miss not having someone in your life that you can share space with. You need to move on."

"Yes, as you've told me a hundred times. I'm working on it. I'm still just not certain about what I want. I see good things in all of the men I go out with. But, I just haven't met the one that has all of those individual attributes."

"You never will." Yasmina walked back into the kitchen and opened the cupboard that had her selection of teas. She found a suitable Earl Grey and carefully placed the teabags in the Lebanese coffee cups that she had acquired thirty years earlier on a trip to Beirut. Yasmina was not much of a coffee-drinker anymore, but enjoyed using them to serve tea, since the cups always generated conversation. "You've seen perfection in all things in the universe, but you must know that there's no such thing as the perfect mate."

Nerissa Khoury joined her mother and moved the notes and books around on the kitchen table. "I know, mom. I just want to make sure that I don't make the same mistake twice."

"Oh, for crying out loud. You've been divorced for twenty years. I think you've grown substantially since then, and I think you have a much better handle on life than you did then. Tell me more about this new guy."

Neri shrugged off the question. "He's just a guy. Pushy, domineering. Too damn sure of himself. He thinks he has all the answers to everything."

"Ah." She nodded. "He's too much like you. What did you tell him you do for a living?"

Neri looked askance at her mother. "Music and culture specialist with State."

Yasmina shrugged as the teapot began to whistle. She poured hot water into the cups. "Not bad. I like it."

She dipped the teabags a couple of times and then sat the cups on the kitchen table. "At least tell me where you're headed so that if I get a frantic phone call from the Red Cross, I'll know if it's real or not."

Even though Neri was not wearing her reading glasses, she tilted her head down and looked at her mother as if she had been. "I told you, Belize. I haven't done any diving in a while, and I thought this would be a good opportunity to take a tune-up and look at some coral."

"Alone?" Yasmina challenged.

Nerissa nodded. "Yes. I'll be diving with a group, but I don't plan on booking it until the last minute."

"That's my girl." Yasmina stirred her tea. "I don't recall you talking about an overwhelming desire to dive again. What brought this on?"

Neri didn't want to lie to her mom but could not tell her the full truth. "Paul thought I should take a few days off. Actually, a couple weeks. Something's going on at the Tank and he thought it best if I was out of DC for a while."

Yasmina stared into her tea for a moment, as if she was studying tea leaves like many of her contemporaries had done through the years. Some looked into crystal balls, some stared at quartz geodes. Some Caribbean cultures tossed chicken bones onto a cloth to get the same effect. "Is there anything you can tell me?"

"No."

"Ah. I see. Can I at least have your travel itinerary?"

Neri nodded, a small smile appearing at the corners of her mouth. "Yes, of course. But, if anyone asks, you don't know where I am."

———— ⫸«◉»⫷ ————

Mathias Karlsson pulled his boots off on the front porch of his single-story adobe home and slapped the heels together to shake lose the reddish Penistaja combination of sand and clay. Common around Santa Fe, the soil was named after a small ranching community in northwest New Mexico. The name itself came from a Navajo word that meant *forced to sit.*

The soils were common in the Southwest landscape of mesas, snow-capped mountains, and desert grasslands. Formed by a combination of water and wind-driven forces on sandstone and shale, it could be separated into three basic materials: sand, silt, and clay, which were present in most local soils in different proportions.

He had fallen in love with the area forty years earlier when he had fallen in love with his eventual wife, Peggy. He had been on field exercises on the McGregor Range, an artillery testing area controlled by Fort Bliss, which straddled the Texas and New Mexico borders. His unit, a part of the Tenth Special Forces Group out of Fort Carson, Colorado, had been deployed there for a month to work through chemical weapons scenarios led by their 82nd Chemical Recon Detachment.

On a well-needed weekend break from the exercises, he and a buddy had ventured north to Santa Fe to get as far away from the action, and the Army, that they could. In one of the cozier pubs the pair had run into a couple of nice wholesome local girls who seemed to be captivated by the warriors now out-of-uniform. Margaret, or Peggy as she was known, worked as a receptionist for a local heating and cooling contractor.

The next day, Mary Margaret Hemingway offered him a private tour of New Mexico's capital and the southern tip of the Sangre de Cristo mountains. She told him of the town's colonization by the Spanish in 1610 and brought him quickly up to speed on its culture and history as they drove the crooked streets past adobe landmarks and stopped at the Palace of the Governors, which had become the New Mexico History Museum. They were both young and very much physically attracted to each other. She had been a high school cheerleader, and he, a first-string basketball player, who had turned down a scholarship to Northwestern so that he could enlist in the US Army.

She was absorbed in his patriotism and commitment to defend the nation, even though she never understood the nature of his work. She knew he was in the *special forces*, whatever they were, and that when problems erupted around the world he was dispatched on a moment's notice to sort them all out. She found it interesting and captivating. A year later, they married and for the next twenty years, they made a life together with her acquiescence to his lifestyle; a different base every couple of years, a new home, new schools, new friends. It wasn't the life she had dreamed of, but she made it work. There were missed birthdays, missed Christmases, and missed family events, as one could expect.

After his time with Uncle Sam had drawn to a close, she looked forward to them being together, welcoming grandchildren into the family, and finally having the opportunity to enjoy life. But, one night in a momentary offering of vulnerability, he confided certain aspects of what he really had done in the Army all those years. She was shocked, and it changed her. It changed them. Forever. The cheerleader-turned-Homecoming Queen of Santa Fe High School was not prepared for the full realization that her husband was basically a government killer.

War, she could understand. Taking out a drug lord in some far-off land, she could understand. But working for various government agencies to do things outside of an official declaration of war was more than she could handle. In her mind, she could not rationalize some of the things he told her and still believe that she could be in love with someone like that. He tried to explain that he was simply a counteragent; a person who was sent in to nullify enemy agents. Sometimes with diplomacy, sometimes with logic. Occasionally by force. He wasn't an assassin, as she had postulated, but merely a soldier. He didn't pick his battles. The US Government did.

The divorce was quick and amicable, and since the kids were fully grown, studying hard in college and pursuing lives of their own, they mutually agreed to the split. His full retirement consisted of a drunken weekend in Puerto Vallarta, and then a week later, he had requested contractor status to get back into the only profession he knew. He was a soldier. Plain and simple. He loved his country but didn't give a hoot about politics or politicians.

Peggy was able to get on with her life. She remarried and after time, Karlsson found that he actually liked her new husband. A stockbroker or financial planner of sorts. The guy was good with her and good with the kids and they all got along splendidly for years. Cards and visits at Christmas. From then on, no birthday was ever forgotten. And then, just a few years later, she was gone. It was some fast-acting cancer that took her before she realized she was sick. He saw everyone at the funeral but deployed to Southeast Asia a day later and was able to put the lost memories, as well as the memories that never got a chance to happen, behind him.

Shortly after his return, a friend of his had alerted him to the sale of US Government property, which included the forty-acre ranch at the end of Old Cañoncito Road, bordering the Pecos National Historical Park. In addition to the main house, the 2,900 square foot Pueblo-style spread offered an additional 600 square foot casita with a full bathroom and kitchen, probably intended for in-laws, or welcomed guests. Located near the north fork of the Galisteo Creek, the main house was large and openly designed with three wings at slight angles. The main wing included a huge kitchen with cabinets and woodwork done in local pine. It had a large island with plenty of space to lay out his cookware, and a large dining area and comfortable master suite. Another wing of the home contained a large family room and two additional bedrooms together with two more full baths. In the opposing wing of the home could be found a full gym, a fourth bedroom and a bathroom with a roomy sauna that could seat six if they were friendly enough. The home seemed to have been pieced together over time, but well-coordinated.

There were gardens and three expansive greenhouses on the

property for those interested in growing one kind of plant or another. But it was the specific type of plant that had caught the attention of the Drug Enforcement Administration and caused the property to end up in their hands thanks to a practice they called *asset forfeiture*. Originally valued at over a million dollars, Karlsson acquired it for just $400,000, and then added a robust Cummins 24kw generator so that he could continue to enjoy the creature comforts of life even if the electrical grid went toes-up. Naturally, the greenhouses had to go to make room for the barn that he had in mind.

There was a grassy area in the courtyard that was created by the wings of the house and the garage. The grass seemed to do quite nicely with little work or water needed on a regular basis. The Santa Fe rainy season ran July through August, with thunderstorms barreling through in the afternoons. And even though most people didn't associate New Mexico with snow, from November through April, they received an average of thirty-two inches of snow in town and up to three hundred inches in the ski areas of Taos and Angel Fire. It was the kind of place he had always wanted. Roomy, private, and well off the grid.

His nearest neighbor was almost a mile away, and most of the residents of the area had lived there for generations. It would have been a great place to raise a family if he'd had one. He had an occasional girlfriend now who dropped in from time to time when she wasn't doing some sort of secretive snooping for the Air Force's Office of Special Investigations, and they enjoyed the scenery together.

Karlsson and Special Agent Jackie Biehn had met on a case a couple of years earlier and were perfect for each other. She was focused on pushing her career, free of social encumbrances, and the two of them made time together when they could. Neither were, at least for the present, interested in any sort of official relationship that might require commitments. Commitments not so much to each other, but simply as to time or expectation.

Karlsson had his horses, two Quarter Horses, and three Mustangs, which had also been acquired from the US Government at great savings. Once a month or so, he had Jackie's company as well. No one was going to write a love song about them, but they understood each other's needs and it worked for them. He was as happy as a nefarious character like himself had a right to be. It turned out that Jackie was quite comfortable riding the hills, even though camping was not her first choice for weekend entertainment. The horses and her seemed to understand each other as much as Karlsson and her did.

Up until the email from Grand Emperor Insurance arrived in his virtual basket, his primary focus had been on his three-year-old, Matilda. The chestnut mare had just arrived, and he was trying to get her comfortable with her new surroundings. She had four roommates in the spacious and environmentally friendly barn, and they needed time to get to know each other. She stood fifteen-two, as they measured in hands, so she was no lightweight, and it was important that she assimilate with her new brothers and sisters gradually. He was still *sacking her out*, as they said in the horse world. At six-foot-four and two hundred pounds, he needed a big horse that he could depend on, and Mustangs were smart, loyal and tough.

Despite his New Mexico upbringing, he was still new to the role of horseman, and welcomed the tutelage of Dr. Velva Capaz, DVM, horse trainer and no-nonsense confidante, as well as her son Aaron, who was in his last year of undergraduate work in Engineering at the University of New Mexico. He had started his studies at the UNM-Los Alamos simply due to the huge difference in cost between in-state and out-of-state tuition. That, and his mother had done her pre-vet work there before attending the College of Veterinary Medicine at Ohio State.

During the early days Aaron served as Matt's part-time ranch hand, riding the fence lines, and checking the water troughs located around the property, and used Matt's casita to crash if he had put in too many hours and too many beers to make the forty-mile drive back to campus. Mother and son had trained Matt's Quarter Horses and then trained him how to break and train the Mustangs.

Velva had also designed the large barn that consisted of a tack room, feed room, and six twelve-by-ten stalls, each with its own adjacent twelve by twelve paddock and water trough. Directly outside the barn was an acre and a half green paddock and a seventy-foot round pen made up of eighteen twelve-foot, six-railed panels for training and breaking in new horses. As she had designed it, the dry lot could also be used for isolating new horses or facilitating the recovery of injured ones.

He had grown up watching John Wayne and Clint Eastwood doing horse things, without ever really understanding the work that it took to make them do the things they did in the movies. Velva took her work seriously and Karlsson enjoyed immersing himself into a pastime that didn't involve killing total strangers. She brought him up from the basics, and though she was well-versed in the equestrian arts, she did not belittle his novice understanding of his new hobby. He was ready to do it right, so she appreciated his commitment, and he hers.

She taught him how to groom, how to pick hooves after rides and how to inspect the horses each time they were ridden, looking for injuries, sores, or anything that might get caught up in their coats or tails. She lectured on the best fly sprays and oils, and what to pack when setting out on a ride. Her lectures on bridles, alone, covered the benefits and drawbacks of various western gear including bosals and mecates, how to apply them and how to store them.

Karlsson poured a cup of black coffee and sat down at the kitchen table. With a combination of trepidation and annoyance, he clicked on the email from Grand Emperor Insurance. It was simple, as the messages often were.

"Need you one more time. Wouldn't ask if not critical. Still at the same number here." It was signed P.

Karlsson stared at the message for a moment as he sipped the resultant brew of the Yellow Brick Coffee that he had picked up in Tucson a couple of weeks earlier. The Kamoini Othaya was a classic Kenyan coffee brought to a light roast, with a subtle red currant and grapefruit flavor. He didn't care how they made it. He liked the smell and the taste.

He arose and looked out the window above the sink at the mountains in the distance. He could not believe that after all this time, Washington still couldn't get its act together. He trusted Paul. But he was incensed that those self-serving narcissists, who called themselves politicians, still had not seen the writing on the wall.

He had a good life. He had everything he needed. A government pension, a great ranch, an understanding girlfriend. Why jeopardize any of that?

He went outside and took a seat in one of the Adirondack chairs on the porch that had been made by Velva's son, a gift for helping him through a tough time. The coffee was like an aphrodisiac for his brain. He considered the options. He considered his love for his country. In the end, the self-doubt was headed only one way.

He dialed Velva's number, and she answered on the second ring. "Hi Matt."

"I have to go away for a few days. Maybe a couple weeks. Can you guys watch the place?" He said, looking at Stoney, his favorite Quarter Horse, poking his head out of the door to his stall. It looked like the horse knew something was up.

"Yeah. You gonna be okay?"

"Absolutely." He sipped his coffee. "But if not, my will and stuff is in my desk drawer on the left."

Velva was silent for a moment but knew not to press him. "Aaron wants the casita if you don't come back."

Karlsson chuckled. "It's not that serious. I'll be back. But, if I'm not, Bennie Haskell, my attorney, already knows. It's all yours. Just take care of Jackie."

He returned inside and sat down at the table and typed. "Long time, no see. What have you got?"

CHAPTER 4

Lieutenant Colonel Jonathan Babic walked out of the general's office, confused and shocked. Two steps down the hall, the full realization of what had been asked of him finally hit home. He was being directed, in peacetime, to meet with an individual known to be a very lethal character, and arrange for the abduction, and possible murder of, a US intelligence operative. It didn't make sense.

In his right hand, he clutched the leather zipper folio that concealed the blank eight-by-ten envelope containing fifty thousand US dollars, while his left hand subconsciously ran down the button line of his dress uniform and over the top of his Command Missile Badge on his left breast pocket. The pewter-colored device with the star and wreath atop, indicated that he had spent at least fifteen years in his career field overseeing units in the operation of nuclear missile systems. Known in the Air Force as the *pocket rocket*, it was one of the awards and devices that transferred with him when he transitioned to the Space Force.

"The plan is already in motion." The general told him. "You're to meet with the team's emissary at this restaurant..." He slid the simple piece of unlined paper towards him across the desk. "...and provide no additional information. Give him the envelope and casually walk out of the place."

Babic had recognized the popular Georgetown establishment on Q Street, having dined there on two occasions with his wife. "That's it?" He asked, pushing the paper back across the desk to his boss.

"That's it, Colonel. No drama. No intrigue. Just do it and go home."

"But how will I recognize him?" Lieutenant Colonel Babic responded.

The General looked at his watch. "It's almost zero one hundred." He spoke in a low controlled voice, indicating one o'clock in the morning, as most civilians would know the hour. "By the time you get there, I doubt you'll find many single male adults that aren't three sheets to the wind. Your guy will answer to the name of Dave Fox."

Babic was tired and needed a shave. The rubber heels of his Corfam dress shoes thumped out an echo against the near-empty halls of the Pentagon. While it was truly a twenty-four-hour business, at this hour of the night, only those senior officers with real world-class problems remained. They were all tired and needed a shave. The male officers, anyway.

The Metro quit running at midnight, so he had a choice between using his own car or grabbing a cab. The cab made more sense, so he checked his cell phone and punched the number for the preferred Pentagon vendor. It would take him several minutes to get around to the front of the building, and he calculated it would be a similar amount of time for a cabbie to pry himself or herself away from the queue at Reagan National and make the trip across the bridge.

When he got there, the yellow cab was waiting. "The Cardigan. Wisconsin and Q."

"Right." The cab driver said in accented English as he dropped the transmission into gear, and they lurched forward with a jolt.

Babic could not believe what he was doing. What had this to do with the exploration of space? How could his career have so suddenly gone off the rails? He was so busy trying to put it all together, that he didn't even recall the route they took. Ten minutes later they rolled up in front of one of the typical Georgetown bars, set into a row of houses that looked like they had been there for centuries, whether they had or not. Babic pulled a fifty-dollar bill out of his wallet and passed it through the bullet resistant screen that separated the front and back seats. "Can you wait for me for five minutes?"

The cabby looked ahead of the row of parked cars towards the intersection and nodded. "Sure. I be up there."

Babic clutched the leather folio under his arm and walked towards the entrance. Once inside, he noted the small gathering of Washington well-to-do's. Men, women, and the non-committed whispering across the tables at each other in conspiratorial fun and frolic. The younger men with younger women trying to impress their dates with their access to the power-elite, or the older ones trying to impress their dates with how powerful they were now and how an evening of bliss would help pass the power to the next generation. Everything was a game here, each player angling for power.

The restaurant wasn't that wide, but it was noticeably deep. On the left were leather upholstered booths with accent lamps near the wall, offering only enough illumination to look into each other's eyes and to sign the check. To the right were tables with four chairs each, and towards the rear was a classy bar with every conceivable libation. Chandeliers were a nice touch that seemed to give the place an air of respectability. He looked quickly around the near-empty room but saw no single men that looked like they might be waiting for him. He wandered slowly back towards the bar, and then stuck his head into the small, but fashionably appointed restroom at the rear. It was empty. He emerged from the restroom and tried again to identify the character that he was supposed to meet. Everyone was coupled for the evening except for the two women at the bar, attired in smart business outfits, drinking martinis, and laughing about something they must have found incredibly entertaining. Disappointed, he headed back towards the front door. There must have been a mix-up.

"Leaving so soon, Captain Kirk?"

Babic turned. One of the two businesswomen at the bar arose from her stool and moved his direction. "Excuse me?" He said a bit uncomfortably.

"I know it's late, but what did you expect to find tonight?" She smiled. She was quite striking, in an outdoorsy kind of way. In her heels, she was almost as tall as him, just shy of six feet. She was strikingly attractive, dressed well in a grey pinstripe skirt and suit jacket, but displaying premature wear-and-tear on her somewhat masculine hands. If it weren't for the absence of an Adam's Apple, he might have wondered if she was trans-gendered. Nevertheless, her voice was quite breathy and feminine.

"Uh...I was looking for someone, but he's not here." He replied softly.

She grinned as she took his arm and steered him to one of the empty booths. "Well, what's his name? Maybe I know him."

Babic was extremely suspicious, if for no other reason than women rarely threw themselves at him, and he was carrying a large sum of cash, for which he was personally responsible. "No. I doubt it. But thanks anyway."

He started to move away from the booth, but she grabbed his hand firmly and sensually. "Please sit-down Colonel and I'll buy you a drink."

"No. I can't. I..."

Still smiling, she nodded for him to sit down. "You're here to meet Dave."

Babic stopped in his tracks. "What? What makes you think that?"

"There's only been one Lieutenant Colonel come through that door in the last couple of hours. And you, my friend, have the anguished look of a Republican who just walked into a room full of Chicago Socialists."

She seated herself and signaled the bartender to bring her another of whatever she was having. "What would you like?"

Babic was a bit taken aback by her assertiveness but slid into the booth across from her. "Uh...nothing. Thank you."

She lowered her voice. "If you don't get a drink, it will look incredibly awkward for both of us."

What was he doing? Was he falling into a trap? "Uh...Jameson on the rocks."

She looked back towards the bar. "Wally, Jameson rocks for my friend!"

He looked at her for a moment and tried to decide how she fit into this unusual operation. She had the look of being ex-military, or ex-cop, or ex-something. "I was supposed to meet a friend of mine."

She smiled ear to ear. "Yes. Dave Fox. Please smile. You look like you're about to get a colonoscopy or something. This is where congressmen and interns come to get laid. No one in here is trying to be serious about anything."

"Uh, yes." The anxious Lieutenant Colonel nervously tried to smile. "Where is he?"

She winked. "I'm him. Well, her."

Babic looked intently at the statuesque brunette. "What?"

She tilted her head to the side innocently. "Or, for fuck's sake, you didn't think we use our real names in shit like this, did you? Not that it matters, my name really is Davina. I tend to like Dave though, because it throws people off. Like your boss."

Babic stared at her blankly. He could not afford to louse up this meeting. "You're Dave Fox?"

"I am tonight. Look, if it helps you to identify me as your contact, I can tell you that an hour ago some general in the Pentagon handed you an envelope containing fifty grand in unmarked bills and told you to bring it to Dave Fox in this bar. Correct?"

Babic nodded.

Wally brought the drinks over and sat them on the table. He had the look of a tall Latin singer, but the drawl of a native Virginian. "Do y'all want to run a tab?"

Babic shook his head and pulled a couple of twenty-dollar-bills out of his wallet. "No, thank you."

Once Wally had returned to his bar customers, she continued. "You have a business deal down south that needs funded before it can move forward. This is the investment capital necessary to get it going. Lay it on the seat beside you. When you leave, I'll pick it up. It's really that simple."

Babic laid the folio on the seat and rested his hand atop it. "I'm told that this needs to happen quickly."

She nodded with an affectionate smile. "I know. We're already in place. We've had our consultant onsite since yesterday and he's just waiting for confirmation of the funds to proceed."

Babic started to perspire. "What...uh...what is the..."

She leaned over the table and put her finger to his lips. "Now, now. I don't know anything about it, and you probably shouldn't either. Take a couple sips of your drink, give me a quick kiss and a hug, and get back in your cab."

—————«(O)»—————

Nerissa was awakened by her biological alarm clock at five-fifteen, which was really four-fifteen local time, and noticed that she had a message on her phone. She did not need her glasses to recognize it as a number from Washington DC. One that she dared not keep in her contacts list.

"NEW INFO ABOUT YOUR VACATION. CHECK OUT RAMON'S AT 0730. ASK FOR DAMIAN. 17.3160 N, 87.5351 W"

She shook her head with a frown. "The nerve of the man to assume I'd be awake in time to see this."

Her room was cool, but damp from the high humidity, exacerbated by the towels and dive gear hanging in the shower that were still wet from the previous day's dive. Actually, she had made two dives, getting a spectacular tour of the Hol Chan Marine Reserve in the morning, and then a visit to Shark Ray Alley, one mile south of the Hol Chan cut, after lunch. They were the most popular dive sites in the area and the divemaster had selected them not only for the scenery, but because they were great spots for new or less-experienced divers. Depths ran from five feet down to thirty, so the water was warm and clear, and the native jacks, groupers and snappers were as curious about the divers as the divers were of them.

Hol Chan was only about four miles from the island's largest town, San Pedro, and was about a fifteen-minute boat ride. Shark Ray Alley, sometimes known as *Zone D* of the Reserve, was a popular dive spot due primarily to the harmless nurse sharks and smaller rays inhabiting the area. Named not for a feature of the environment, but rather due to its history of the locals using the area to clean their catches. This practice resulted in the waters being filled with easy dinner for the aquatic predators. Once the pattern had been established, it didn't take long for the sharks and rays to realize that it was a great spot to meet for dinner.

She rubbed her eyes and squinted at the text. Ramon's Beach resort was about five hundred feet south of her hotel, off Coconut Drive. It was one of the most popular dive resorts on the island, distinguished by its tropical atmosphere and thatched huts. It welcomed divers from all over the world and ran a fleet of boats ranging from twenty-eight to forty-six feet in length, accommodating a variety of dive groups.

Purchased and completely renovated by adventurer Richard Headrick and Ramon Nunez in 1987, it had become Belize's oldest and most respected dive resort and was uniquely located near the world's second longest barrier reef, stretching one hundred eighty-six miles, and was also home to three out of four of the western hemisphere's living atolls.

She donned her gym shorts and a t-shirt and set out north along the dirt streets to take the morning air. The shops were closed, and the streets were empty except for a couple of other runners she passed along the way. She ran a mile north and then turned to head back. It wasn't her normal distance, but she did not wish to venture too far out of her zone of comfort. She was back in her room about eighteen minutes later and rummaged through her suitcase to find dry clothes to wear on the morning's dive. Apparently, for reasons yet unknown, Paul had something special in mind for her. She entered the coordinates into her iPhone and a moment later saw that they centered on the famous Blue Hole.

The Great Blue Hole was a giant marine sinkhole off the coast of Belize, lying near the center of Lighthouse Reef, a small atoll forty-three miles from the mainland. The attraction was circular in shape, over a thousand feet across and more than four hundred feet deep.

Formed during several episodes of glaciation when sea levels were much lower, it featured unusual ledges at various depths with submerged caves and stalactites, indicating that the hole had to have been formed when the area was still on dry land. The geological puzzle was that some of the stalactites were consistently off vertical by five degrees demonstrating that there had been some geological shift in the past with a tilting of the underlying plateau. Proof to some that the planet had already *globally warmed* at least once or twice in its lifetime.

In 1971, famed explorer Jacques Cousteau, brought his ship, the *Calypso*, to the Hole to chart its depths. Investigations by this expedition confirmed the hole's origin as a typical karst limestone formation, formed over thousands of years. He brought international attention to the area and naturally, tourism exploded. Divers attacked the Hole with a fervor, but sometimes, the Hole won.

A privately chartered submarine, years after the Calypso visit, managed to locate some of the bodies of divers who had gone missing after succumbing to nitrogen narcosis; rapture of the deep, the momentary alteration of consciousness caused by breathing normally safe gases at depth. But below a depth of three hundred feet the water became anoxic, due to a layer of hydrogen sulfide, so rather than attempt a recovery, the bodies were left where they were found, and the Belize government notified of their discovery.

After her return, she switched on the television set to catch the news, and then started the shower. Her research indicated that the Blue Hole was at least a two-hour boat trip from Ambergris Caye, longer on days when the weather failed to cooperate. When the water was particularly rough, a boat trip to Lighthouse Reef was near impossible for the average landlubber. Nevertheless, she grabbed her regulator bag and a bottle of water and started out.

Ramon's was modeled after a Tahitian village, with tikis and totems throughout the lush tropical jungle foliage, immaculately kept. Sandy paths led up to wooden-planked sidewalks around the buildings; sixty-one thatched roof cabanas, a hotel lobby and restaurant and of course, one of the finest dive shops anywhere.

She stopped briefly to look at the large, laminated schedule posted on the wall and saw that Blue Hole tours were not run every day. Weather, and tour size were the most common factors to affect departure times, but it seemed that the Blue Hole dive boat would not leave until 0900 and took about two hours to reach the site. She remembered from her tour literature that air tours left at 1000 and lasted for a little over an hour, out and back. With the weather predicted as mostly sunny with a high near eighty-seven, she anticipated a crowded dive boat.

She wandered up to the young man standing behind the kiosk station in the makeshift office on the dock. "Good morning. I'm looking for Damian."

The dark young man looked up with a smile. "Damian? Yeah. He's over there." Gesturing to a tall slender man in his twenties, darkened by the sun and hardened from a life outdoors. "Damian." He yelled pointing at Nerissa. "This is the lady you've been waiting for."

Damian grinned with the smile that was reasonably genuine, but obviously quite practiced and refined over the years with the tourists. "Hi! Are you...Neri?"

"Yes, I am." She returned his smile. "I was told to see you about a dive this morning. I think I'm headed to the Blue Hole today."

He nodded and reached for her arm. "You are, but not with us." He led her back up the way she had come. "You're going out with Eric today."

"Eric?" She asked, surprised and still not sure what to expect.

"Yes. You must be well-connected because we don't see Eric in here every day."

"He's not one of your regular skippers?" She asked with a bit of uneasiness.

Damian laughed. "He's not one of our skippers at all. At least not on boats. He flies the seaplane. Someone booked you on a VIP tour. Eric will fly you out to the Hole and meet up with your friends."

"My friends?"

"Yes. We were told there's a boat waiting for you out there, so he'll fly you out and then you can sync up with them for your dives and lunch. They'll bring you back this afternoon." He turned the corner and saw the large man in the shorts and flip-flops chatting up one of the female staff members. He wore a light straw hat with a pink band emblazoned with *Belize Yacht Club*, that looked like it was more suited for a golf club pro than a pilot. "Hey Eric. This is Neri." He turned back to her with a smile. "Eric will take care of you from here. You'll have a blast!"

Eric was indeed a large man, at least six foot one and close to two hundred fifty pounds. His dark brown hair was cut a little longer than was the fashion and was accented with just enough gray to allow his passengers to trust that he was sufficiently experienced to be taking them where they wanted to go, safely. He took one look at Nerissa and forgot about the woman he had been talking to. "'Ello, luv!" The British accent was obvious. I'll bet you're Nerissa... uh...Neri?"

"I am." She said and shook his outstretched hand. He was not what she might have expected for a pilot. But then, with Paul's text, she was not sure what to expect.

"I'm Eric Gates. Let me take your gear." He said as he lifted her regulator bag off her shoulder. "Sorry to make you walk all the way down here, but I'm afraid we have to walk back to the airport. It's not far." His grin widened. "But if you're here, you already know where the bloody thing is, don't you?"

She shrugged with a nod. "I suppose so." She followed him back up the planked sidewalk down which she had just ventured. "Been flying long?"

He glanced over his large shoulder at her. "Yeah, luv. About thirty years. I was here with the RAF...the, uh...Royal Air Force. I was a Squadron Leader...what you'd call a Major in the States, with Fifteen Sixty-Three Flight. We ran Whirlwinds and Pumas; helicopters on support missions, back in the nineties when I was just starting out. Moved around a bit, but after I retired, I got divorced, and I couldn't wait to get back here. It's quite the dream for any man who's never really grown up."

She was cautious, as was her nature, but he had an innocent and disarming way about him. "You look like you played some ball in your time." She changed the subject.

He nodded his head vigorously. "Oh, you bet. I still love football! But what we call football back home, you call Soccer in the states." He smacked his stomach, "Of course, that was a few pounds ago." They emerged onto the street, and he turned again. "Sorry about the walk. Seaplanes and amphibs usually put in at the Boatyard on the other side of the island, but Ramon's is a good customer so it's just as easy for me to land and refuel here. Besides, everything is walking distance to the hotels. No need for a cab!"

They crossed the street and she hastened to ask. "So, how did you book this reservation?"

"Phone call from the states. I think it came from your employer."

"My employer?"

"Yeah. Grand Emperor Insurance or something like that. We get these types of bookings from time to time. Usually, salespeople who've done something magnificent and the boss wants to reward them and their families. Come to think of it, you're the first single I've gotten from them." He slowed and turned with a raised eyebrow. "You are single aren't you?"

When she gave him the look that he had received from other female passengers, he continued. "I mean, are we picking up another passenger? You know, weights and balance. That sort of thing."

She laughed, knowing that she was being hit upon. "I'm single. For the flight. I'm meeting friends on the boat, and I'm not sure that they have room for another." She grinned and added, "No offense."

He grinned back. "None taken. I just like to know."

They walked into the Tropic Air terminal, and he waved at the thin man who returned his smile. "We have an arrangement with Tropic. Two hundred cash for landing fees, plus whatever fuel they put in. Follow me."

He walked through the glass door onto the flight line and motioned her to follow. "It's okay. You're with me. Security is not as big a deal down here as it is in the rest of the world. We all kind of know each other and the presumption is that I'm not picking up a terrorist."

He waved and nodded at Rafael, the ramp technician he had entrusted to fill the wing tanks with fuel. Rafael nodded back. "I topped her off with eighteen gallons of one hundred double-L and towed her back over here. You're good to go." He said as he handed him a receipt for the fuel.

"Tell Carlos I hope he feels better." Eric said.

"What?" Rafael replied.

"Carlos. You said he was out today with the flu or something."

"Oh. Yeah, I will." He commented and walked quickly back towards the building.

Almost oblivious to the exchange between the two men, Neri slowed her step as she looked at the single engine Cessna that appeared taller than normal due to the pontoon assembly on which the airframe rested. "This is it? What is it?"

He chuckled, "It's a Cessna 182 with Wipaire Amphibious floats. It looks a bit tall from the ground, but she's a good solid aircraft and will get you where you need to be. Here, give me your bag." He took her regulator bag and opened the starboard door of the aircraft to toss it up inside, and then climbed in. "I have to do a quick pre-flight so you can either have a seat inside or follow me around. Up to you."

"I'll watch." She smiled. "There's nothing else to do, and I might learn something."

"You're the boss!" He smiled.

Eric grabbed a laminated card out of the pocket on the door and ran through the cockpit checklist verifying the brakes, fuel selector and a variety of other points were as proscribed. When he was satisfied that everything was much as he had left it an hour earlier, he found his fuel-drain tool and emerged from the cockpit. He checked the fuselage, hatches and control surfaces and then returned to the nose of the aircraft to check the propeller. The inspection was quick simply because he had done the more thorough inspection on the mainland before arriving at San Pedro. As he wandered around the tail of the aircraft, he used his knuckles to thump on the aluminum floats to see if they sounded any different than they had an hour earlier. Then he used the clear plastic tube to check the fuel to ensure that it was water free, and the right color for 100LL, the bluish-colored low-lead, one-hundred octane juice he needed to safely operate his engine. He dumped the liquid on the ground and climbed back inside to flip through a couple of pages on his iPad and then clipped it into its holder on the yoke.

"All set. Why don't you slide into the right seat and buckle in? Since it's just the two of us, you might as well enjoy the view from the front."

"Is that allowed?" She asked, uncertain about local aviation regulations.

"Yeah. No big deal… just don't touch anything." He laughed. "The general rule in military aviation is that if a switch is red and dusty, don't touch it."

"Red and dusty? As in, not often used?" She laughed a bit nervously. "I promise. I'm assuming you want me to keep my feet away from the pedals as well?"

He nodded as he looked through his checklist. "Uh huh. That's what keeps us flying straight. Or pushes us in the direction we need to go."

"We can take off from here?"

"Excuse me?" He looked up.

"Well, the pontoons." She continued. "I didn't realize that seaplanes could take off from dry land."

"This is an amphib luv. We can take off from water or extend the gear and land on dry pavement like any other aircraft. The difference is the drag. The pontoon assembly adds drag to us, so it takes us a bit longer to get airborne. The trade-off is that when we land on water, we can stop much faster than we would on pavement." He smiled. "But we still need extra space to get back in the air. The difference when taking off from the water is that we can do part of our run-up on step, and actually start out one direction and then turn into the wind when we're powering-up for takeoff."

She shrugged. "If you say so."

The reality was that if they had been taking off from water, Eric might have noticed the aircraft sitting slightly lower in the front than normal and done a more thorough inspection of the floats. They had been dry that morning when he left Belize City and since he landed on dry pavement in San Pedro, he had not bothered to unscrew the inspection caps on each of the pontoon compartments. It would not be for another half hour before he realized that Rafael had not been an employee of the airport after all and had dumped about two and a half gallons of muriatic acid into the forward compartments of each aluminum pontoon.

When Eric completed his preflight checklist, he returned the laminated card to its pouch. "Ready to go?" He asked, looking at Neri, who was busy taking in the instruments on the dashboard.

"I suppose so. Let's do it."

Eric opened his window and looked behind and in front of his aircraft and yelled, "Clear prop!"

The engine roared to life and the propeller began to spin. The vibration was mild, but just enough to let them know that things were working as they should. He depressed the microphone switch on the yoke. "Cessna Victor three three Zulu Zulu, ready for departure."

From somewhere, someone squawked back, "Three three Zulu Zulu cleared to taxi, turn and depart on runway two-five. Left turn and advise tower on one two-two decimal five."

"Roger that. Taxi, turn and depart on runway two-five. Cessna Victor three three Zulu Zulu." He replied and checked out the windows once more to make sure no one was in the way. He adjusted his headset and indicated for her to don hers.

"You buckled in?" Eric looked over towards her lap.

Nerissa checked her seatbelt and fought the uneasy sensation that had been building inside her. She enjoyed flying and had often thought about taking lessons. However, this time, she was thinking about Paul's last-minute instructions to divert from her plans and to meet out in the Caribbean, at some coordinate, with people she did not know. She fought the voices in her head that told her that potential danger loomed ahead. She balanced those thoughts with the clairsentient feeling that if she did not go, then trouble awaited her here in the touristy island-town of San Pedro. Nothing she could put her finger on, but rather a general feeling.

After the taxi to the other end of the runway, Eric did a last-minute check of the cockpit and instruments and called the tower to report he was ready for takeoff. He raised his eyebrows and winked at her as he pushed the throttle forward. The aircraft began to move, slowly at first, and then with enough inertia that she could feel herself being pushed slightly backwards in her seat. As the ground whizzed by, he muttered to himself, "Vee One!"

"What?" She looked over at him. He was focused on the technical aspects of the takeoff and ignored her. Extraneous conversation in the cockpit during takeoffs and landings was forbidden. For good reason. Many seasoned pilots had done stupid things because of unnecessary distractions, which lead to horrific results.

"Vee Two." He said with a smile. "And...rotate." He pulled slightly back on the yoke and the nose of the aircraft lifted into the air, temporarily blocking the view she had of the ground in front of them. She adjusted her posture a bit and could see that they were airborne. "Gear up." He reached for the lever on the dashboard and then did a quick sweep of the horizon to ensure that he was not about to run into anything trying to share his airspace.

A few minutes later when they had completed their turn and were safely over water, he looked at her again with a grin. "Sorry angel. I get a bit preoccupied during takeoffs and landings. Did you say something?"

"No." She shook her head, a bit more relaxed. "You said something about Vee one and Vee two. I wasn't sure what that meant."

"It's nothing. Pilot talk. We try to verbalize what's going on as if we were talking to a co-pilot, whether one is sitting there or not. It's like, you know, muscle memory. Vee one is the speed at which we can still stop the aircraft if we need to abort the takeoff, and vee-two is the airspeed where it's safe to put us in the air, even with an engine out. Assuming we had more than one. No big deal." His grin widened. "You can relax now."

"What?"

"You can release the death grip you have on your seatbelt. We're airborne." The grin turned to a laugh.

"Oh." She was embarrassed. "I'm sorry. I...uh..."

"Don't worry about it." He comforted. "It happens all the time." He made some adjustments to the instruments and then tried to calm her. "So, what do you do for a living?"

Neri looked at the beautiful blue-green sea below. It was so clear, she could see the bottom and delighted at the view of submerged coral. "I'm a...uh...arts consultant for the State Department."

Eric nodded with a smile. "Arts consultant? For the US State Department? So, what's that then? You tell them what kind of music to play at embassy gatherings?"

She looked back at him with a nod. "Actually, yeah. Something like that."

He chuckled. "Sure. I'm sure we really need those, pet." He touched in the coordinates on his GPS that he had been given for the Blue Hole. "No offense. I'm sure my government has something like that as well." He turned southeast and did another visual sweep of his airspace to make sure they were not on a collision course with anything.

After a few minutes, Nerissa finally asked, "So with all of this ocean, what exactly are we looking for?"

"We are looking for a forty-foot Sea Ray Sundancer. Quite an expensive toy for many. If we find more than one when we get there, I'm told that this one is named the Proteus."

"Proteus? As in, the Greek god of the ocean?"

"I'm guessing that's the one." Eric replied looking at his instruments. "By my calculation, we should be right over her in about twenty-two minutes."

After a moment of silence, Nerissa asked, "I'm assuming we have enough gas to get out there and back? Well, to get you back?"

"Absolutely! With this configuration we could get about four hundred eighty miles. I could get you to Mexico if you needed." He winked again. "You got a boo?"

"A boo?" She asked with a smile.

"You know, love, a bee-eff...a boyfriend. Attractive young thing like you darting around Washington with all those politicians mucking things up every day, you must have someone to cry to?"

Nerissa liked the guy but was not the type to become involved with a pilot on a vacation. "Yes, I have a boo. We're working things out, but we're taking it easy. Besides, I never discuss personal matters like that with the people making my food, or pilots in whose hands my life rests."

He laughed. "Brilliant! I get it." He reached between his legs under the seat and brought out a walkie-talkie and handed it to her. "This is a marine radio that we'll call her on. Technically, we're not supposed to have a marine radio unless we have a boat, and Proteus isn't supposed to have an aircraft radio unless they have a plane. So, when you spend as much time as I do on the water, you'll find we have to bend the rules a bit."

Twenty minutes later, they could make out the familiar lines of the Great Blue Hole, the coral-encompassed dive site that was so popular with divers. "We're in luck, love." He pointed ahead of the aircraft. "Unless my eyes deceive me, that's the only boat down there, so this should be easy. Turn that knob to the right." He gestured at the walkie-talkie he had given her. "It should already be on channel sixteen."

"It is." She confirmed.

"Do us a favor and turn it on." He said, sweeping the horizon for signs of other aircraft.

She complied and he took the portable radio from her. "Proteus, Proteus, Proteus...this is Skylane on channel sixteen."

Though muffled by her headset, Nerissa heard the reply. "Skylane, this is Proteus. Winds East at four knots, sea calm. Bring it on in. Switch to channel six."

Eric rested the radio between his legs while he found channel six on the selector, keeping one hand on the yoke. "Proteus, this is Skylane. We'll circle on descent and have her to you in a minute."

"Proteus copies. We'll stay on channel six. Happy landings." The voice responded as Eric cut the power and added flaps to allow the aircraft to glide in at a speed suitable for landing.

"GUMPS check, love. All routine." Eric said to her as he ran through the final checklist of confirming his aircraft's profile for landing. "Gas, check. Undercarriage...I think we'll be leaving the gear up for this, check. Mixture...rich. Propeller position, check. And, of course, seatbelts." He smiled at her again. "I'm betting you're still buckled in?"

She nodded, as she reached for the shoulder harness to give it a quick tug.

"Then, mum, we are ready to land. You'll feel a little more bump from the deceleration than you're probably used to, but with the seas this calm, it should be a piece of cake!"

Nerissa nodded and watched the horizon tilting as he banked the aircraft around to the left. Below, she could see the huge white Sea Ray that she had been told to meet. From the air, it looked quite luxurious and no doubt expensive. Her excitation of having reached their destination was being quelled by a sense of foreboding. Something was wrong.

Eric continued his descent and reduced power to bring the airspeed down to just above stall speed. He added flaps so that the safe landing speed would be just above fifty-eight knots. It was then that he felt another vibration in his seat and the yoke. Instinctively, he ducked his head to check the underside of the port and starboard wings, and then risked a glance out his window to see if they had hit a bird with one of the floats. Everything looked normal, but there was the slightest buzzing of wind around the undercarriage that seemed unusual.

What he did not realize was that over the last twenty-five minutes, the hydrochloric acid that Rafael had secreted into the floats had begun to dissolve the aluminum and was now eating its way through the bottom portion of each float. Even if he had known, the affected compartments included the one where the landing gear retracted, so even if he had aborted the landing and made a break for dry land, the hydrogen gas that had been building up inside could have sparked and ignited upon impact with the pavement if the compromised gear mechanism and floats failed. Being a seasoned pilot, Gates reckoned that the noise and vibration were something that he could check out later, but there was no reason to abort the landing now.

He looked over at Neri and saw that she had a concerned look on her face. "It's okay luv. All is well."

He had completed his turn and was now bringing the aircraft in southwest of the geologic phenomenon so that he could land into the wind and taxi right up to the Sea Ray and the light gray Zodiac tender that he could see rafted off the stern. Satisfied that he was lined up with the right airspeed and altitude, he reduced power again and allowed the aircraft to glide in over the exposed coral on the southwest side of the Hole. Piece of cake.

Inches above the water, Nerissa suddenly saw a violent impact in her mind and to Eric's surprise, she thrust both of her hands up on the dashboard. A second later the pontoons touched the water, and the aluminum that had been in the process of dissolving, immediately gave way under the force of the impact and trapped the water as if they had been metal parachutes. The jerk caused the aircraft to lurch to the left as the left pontoon failed first. The Cessna cartwheeled and then nose-dived into the water and flipped.

Nerissa lost track of time. Though the aircraft was sinking nose-down, she was not afraid. She felt no pain. She was no longer in the physical universe, as it were. She was aware of the slow-motion impact, and their bodies violently jerking about the aircraft cabin, confined in their seatbelts. It was something that psychologists called tachypsychia; the neurological condition that distorts the perception of time during crisis. She was only vaguely aware of the coolness of the water as it filled the cabin, and the noticeable change in ambient pressure as it sank past twenty feet.

Yet, she was calm. It was if she had expected the tall lanky man in the Lycra wetsuit to open the starboard door, release her seatbelt and bring her to the surface. Once on the surface of the water she was passed to another man, who to her surprise, walked down a flight of stairs to meet her. Stairs? In the ocean? Nothing made sense. She was somewhere else, floating among the planets. Beautiful planets. Gas giants, but not Jupiter or Saturn. There were no rings. While Saturn's rings were bright and visible, she knew from her previous psychic visitations that Jupiter had dark rings which were made up of dust and tiny pieces of rock. A previously unknown fact before the flight of Voyager 1 back in 1980. This place was somewhere else entirely. There was a hum. Musical instruments tuning. Poorly. An obnoxious cacophony that prevented her from relaxing and enjoying the moment.

She could see the surface of the planets beneath the gas clouds. There were people there. Civilizations. They were speaking to her. She felt comfortable that she could stay as long as she desired but would eventually have to return from whence she had come.

In the recesses of her semi-conscious mind, she could hear a deep baritone voice, "Have you got her? I'm going back after the pilot."

CHAPTER 5

I t was sometime later when Nerissa awoke with a gagging cough and struggled against her bonds. She quickly determined that she was not tied up, but rather just covered in a blanket with something rigid around her neck.

"Easy, young lady. Easy." A calming voice assured her. "You're okay. We just covered you up and put a cervical collar on you because we weren't sure if you'd broken anything or had gone into shock."

"Where am I?" She asked, disoriented.

"You're okay. You're on the Proteus. My name is Ernesto... Ernie, and this is my boat. You were in an aircraft crash. Do you remember?"

She thought for a moment. A second before the crash, the discomforting feeling of something bad, followed by the reality of the aircraft striking the water and going end over end. The cabin filling with water as she looked at her unconscious pilot. "Eric? Is he okay?"

The baritone voice that seemed familiar to her replied. "The pilot? No. I'm sorry. He didn't make it."

She opened her eyes to see the two men kneeling beside her. The shorter, heavier-set one held a laminated nautical chart above and beside her head to block out the sun. "What happened?"

The tall skinny one who looked to be fit, but in his leathery sixties, answered her. "After we pulled you out, I went back after him, but the aircraft was already sinking too fast. I had an eyeball on it for a moment, but by the time we got to a hundred twenty feet, it was sinking too quickly, and I knew I couldn't get to it. I'm afraid it's on the bottom of the Blue Hole."

She rolled to her side to cough up a combination of phlegm and seawater. When she finished. She pushed herself up into a sitting position. Ernie reached for a cushion and slid it behind her back.

"You got thrown around pretty hard in there, so we put the C-collar on you. If you can feel your hands and toes, we might be able to take it off. That is, if you like. Can you breathe okay?"

Neri wiggled her toes and then moved her fingers, making fists with both hands and then releasing them. "Yes. I have a headache, but I think I'm okay."

Ernie leaned forward and carefully released the Velcro straps that held the plastic collar in place. "Don't move. Once I take this off, I want you to take it easy, and slowly see if you can sit up by yourself."

The Velcro made the characteristic ripping sound as the tall skinny man stepped over her and put his hands on either side of her head to hold it steady. Ernie carefully slid the collar out from around her neck and laid it aside. He nodded, and the man with the baritone voice said softly, "Good. I'm going to take my hands away and let you see if you can hold your head up without support."

Nerissa opened her eyes and looked around. She was on the aft deck of the Sea Ray. "I...uh...I'm thirsty. Could I get some water?"

Eric smiled, somewhat relieved. "Yeah, we can do that."

After he departed, she looked at the lanky one beside her. Tall, dark, weathered, looking something like a theatrical version of the cowboy who used to sell cigarettes. "I guess I have you to thank for getting me out of there?"

"I guess." He smiled. "If it matters, I was already in the water. It was part of the ruse to make your arrival look like nothing more than a fun-filled SCUBA rendezvous. That, and it was a way to provide additional security to cover your arrival, such that it was. While more formal introductions will be forthcoming, let's just say that we work for the same guy in Washington. Well, Virginia, if you want to split hairs."

She looked at him blankly for a moment. "And this is his idea of a vacation?"

He grinned. "People who know Paul know that he is not a real people-person and doesn't give a damn about your enjoyment. My understanding is that he is in possession of some information that indicates that your life might be at risk. He asked me to look after you for a couple of weeks until the threat can be better identified."

"I've never seen you around the office." She pushed herself further upright with a bit of pain showing on her face. "You're one of us?"

"Not really. Same boss, different department. When your team finds something that requires...uh, intervention, so to speak, they send in one of us."

She slowly nodded. Partly to see if her neck muscles still worked. They did. "I've heard about you guys. Is *counter-agent* the correct term?"

"Good enough for now. Ernie is a contractor that I knew when I was with SOCOM; the Army Special Operations Command. He was an eighteen-Delta with a B team." When she looked up questioningly, he continued. "He was our Special Forces Medical Sergeant. Paul asked me to find a guy who knew boats, and Ernie was the guy I picked. He was the guy they'd send in to set up medical treatment in hot zones when doctors couldn't get in. He's not a licensed medical doctor, but he can take out your appendix in the dark, or about anything else if necessary."

Ernie came back up from below deck and uncrewed the bottle of water before handing it to her. "Sip slowly. You got a good shakin' and we don't want to rush your recovery. However..." He looked at his yachting partner.

I was just starting to work on introductions. "Ernesto Heigel, Sergeant First Class, United States Army...retired."

Nerissa smiled and raised a shaky fist to give him a bump. "Ernesto...Heigel?"

"Yes, Ma'am. German father, Puerto Rican mother. It's a pleasure to have you aboard."

"And you?"

"Matthias Karlsson. Matt, to my friends." He offered the same fist bump, but she opened her hand.

"Nice to meet you both. Can you help me up?"

Karlsson took her hand with his right and used his left to steady her forearm as the two men carefully helped her to stand. They were on a hydraulic swim platform that extended the aft portion of the boat by another three and a half feet and could be raised and lowered by a switch. When lowered into the water, a set of stairs appeared, which compressed and went level with the platform when brought back up to deck level. The assembly made it easier to get swimmers and divers into or out of the water, and when underway, allowed the gray inflatable Zodiac Cadet to be tied down sideways for secure transport.

"Everything was going fine. He seemed to know what he was doing, and I felt very safe." She paused. "Until the last second. Right before we hit the water. I don't know what happened."

Karlsson looked at her. "From what I could see as it was sinking, it looked like both of the floats failed."

"Failed?" She asked.

"I couldn't tell that anything was wrong from my vantage point. It looked like a pretty normal descent...and I've seen a lot of seaplanes land." Ernie injected.

"The front of the pontoons ruptured somehow." Karlsson exhaled through his lips and continued. "There is no way that happened by accident. Those things are constructed to take almost twice the weight of the aircraft without failing. So, if it was just one of them, I might be able to call it bad luck. But both of them? At the same time?" He shook his head. "Huh uh. Someone tampered with those floats somehow. Someone that had access to them when your pilot wasn't around."

She was quiet for a moment. "Rafael."

"Who?" Karlsson asked.

"Eric flew in from the mainland to pick me up in San Pedro. He told me that he'd done a thorough inspection, what he called a preflight, before he left. The only person who would have had time to tamper with the pontoons would have been the kid who called himself Rafael. While Eric was meeting me at Ramon's Resort, he was away from the aircraft for about an hour. And Rafael was the guy who met us and told him that he had topped off the fuel tanks." She shook her head cautiously. "Eric asked him how the other guy was doing, the regular guy that usually services the aircraft there, and Rafael hesitated for a moment. Earlier, he'd told Eric that the regular guy was out with the flu. It had to be him because he was the only person around the aircraft. He towed it over to the pumps to refuel it. No one else could have gotten access to the plane."

The two men looked at each other before Ernie spoke. "We need to put a whole lot of *gone* between us and the Blue Hole. He probably filed a flight plan to get out here, and if he doesn't take off again in the next hour or so, someone may start looking for him."

Karlsson was pensive, looking out over the water. "How much fuel do you have?"

"Enough to get us a couple hundred miles. What are you thinking?"

"Considering what we're here for, I think it's best to head north and get as far away from here as we can. Even if the government, or whoever sent Rafael, knew where the plane touched down, how long do you think it would be for them to get a salvage operation together and raise it?"

Ernie frowned. "Weeks. Maybe longer. That hole is over four hundred feet deep, and at three hundred feet there's a layer of hydrogen sulfide. Divers can't go down there. The last thing to get to the bottom of the Blue Hole was a commercial submarine a few years ago."

"That's what I heard." Karlsson looked at Neri sadly. "I'm sorry about your pilot. My only thought at this point is to get out of here, and if asked, we didn't see anything. For all intents and purposes, two people were in that aircraft when it sank. We need to get you out of here, report to Washington and then take it from there." He paused for an afterthought. "But we can't use the radios or phones in the clear. Whoever knew you'd be on that plane had to have intercepted Paul's communication to you. We have to get somewhere else." He paused and looked out at the beautiful clear sea. "We can't go back to the hotel. What did you leave in your room?"

Neri shrugged. "My clothes, my luggage...my purse and wallet."

"Cell phone?" Karlson asked.

She shook her head again. "It was clipped to my regulator bag, which is now at the bottom of the Blue Hole."

"Passport?"

She sighed poignantly. "There was a color copy of it in my luggage back at the hotel, but the real one was in a waterproof envelope in my regulator bag."

Karlsson nodded with a slight smile. "Perfect. So, for all anyone knows, you're at the bottom as well. This could work."

He looked up at Ernie. "Do you know this area?"

Ernie nodded in agreement. "Yeah. There's a place up the coast where I've berthed before. El Placer in Quintana Roo. It's about a hundred fifty miles give or take. We could refuel and provision there and then get to Cozumel or someplace where we could blend in better. Cancun is about fifty miles further north of there."

"Neri, can you walk? We need to get below and have a look at the charts and figure out how we're going to communicate with the Office."

Together, Matt and Ernie got her into the salon and helped her sit on one of the luxurious white couches with the intricate stitching. She did not really need the assistance, but with the rocking of the boat, neither man was willing to let her walk on her own until they were sure she wasn't going to take a dive.

"What types of commo do you have onboard?" Karlsson asked.

Eric, the consummate Special Ops operator frowned. "Everything. Who do you want to call, and how?"

"Satellite and SSB?"

"Of course."

"Okay. Get us out of the coral and start us north. We'll figure out the details when we're underway."

"Roger that." Ernie said and turned to slide into the captain's chair. "Stow the Zodiac."

Karlsson nodded and headed aft to the back deck where he pulled the line in and got the Zodiac in its sideways position before he lashed it down across the swim platform. When he got back inside, he saw Nerissa leaning forward, face in her hands.

"You okay?"

She chuckled lightly, "If you mean, am I okay after surviving another attempt on my life, a horrific crash that killed my pilot, and left me with the realization that someone with access to our secure communications is trying to kill me? Well, if you mean physically, I think I'm fine. Emotionally, I'm afraid I'm a wreck."

Karlson sat his tall, lanky frame softly down on the couch next to her. "Another?"

"Yeah. A couple days ago, a cement truck ran through a red light and broad-sided the pickup truck in front of me. I thought it was just a weird accident, and now, I'm not as sure."

Ernie maneuvered out of the shallows surrounding the Blue Hole, and once in open sea, set the autopilot for a point that would bring them in southeast of the spot in El Placer where they could get diesel for the boat.

He was a pro. In the event that something happened to the GPS, if they missed their landmarks, he knew that he could simply turn west and follow the coastline north until he found his destination. In the Navy, they called it GIGO; Garbage In Garbage Out. When dead-reckoning, only a true gambler would plug in the exact coordinates because if for some reason they missed their spot, when they hit the coast, the boat-driver would not know whether to turn north or south. By picking a point which was well south of the marina, he knew that he could go north and follow the coastline. GPS brought more science to the art of navigation, but one never wanted to depend solely on electronics because of Murphy's Law. Whatever could go wrong, would go wrong. And, at the worst possible time.

"When did you eat last?" Karlsson asked their new ward.

"What?" She looked up. "I had an energy bar after my run."

"Are you hungry?" Karlsson asked out of courtesy, but also to see if she was showing signs of a concussion.

"I don't know. I suppose I could eat something. What do you have?"

Ernie looked over at her from his seat at the controls. "Well, we packed mainly for the male appetite, but we might find some fruits and vegetables down below if that interests you?"

She smiled. "Anything would be nice. An apple for starters if you have one."

Captain Heigel checked his autopilot to ensure that it was working and that they were headed the way they wanted to go. "I think we can find that. Matt, can you mind the controls for a minute?"

Karlsson got up and walked over to the pilot's station. "Yeah. Can I use your Sat phone?"

"You sure?" Eric's eyebrows came up just slightly.

"Yeah. We have to figure that everything is compromised, but we need to make a report. I'll make it in code so that Paul will know what's going on, but anyone else will think we lost our customer."

Ernie disappeared down the ladder for a moment and Karlsson studied the dashboard of the impressive craft. The Raymarine electronics suite included a forty-eight-mile color radar screen integrated with the RN300 GPS chart-plotter, and a multi-function Tridata suite that told them everything about the speed of the boat and the depth of the water they were transiting. He determined that the VHF radio and ST7001 autopilot were far too complicated for his basic seamanship skills and decided that he wouldn't touch anything until the captain returned. The other instruments included relatively simple analogue tachometers, compass and monitors for the engines. And, of course, the switches for the entertainment system and other such expensive niceties. It was a Sea Ray. It had to have the toys.

Ernie returned up the steps with an apple and the satellite phone. The apple he handed to Nerissa and the phone to Karlsson. "Here, trade me places before you run us aground."

"Can I send a text from this thing?"

Ernie stifled a grunt. "Of course. You have to remember that this thing thinks internationally, even if you're ordering a pizza from up the street. You have to dial the country code and the area code and then the number. Here…" He pointed to the keypad.

Karlsson thought for a moment and then mentally composed his message. He dialed Paul's private cell number and sent, "RUSTY SABER. AIRCRAFT CRASHED ON LANDING AND SANK IMMEDIATELY. NO SURVIVORS."

Satisfied that the text had gone through, Karlsson switched the satellite phone off. If someone was tracking it, then he certainly didn't want to provide location updates.

Ernie asked quietly with a poker face. "Rusty Saber?"

"Yeah." He laid the phone on the dashboard of the control station. "It was a one-time code that Paul and I used on a job about ten years ago. It meant that the mission was accomplished, but that communications were compromised, and he should ignore the content of the message. No one but him will know what it means."

Ernie nodded and looked past Karlsson at the demoralized figure on the couch. "How would you feel about an omelet? I heard that Matt is one of the truly great chefs aboard the Proteus."

Neri offered the first genuine attempt at a grin since they had fished her out of the water. "I'd have to say yes. At this point I'd take anything."

<hr />

Lieutenant Colonel Jonathan Babic watched his shoes thump the granite floor as he made his way to his boss' office. He was in a daze and said *excuse me* to at least a half dozen other military powerbrokers as they pursued other global crises in the opposite direction. When he got to the door he was looking for he went in and started to speak to the middle aged, gray-haired gatekeeper sitting at her workstation.

She looked up without emotion. "You can go in. He's expecting you."

Babic closed the door behind him and looked at the man he had once considered a mentor.

"Yes?" The General said without diverting his attention from his computer screen.

"You said to let you know when we heard something."

"I know." He responded with borderline contempt. "What have you got?"

"Signal from VESUVIAS, sir." As his contact had been dubbed.

"I figured that, Colonel. What is the fucking message?"

"VESUVIAS said *acquisition complete, send final payment.*"

The general looked up with a smile. "Really? They got her?"

"That's the message sir. Nothing else."

The General nodded and pecked away at his keyboard. "Just a minute. I need to check the comms mask to see what her recovery crew had to say." He typed in a string of letters and phrases that would find their way to the National Security Agency post that had been assigned to monitor that area for radio traffic.

He clicked on an area about twenty miles Northwest of the Blue Hole and dragged his mouse Southeast, forming a dotted square on the screen that encompassed the area in which he was interested. Then in the drop-down filter menu for RF bands, he selected *Cell, Satellite, Marine,* and *Aviation*, and clicked on *Apply*.

By estimating the time and location of the drop, he was quickly able to distinguish the message he was looking for from all the rest. He read the message twice just to be sure he was interpreting the data correctly. He had never heard the phrase *Rusty Saber* used on an operation but was content from the rest of the message that the team in Belize had successfully engaged the target. No survivors. He exited his program and stood with a single clap of his hands. "Fantastic! Colonel, a job well done!"

"Sir?"

"The target is down, and the recovery crew is leaving the area. I think you've earned yourself a day off."

"But sir, what's this all about? What have I done?"

"Babic, don't be such a pussy! You have done your duty and

helped secure our nation. We don't often have all the facts when we're asked to do what we do. We just do it with the knowledge that our superiors are making decisions that protect us all."

"But sir..."

The General looked up across the desk. "You have fulfilled your mission. I am upgrading your current assignment to require an O-Six in this post and sending through your paperwork for immediate promotion to full Colonel." He smiled just a bit. "Now take the rest of the day off and celebrate with your wife. Dismissed."

Soon-to-be *bird* Colonel Babic instinctively snapped to attention. "Thank you sir!" His right toe came back and touched down just behind his left heel, and spinning to the right, he executed a perfect about-face maneuver before smartly walking out of the office. His head low, he walked past the gray-haired gatekeeper without a word and exited the suite into the hallway. He was just another military officer on his assignment, just like the other twenty-three thousand anonymous faces around him. He had worked hard to get where he was, and now he was being bought off in exchange for his cooperation and silence. He was disgusted with himself. The General was right about one thing though. He needed to take the day off.

—⊶((◍))⊷—

Stan Marchand rolled over and as quietly as he could, slipped out of bed and headed to the bathroom. Tricia and he had gone to dinner at Gleneagles the night before and run into friends who insisted on closing the establishment down. By the time they returned home, neither was interested in a physical liaison, but around two in the morning he had awakened to her touch. Her special touch, indicating that she was ready if he was. After a frenzied encounter under the sheets, they had both drifted back off to sleep, with nothing on their calendar that necessitated their presence before lunch.

He looked at his watch and saw that it was nine o'clock, and as he stretched and looked at himself in the mirror, he felt just a bit guilty that his younger friends were still on the job and had already started their day hours earlier. "The joys of civil service retirement." He said to his image in the mirror. He flushed the toilet and returned to the bedroom to see his Tricia rubbing her head, her beautiful blond hair askew.

"You know, Mr. Marchand, if you continue to keep a membership in that club, they're going to turn you into an alcoholic?"

He sat down on his side of the bed and looked at his phone. Two emails from Grand Emperor Insurance caught his eye, but when he opened them he could tell that they were not taskings. They contained some kind of narrative that would require him to have a cup of coffee before reading. He tossed the phone back on the nightstand and slid under the covers. "I know. It's an occupational hazard. Most of them are good people, and when you're not around, they fill the void. They're my social network now."

She tilted her head and looked at him with one eye open. "You're so full of shit! Maybe that's why I love you."

"Uh huh." He sighed. "Maybe that's why I love you too. You can see through the superficial façade that is Marchand."

She rolled over and smacked him on his shoulder. "One of these days…" Her voice trailed off as her fingers traced lightly across his shoulder, down his arm. "Some woman is going to make you wish you'd been a stockbroker or welder or something."

"What's wrong with being hooked up with a retired Secret Service agent?" He smiled.

Her fingers dropped down to his rib cage. "Naw. You guys aren't the white-picket fence types. I can't see you making lunches for your kids before sending them off to school."

He rolled over and looked at her. "Uh huh. Like that's where you saw your life going."

Her touch went from a light tracing to her digging her nails into his stomach. "Maybe ten years ago. Where were you then?"

"I was protecting people who thought they were entitled to

it. Where were you? Sucking your thumb and asking your mother what intercourse was?"

She smacked his solid abdomen with a resounding clap. "You fuck! I'm not that much younger than you. If you can stay alive and out of diapers for six more years, we'll have two pensions to live on!"

"Okay." He smiled and pulled her close to him. "I'll wait. In the meantime, you better learn how to play golf because Griffiths isn't getting any younger and I'm eventually going to need another golf partner."

"You mean a drinking partner. Everyone plays golf, but I don't think I can keep up with you guys when you get going."

He brushed her hair aside and kissed her ear. "Well, I'll drink less if you take golf lessons."

"I did take lessons."

"I mean, more lessons!" He glanced over at his phone on the nightstand. "Sorry to break the mood, but I need to get some coffee and answer these calls."

She nodded and pushed herself up so that she could swing her legs out to the floor. "Something big brewing in Washington?"

He inhaled hard enough to flair the nostrils on his aquiline nose. "Who the hell knows? It's usually nothing, but they run around with their hands in the air like the sky is falling."

"Uh huh. Do what you've got to do." She stood and started to the bathroom; her naked form accentuated by the light coming through the blinds. "Let me get cleaned up and I'll make us coffee and breakfast."

She disappeared into the bathroom and closed the door behind her. He picked up his phone and opened the email from Grand Emperor. The first email consisted of a one-word message. "PAN."

It took him a moment to realize where he had heard the term before. In aviation and boating circles, *Mayday* was the phrase sent when there was something wrong, an emergency was being declared and the sender needed assistance right away. However, if there was something wrong and the crew was working through whatever problems might have presented, they sent *Pan*. It meant that listeners needed to stand by in case their attempts to correct whatever was wrong, failed, and they had to escalate their status to a full scale emergency.

He opened the second email but noticed that it had been sent from an address with which he was unfamiliar. It still came across as Grand Emperor Insurance but had not originated from the same device. It caught his attention and stimulated his curiosity.

"ADVANCE: VERACRUZ, TAMPICO AND BROWNSVILLE. NEED DIESEL, ON THE WATER. USUAL RATE PLUS BONUS IF U CAN LEAVE IMMEDIATELY"

"Diesel on the water?" Someone important was coming up the Mexican coast by boat. "HEADING SOUTH IN FOUR HOURS." He tapped. Tricia was not going to be happy.

———◈———

Nerissa felt the momentary weightlessness as the aircraft descended the final few feet and knew something was wrong. Some might call it clairsentience, and others would say that she was simply situationally aware. There was a noise that seemed to alarm the pilot as well and she saw him take note of the underside of the wings, before looking out his window at the floats. He had begun to instinctively pull back on the yoke to keep the aircraft airborne for a fraction of a second longer than he normally would have. It was evidence that he too suspected something was amiss.

She was not alarmed. She was curious. She braced for the impact that she knew was inevitable. As the left float imploded and began to toss the aircraft into a cart-wheeling motion she saw them. Standing proud and tall against the blinding white light of dawn she saw them standing there as they had for centuries. The jury who sat in judgment of the newcomers, expressionless but diligent in their duty. She felt comfortable among them but knew that it was not yet her time. She felt warm and at peace, but knew she had to go back.

She suffered through several more jolts before the aircraft came to rest, nose down in the water, the cabin filling quickly. The tall skinny one opening her door and releasing her seatbelt. She held her breath as they climbed slowly towards the surface. Then, more jolts. Softer than the first. More cushioned, they came in a rhythmic patter that accompanied the noise outside of her consciousness. The smell of the sea. The voices of earth-bound humans.

She awakened to the feeling of motion but sat slowly up until she could focus on her surroundings. "How long was I out?" She asked as she looked at the now familiar cockpit of the Sea Ray.

"Couple of hours." Ernie replied from the helm. "You were breathing pretty normal, and your vitals were normal too, so we just let you sleep. How do you feel?"

She quickly took stock of her physical self. "Like I went a couple of rounds in the cage with that Scottish guy. The...uh..."

"Conor McGregor? The MMA champ?" Karlsson replied. "I think he's Irish, but I get your drift." Karlsson and Ernie laughed.

"Where are we?" She asked looking out over the water.

Ernie glanced at his instrument panel. "About an hour south of El Placer. We're making pretty good time, but we wanted to conserve fuel and didn't want to jostle you around too much. So, we're running about two thousand RPM burning forty-four point eight gallons per hour. That gives us about twenty-four and a half knots in speed."

She looked at him with her head tilted just a bit. "And, how fast is that in regular miles per hour?"

Ernie grinned. "About twenty-eight miles per hour. We want to get there, but we don't want it to look like we're in a hurry."

Karlsson added, "We're just a happy group of American taxpayers out for a vacation experience, diving our way up and down the Mexican coast."

Neri rubbed her head. "What happens after we get to El Placer?"

"We're tourists!" Ernie exclaimed. "We're going to have some drinks and lunch and then head up the coast to Cozumel or Cancun. Just like all the other tourists."

"And from there? Do we have a plan, or are we just winging it?"

Karlsson jumped in. "From there, we'll turn west and then south to follow the coastline towards Campeche, and then check for messages. Paul knows we are making our way back and is planning some assistance for us."

"When we get to El Placer, though, you can call your friend and let him know you're okay."

"My friend?"

"Yeah." Ernie looked over. "While you were out, you called out the name *Mark* a couple of times. I figured that was a boyfriend or something."

Nerissa thought hard for a moment. "Mark? You're sure?"

Matt Karlsson nodded. "I think so. It sounded like you said *Mark*, but it could have been something else."

Neri thought for a moment. She could only think of one man named Mark with whom she shared any type of past. A man she met in the physical existence only briefly but had shared a psychic journey, which changed the path of history. She had not seen him in two years and had tried not to think about him, for both of their own good. "Oh. I must have been really out of it. Sorry."

No need to apologize." Ernie said. "If you want to call him, we can make arrangements for that. If it's important, we can figure out a way to get you through to whoever you need to call."

"Well." She thought. "My son and mother."

"That's being taken care of." Karlsson interjected. "In person. Paul thought it best if we avoided the use of electronic communication as much as possible."

Her mother knew that she was on assignment. "He's going to send someone by her apartment?"

"Yeah. But we want the rest of the world to think that you are at the bottom of the Blue Hole. It will take us the better part of your vacation week to work our way around the Mexican coastline, back into the US of A. We don't think that any of us should be in a hurry to suddenly show up somewhere."

"Then what?" She asked.

"Well," Karlson continued. "Then we keep you out of sight and out of mind until Paul can figure out what's going on and who wants you dead."

She shook her head quietly. She knew that something she had done had upset the Washington equilibrium, but she trusted the two men who were now assigned as her travel partners. "I'm going to need some things. My luggage is back in San Pedro and will probably be in an evidence locker by the end of the day. Personal things." She frowned. "And a US passport. I won't be able to re-enter the United States without one."

"Paul's taking care of that too." Karlsson replied. "At some point in the next forty-eight hours, we'll have a new passport for you. But I'm not sure what name will be on it." He smiled knowingly. "I assume that you've had a cover dropped on you at least once or twice before?"

She squinted at the sun and then looked back into the cockpit of the Sea Ray. "Once or twice."

Two hours later, she walked along the streets of El Placer, a relatively modern tropical stopover amidst the reality of Mexico. The beautiful aqua water and sandy beaches, the modern high-rise hotels, and of course the shops that offered everything the female tourist needed to make her stay a pleasant one. Her gangly-but-fit escort in tow, they returned to the beachfront bar for an afternoon cocktail, while Ernie stayed aboard and supervised the refueling and reprovisioning. Once they had determined that Eric's plane had been sabotaged so easily in front of an airport terminal building, none of them were going to take any chances now.

Near the pier there was a quaint little bar named Candelarias hidden under the palm trees with the ubiquitous sign in English that stated, "No shirt, no shoes, better service." It was still relatively early, so they ventured in to the near-empty venue and had a seat.

The sinewy, dark-complected bartender named Carlos greeted them with a smile. "Good afternoon! What can I get you?" His English was flawless and seemed incongruously out of place in this locale that, after a plane crash and four-hour boat ride, seemed so far from home.

Neri smiled. "Your English is very good. Are you a local?"

"I am now." He grinned. "I was born in McAllen and went to Texas A&M before realizing that all of that education was taking me further away from what I wanted in life." He used a small towel to wipe the bar surface in front of her. "This is the life everyone aspires to, so I thought, why waste thirty, forty years working towards it, if I could have it now?"

Karlsson nodded knowingly as Neri laughed and commented. "I can't fault you for your vision!"

"What can I get you Bonita?"

Neri glanced at Karlsson with a questioning look, and then back at Carlos. "What do you recommend?"

"Today, the *especialidad* is *The Press Secretary*, or better known as the Gin P-Sake...one part gin, one-part saké, extra bitters, artificial red coloring like its namesake, a drop of Tabasco to simulate snake venom and garnished with a slice of red pepper. It tastes like pee and is guaranteed to leave a bad taste in your mouth for days. Two of them will leave your stomach turning and your brain scrambling to understand common logic. Again, like its namesake."

They both laughed at the political humor. "You seemed to be well-versed in American politics!" Neri commented.

Carlos rolled his eyes. "They think we're such ignorant morons down here. They continue to import voters who will contribute nothing more up there than they did down here. With the exception that your left-wing will certainly be able to stage a socialist coup in the next four years."

Neri considered her options. "What the heck. We're in Mexico, so how about a Press Secretary?"

"You got it!" Carlos said. "And for you sir?"

"The same, thanks." Karlsson reached into his pocket. "I'm a little light in Pesos. Any chance you'd accept US currency?"

"Naturalmente, señor!" Carlos said with a furtive grin. He lowered his voice. "I actually prefer it."

Carlos grabbed a shaker and added the necessary amounts of each ingredient and dumped in enough to make a couple of drinks with a dividend left over. People, especially Americans, tipped bigger when they thought they were getting something extra for free. "Where are you from?"

Nerissa quickly looked at Karlsson, who answered. "Albuquerque. Down for some diving and relaxation."

Carlos sliced a piece of red pepper and tossed a strip into each glass before he poured his concoction. "Sip these gently. They might be a little stronger than the martini's you're used to up north."

"Thanks!" Nerissa said as she brought the glass to her lips.

Carlos looked out towards the pier and the gas dock. "Is that your Sea Ray out there?"

Karlsson looked across the water at the boat glistening in the sun. "Yes. It belongs to a friend."

"Nice. I bet it costs a fortune to fill it up."

"I'm sure it does. Twin diesels. It has quite a range, but it is definitely not the most economical way to get from point A to point B."

Karlsson sampled his drink and nodded his approval. "This is good! I'm glad I'm not driving, though!"

"Like I said, amigo. Not what you're used to up north." Carlos rinsed out the shaker and carafe. "I saw you come up from the south. Ambergris Caye?" He asked innocently enough.

Karlsson nodded.

"You guys dive the Blue Hole?"

Nerissa jumped in. "No. I'm just learning to dive so we stayed in the Hol Chan area."

Karlsson was impressed. She was no novice at the game.

"Where you headed?" The bartender asked.

"Up to Cozumel and Cancun. We thought we'd check the dive sites out there and then catch a plane home." Karlsson replied, just as innocently. "Just some fun in the sun." After a brief pause, he continued, "Any other Americans around?"

"Mostly younger people. Destination weddings with bachelor parties attached. That seems to be the current thing. They come to town, have their fun, and then leave. Are you looking for anyone in particular?"

Karlsson responded quickly. "No. Just curious who's around."

Carlos was more than moderately streetwise. "No one that you'd be interested in meeting. We don't get a lot of attention here."

Karlsson did not want to under-estimate the opposition, whoever they might be, and whatever they might be capable of. Depending on how deep any type of conspiracy was being planned for them he wanted to err on the side of caution. He slid a one-hundred-dollar bill across the counter. "We're not looking for a lot of attention, ourselves."

Carlos slid the bill off to the side. "And, if anyone asks, I didn't see any extranjeros here today arriving by boat. And, if any did, it wasn't an attractive middle-aged couple who came in on a million-dollar Sea Ray."

Karlsson smiled. "You most certainly are the man!"

An hour later, with one drink behind them, Nerissa noted the small stage in the corner with the microphone and speakers. "So, what time does karaoke start here?"

Carlos grinned as he passed by them to attend to a young couple who were in the process of seating themselves at the end of the bar. "Si ustedes son cantantes muy bueno, entonces cuando quieran!"

Karlsson translated using his limited understanding of *Texican*. "I think he said that if you're a good singer, then whenever you want."

Nerissa smiled and from her stool started into an acapella cover of Doris Day's version of Secret Love, the Webster-Fain piece from Calamity Jane. It was as if Doris Day was in the beach bar. Even the young couple at the end took note and listened. It was quite a show of respect considering that they weren't yet alive when Doris Day was an international sensation.

"I thought your team didn't drink." Karlson asked quietly when she finished.

"We don't when we work. When we're trying to put a plane crash and a horrific day behind us, we resort to the same depressants that ...people in your line of work use."

Karlsson raised his eyebrows ever so slightly. "My line?"

Nerissa looked at him with eyes that were bit glassier than they had been earlier. "I know what you do. Just like you know what I do. Sometimes we have to work together. Sometimes we don't like to admit that either of our jobs exist. I started out as an idealist. As did you, I'm assuming?"

Karlsson nodded and raised his glass. "Yes. Here's to idealism!"

Carlos brought them another round with the request that neither of them should be operating a motor vehicle for at least eight hours. As he poured the drinks, Neri finished her impromptu set with *The Way We Were*. Something Doris Day had performed in her 1975 TV special, with photos of the leading men she had worked with in her time, floating past behind her as if in a dream. The young couple applauded and Karlsson paid the tab.

"And that, my dear is our swansong. Time to go."

She smiled and carefully pushed the barstool back enough to graciously make her exit. Admittedly, she was not a drinker, and Carlos' drink-of-the-day had anesthetized her to the degree that she could have held still for an appendectomy.

Karlsson gently steered her towards the boat at the end of the dock, carrying her shopping bag from the day's excursion. She leaned her head against his shoulder and sang a song that she had sung to her son, Hunter, when he was a young child. Doris Day's Twinkle Lullaby, a song from the 1963 movie, *Move Over Darling*, about a woman presumed lost at sea who unexpectedly returned to her family several years later.

—◦((◦))◦—

Lieutenant General Nelson Scott replaced the handset of the secure telephone unit in its cradle and collected the papers on his desk. He shoved them into his leather folio and walked out of his office. "Glenda, I'll be out for a while. If anyone asks, I'll be back around four."

"No problem, General." The gatekeeper replied without looking up from her computer screen.

Five minutes later, he was in the back seat of his staff car, an unmarked black Ford Explorer, headed towards Lee Road in Chantilly, Virginia. The Headquarters of the National Reconnaissance Office. A large glass and steel building, built in secret until a news article outed them in 1992 as they emerged from the bureaucratic closet to fight for funding like every other government agency. During his first trip there he had remarked to a coworker that only an idiot would have built a spy building that close to a major freeway that fed into Dulles International Airport. With all that glass, it was a certainty that someone was eavesdropping with laser interferometry. Even though the SCIF's were located towards the inside of the building, the volume of seemingly harmless chatter that went on in the halls and outer offices still had to make for good copy.

The driver of the staff car paused at the gate on the north side of the complex to identify himself and his sole occupant. "GUARDIAN THREE. We're expected."

The guard glanced in the back of the vehicle and pressed a button, raising the gate. "You know where you're going?"

The driver nodded and the Explorer drove through. It pulled up in front of the building and stopped in front of the single pedestrian standing on the sidewalk. The forty-something man in the dark gray suit opened the right rear door and slid in next to the general.

When they were safely underway, the stranger said to the general, "So, what's this all about? I thought you wanted to keep this strictly off the books?"

General Scott looked out the window at the late summer afternoon. Virginia truly was a beautiful region of the country. Hills, trees, and history. He knew he would have to temper his remarks for his elite audience. His guest oversaw the Mission Operations Directorate, which reported directly to the head of the NRO. The man in the gray suit was no political lightweight, but like himself, he was in a position that although it offered access to many secrets it was also on the chopping block if someone needed a scapegoat. Scapegoating was a regular practice in Washington.

As a member of the United States' so-called *Big-Five* players in the intel community, the organization reported into the Defense Department and was responsible for the operation of all the US reconnaissance satellites and the information they processed. They developed, built, and launched the birds that supposedly kept us safe from our enemies. They saw much. On the earth below and the busy space above. It bore an eerie resemblance to the Hermetic textual passage, which referenced the effects of celestial mechanics on terrestrial events.

"I do." The General replied with a quick glance towards the driver, as if his guest had not noticed him. "It's contained. What about your side?"

"Because of the location I assigned it to a team that spends most of their time tracking drug runners for the DEA. They get dozens of taskings every day, so this one would not have appeared any different."

"Good. So, if we take it down today, there shouldn't be any questions?"

The man in the gray suit glanced quickly at the driver. He assumed that like most in that role, he had been cleared for Above Top Secret. "None. No problems. Do you expect any questions later?"

"None. But…" His voice trailed off as he looked out the window at the beautiful sky and the buildings symbolic of their democracy. "You just never know." The General inhaled briskly through his nose as his tight lips turned down to a frown. "You just never know."

CHAPTER 6

The trip to Cancun had been uneventful except for the nominal amount of cabin fever that was to be expected from a group of three strangers sharing a forty-foot boat. Then again, it was not a vacation, but rather a group of professionals thrown together for an indeterminate period. Like astronauts training for a mission to space. They had gotten to know each other to a limited degree and had melded well. They knew their roles and discussed many of the obstacles they might meet before they got back to US soil. So, it wasn't a surprise that Mexican Customs would want to inspect the boat upon arrival, but what was a surprise was the level of cooperation received during the initial inspection.

"Pasaportes, por favor." The young officer requested after the Proteus had tied up at the dock.

Nerisa had been hidden in the head below deck, with the hopes that the usual cash payment would help speed the inspection along. The young officer named Dominguez glanced at Ernie's and Matt's passports and then pulled a packet out from under the clipboard. "I believe you have a female traveling with you. A Mary Ann Taggart?"

Both men looked at each other, as the officer handed Karlsson the manila envelope, sealed with a piece of transparent tape across the opening. On the cover of the envelope. Someone had written the word *Emperor*. Karlsson opened the envelope to find a US Passport, a stack of hundred-dollar bills and a Corporate VISA card made out to the same individual, an employee of Trundle Engineering. He opened the US Passport and saw Nerissa's picture with the new name.

"Your documents appear to be in order gentlemen. I hope you

enjoy your stay in Cancun, but I must ask if there are any drugs or firearms on board?"

"I certainly don't have any drugs." Ernie replied as completely as he dared, with a bit of confusion.

"Me neither." Karlsson added without knowing what types of firepower his skipper might have stashed, to be close at hand if necessary.

The Customs official nodded and winked at Karlsson. "Then, if you will forgive the intrusion, we would like to have our dog board your craft. It will only be a minor inconvenience and then you will all be free to disembark and enjoy your stay."

Karlsson carefully withdrew Neri's new passport and handed it over to the officer, who flipped through the pages and handed it back. The Customs official had to have been someone on Paul's payroll. The first scheduled contact was not for several more days when they made it to Veracruz. But Paul was always full of surprises. Nevertheless, Karlsson palmed two of the one-hundred-dollar bills and passed them to the young officer as they shook hands, in such a manner that his partner, standing on the dock next to a rather bored looking German Shepherd, could not see.

As the Customs official signaled his partner to bring the dog aboard, Karlsson slipped below and tapped softly on the door. "Customs inspection Ms. Taggart."

Nerissa opened the door slowly with a puzzled look on her face. He slid the envelope to her through the crack of the door. "Here, Mary Ann. Customs wants to bring the dog aboard, so when you finish in there, why don't you come up on deck and join us for a drink?"

She took the manila envelope with a frown and closed the door. A moment later, he could hear the toilet flush, and the door opened again. "Thanks." She whispered. "I'm not sure how we just got this, but I never look the gift horse in the mouth."

Karlsson shrugged. "I'm pretty sure this will be a routine sniff. When the dog doesn't find any weed, we'll be free to join the rest of the revelers in town."

"Can they sniff out the currency?" She asked now that she had about ten thousand dollars in the envelope, stuffed under the tee shirt in the small of her back.

Karlsson waved her up the ladder ahead of him. "That dog doesn't look as if it could smell anything other than a steak and another dog. The Customs guy is the person who carried the envelope. If we get pinched now, it will mean Washington has a bigger problem than what they'd thought."

Karlsson and Nerissa joined Ernie on the back of the boat as the Mexican Customs team let the dog run around the area below decks. About four minutes later, the underwhelmed canine returned from his search and headed back to the dock to await his treat for a job well done. The official who had passed the envelope to Karlsson waved and they headed back down the dock to greet the other new arrivals.

Nerissa flipped through her passport to find out who she was and where she had been for the past three years. "That son of a bitch." She smirked.

Karlsson looked at her with a raised eyebrow.

"Mary Ann is from Pawtucket Rhode Island." She mentioned with a tinge of exasperation.

"So?" He asked. "Is that a problem if we get stopped?"

She closed the passport and shoved it into one of her back pockets. It might as well look used if anyone else asked her for it. "That's where my *ex* and I went on our honeymoon. We were there for a week, and he fell in love with the place. Only Paul would have been ornery enough to pick that as Mary Ann's city of residence."

She looked at the VISA card. "Trundle Engineering?"

Karlsson grinned. "One time he dumped a cover on me that said I was in pest control. Really cute! Are you okay with this?"

"Paul knew that on our honeymoon there, we rented a room in a Bed and Breakfast place and our room had a faulty trundle bed. We slept on two levels that entire week. Very funny!"

Karlsson smiled. "And yet many people think he doesn't have a sense of humor."

They decided to watch the Proteus in shifts and since Ernie had not had the chance to get any recreational time in El Placer, he was selected to go ashore first, have some dinner, and scout out the town. When he returned two hours later, Nerissa and Karlsson had their turn. They were in no hurry as Ernie would need time to refuel.

After cabbing a few blocks, they walked among the vacationers, with Karlsson frequently checking to see who might be interested in them. The trouble with tourist destinations was that one could not be sure if unwanted attention was indicative of hostile surveillance or a simple pick-pocketing scam. But this time of year, it was still hot and not drawing the number of tourists that it would see in a couple of months.

They ended up at one of the top nightspots in Cancun, that was more reminiscent of Las Vegas than Mexico. The Coco Bongo offered a unique experience; stage shows complete with all the special effects one would expect in Sin City USA. Multi-level seating throughout the venue allowed each patron to enjoy a performance from anywhere, no matter where they were seated. Karlsson recalled a visit to the Imperial Palace in Vegas where he had tipped the Maitre'd a mere twenty dollars and was surprised to be seated behind a pillar that necessitated him and his wife at the time, to lean out around the damned thing to see the stage. This was much better. Conga lines, trapeze acts, live bands and integrated video made it a fabulous experience. It was obvious from their behavior that many of the customers near them had been there before and had purposely planned a return visit.

Karlsson largely ignored the entertainment and without being any more obvious than he had to be, scanned the crowds for any sign of interest. It was what he did. He was looking for anomalies. Anomalous behavior. Anomalous appearance. Something or someone that stood out. Regardless of outward appearances, he was working. If someone was planning a surprise, then he had to know from where and from whom it was coming.

People who engaged in acts of *targeted violence*, as the Secret Service had defined it back in 1998, tended to identify and observe their target for a period of time before striking. Otherwise, there were too many variables that might affect their ability to act out. This meant that assassins had to engage in somewhat predictable patterns of surveillance in order to know where their target might be on any given date and time. Thus, most security details included surveillance detection as a part of their overall protection plan. Surveillance that could be spotted by a trained observer.

When they entered, he took note of the exit signs. He took note of where the security people stood. He took note of the people seated around them. He took note of the people who were present when they arrived and who came in after them. While it was a chance for Neri to relax, he could not drop his guard until they were back on the Proteus. He had to be situationally aware. Hyper aware.

They were seated on the bar rail on the second level. The mass of humanity was energized and had driven the occupancy below to standing-room-only near the stage. It was loud enough that one had to lean in and yell in the ear of their date if they wanted to be heard. The place was packed and dark, and noisy. It was the kind of place Karlsson hated since it was impossible to protect someone adequately with such limited resources. Nevertheless, his scan of the venue seemed to indicate that they were as alone in the mob as they could be and after a few minutes he found himself de-stressing a bit and enjoying the surroundings.

It was after the waitress had replaced their first drink with their second that Nerissa leaned in close to him. "You seem like a guy who might be fun to be around when he wasn't looking for potential threats."

Karlsson allowed a corner of his tightly pressed lips to turn up in a smile. He needed to blend in and to make everyone else think that he was on a spectacular excursion with an attractive younger woman. He had a role to play, and it wasn't much different than the other roles he had been asked to play over the years. If they did not speak, someone might get the idea that they were the anomaly. "That obvious? Uh huh. Sometimes. But my idea of fun isn't a place where the music is at a hundred twenty decibels and the people are packed in butt-to-belly button."

She took a sip of her Margarita and smiled back. "Yeah? So, what do you and your wife do for fun, when you're not doing clandestine things for the government?"

He glanced over her shoulder towards the stairs and then back into her eyes. "She's gone. She died several years ago."

Nerissa squinted, the anguish showing on her face. "I am so sorry. I didn't mean to pry. I..."

Karlsson touched her arm. "Don't worry about it. We had been divorced for a lot of years and she had remarried. But even though she was married to someone else at the time we lost her, it still hurt. Our kids were grown, and had already adjusted to their new family dynamic, so to speak. It has been a long time now, but, she was a part of my life, and I really just never found anyone to take her place."

"No girlfriend?" Neri asked. The Margaritas were relaxing her, and she was obviously in the mood to talk.

"Mizzz Taggart," He drawled, using her assigned name in case anyone important was listening in. "Despite what you might think, I do manage to keep a social life, such that it is. And, if it matters, before this, I was trying my *damndest* to be officially retired. However, since you asked, my previous occupation has not exactly lent itself to meeting members of the opposite sex for purposes of fraternization. Nevertheless, if I told you I was dating someone in the business, I'm sure you would understand."

She sighed. "Understood. My occupation is no conversation starter, either."

"I can imagine. Boyfriend?" Karlsson asked. Turnabout was fair play.

She shook her head. "Not in a while. My mom says I'm too picky and that I'm waiting for someone who doesn't exist in this realm."

"In this realm?" Karlsson asked, amused at her choice of words.

She smiled. "You know what we do. If we can go anywhere in the universe, wouldn't it seem feasible that we could develop relationships with people outside of our current space and time?"

Karlsson grinned at her. "Now that would be a difficult role for a guy to compete in. Most people think that it would be tough enough to follow a dead spouse. You're adding a whole new dimension to dating expectations."

They both laughed and she tried to explain. "In a matter of speaking, yeah. It does. If you think about it in the physical sense, for me, it's like watching a movie from the seventies or eighties, and out of curiosity, you Google the performers to read something about them, or to see what they're doing now. Depending on the actor, and the date the movie was filmed, they might be years dead. You can see what they accomplished before or after they made the movie you're watching, and many times, how their lives ended, or what they accomplished throughout their career. There is no forward-moving time as we know it in the psychic realm."

Karlsson digested what she was saying. "So, you can look at a person's life as if you were reading it in some sort of encyclopedia years later?"

She nodded with a polite shrug. "Much of the time."

He considered the ramifications of what she was saying, and he began to understand why Paul might consider her such a valuable asset. "And I suppose there are others like you out there? People with your...uh...attributes working for our government? Or others?"

She took another sip of her Margarita. "Of course. For years now." She carefully sat her glass on the cocktail napkin. "For many years, our government resisted research into this field. Hell, think back in history. For the longest time, simply referencing a phenomenon like this would have gotten you burned at the stake or thrown out of your country club. Our civilization, our culture was ingrained with the idea that the biggest dichotomies in life were whether we believed in God or whether we were atheistic. The reality is that there are many belief systems grounded in something real or what we call actuality. However, to be totally atheistic means that you not only don't believe in anything, but that you are doomed to a closed mind and your spiritual growth simply cannot advance."

"And agnostics?"

"We used to say that agnostics were simply chicken-shit atheists who were afraid to take a stand for fear that if they were wrong, they'd end up in hell or purgatory or something." She smiled. "Actually, some agnostics are simply skeptics who are looking for proof of something to push them over the line. To believe or not-believe, as they say."

"And you have the answers?" Karlsson winked.

"About some things. Not everything. I can see what I need to see. Sometimes, what I'm told to see. What I do isn't a carnival game. Everyone has some capacity to be psychic. It's like golf. Everyone can swing a club, but if you're serious about it and take lessons, and practice, you'll be really good at golf. But some people will be naturally better at it than others. Like playing the tuba or welding a pipe. If you have no interest in learning...like the atheist, then you probably won't find the secrets or life that you want. The agnostic, at least, has a chance at discovering something, even if by accident."

Karlsson was silent for a moment as he looked around the room. There was a couple in their late sixties or early seventies that seemed to be looking for a spot to land. His bald pate was accentuated by the flowing gray locks raining down across his ears. Karlsson figured him for a hipster from the sixties who was still trying to celebrate his youth in this noisy place. He had made his fortune in a capitalistic world but would stubbornly vote democrat until the day he died. His wife had given up coloring her hair and was comfortable draping a misshapen sun dress over her thin frame. They had to be from a herb farm in northern California. Karlsson ignored them and returned his gaze to Neri's eyes.

"Well then, the elephant in the room is...what about us?"

She took his hand across the table and squeezed it lightly. "I'm not worried. This isn't where we end. You live on a farm somewhere out west, where it is reasonably dry. You have animals. You will see them all again. I will see my mother and my son again. You will do your job, even though it may cause pain to others. But, to answer your question, I am not worried. But you need to be. At least, for a while."

———— ‹‹(●)›› ————

Jonathan Babic found a space about three doors down from The Cardigan, on Wisconsin Avenue just past Q Street. Certain that he had not been followed, he locked his car and tucked the leather folio under his arm. The place was busier than it had been the last time, but then again, it was earlier, and people were still working at finding a suitable partner for the evening. It took him a while to find the woman who called herself Davina, or Dave Fox, depending on her audience. She was seated in a booth along the left side of the room, chatting with an attractive woman in her mid-fifties. Tonight, though, she was a blond.

"Good evening." He said with a smile so fake a third grader could have spotted it.

"Hey, Captain Kirk! I've been waiting for you." She gestured across the table. "This is Francine. I asked her to stay but she has to get home to take care of her dogs and cats."

Francine, like her partner for the evening, was an attractive woman, well-attired, but there was something about her that indicated that she had had a rougher life than most of her Washington contemporaries. Lean and fit, she used makeup to cover the hairline scar than ran up and down just along the outside of her left eye. Whatever injury had caused it, also caused her left eye to droop just a bit when she smiled. Her hands gave away her age and hinted at a life in the trades. Had she been wearing jeans and boots, sans makeup, she could have passed for a truck driver or wrangler. However, the shape of her legs was entirely feminine and her choice of dress and heels indicated that she had style and taste.

Francine smiled as she slid her way out of the booth and stood to shake his hand. "Nice to meet you, but I have to catch an international flight first thing in the morning, and I'm already half in the bag." She gave him the cursory hug that substituted for a handshake in modern Washington and blew a kiss to Davina. "Ciao, Bella!"

"See you next week." Davina grinned and touched her fingertips to Francine's palm as she walked past.

"Don't tell me, congressional aid from Kansas?" Babic said, trying to be humorous.

Davina laughed. "Hardly. Civil servant. Ex-Army or something-or-other." She looked over at the bar. "Wally must be falling down on the job. I ordered you a Jamesons rocks a few minutes ago and I think I need to remind him.

Babic tried to stop her. "Wait. I really don't..."

She ignored him and stood. "Oh, come on Captain Kirk. You've got to play the game. Sit tight, and I'll be right back."

Babic was facing the door and had a reasonably good view of the people coming and going. None of them looked suspicious, but he felt, under the circumstances, that he was supposed to be at least a little tactically competent and so he continued to look around the place.

Davina was back in a few seconds and set his drink in front of him. "Now we can toast."

Babic looked over his shoulder, back towards the bar, and then returned his focus to the unusual woman across the table. "What are we toasting to?"

Davina raised her glass. "Mission accomplished!" She waited for him to raise his glass.

A very long day behind him, Babic was ready to unwind, and lifted the Jameson's in her direction before taking a good slug. "Right. Mission accomplished."

She studied him for a moment before offering her psychological evaluation. "You don't look all that thrilled. What's the problem?"

"No problem. I'm just not used to...you know. All this."

"Listen Colonel, we're just doing our jobs, protecting and defending the Constitution of the United States against all enemies foreign and domestic." She smiled, reciting the passage from a military officer's oath of office. "We're all idealists when we join up, but over the years, things change. Reality sucks. There's no question about it. Come on, drink that up and I'll get you another, and in no time you'll feel like you were back in Iwo Jima."

Babic took another sip of his drink and felt the alcohol pulse through his veins. "That was the Marines. I was Air Force before... this."

"Air Force, Marines...we're all fighting the same wars, whether CNN gets it or not." She finished whatever it was she was drinking and signaled Wally for a couple more libations. "Even though we're...uh, what's the word? Compartmented! We're all compartmented. We have to do our own jobs, but only occasionally do we know what everyone else is doing. It doesn't matter. You put in your time, collect your pension, and then find a nice quiet place to retire to and get forgiveness from your local priest."

Babic smiled for the first time that day. "I'm not catholic."

Davina leaned in close with a sly grin. "Well then, is there something you'd rather confess to me little boy?"

She was obviously drunk, it was nearing ten o'clock, and he had a long drive to get home. "I'll pass. Maybe some other time." He slid a hundred-dollar bill across the table with a polite smile. "Please tell Wally that I've had enough, and I have to get going."

Her grin turned to a playful smirk. "Awww...I didn't scare you away, did I?"

"Not at all." Babic stood, perhaps not as steadily as he had when he'd come in. "Perhaps a raincheck?"

She winked at him as he walked out into the evening air, leaving the folio with her final payment on the seat. He inhaled deeply and tried to separate the fresh air from the smells of the other restaurants along the row. The temperature had cooled, and despite the humidity and haze, he thought he could see a couple of stars breaking through as he walked to his car. Beautiful stars. He had hoped to get to them one day. Maybe only as far as Mars. One never knew, but at the very least, given the pace of technological acceleration, he had hoped to be able to tell his kids that he had experienced weightlessness somewhere in the dark vastness of space.

He made his way south on 35th Street Northwest, looking for the bridge that would take him across the Potomac and onto Interstate 66. He was feeling better now. The job was done, and he had just enough of a buzz from Wally's cocktail that he was feeling more positive about life in general. Better, hell! He was elated. He turned the radio up and tapped a couple of icons to find a satellite station that mirrored his mood. Someone was singing *Fly Me to the Moon,* and that suited him just fine. He turned the volume up as he entered the busy freeway, which was now slightly less busy than it had been two hours earlier.

He punched his accelerator and the speedometer climbed past eighty. His wife, Darlene, might still be awake, and he could tell her how wonderful she looked. Maybe she would feel amorous enough to try to make love. How long had it been? His heart rate climbed, and he felt himself passing slower motorists who obviously had nowhere to be in any real hurry. He felt alive. He felt on top of the world.

But, in his euphoria, he had neglected to check his rear-view mirror with the same alacrity as he had before the drop. For if he had, he might have noticed the blue Toyota that had been tailing him since he left The Cardigan. He might have been suspicious enough to slow down and try to see if it was, in fact, a surveillance or not. He pressed on and whipped between two more cars.

Then, as he crossed over Lee Highway, the loud noise and the awakening jolt coming from the area of his Honda's left front wheel brought him to his senses, albeit a bit too late. The small explosive device that had been planted on the suspension near the steering knuckle and control arm had disintegrated the metal, blown the tire, and caused the frame to dig in and pivot the car into the cement divider. It bounced once and then ricocheted across the westbound lanes of traffic before flipping end over end and sliding over the embankment. He didn't care. The Jameson's-rocks and whatever narcotic Davina had added, had done the job. He was at peace, weightless among the stars at last.

━━━━━》《◎》《━━━━━

"Would you folks mind if we joined you?"

Karlsson looked up and noted the balding man with the skinny wife in the sun dress, behind him. They had circled the room and decided to seek out two of the last few seats on the second level. His earlier analysis put them pretty low on the threat scale, so he nodded and gestured to the two seats beside him and Neri. "Be my guest."

"Thanks." The man said as he pulled out a stool for his wife to sit. "I used to think this place was too loud for me, but now that I'm losing my hearing, it might turn out to be just the right volume, after all. Trevor Maxwell." He extended his hand. "Most people call me Skip."

"How do you do, Skip?" Karlsson shook the man's hand. A light handshake with soft skin that revealed that he hadn't made his living breaking bricks. "I'm Matt, and this is Mary Ann." Using her new alias.

Nerissa smiled and reached over to shake his wife's hand. "Mary, hi."

"Justine." The woman smiled back, her sundress falling a little more open across the wrinkled skin of her chest. The skin was bronzed and weathered. She had spent her time outdoors. "Are you kids celebrating something tonight?"

"Not really." Karlsson replied, thinking quickly to construct a cover that would hold up to a social encounter with people that he didn't really need to impress. "Down here with a group; a friend of mine's son is getting married and destination weddings are quite the thing now. You?"

"My birthday. Well, in a couple of days." Skip replied.

Justine cut in. "We wanted to do something different this year, so we're travelling the nineteenth parallel. Following the sacred geometry."

Karlsson looked at her with a quizzical look for a moment and then to Skip and back again. "Excuse me?"

"It's where the energies of the planet align." She smiled.

"You lost me." Karlsson admitted.

"When a star tetrahedron is placed inside a sphere, or a planet, like the Earth, two of its opposite apexes will touch the North and South poles. The other apex points line up on the planet's surface at nineteen point five degrees North and South latitude. It is one of the sacred geometric shapes, through which energetic, inter-dimensional power manifests. At this specific latitude we experi-ence the intersection between the light body of the planet and its surface. Since these energies can connect us to other dimensions, there exists an energetic predisposition for inter-dimensional ex-periences." She paused. "And it enhances the hell out of orgasms."

Karlsson laughed politely and looked at her for a moment to try to determine if she was being serious, or merely teasing them with some sort of campy performance.

"Dragon lines." Neri added as if she understood what the wom-an had just said. "Portals, stargates, and the ability to communicate with that which is outside of our physical realm."

"Your wife is a very sharp lady!" Justine said. "Volcanic activity, plate tectonics, the witnessing of interdimensional phenomenon, all seem to happen around this latitude."

"We were visiting Teotihuacan yesterday; to purify our souls." Skip rolled his eyes. "I decided that a two-hour plane ride to Cancun would help me purify my soul and pollute my kidneys even better. It is, after all, my birthday!"

"We've been married for forty years, and he still doesn't get me!" She wrapped her arm around his and pulled him in close for a kiss on the cheek. "People don't understand the significance of the number."

The waitress broke up the unusual introduction and took their drink orders for Gimlets, a concoction of gin and lime juice. She glanced at Karlsson and Nerissa, who both shook their heads, and then departed in a hurry. She was busy and did not have time for idle conversation.

"There is so much in life that we take for granted. We never question the significance of things. Especially numbers." Justine continued her lecture. "Take the inauguration of the President. This ritual, based on Masonic tradition, is conducted by the Chief Justice on the twentieth day of the January just before noon wherein at precisely this time, which is 19.5 days into the new solar year, the President-elect becomes the new president of the United States of America. Interestingly an oath must be taken for each term of presidency. If the 20th of January falls on a Sunday, the President-elect is sworn in in a private ceremony that day and then again publicly the following day. It's perhaps a quiet part of our heritage that isn't often captured by the media."

"I've heard that." Neri nodded, exhibiting no particular emotion. "I was in Sedona a few years ago and had the opportunity to take one of their metaphysical tours. I found it to be quite enlightening. I think someone spoke about that."

Karlsson looked at her. He didn't want to stifle conversation, but on the other hand, he didn't want the conversation to lead down a path that might draw attention to her profession. He rolled his eyes with a grin. "Oh, sweetie, you know that stuff is way over my head."

Skip rested his hand upon Karlsson's shoulder. "Glad to see that there's a fellow realist out there." He looked around the room as he spoke. "I like to keep an open mind about her hobbies, but I have to confess that I'm a bit of a closet conservative. I like to see a bit of tangible evidence before I'm willing to go all-in on the spiritual thing."

"Me too." Karlsson nodded. It was time to re-direct the conversation. "Are you from the Southwest?"

Skip shook his head as he returned his attention to the table. "No. We're actually from the Mount Shasta area now. Originally from Sacramento. I grew up a typical idealist through college, out to bring peace to the world, and then suddenly got the urge to get into computer languages. Before I knew what was going on, I'd inadvertently made a success of myself, and caught the attention of some of the big boys in Silicon Valley. They bought my ideas and my company and left us pretty well off." He smiled as he saw the waitress returning with their drinks. "So, like any good convert to capitalism, when they dangled more money than I'd ever imagined in front of me, I sold out."

"You didn't sell out." Justine corrected. "The stars and planets aligned, and you saw an opportunity to live comfortably on what the universe provided."

They backed up to allow the waitress to set the Gimlets on the counter in front of them. Skip produced a Mexican bill of unknown denomination and said, "Thank you. Please keep the change."

For the next hour, the ladies seemed to speak their own language while Skip and Karlsson nodded, shrugged appropriately, and looked around the room at the performers and audience members who were in various states of awe and inebriation. It was obvious that Skip was a people-watcher as well, but Karlsson could not tell if it was simple curiosity or if their new friends were as interested in those around them for the same reasons as Neri and him. Certain key words would occasionally draw him back into their conversation.

"You have to meet Madam Twyla. She has the best deals on crystals that I've ever found, and their resonance is impeccable." Justine smiled affectionately as the waitress stopped at their table to see who was ready for reinforcement. "Have you studied resonance?"

Neri touched Karlsson on his forearm. With a smile she replied, "A little, but I have to tell you that I've had enough alcohol for tonight and think we should probably be getting back soon to see how the rest of the party is doing. I'm afraid I'm getting a bit buzzed!"

Karlsson grinned, taking the hint. "Yeah, You're probably right. We've been at it all day." He flipped through the Peso notes in his pocket until they added up to a thousand Mexican Pesos, about forty-eight dollars, and left them on the counter. "Skip, it was a real pleasure meeting you guys, but I think we'll be making our exit."

"But you haven't seen the finale. It's really something." He said with an almost genuine smile.

"Thanks, but we're on the hook for any damages if the kids get out of control tonight."

"Oh?" Justine asked. "Where are you staying?"

"The Grand Park Royal." Karlsson lied with a perfect smile as he grabbed Neri by the arm. "Hopefully, it's still there when we get back. Again, very nice to meet you. We'll be back tomorrow if you're in the neighborhood."

Skip and Justine gave them each a big hug. "Hope to see you tomorrow!"

They made their way to the exit and when they were again under the stars, Karlsson looked around before leaning in to her close. "Something wrong?"

"I suddenly got a feeling about her."

"Suddenly?" Karlson quipped as he searched the street for a cab. "I had a feeling about her the second they sat down. She went right to the spiritual thing."

Neri frowned at him. "I thought they were nice people, but the conversation was getting closer and closer to harmonics, and it made me thing about a recent tasking Paul gave me. I was suddenly uncomfortable."

"You think she's one of the bad guys?"

"I don't know. It was just a feeling. I felt like she was trying to reach me on a psychic plane while we were talking. It was strange."

"Maybe she's just another psychic, and she was plying her trade to see if you had some sort of gift?"

"I don't know. I just felt like it was time to get back to Proteus."

"Cab mister?"

Karlsson eyed the white Honda cab with the green horizontal stripe running along the side under the windows. It had pulled to the curb a little too conveniently. He hadn't seen any cabs in the line of traffic and could not tell from where it had come. His professional training kicked in, and he smiled. "No, gracias! Decidimos camiar." He replied and waved the man ahead.

"I thought we..." Neri asked.

"Not that one. He came up too quickly and I didn't see him before. Too coincidental."

Neri took his arm up above his bicep and pulled in closer. "Professional paranoia or do you suspect something?"

He grunted, looking around. "Probably both. I've been in this business too long not to be paranoid. There are no coincidences in this job. If a cab suddenly rolls up to you after passing a dozen other couples on the street, they're either on our side or the opposition's."

She looked around him to see if she could see anything suspicious. "Maybe Paul sent someone to look after us."

When they reached the intersection, Karlsson spun her around so that they could go back the way they had come. "Paul wouldn't do that. He knows that it could be dangerous for the people following us. I might mistake them for the enemy, and it wouldn't be pleasant."

They walked back East on the Boulevard Kukulcán and were close to passing the Coco Bongo again when he saw the same cab for a second time, its driver eyeing them as they walked on. "Same guy."

"What do you mean? Are you sure? All of the cabs down here look alike!" Neri glanced around.

"But they aren't numbered one seven four one, like the one that stopped for us. He must have made a loop and come back."

"Maybe he's just a good businessman and this is where he gets his best fares?"

Karlsson nodded. "I'm sure that's what it is. Let's grab one of these other cabs and they'll get us back to the dock. Ernie must have had enough time to get refueled and get back there."

They rode in silence and ten minutes later they were back aboard Proteus. The first thing Karlsson noted was the smell of coffee overpowering the salt air and dead fish odors they had come to know.

Ernie greeted them with a smile. "Well guys? How was your night on the town?"

Nerissa smiled back. "Great!"

Karlsson replied with less enthusiasm. "Good. How long would it take to get underway if we needed to?"

"Problem?" Ernie asked.

"No. Nothing concrete. Just a feeling. Maybe due to my

overworked, over-developed sense of adventure, combined with a couple of cocktails and a rather questionable piece of Mexican steak."

"Ten minutes or so."

Karlsson looked up and down the docks. People were in various stages of tidying their boats after a day at sea or celebrating the Cancun experience with laughter and song. Most were oblivious to the world around them. "How are we on fuel?"

"We can make San Felipe on the northern tip of the Yucatan. It's a small fishing village. Not many tourists, but we can get fuel and food there. Probably a couple hundred miles."

Karlsson sighed. "I'd hate to waste that coffee. Let's get out of here." He looked back towards the lights of the city. "Once we get to sea, I think I need to make another phone call."

CHAPTER 7

Nerissa had grown accustomed to the sounds and sensations of the gentle slapping of the hull upon the water, and the cozy feeling that they were safe in their own space enveloped her as she gently shut out the other noises around the fringes of her consciousness. She drifted into the regions of space-time that very few knew and freed the percipience that might provide the answers for which she had been searching.

While not on an official tasking, she tried to bring her mind back to that place she had been a week before. She floated peacefully in space and clearly saw the moon and the stars. Far below was the brilliant blue marble that she called home. After a carefree orbit, she knew where she was and where she needed to be and descended through the blackness of space into the warmth of the familiar orb like a child rotating a globe for a class on geography. In a gradually descending spiral, she focused on the patch of green earth that contained the square concrete layer cake. It was there and she found herself in daylight. The time was not right, so she took herself back to the period in which she had heard the unusual humming sound coming from an unknown source.

Someone, or some group had wanted to know about it. Someone out there knew what it was, but they were afraid to admit it. That is, if they even knew more than one piece of the puzzle themselves. It was a strange sensation. She was in the past. The air was fresh and clean. It felt like early summer or late spring. The people knew to expect something but had no idea what was supposed to happen. The people that were assigned to protect the building and its contents were called in to the lobby. Steel shades were drawn. A feeling of static electricity enveloped the building and the occupants, who had been well-trained to follow orders. They were anxious, but they knew better than to disobey instructions.

A soft hum crescendoed in volume and intensity. A discordant hum. But it gradually evolved into something more pleasant. The violins and other instruments were tuning, and they were going flat or sharp to bring their individual instruments into perfect tune. They would play together, so they had to get from cacophony to symphony. Perfection of harmonics.

She felt the electric charge pulse through her body and could sense the approach of entities that were not of this world. Maybe they were related by some far-off kinship, but they were strange, indeed. The sensation of weightlessness overtook her, and she could see some sort of vapor rising from the layer cake. A pale-yellow mist. It was what they came for. It was agreed when they would come and how much they could take. Their presence and activity were not for any type of personal enrichment, but rather for their survival. They needed what they were taking for the continued preservation of their planet. They had no hostile intentions toward the people at the site, or anywhere else on the planet. It was more a matter of one hand washing the other.

From a physical sense, though, it did not seem feasible that they could take that much of the substance out of the layer cake, fit it onto their craft and then fly away. Her knowledge of aviation fundamentals was elementary. Lift versus drag. It confused her, but she fought hard to avoid trying to solve the puzzle. She was there simply to draw perceptions as they came to her.

But what they were taking would add several thousand pounds to their aircraft. Her mind jumped to an analytic overlay; she was trying to extrapolate and rationalize the input that was coming into her subconscious, even though it did not make any earthly physical sense to her. Nevertheless, she began to understand and accept that they knew how to manage their cargo.

Inside the layer cake, other people concerned themselves not with the accounting of what they had provided, but rather with the establishment of a firm custodial control of the content of the rooms from which the material had come. They did not open the individual doors to the rooms from where the product had been atomized and removed. Instead, they clipped formal looking certificates, with official seals properly affixed, to the door to indicate that everything inside was still there. It was all terribly confusing and seemed to her like a bank robbery had just been committed, with the cooperation of the bankers, and was about to be covered up.

Her focus was momentarily directed to another location. Somewhere near the center of power. Government. Someone, in a leadership capacity, has knowledge of the event and wants to share it with the public. He has grown weary of keeping secrets and others must stop him. He is in a hospital of sorts. A tall building. He is drugged and thrown from a window, and the others in his circle will claim it to be suicide. While passing over, his spirit makes a brief contact and lets her know that there is much knowledge to offer when the time is right. Her curiosity grows and she wants to learn more about this, but the discordant hum returns, causing her to move back to the building in the field.

She pulled back from the concrete layer cake and searched for the entities that were preparing for a long trip home. Once again, she saw them standing there, silhouetted against the blinding white light of dawn. Standing proud and tall as they had for centuries. They recognized her and tried to communicate. They knew the reason for her presence.

"Why?" She asked telepathically. She needed to know herself.

An indistinct entity that blended into the brilliance of light behind, replied simply, "Zack in stitches."

Bewildered by their response, she was once again aware of a change in the motion of the boat and the smell of the sea air. Ernie had proven his formidable navigation skills as the Proteus came in at the appointed time with Salmedina Island off to starboard and the Hotel Isla Bonita to port. Boca del Rio was just ahead on their left. Pursuant to the instructions that Karlsson had received earlier, they jumped on their radio and hailed accordingly. "KINGFISH, KINGFISH, KINGFISH, THIS IS THE PROTEUS."

As if someone had been waiting for their call, the answer was immediate. "PROTEUS, THIS IS KINGFISH. WE HAVE A BERTH FOR YOU, SLIP BRAVO-TWELVE."

"PROTEUS COPIES. SEE YOU IN A HALF HOUR, BRAVO-TWELVE." Ernie acknowledged succinctly.

He scrolled through the pages on his tablet to find the chart relative to the approach and docks and looked around to see if there were any other boats nearby. Now off to port was the Aquarium of Vera Cruz, and beyond that was the busy Boulevard Manuel Avila Camacho. It was an easy place to navigate. Minutes later, he found the slip he had been looking for, and began his meticulous process of backing into the dock. The well-tanned gent in the shorts and University of Cincinnati tee-shirt watched with appreciation from a neighboring boat as Ernie backed in and Karlsson dropped the fenders over the side like a professional. They had been at sea for several days and had gotten the routine down to a choreographed performance.

As Karlsson focused on the stern line, the man who had been watching from the forty-three-foot Tiara jumped off and headed to the bow of the Proteus and reached out to grab the bow rails as Ernie idled the engines. Karlsson did a quick clove-hitch knot on the stern and then raced forward to secure the bow lines. It was a moment before he looked up and recognized his friend, whom he had last seen in the snowy Cleveland winter more than a year before.

With a wide smile he said, "You look familiar. Have we met?"

"Stan Gable. Dallas." The dark complected man returned the grin. Someone in Virginia said you might need a hand, and I guess I'm it."

Karlsson moved the air-filled fender around and secured the line. He lowered his voice. "Gable?"

"For now." Marchand smiled. "This is one of those gigs where Paul pays in cash, and we don't leave anything behind that might connect the Tank."

Karlsson extended his arm and laughed. "Come aboard. I'll introduce you to the team. It might be time for a drink."

They checked the lines and then moved aft to meet up with Ernie, and Nerissa, who had by now rejoined the physical plane and was shaking off the remnants of a good rest.

"Ernie, this is Stan. He and I worked a job last year and I believe that he is the person we are to thank for the passport for Neri. Well, Mary Anne."

Stan shook hands with Ernie and then turned his attention to Neri. He and Neri shook hands and then a smile began to form at the edge of his mouth. "It's been a while."

Nerissa tilted her head with a questioning look on her face. "We've...we've met?"

Stan nodded. "A couple years ago. Gleneagles Country Club in Texas. I was playing golf back then with a retired Marine officer named Reynolds. Mark Reynolds."

Her mind raced for a moment, and she grinned when it came back to her. Had it been coincidence or clairvoyance? Somewhat embarrassed, she replied, "Oh yes. Mark. I remember now." Her eyebrows narrowed slightly. "Were you...on the job then?"

Marchand chuckled. "Hardly. As a matter of fact, I'm not sure I'm on the job now. I do the occasional thing for Uncle Sam, and then return to my well-earned retirement. Just like most of us on this bucket."

Karlsson smiled and headed for the cabin. "Drinks anyone?"

Marchand released his light grip on Neri's hand. "Of course. What are you pouring?"

⸺◈⸺

Lieutenant General Nelson Scott, the career Air Force executive being groomed to eventually take over the Space Force, looked at the situation report that had been sent from their agents on the ground in Belize the day before. The first time he had read it, he felt satisfied. But a good night's sleep brought with it an uneasy sensation that total confirmation may still be lacking.

"At 0810hrs CST, a Cessna 182 configured for amphibious operations, registration V33ZZ, departed Belize Efrain Guerrero International Airport (MBAC) on Ambergris Caye, having filed a flight plan for a dive destination known as the Blue Hole. Piloted by a local resident of British citizenship, Eric Gates, the flight was to land at sea and transfer a female passenger to a private yacht anchored near the Blue Hole, before returning to Barry Bowen Airport in Belize City. After departure, no further contact from the pilot was received. The transponder quit squawking at 0834 CST. The operations manager at Barry Bowen reported the aircraft overdue at noon central time. At 1345 CST, a Belize Coast Guard crew out of San Pedro searched the area around the Blue Hole and interviewed crews of three boats on station, but reported no sign of wreckage, and no witnesses."

He paged down and continued reading. "Coast Guard investigators suspect that the aircraft crashed due to mechanical issues, but question why no distress signal was sent. Further, the pontoon structure should have kept parts of the aircraft afloat or should have been visible during search if components had become detached. No reports were filed by any pleasure craft that might have been overflown on flight path or at the rendezvous site at the intended time of landing, leading investigators to wonder if the aircraft was hijacked and the transponder intentionally switched off, or if the flight had been intended for illegal use."

General Scott exited out of the report and considered earlier communications from the recovery team that indicated that the aircraft crashed on landing and there were no survivors. Was it possible that the aircraft could have sunk without leaving any floating debris? The fact that there were no witnesses made sense considering the time of day and remoteness of the rendezvous site. The operation would have been so much cleaner if there had been bodies. Then again, bodies and wreckage were evidence. Evidence that could be used to follow a trail.

He couldn't take another sleepless night. He opened the small safe beneath his desk and pulled out one of the burn phones he kept for just such a purpose. Hesitantly, he sent a text to the number that he had been given by a man he had never met, who probably didn't officially exist. "NEED TO CLOSE THE LINK DOWN SOUTH. SEND PROPOSAL AND TERMS."

Out of nervous habit, he switched over to another screen on his desktop and typed in the coordinates for right ascension and declination. He used his mouse to click and drag a mask around a segment of a starry black sky, which he enlarged. It was there. It had to be. Niburu had reached aphelion fifty years earlier and was headed back. Sooner or later someone, somewhere was going to see it. The crew at the Vera C. Rubin Observatory in Chile, had the LSST; the Large Synoptic Survey Telescope, aimed at a portion of the sky where they expected to find it. Certainly, within the next year, the secret would be out. Now that the James Webb space telescope had reached its L2 Lagrange point, the large body might be visible even sooner.

Sitchin's translation of Sumerian cuneiform had been close, but as Cal Tech planetary scientists had mathematically discovered some years earlier, it was more likely that the illusive ninth planet orbited the sun once every 15,000 years. Not the 3,600 years that Zecharia Sitchin had postulated, based on his controversial translations. Regardless, it was headed back towards the inner solar system. It was coming back, and nothing was going to stop it.

He knew the Russians were looking for it too. However, the covert US listening post in the abandoned LORAN-C station on Saint Paul Island had not picked up any chatter about it. Located seven hundred seventy miles southwest of Anchorage, in the middle of the Bering Sea, it was a fourth of the way to the Kamchatka Peninsula and had an eye on everything sailing through or flying over the area. For the Coast Guard personnel assigned there before the site was officially decommissioned in 2010, the twelve-month unaccompanied tour was an exercise in isolation. For the covert intelligence analysts there present day, it was an excruciatingly insufferable steppingstone to a better posting.

He shook his head as he pursed his lips. It was a few minutes later when he received the reply from the man he knew as Dave Fox.

"HOW CLOSED?"

General Scott thought for a moment and then thumbed in his instructions. "LIKE IT NEVER HAPPENED".

He watched as the ellipsis morphed into a response. "20K INCLUDES TRAVEL".

The General was ready. "DONE - $ TOMORROW – 2100 USUAL PLACE". He powered down the phone and replaced it in the safe. He didn't like having to break cover to keep the meeting but had no one else to send. Babic was gone, and he had no one on his staff to replace him. At least he and the illusive Mr. Fox would finally be on equal terms.

⸺⬦((◊))⬦⸺

Lenny Hart slipped off his loafers and pushed himself back in the beige leather recliner in the corner of the cage. He donned the Sennheiser headphones connected to his tablet and selected a hemi-sync track that would help him clear his mind of all the garbage; the drunken monkeys that Buddha claimed were running wildly around in human minds. They were the random thoughts of the physical universe that were equated to monkeys jumping around, screeching, and carrying on, that kept mortals from relaxing into a meditative state.

In the outer room on the other side of the foam-insulated and electronically shielded wall, Paolo Aguilar looked at the eight-by-ten manilla envelope and compared the tasking number printed on the outside with the number he had written on his notepad. He looked through the notes he had made during the brief conversation with Paul and ensured that he would be able to pass the information to Lenny without cueing him to respond in any particular way. To protect the protocol, both the viewer and the monitor had to be blind to the target. Nevertheless, the monitor had to be able to determine when the viewer had effectively locked on and was producing valid information.

When he felt he was psychically prepared, Hart powered down his tablet and placed it in the drawer. He moved to the table and organized his pens and blank sheets of paper, and then flipped the switch under the desk that alerted his monitor that he was ready.

On the other side of the wall, Paolo spoke softly into the microphone. "On the desk in front of me, I have an envelope, which is numbered CV27229. Please tell me what you can about the contents."

Hart wrote his name and the date in the upper left-hand corner of the page, and then wrote *CV27229* underneath. Immediately right of the task reference number, he allowed his hand to quickly draw an ideogram, which to another individual might have resembled two figure 8's clumsily superimposed on top of each other. He lightly tapped the ideogram with the tip of his pencil.

A chill ran down his body as the first perception hit him physically. He spoke aloud for Paolo's benefit as he made his notes on the page. "Cold." He wrote on the paper. "Hollow, empty...vastness. Silence."

"Eternal." And then in parentheses, he noted "Death?"

"Forever, eternity." He paused and then wrote "Always was... no...was there first. But not always."

"Distant...hollow. Emptiness. Far away." On the lower left corner of the page, he drew a small circle about half the diameter of a dime. He drew lines radiating out from it to signify heat or light. Then around the circle he drew a shallow oval that stretched across the page and back. Near the lower edge of the oval, he drew an arrow to the right and wrote "Movement." He felt as though he were sketching an orbit. A large elliptical orbit.

<hr />

Despite the seriousness of the mission, the group seemed to

bond energetically. Ernie turned out to be quite the bartender and had become most adept at manufacturing the Tequila Sunrises with the local Añejo libation that Stan had found in a shop earlier in the day. By the time they were finishing the second round, the group had become old friends.

In addition to helping the travelers blow off some steam, the small party on the back of Proteus helped them blend in with other boaters and avoid standing out as anything other than a group of extranjeros getting together for some fun in the sun. Their casual positions around the small table allowed them to visually cover the area three hundred sixty degrees around their boat, hyper-alert for anything or anyone who might have appeared suspicious. Someone who knew the job and had a sense of humor might have called it *tactical-casual*.

"Well, Mary Ann," Stan eased into business using her cover name. "I think I've got great news for you."

She smiled back, somewhat glassy-eyed. "I could use it."

Stan raised his glass to the others. "This is your last night on the water. We're out of here tomorrow on a private flight to Panama City, Florida. We take on fuel there and then we're off to Chicago."

"Chicago?" She squinted her eyes playfully. "Why Chicago?"

"Why not Chicago?" Stan responded. "Unless you think I'm being too invasive?"

"I think you mean intrusive, don't you?" Karlsson interjected, enjoying the relaxing interlude.

"What's the difference?" Stan smirked.

Karlsson used his index finger to methodically swirl the ice cubes around in his drink before answering. "If you ask me about my bowel habits, that's intrusive. If you slip on a pair of rubber gloves and go in for a look yourself, that's invasive."

Nerissa and Ernie squinted and exclaimed simultaneously, "Eewww... yuck."

Stan Marchand shook his head with a smile and continued. "Not actually Chicago. We're bringing you in to the Executive Airport that's about twelve miles north of O'Hare. From there, we take a clean car, head north and cross into Wisconsin. Paul gave us the keys to a nice little four thousand square foot place near the border, with its own boat dock and open access to Lake Michigan."

Nerissa eyebrows raised. "His vacation home?"

Stan grunted. "Hardly. The property was acquired by a Chinese gentleman last year who...uh, no longer had need of it. The Secret Service had the place wired for surveillance, but after the case was over, they felt it best to allow another agency to take possession of it." He exchanged knowing glances with Karlsson, who had been involved with a portion of the assignment. "They didn't want it on their books for any GAO auditor to question at a later time."

Marchand savored his Tequila Sunrise. "Waukegan was a few miles closer, but we thought it would be easier to disappear from the Exec airport. It's about a twenty-five-minute ride to the house by car. I have a guy on the ground there and if it looks like we're compromised, we can divert to Waukegan as a back-up plan with just a radio call."

Mary Ann né Nerissa nodded thoughtfully. After a moment she asked, "Has anyone figured out who wants to kill me?"

Marchand's eyes darted quickly to Ernie, who took the cue and stood up. "Well, kids, this looks like the time for me to go sightseeing for a couple of hours." With a big grin, he shook hands with Stan. "This sounds like it's about to become a classified conversation, and I've already had enough secret shit this week to hold me for a while!"

Nerissa stood and gave him a long hug. "I can't thank you enough!"

Ernie winked at her and climbed up to the dock. In moments he was gone. Just another Yank spending money on holiday.

The sun was setting and Karlsson brought a lantern up to provide some light around the small portable table. As the light of the day faded, it seemed appropriate to lower their voices to a more intimate level. Stan leaned forward and rested his elbows on his knees, his hands clasped with his fingers making a steeple. "This is all conjecture at this point, but we think the threat is internal. The interest in you started after you were assigned an RV target by our own Space Force. The officer who assigned the task to the Tank...to you, was killed in a suspicious traffic crash the other day."

"Oh my." Nerissa shuddered, putting her hand to her mouth.

"We believe that the person or persons who orchestrated the plane crash in Belize had to have had access to your communications, and from that were able to deduce, your itinerary. To us," he paused, "that suggests government involvement. Perhaps, the guy killed in the traffic incident was involved."

Nerissa ran her fingers through her thick black hair and pulled it back behind her head. "But why?"

Marchand took a sip of his drink and returned the glass to the table. "After I left the Secret Service, Paul invited me to join his team as an occasional set of eyes and ears. A part-time viewer. He provided me a couple of tasks in the past week, and while I'm nowhere near as good a viewer as you or the rest of them are, I think we've been on the same project. He wants us to compare notes so to speak."

After a few moments of reflection, she proposed, "Something about Fort Knox. Something in the past."

Marchand nodded. "We gave them gold."

Nerissa responded. "It had to be in the past. I was thinking Truman or Eisenhower?"

"Yeah...maybe Eisenhower. No one's audited the gold since 1953. Hell, the last time anyone saw a portion of it was in 1974 when they opened one of the rooms to a couple politicians and reporters. And, for whatever reason, Paul asked me if I'd ever worked with the Mint Police."

Nerissa agreed. "The public explanation for all the secrecy was that the head of the mint conducted an audit every once in a while and then oversaw the seal process."

Karlsson, who had been looking back and forth at them across the dimply lit table, like a spectator at a tennis match finally joined in. "Wait. Are you saying that someone has taken the gold out of Fort Knox?"

"Not all of it." Nerissa answered.

"Just enough of it that it would raise concerns on the global currency market if we had to produce it and couldn't." Marchand added.

"But didn't I just hear you say that we gave it to them? Who's *them*?" Karlsson asked.

Marchand looked at Nerissa. "How sure were you that you locked on to the right target?"

Neri shrugged. "Probably about ninety percent. You?"

Marchand shook his head. "I can't be sure. Paul said my report was helpful and that parts of it could be confirmed, but I really don't know."

She shook her head. "And there's no way to confirm all of it. The President of the United States can't get in there, so the chance of us getting a tour is pretty remote. No pun intended."

Karlsson interrupted. "Wait. If the POTUS can't get in there, then how did someone else go in and haul out a bunch of gold with the Mint Police and US Army standing by? Who is your source?"

There was a silence around the table for a while before Stan finally looked at Karlsson and spoke. "I know you're not a firm believer in the remote viewing thing. All I can tell you is that the United States Government got into it back in the seventies after reports came in from our intelligence agencies that the Soviets were using psychic warfare to spy on us. We found some science geeks out at Stanford that were already working on it in a lab."

Karlsson nodded. "I know. We had this talk a year ago."

Marchand noted Neri's approving nod and continued. "Nerissa and I were both given remote viewing tasks that appear to be related. Psychic research if you will. Obviously, adhering to the protocols, neither of us knew that anyone else was being given the same task. And, to that end, there could be other viewers that are currently working on it, and we wouldn't know."

"The take-away is that both of our targets were Fort Knox, at some point in the past; say the nineteen fifties. The difference is that she filed an official report on her findings, and I didn't. Someone wants her dead, but no one has tried to come after me. So, we need to know who saw the report, and why it pissed them off."

Nerissa continued. "Here comes the hard part. A few years ago, I had an assignment that involved the government's release of information about Unidentified Aerial Phenomenon...what you used to call UFO's. You see, there was an Army Lieutenant Colonel named Corso...Philip Corso who wrote a book about the Army collecting crash debris from an extra-terrestrial vehicle that crashed out in the Roswell-Corona area of New Mexico in July of 1947. He said that the artifacts were funneled into the private sector, where civilian scientists were able to reverse engineer them and use the technology to our...our government's benefit."

"Since that time, other military officers, including a couple of US astronauts, stated that at least one species of extra-terrestrial life form had made contact with our government and arranged to trade their technology as long as it was used for peaceful purposes. One source said that Eisenhower made a trip to Edwards Air Force Base to meet with a...uh...foreign visitor and see a demonstration of their vehicle in 1954. Another source said Ike snuck out of a Georgia hunting trip to see another alien air show at some other base in 1955."

Marchand cut in. "On the 1954 trip, he left his Palm Springs golf weekend with the excuse that he needed emergency dental work after biting into a piece of duck that still had lead shot in it. He really did have the dental procedure, but it was the night after his team spirited him off to Edwards. The Secret Service left most of his security detail in Palm Springs, so the press never knew the difference."

Karlsson thought for a moment after allowing the message to sink in. "You're telling me that our presidents are in contact with beings from other civilizations in other parts of the universe?"

Neri grimaced. "Well, not all. Truman and Eisenhower started the contact in the late forties and early fifties. Kennedy was made aware of the program and when he tried to take it public, well, you know what happened. Johnson never asked to be read in, and just plain didn't care as long as he could make money on Viet Nam. Nixon knew about them because he had been Ike's VP. But he's probably the one that screwed it up for other office holders after taking Jackie Gleason on a tour of the lab facilities at Homestead Air Force Base in 1972. "

"Gleason, the comedian? The actor?" Karlsson asked, squinting.

"Yeah. After that, the program was turned over to the CIA and the clearance was raised to where the POTUS no longer had an automatic need-to-know. Carter and Clinton desperately wanted to know the truth about it, but George Bush the First denied them access when he was head of the CIA under Reagan. Then, later when he was in the Oval Office, he was probably the last of our presidents that knew the whole story. George the Second might have known when he was in office, but he obviously knew better than to talk. We think his father probably briefed him before he died."

"So, Reagan knew?" Karlsson asked with genuine curiosity.

Marchand smiled. "Reagan was the president that pressed for the Strategic Defense Initiative, sometimes called the Star Wars Defense Initiative, an anti-ballistic missile system designed to shoot down things in space. And, before you ask, consider that Trump was the President who separated the Space Force as an individual military organization, for the specific purpose of dealing with threats in space. While we don't know for sure, we have to speculate that he might have known something."

A pensive Karlsson speculated. "Wow, if I was political, I might come to the conclusion that the Republicans had control of the UFO secrets."

"Not really." Nerissa answered. "Political parties themselves have no control. Neither do their candidates. The entire program is blessed by the government but run by private industry. The *defense industrial complex* as Eisenhower mentioned in his farewell address. The Black Ops budget is more than fifty billion dollars a year. That's almost ten percent of our total defense spending. Access to each funded program is extremely restricted, so Congress and the presidency aren't read-in to most of the specific projects. They understand that these programs are necessary to our defense, but they actually welcome the plausible deniability."

There was silence around the table before Karlsson brought up something that had slipped past earlier. "You said *traded*. If they were giving us technology, what were we giving them?"

Nerissa shrugged, "Back in 1976 there was a fellow named Sitchin who was studying Sumerian cuneiform texts and somehow determined that the ancients were aware of another planet in our solar system that had a long elliptical orbit around the sun. This planet was called Niburu and supposedly took about thirty-six hundred years to make a complete lap."

She regarded Karlsson's speculative look. "As you can imagine, mainstream astronomers and recognized Sumerologists rejected his research saying that his methodology was flawed, his translations askew and his science incorrect. They basically lambasted him in the professional journals."

"Nevertheless, he published a book that went viral and told the story that a half million years ago, a group called the Anunnaki came here from a planet called Niburu and decided to plunder our natural resources. However, because they considered the work too tedious, they brought slaves. When the slaves didn't work out, they eventually decided to re-engineer the DNA of certain creatures that walked the planet and turn them into a working-class being that could follow orders and perform manual labor. In effect, they colonized Earth with what is now humankind. Homo Sapiens."

Karlsson examined her to see if she was being sincere or conning him for reasons unknown. "Uh huh."

Nerissa continued. "If Sitchin's translation was correct, these cuneiform texts tell us that about four hundred fifty thousand years ago we were visited by an advanced civilization from another planet who came here to explore Earth, because their climate and atmosphere were changing rapidly, and they needed materials to slow the changes. When they got here, they found the earth to be inhabited by a bunch of wild animals but alas, no sentient life. They realized the enormity of their task, and the difficulty of their assignment, so they decided to genetically engineer a new species that would help them dig and load."

"They happened to have landed in an area that we later came to know as Mesopotamia and named their colony *Eridu*. In a later recorded book of wider distribution that you might have heard of, it was known as *Eden*. Like I said, they had brought some slaves with them to help with the mining but eventually the slaves revolted and turned against their masters. The slaves started a war but were ultimately wiped out. This left the Anunnaki with no one to dig for them. Thus...the need to engineer a new species." Marchand stood and began to rotate his torso to the left and then to the right until the creaking and cracking of his spine signaled the fact that he was loosening up after a long day on the water. He had heard the story before, and maybe even experienced parts of it himself in another dimension. He nodded at Neri to keep going, but his eyes flashed to the two noisy couples going aboard the next boat over, returning from a night of frivolous gaiety. Their conversation would have to be cut short.

Neri lowered her voice. "The solution was to create a new race of human beings, eager to work, but more harmless than the Egigi, the original slaves. They engineered and combined their DNA with early man. Unfortunately, there were several lab failures that resulted in uncontrollable species, like the Nephilim, a bunch of bone-headed giants, but eventually they found a suitable pathway with one experiment that they called Adamu."

"Adamu?" Karlsson repeated. "Like Adam? In Eden? I sense this is going somewhere biblical."

"Yes, I'm afraid so. The first man." Nerissa sipped her drink. "After years of successful mining, the Niburu returned to finish their mission, which caused an increase in the global temperature, an erratic climate, the melting of glaciers, a great flood. I think you've heard this somewhere as well. The Anunnaki created great boats to withstand the floods. They gave humans knowledge of architecture, math, music, and writing...politics; a monarchical system of government to lead through a blood line. Mankind built temples to align with constellations, which were designed to guide their fore-bears back to earth."

Karlsson glanced at Marchand and then back to Neri. "You're fucking with me, right?"

Neri smiled. "I wish I was. I can't prove any of this, but you must realize that I'm not the only person who has been tasked with the origins of our civilization over the years. It's what we do."

Karlsson shook his head and looked past the harbor into the Gulf. "You guys talk about this like it was fifth grade history or something. What you are suggesting is totally contrary to every-thing mainstream science tells us." He rubbed his beard stubble. "And, it destroys every religion we have on our planet."

"Not really." Nerissa replied. "The Annunaki worship the same God that we do."

Karlsson was overwhelmed. "So, what was it they were mining?"

"Gold." Marchand said quietly.

"Gold? They came how many light years to steal our gold?" Karlsson asked whimsically.

Marchand shrugged. "Well, they technically didn't steal it. Four hundred fifty thousand years ago, we really didn't have a claim to it. And sometime in the 1950's, we...uh...gave it to them."

"Zack in Stitches." Neri added quietly. "Zecharia Sitchin."

CHAPTER 8

Lenny Hart was completely relaxed and totally absent from his current time and space. He hovered weightlessly over the box with the gold light radiating upwards from the forest to the dark sky above. He tried to perceive the purpose of the event, but the harsh humming noise grew disagreeably louder and then seemed to dissolve into individual musical notes. Notes that made a tune of sorts, but nothing at all pleasant or predictable. It was completely unfamiliar to him. A nonsensical arrangement with ill-conceived orchestration.

Once the obnoxious melody had played through, Hart could feel himself losing his psychic connection and returning to his reality in the small, shielded room. He was losing his attachment to the target he had been chasing in another realm.

Chief Warrant Officer John McMaster leaned in towards the microphone on the desk. "It looks like you're ready to end the session. Do you need a moment to organize your notes before we debrief?"

Lenny rubbed his bald pate. "Yeah. Just a couple."

Hart looked at his notes spread haphazardly across the desk and organized the sheets of paper into the order in which he had completed them. Then he flipped through them one at a time to see if sketches or perceptions he notated earlier in the session made any more sense to him now that the session was concluded. He hadn't felt a strong connection to the target until the very end, and by that point he had lost his concentration. "That damn music." He thought to himself.

He finally stood and stretched his arms and torso before collecting the materials on the desk and switching off the desk lamp. On the other side of the door, McMaster looked up from his notes with a smile. "How's it going?"

"You tell me." Hart grunted as he sat down in the empty chair at the corner of the monitor's desk. He adjusted the side chair a bit so that he could walk the Chief Warrant Officer through his perceptions. Heaven knew that he wasn't the best artist in the world. Maybe the Chief could help him put the lines and circles together to make more sense of it. It was a silly thought. McMaster had no idea what the target was any more than Hart did. To ethically follow the Remote Viewing protocol, the monitor had to be blind to the target to prevent any type of information leakage or cuing.

"Do you want some water? Coffee?"

Hart shook his head. "Not right now, thanks. Maybe later."

He rubbed his head again and then began. "I'm not sure what I got from this. I had so many images passing through my head that I couldn't tell which ones were important, and which ones were not. My first gestalt was a structure. High in the air...like on a mountain."

Hart flipped to the next page. "It seemed like a hardened structure...like concrete and steel, but a strange shape." He pointed to his elementary sketch. "Like an elongated shoebox, with something mechanical on the top of one end...and maybe a second story underground on the other end. It has some scientific purpose, but it hasn't been there that long."

McMaster made some notes in his folder. "Go on. Tell me more."

"It is important. It has a purpose. But when I tried to learn more about it, I kept getting...uh...kicked out of there. I kept finding myself in a forest moving around another building. It's just a box-like structure. One, maybe two stories tall. There's some kind of gold-colored beam that comes out of it and goes up into the sky. I can't get close to it either because the closer I try to home in on it, the louder that humming noise."

"The humming noise?" McMaster was curious. This was the second viewer who had reported a hum associated with this target. "Tell me more about that."

Hart shuffled through his stack of notes and found the page on which he had scribbled a musical staff, beginning with a treble clef and then a series of quarter notes and half notes on different lines. "It's like a band or orchestra are tuning their instruments, getting ready for a concert. They start out, you know, really out of tune, and gradually each musician sharpens or flattens their instrument until everyone is in tune. Then, they go out of tune again, before individual musicians start playing some kind of solo parts. It's all loud and obnoxious. Really weird!"

McMaster jotted down Harts comments in his log. "Keep going."

"I don't know." Hart said, looking at the floor. "The music means something. I feel like it's trying to tell me something. But…"

After a lengthy pause, McMaster looked up. "But what?"

Hart shook his head. "The music is trying to tell me something. But it's also doing something."

"Doing something?"

"Yeah. It's communicating some kind of message, but it's doing something. It…makes something happen. The vibration of the different notes…at different speeds, has some sort of effect on something else. Is that crazy, or what?"

"Not crazy. When you're done with your report, we can come back to that. What else have you got?"

During the next ten minutes, Hart explained the rest of his notes and then reassembled the stack of pages the way they had been when the two men first sat down. CWO McMaster then took all of the pages and inserted them into a large manila envelope with the task number on the front, and then sealed it with security tape. He used a fine-point marker to sign his name across the tape.

"Why don't you relax for a minute while I drop this off with Jillian and grab a couple of coffees out of the galley. Now that the tasking is wrapped for the day, we can talk about that hum you heard."

Hart nodded. "Thanks! I have to make a quick trip down the hall but will meet you in the conference room."

Five minutes later, Chief McMaster joined Hart in the conference room with two cups of black coffee, and softly pushed the door shut with his foot. He eased himself into one of the faux-leather chairs. At seventy years of age, and twenty-pounds heavier than he should be, he was now the oldest, and largest member of the Tank. It didn't matter. A person's age had nothing to do with their psychic functioning. However, the associated slower metabolism did mean that he needed to exercise more and consume less if he wanted to remain a live psychic into the next decade.

"We're off the record." He began. "I'd like to know more about the hum you heard. You see, you're not the first viewer to hear it and your perceptions are very similar to what others have reported. Especially on this particular target. It's been described as musical instruments tuning. And it moves from cacophonous to symphonic, and back again. And, while others have talked about the fact that this music...or vibration, may be actually doing something, you're the only one that reported hearing individualized notes. A solo, if you will."

Hart sipped his coffee and chuckled. "It wasn't anything I've ever heard before."

"I understand." McMaster replied. "But could you tell me, you know...if you heard it somewhere out on the street, would it sound like modern Hip Hop? Country? Classical?"

Hart looked at a blank space on the wall. "None of that. It sounded like just random notes being played on an instrument. Like someone who didn't really play just making noise. Not pleasing to the ear. Like a kid trying to figure out piano keys...or find specific notes on a sax."

"So, the instrument...like a piano? Guitar? Saxophone?"

"At first, it sounded like violins and cellos. But it seemed to morph into...maybe, yeah...a clarinet or alto sax."

"If you had a keyboard, could you play what you heard?"

Hart laughed. "Hell no. I'm not really musical. But maybe if you put me with a professional keyboard player for a few minutes, I could describe it and see if he could pound out something close. Why?"

McMaster sat his coffee cup down on the table. With a shrug, he answered, "Well, something's been going around in my mind about this case. Different psychics seem predisposed to focus on specific types of stimuli or clues. Some see things, some hear things. Some viewers have olfactory sensations. But what we've found is that sometimes a target actually *wants* to be found and will present itself to a viewer more strongly in the manner in which the viewer is most comfortable. So, if viewers are hearing something, then it's possible the target might be trying to communicate the importance of the message through sound. Or song, so to speak."

Hart was still learning his craft and wanted to know more. "Okay."

McMaster thought out loud for a moment. "I want to put two ideas into your head and then let you go away and think about whether or not either idea makes sense to you. First, back in the later seventeen hundreds, a British marine officer and small-time politician by the name of Philip Thicknesse wrote a book about using ciphers embedded in music. What later came to be known as musical encryption."

"A lot of the composers of that time did it. Johann Sebastian Bach spelled out his own name in several of his compositions using a succession of the notes B, A, C, and H, the H was really a natural B in the German system. B flat was considered to represent the letter B in these cyphers. This short music monogram is now called a Bach motif. Brahms and Schumann did the same thing. Not for any type of espionage or intelligence purpose, but rather to just put their names or sometimes their friend's names into a piece for the fun of it."

McMaster took another sip of his coffee. "If you saw a movie called *Close Encounters of the Third Kind*, composer John Williams used a five-note motif as a form of a greeting with the alien visitors. You hear the motif throughout the movie, but it's what they play on top of Devil's Tower to say hello to the spaceship. Over and over again they play B flat, C, A flat, another A flat an octave lower, and then E flat."

The truth is, Williams went through more than three hundred

different five-note permutations to arrive at the jingle, that once you get it in your head, it stays with you. The directors then used the Curwen hand signs to symbolize the basic solfege notes."

Hart's left eye squinted involuntarily. "Solfege?"

"It's a form of solmization. Uh, you know, like Julie Andrews in the Sound of Music? Do, re, mi, fa, so la, ti, do. A Hungarian composer, Zoltan Kodaly, was teaching music this way as far back as the nineteen-thirties, but after World War II, he put it to hand signals."

McMaster shrugged. "Anyway, people listen to music every day and don't understand the origins of what they're listening to. I know that the CIA experimented with embedding cyphers in music long before steganography embedded messages in analog and digital communications covertly. It's just something to think about."

Lenny nodded. "And the other? You said two ideas."

McMaster reflected. "Yeah. The way the Tank got its start was from the work that a bunch of science geeks had started out at Stanford in the early seventies. They were physicists and engineers. Not paranormal crackpots. They were doing some next-level research on quantum mechanics and as a part of their research, they focused heavily on wave patterns and vibration."

"And?" Hart mused as he sniffed his coffee and decided that it had been on the burner for too long.

"Among the things they found was that you could point two horns at each other and transmit high energy sound in the twenty-two kilohertz range. The vibration causes a standing wave that will support or suspend a small object, like a bead. The sound needed for that is about equal to what's generated at a rock concert. But it's at a frequency that humans can't hear. So, I suppose, if you could generate more power, more sound, you could levitate other objects. Maybe even change their form. Depending on the frequency of the sound or the magnitude of the wave pattern, something like that might easily make a humming noise and cause things to move."

"Like the electro-magnetic rail systems."

"Yeah. A lot like that, except, Maglev systems can only suspend solid objects, while acoustic systems can suspend liquids as well.

Droplets, anyway. I've met some of the guys out at Argonne Labs who are doing this stuff every day."

"And your point?" Hart asked respectfully.

McMaster thought for a moment. "You said that the sound meant something. It could be a message, or as you said, it could have had some other functional purpose. They could have been using the vibration to move something."

"Einstein." Hart replied pensively. "Everything in life is vibration."

⸺ ((◉)) ⸺

Despite the core evil that emanated from the wasteland occupying the space where his soul should have been, Lieutenant General Nelson Scott stopped abruptly in traffic and allowed the elderly woman to push a cart containing all her worldly belongings across the street. She was close to the crosswalk anyway, but his sudden yield afforded him the opportunity to see if anyone was following him. He was not formally trained as a covert operator. However, some of the things he had seen in adventure movies made him think that he was doing a stellar job of identifying any type of potential surveillance. The reality was that he wouldn't have recognized a tail even if it drove over the curb to avoid rear-ending him. Plus, in these days of miniaturized electronics and out-of-control budgets for federal agencies, if he was as important as he felt, *they* would have assigned a dozen cars and two satellites to follow him. He would never have known if anyone who happened to be behind him was part of a surveillance or not.

With him, it wasn't paranoia. It was arrogance. He viewed himself as indispensable and gifted, but in the event he had aroused suspicion somewhere, he wanted to prove that he was as good as any of the Agency's players. For thirty years he had existed in a microcosm of power that placed others at risk, while he retained the safety and sanctity of deniability. Regardless, he instinctively placed his hand on the leather folio on the passenger seat to keep it from sliding off onto the floor as he braked.

No relation to the family of the WWII flying ace, the *Scott* name had nevertheless been identified with excellence in the military aviation community for many years. Ever since there had been an aviation community, for that matter. Now, as he was nearing the end of his career, it was his time to make something of himself and to rise to the pinnacle of success. Well, in this new Space Force anyway, he reckoned. The truth be told, when he left the Air Force Academy in Colorado Springs decades earlier, he'd had his heart set on being the Air Force Chief of Staff. Maybe even Chairman of the Joint Chiefs. There was still time. The transition had been a mere uniform change and actually accelerated his progress considering the smaller size of the agency and his proximity to the top. He was now third in line to the throne. Had he stayed in the Air Force, with his lack of political connections on *The Hill*, he would have been thirtieth.

His transformation included a month at Nellis Air Force Base and a few side-trips to the non-existent place known to many as Area 51, with the 328th Weapons Squadron. WPS, as it was referenced in official memoranda, was the United States Space Force's weapons school, and featured the Space Superiority Weapons Instructor Course as well as the Space Warfighter Advanced Instructor Course. As a senior officer, he had to know what his Guardians were learning and what was expected of them in their new roles. And, he needed the so-called street credibility, the *street-creds*, to earn the respect of his subordinates.

He felt lucky today. About three doors down from the Cardigan, Q Street presented him with a recently freed parking space. He pulled up quickly, slammed his government Ford into reverse and backed sharply in, chafing the tires on the curb in the process. He gave his parking job a cursory look and then keyed the dongle to lock it up. The neighborhood looked okay, but with the reductions in police staffing over the recent past few months, street crime had predictably climbed. Even in the nicer areas of Georgetown. He wouldn't be that long.

It was a few minutes before nine and even though there was

still some daylight left in the western sky, he had to give his eyes a moment to adjust to the dimness of the bustling establishment. He kicked himself that he had never asked Babic for a description of his contact there. Dave Fox. Babic had done what he'd been told and had been a good troop. Up to a point. But, once he had developed a conscience, he was no longer of use. There was much to be done and Scott could not afford to have some self-righteous Boy Scout playing a part in what could be the end of the world. For many, anyway. There would be survivors, of course, but it was Scott's job to ensure that they were the right ones.

General Scott wandered down the steps and through the dining area but did not see anyone who resembled a nefarious character there to collect blood money. After a self-conscious moment of standing in the corner of the room, surveying the diners, he broke off and headed towards the bar in the rear. A quick glance at the bar patrons indicated only couples or small groups that seemed to know each other, and they expressed little interest in him.

He was about to head towards the restrooms in the back when the voice in his four o'clock position said, "Hey, General. Are you looking for Dave?"

He turned with a snap of his head to see the bartender, smiling in his direction. "You looking for Dave?" The bartender repeated.

General Scott's head instinctively rocked to the left and then to the right to see who might have heard the exchange. This was to be a covert meeting. The kind of meeting that his contemporaries in the intelligence community might have put together, to pass important secrets. A bartender yelling his name loudly in the busy club, made him most uncomfortable.

Scott took note of the elaborate nameplate on the man's left shirt pocket, with the name Wally clearly visible, and moved closer to the bar to stand between two empty stools, which seemed to separate the other packs of revelers. "Uh, yes. Why?"

The bartender had finished drying some Old-Fashioned glasses and was in the process of returning them to the shelf so that they would be ready for the next customer. "Dave got called away and can't be here tonight. I'm told that you have a folio that you can leave with me."

A native of Westchester, the General hadn't exactly grown up in the streets of Brooklyn, but he was nevertheless suspicious of what he had just heard. "You want me to leave *what* with you?"

Wally wiped down a wet spot on the bar in front of him and leaned over, his elbows on the well-varnished surface. "I believe you have twenty-five grand in there as seed money for a project. If you want the project to move forward, leave the folio. If not, no big deal. I'm just helping a friend and don't give a shit either way." A conspiratorial smile formed at the edge of his mouth.

Scott looked around the room again. He had fully expected to meet the nebulous Dave Fox at last. The person to whom he had given so much in exchange for so much. "He's not coming tonight?"

"*He* was unavoidably detained. Is that the right password?" The bartender mocked sincerity.

"Sure." Scott glowered uneasily.

General Scott instinctively glanced around the room one more time. He had a decision to make, and he made it. He laid the folio on the counter, nodded, and walked away. If this was some sort of sting, he didn't want to be stung. On the other hand, if this was Fox's idea of additional security, then he could play along. Either way, he needed to get out of there. The bartender was entirely too cavalier about what should have been a very serious meeting. "Civilians!" He muttered to himself on the way out.

Once back inside his Ford, with the air conditioning running full blast, he retrieved his cell phone from his belt carrier and scrolled through the contacts until he found the anonymous one with the 808-area code. He buckled his seat belt and shifted the transmission into drive. As the car lurched forward, he depressed the green *send* key and listened for the ring through the speakers of his car.

After the third ring, Lieutenant Colonel Darren Baronowski, US Army Reserve, answered. He was a reservist with an important position within the JAG Corps that mirrored his civilian occupation, as well as being a long-time friend of the General's, and was influential enough that felt he didn't have to play the yes-sir-no-sir game with anyone who called his personal cell.

"Hi, Nels. Long time! To what do I owe the pleasure?"

General Scott chose his words carefully. They were on public cellular service, and Hawaii was a long way from Washington, DC. "I was just checking in to see how things were with your brother...and his counterpart down south."

The line was quiet for a moment. Baronowski's brother, Thomas, had reluctantly accepted an unaccompanied posting at the most isolated and desolate location in the Space Force's intelligence network. Masquerading as a Coast Guard Chief Warrant Officer, he and two other intelligence analysts occupied the presumably abandoned LORAN-C station on Saint Paul Island, Alaska. They were ostensibly working with NOAA and various wildlife agencies to study the impact of climate change on the local fur seals. The reality was that their attention was focused on the environment above the stratosphere. Watching, and listening, their only respite from the voluntary internment was a four-day trip each month to Kodiak.

"I haven't spoken with Tom in a few weeks." Baronowski replied. "However, I do know that our CG-USARPAC will be visiting Chile this week." Referring to the Commanding General, US Army Pacific, General Jason Keyes. "Is there something I need to know about prior to that visit?"

"Do you know if he'll be visiting Vera?" The general asked carefully.

Baronowski frowned at the phone. "Well, the invitation actually came from the Chilean Army Commander, a chap named Renato Olvera. Our CG is supposed to spend two days there meeting with military and civilian government officials to discuss bi-lateral topics relating to humanitarian assistance, disaster relief and the importance of the Indo-Asia Pacific region to both our countries. No mention of...uh, a trip to the mountain came up, but it might be worked-in if you feel there's a need."

"I do," was the General's response. "We need a face-to-face contact with our agent there to see if there is any information which they've felt unsafe to transmit. It's probably a good idea to meet with your brother as well."

Baranowski was quiet for a moment. "Well, considering the nature of this, I think it would be easy for me to ride along with General Keyes and his entourage and then break off for a few hours to meet with your chap." He had phrased it as delicately as he could. "I'm sure I can think up a reasonable scenario to justify a need for me to accompany them down there."

General Scott thought about the complex logistics of debriefing an agent on the bottom end of the world and realized he would have to take a chance that Baronowski was a loyal and professional confidant. "Yeah. That does make sense." He paused. "Then what about your brother? We're going to need a similar update from him. Is he scheduled to come home anytime soon?"

Baronowski shrugged at the telephone. "No, but I would agree that we need to know what kind of chatter the Chinese and the Russians might be tossing back and forth. If this is not time sensitive, I could easily work out a military flight through Kodiak as soon as I finish in Chile."

"It can wait for a few days." General Scott agreed. "No one from the GAO would think twice about a senior officer bumming a ride to visit his brother, especially if the brother is on an unaccompanied tour. At it's worse, it would appear as just another attempt to get as much as possible out of Uncle Sugar's travel reimbursement policy. But obviously, I don't want to draw any more attention than I have to." He couldn't afford to alert any outside agencies to his network. Yet.

⎯⎯⎯«◉»⎯⎯⎯

Nerissa unconsciously popped her jaw a couple of times to equalize the pressure in her head as the Challenger 350 descended over Lake Michigan on approach to Chicago Executive Airport. She had been deep in sleep. It was perhaps the best sleep she had had in days. She was comfortable in airplanes. Boats, not as much. She glanced at the dive watch on her slender wrist and noted the time as 21:30; or nine thirty at night, Central Time. Even though Belize had been on Central Time, her nautical trip around the coast had taken her through Cancun and Cozumel, which were in the Eastern zone and had therefore necessitated that she adjusted her watch once again.

While some people who experience the trauma of an aircraft crash are demonstrably anxious about boarding another aircraft, Nerissa knew that she would be safe. She knew that the reason for her earlier crash was due to intentional sabotage. Not fate. Not poor mechanics. Of course, she was also clairsentient, which helped. She knew things about the present, past and future, and simply knew what was safe or not. Most of the time. She glanced over at Karlsson reclining in the luxurious beige leather seat on her left, *port* as it was often referenced on aircraft as well as boats. He was grinning at her.

"Welcome back! You've been motionless since we went wheels-up from ECP." He said, using the FAA's designator for the Northwest Florida Beaches International Airport in Panama City.

The brief stopover was necessary for fuel as well as the traditional US Customs inspection and processing to ensure that they were not drug smugglers or fugitives of one kind or another. It was ironic. Almost five million undocumented individuals of various nationalities had waded or walked across the Southwestern borders in the previous two years, with virtual impunity and free lodging. But a couple of thrill seekers on a twenty-million-dollar private jet came back from a Mexican vacation and US Customs went totally berserk with formalities. Naturally, a search of their aircraft and luggage gave up nothing. The passports were genuine, and their names did not appear on any of the *lists*. So, with stern, speculative looks, the US Customs agent welcomed the weary travelers back into their own country.

Neri rubbed her eyes and found the button that would allow her to return her luxurious seat to its upright and locked position, as the commercial flight attendants would have directed. Things were different in general aviation. The pilot simply told the passengers that they were landing. That was about it. There were no instructions to turn cell phones and other devices on or off. As a matter of fact, in the annals of aviation history there had never been a recorded incident of a cell phone actually interfering with any aircraft system during a flight. And one had to consider that there was usually a small percentage of passengers who just forgot to turn them off and perilously traveled the routes of the world with a live cell phone in their purse or on their belt. Nothing happened. Nobody crashed.

When the intercom squawked to life, the pilot merely directed their attention to the screens mounted on the forward bulkhead which gave continuous location, airspeed, and altitude information, with a time-to-destination in the lower right corner. "We'll have to circle to line up on runway one-six but should be on the ground in a few minutes. Welcome to Palwaukee!" He said with a certain amount of genuine cheer in his voice.

To be accurate, there was no city called Palwaukee. The Chicago Executive Airport had formerly been known as the Palwaukee Municipal Airport, simply because of its proximity to Palatine Road and Milwaukee Avenue. And, of course, Milwaukee Avenue was also known as US Route Forty-Five which ran north through Wisconsin and South past the former Chanute Air Force Base and on through the University of Illinois in Urbana to the southern tip of the state. It was the longest numbered US-route in Illinois running from Lake Superior to the Gulf of Mexico and had many nicknames along the way.

"Strange." She yawned. "This is the most rested I've felt since Belize!"

Marchand emerged from the galley area just aft of the cockpit and eased himself into the starboard rear-facing seat and fastened his seatbelt. "Yeah. In this business, you have to catch up on your sleep when you can." He looked across to Karlsson, "I just spoke with our guy on the ground. Everything looks good. He's waiting in front of the Signature FBO."

Signature Flight Support was one of the three nationally recognized Fixed Base Operators at the airport who provided fueling and handling for hundreds of transient and locally based aircraft. With the inclusion of Atlantic Aviation, and Hawthorne Global Aviation, the cozy airport thirteen miles north of O'Hare was one of the busiest in the region. They had enjoyed a close working relationship with the Secret Service and State Department Diplomatic Security Service for many years, so it was no problem for Stan's associate, another retired agent, to charm his way into the manager's office and get the arrival choreographed as well as if the King of Siam had been arriving.

As a part of his *advance*, former special agent Daniel Noble had been able to determine that the arrival could be carried off unimpeded and that no one had expressed any interest in the private flight or its occupants coming in from Panama City. Nevertheless, in order to keep a low profile, rather than a large Suburban like he was used to driving, he opted instead for an imported minivan that looked as if it belonged to a mom taking her kids to soccer.

As the wheels of the Challenger chirped on the runway. Stan Marchand sent two text messages. The first to Dan who was waiting for them in front of the building. "WHEELS DOWN."

Then after a moment, he sent another message to a number he had been given at the start of his trip for one special purpose. It was only to be used when his Protectee was officially back on US soil. "CONSONANCE."

———⟫《◉》⟪———

Marco Pozos had spent most of his life as Mark Wells, the son of an Air Force Officer stationed at the former Homestead Air Force Base near Miami before hurricane Andrew wiped most of it out August 24, 1992. His father, of English lineage and his mother Cuban, he had learned Spanish early on, but with the Caribeño accent.

His fascination with the cosmos drove him towards a bachelor's degree in Astronomy from the University of Florida Gainesville. But after graduation he became conflicted between continuing for his master's degree somewhere or finding gainful employment that would enable him to start paying off his student loans. Of course, the math work in his undergrad program had been complicated, but he got through it. However, he wasn't sure if he could handle another eighteen to twenty-four months of academics. He just liked looking at stars and thought of himself as one day finding the truth to the universe. Or something like that.

It was at a job fair sponsored by the US Government that he began to think of his calling in a different light. Because he was a fluent Spanish speaker, most of the federal law enforcement agencies found him an attractive candidate. However, the thought of chasing someone down a dark alley to handcuff them wasn't as appealing to him as it might have been to others pursuing the field and he found himself gravitating more towards intelligence opportunities. He spoke with an attractive woman from the CIA for about a half hour and even though they had a great meeting across the table in the large lobby of the college's engineering building, he found himself more interested in exploring her naked body rather than exploring what she offered in terms of a career. Once he realized that he was not going to get her out for a drink, he moved on down the row of tables and came across the two guys with cheap haircuts, fronting for something called the Space Force.

Like most recruiters, they spun a tale of opportunity and reward and were certain that they could find a place for him in their ranks. They were equally certain that they could get him approved through the Officer Training School Selection Board and from there, into one of the next available Basic Officer Training Courses, held in February and August each year. They assured him that there would be plenty of ways for him to earn a living staring at stars.

His aptitude tests had been superior, and his general physical fitness helped place him in the top five percent of his class. During the eighth week of the ten-week program, a Colonel had him called into the Wing Commander's office for a private chat about his interests. It was during this conversation that the Vera Ruben Observatory was first mentioned. The Observatory was still under construction, and he would not be able to travel there for another couple of months, but it sounded like an ideal position for him. The only thing about the offer that he questioned was the need to go to someplace called *The Farm*, near Williamsburg, Virginia for two weeks.

"It's for intelligence training." The Colonel shrugged.

"Intelligence? I thought this was a multi-national effort that was funded by private organizations. Why do I need to go to spy school...sir?"

The Colonel pursed his lips. "Our assumption is that other governments will be sending intelligence personnel into this site, having quickly trained them to be astronomers. We're coming at it a different way and training an astronomer to be a spook, just in case."

"In case of what?" Wells had asked.

"You're going to have two missions, Mark. One is the overt one that everyone else is working towards as a multi-national team. The other is an off-the-books assignment. I can't tell you any more than that right now, but I can say that it is vital to our national security, and in general, you'll be looking for something."

"Something like what?" Wells pushed, unsure of what he had gotten himself into.

The Colonel stared out the window at the cobalt blue skies and the white cumulous clouds above. "Something that's been missing for a long time and is headed back home."

CHAPTER 9

General Nelson Scott had worked well into the night, as had become his custom of late, and made the decision to sleep on the couch in his office rather than driving back to his luxurious home in Woodbridge, which overlooked the Occoquan River. Seven months earlier his wife had taken their cocker spaniel and moved to a condominium in Bradenton, Florida with the admonition that if he intended to visit, he should call first. She'd had enough of military life. Since the housekeeper did not care where he spent the night, his plans caused little inconvenience to anyone else.

He awoke a little after five and made the trip to the Pentagon Athletic Center to try to wake up a bit. Located in the E Ring, 7th Corridor, Mezzanine Level of the Pentagon, the PAC offered everything a modern gym should, including a swimming pool, elevated track, basketball, racquetball, and squash courts, and naturally saunas, and steam rooms. After a cursory cycle through some of the upper body equipment, he shaved and showered and considered himself to be as awake as he was going to be.

He had already started the coffee before he left, so by the time he returned to his office, the bracing aroma was in the air, signaling the official start to the new day. He tossed his shirt into the bin and found a fresh uniform to slip into before sitting down at his desk and jiggling his mouse to awaken his computer.

He immediately clicked on the icon to take him to his email and froze when his eyes landed on the top line. "Vesuvius. Small problem. Deal not complete. Other party has moved. Researching now."

"Moved?" He said loud enough that had anyone been in the outer office they would have easily heard.

He looked at the time stamp and realized that the email had been sent only minutes before. He hastily typed back, "My understanding was that other party was a regular contractor."

General Scott sipped his coffee and watched the screen for a full minute before seeing a response. "Waited all night. No explanation. Will investigate aggressively and advise later today."

He should not have been anxious. They had run the mission with the proper cut-out. No one could possibly connect his office to the airplane crash in Belize. Still, it was a loose end. "UNSAT!" he typed.

"Regrets – more to follow" The conversation ended.

He exited out of his email and threw his mouse at the wall. After a moment, he realized what a futile and juvenile gesture it had been. His marriage therapist had warned him about these outbursts of anger and what to do when he felt one coming on. As he walked across the room to retrieve the mouse, he inhaled deeply through his nose and exhaled through his mouth. "I am okay. This is just life. I am coping."

<hr />

Nerissa Khoury awoke to the smell of bacon lightly accentuated by the fresh and exhilarating ionized air blowing in across Lake Michigan. It had rained during the night, just enough to purify the atmosphere and create a spectacular sunrise over the water. As she wandered down the back stairs towards the kitchen she saw Karlsson at the stove carefully turning sizzling strips in the cast iron skillet. Out on the deck Marchand was chatting away on his cell phone and appreciating the vibrant hues coming up over the lake.

"I'm not normally much of a meat eater, but that smells heavenly!" She said as she selected an empty mug from the cupboard and poured herself a cup from the carafe on the coffee maker.

"Yeah, we figured we'd get a good breakfast down this morning because we're still waiting to hear from Paul about our near-term and long-term plans. We don't know if we'll be here an hour or a month. Scrambled?"

"Yes, thanks." She nodded as she looked around the room at the layout of the main floor and the luxurious appointments. "I guess I didn't realize what a fabulous place this was when we got in last night."

Karlsson glanced over his shoulder briefly before returning his attention to the bacon. He enjoyed cooking and always took pride in the finished product. "Yeah. Stan said it was a seizure from a Chinese gent last year. I guess he won't be needing it anymore." He chuckled, reminiscing about how he had acquired his own property some years earlier.

"Mind if I look around?" She asked as she peered into the suite beyond the back staircase. It was an ample master suite with private bath and huge walk-in closet. Across the kitchen in the other direction was a wing that contained the family room, laundry room and another master suite. The rooms were not really disheveled but the sheets were strewn about, and the rooms smelled subtly of men. Not so much like a locker room, but rather like male inhabitants of any household.

She returned to the kitchen and rested her coffee cup on the large granite island, slightly curved, which seated six at its smoothly beveled surface. "Who got what room?" She smiled.

Karlsson folded a couple of paper towels and placed them carefully on a platter so that he could begin to spread his bacon out. "I gave Stan the larger suite out of courtesy." He grinned. "After all, both Stan and the house were once property of the Secret Service."

Nerissa had spent the night in one of the two bedrooms on the second floor. The upstairs had another full bathroom and a recreational area which not only insured her privacy, but offered more in the way of security, considering that any aggressor would have had to get past both a retired Secret Service agent and a lethal government assassin on the first floor before ever hoping to get up the stairs.

The contemporary custom-build house totaled almost four

thousand square feet and included a partially finished walk-out basement that opened to a stone path, which led to a fifty-foot private dock. The basement had been designed for someone who liked to entertain. There was a full kitchen and bar and another full bathroom, along with two leather fold-out sleeper sofas for guests who ultimately decided to stay over. She climbed the front stairs and found herself in the kitchen again. The table was set. The bacon was ready, and chef Karlsson was agitating the eggs in a skillet on the large Jenn-Aire range.

"Get Stan off the phone and tell him breakfast is ready."

Nerissa nodded and tapped on the glass sliding door. When Marchand turned, she smiled and flipped her thumb over her shoulder. "Breakfast!"

Stan ended his call and entered with a smile. "Tricia says hello to everyone."

"Back at her!" Karlsson replied as he used a spatula to slide his finished product onto a plate. Stan had met Tricia on the same assignment that he'd met his paramour, Jackie. Thus, they regarded each other as family. As close as one got to having a real family in the business.

Nerissa smiled. "Tricia? Is this the someone special you mentioned on the boat?"

Stan shrugged. He hated discussing his personal life with anyone. Even those with whom he had shared a small boat for too many days at sea. "Yeah. Yeah, the one I met last year on a job. She was an Air Force techie-turned contractor, and after the job was over she decided to go back to the Air Force and finish out her time to qualify for a pension."

"Are wedding bells in the future?" Neri probed with a grin.

Marchand avoided eye contact and made his way over to the sink to wash his hands. "Who knows? We've both been married before so it's not like either one of us really needs that sort of legally binding agreement. Of course, I love her, but I really love my free time and space as well."

He reached for a towel to dry his hands and quickly changed

the subject. "As you know, Jonathan Babic, the Space Force guy that originally ordered your RV task was killed in a traffic crash last week. It turns out that someone did in fact tamper with his car. The forensics team found that someone had placed a command-detonated device on the steering components down by the wheel. That's what caused the car's left front wheel to dig in and spin it into the guardrail. The tox report from the medical examiner showed that he had alcohol and barbiturates in his system. Not enough to be lethal, but certainly enough to relax him behind the wheel."

Karlsson carefully laid the plates with the eggs and bacon on the table. "So, they drugged him and sabotaged his car? That sounds fairly sophisticated. Slightly more panache than hiring a couple of gangbangers to stage a drive-by and spray him with automatic weapons fire."

Stan agreed. "Yeah. The Pentagon Police had video of him leaving the property and he looked like he was in complete control. From the time he left the party until he smacked the guard rail was less than an hour and his blood-alcohol content was point oh three. Hardly enough by itself to cause significant impairment. The Inspector also said that a search of his office and home failed to locate any barbs at either location. His wife told them that he wasn't on anything, and she'd never filled a script for him."

"Someone spiked his drink, maybe? They wanted him relaxed."

Neri had been pensive but felt compelled to ask. "Is this the man that assigned the Fort Knox tasking? Why would anyone want him dead?"

Karlsson interjected, "Because he wasn't the boss. Someone above him ordered that tasking and now they are cleaning up their tracks."

"Yeah." Stan tossed the hand towel on the kitchen counter. "Paul is digging into their organizational structure to learn more about the General he worked for. He also said that they sent him another task a day after the one that sparked this mess. He said it had nothing to do with Fort Knox. But, it had everything to do with

Cydonia. Apparently, some place on Mars? He said you might know what that means."

Nerissa nodded. "Yes, a couple of years ago we got a tasking, and it was of big interest for a while. Cydonia is in the northern hemisphere and was originally photographed by the Viking orbiters. The big deal was that there was a structure there that seemed to resemble a human face. Once the photos leaked, the speculation was all over the internet and dominated conspiracy folklore. NASA distributed another photograph later, which they dumbed down, and said it was nothing more than a trick of light and shadow on a natural surface."

Stan was expressionless as she continued. "The trouble was, that in the blind experiment, we had a half-dozen viewers describing civilizations that existed there thousands of years before sentient life was emerging on our planet. There were societies there, mining something. Needless to say, they're not there now."

Stan looked past her through the windows at the sun creeping up above the horizon. Lake Michigan seemed to glitter with energy. Off in the distance he could see a cabin cruiser drifting with the currents, the couple on the back deck sitting quietly as they waited to snag a salmon on their line. Maybe a bass or a muskie. "I'm just thinking out loud, but was that the only other tasking you got from the Space Force?"

Neri nodded. "As far as I know. They are brand new and not a regular customer."

Stan slid a chair out and seated himself as Karlsson pushed the platters closer to him. "Paul said that he was suspicious of the request right from the start. When he tried to pin Babic down, he was told that they wanted to know if our psychics could see into Fort Knox better than Chinese or Russian satellites. But he had a feeling that they were bullshitting him."

Karlsson passed the bacon to Neri. "You think the Space Force has a secret involving Fort Knox that is worth killing over?"

Nerissa slid a couple of strips of bacon onto her plate and then passed the platter to Marchand. "Maybe. Not that the two taskings were necessarily related in any way, but when we viewed Cydonia a couple of years ago, almost everyone got a perception of the presence of gold."

"Gold on mars?" Karlsson asked.

Stan nodded. "Yeah. Nothing that's been proven. Well, yet." He reached for the pepper shaker in the center of the table. "Whatever might have been there a hundred thousand years ago, would probably be long gone by now."

"Gold on mars. Gold in Fort Knox." Neri used her fingers to pick up a bacon strip and chew off the end. "The Fort Knox viewing... we both saw some sort of extra-terrestrial entity taking gold away."

Stan nodded. "At some point in the past." They had been unable to discuss their activity in this much detail earlier simply because Ernie had not been completely read-in to the project and did not have the clearance. Neither did the pilots who brought them to Chicago.

"The nineteen fifties." She recalled her feelings and perceptions during the viewing that now seemed so long ago with all that had transpired. "Eisenhower."

Stan looked out at the beauty of the lake and thought about a similar morning long past, when he was a young kid just out of college. He was in Officer Candidate School on the back side of Quantico, overlooking the Potomac River. Standing at attention in formation as the choppers from HMX-1 took off, headed up to Washington to pick up their precious cargo. The sounds of powerful engines, the smells of wet autumn leaves, the bracing crisp air in the cool November morning.

"Holloman." He said.

"Who is Holloman?" Karlsson asked.

"Holloman Air Force Base." Neri answered. "I couldn't remember the name of that base. Sometime in February 1955, Ike disappeared from a quail hunting trip in Georgia for about thirty-six hours. His press secretary said that he had a case of the sniffles and would be back on schedule in no time. An Air Force hospital staffer, stationed at Holloman, later said publicly that Ike's airplane, the

Columbine, landed out there around nine in the morning, taxied to the end of an active runway and parked." Marchand and Neri exchanged glances.

"Supposedly, according to the corpsman, a UFO landed nearby, Ike got out of his airplane and walked over to it, and spoke with... uh, someone or something, for about forty-five minutes."

"While another UFO hovered above them." Nerissa finished his sentence.

Stan grimaced. "We're doing an awful lot of analyzing here. This is some serious overlay!"

Neri shrugged. "Paul put us together for a reason. He wanted us to compare notes, and this is what we're doing." She took a sip of orange juice and reached for a napkin to jot down some notes as they spoke. "There was also the visit to Edwards the year before. Almost exactly a year before."

"Edwards Air Force Base?" Karlsson asked. He knew the conversation that had begun on a boat in the Gulf of Mexico, was well over his head but wanted to feel like he was participating, nevertheless.

"Yeah." Stan scooped a helping of scrambled eggs onto his plate and reached for the pepper shaker. "That one was actually the first contact. Supposedly. Ike had excused himself with a complaint of a toothache and was whisked away from Palm Springs for some sort of emergency dental surgery. There were still rumors about this when I was just starting out in the Secret Service."

Karlsson considered what he was hearing again. When he had heard it earlier, he played along, somewhat interested. However, as a devout realist, he was still not on board with the topic. "So, you're saying that Ike had two apparent meetings with some sort of alien ambassadors, and then we gave them our gold?"

Neri swallowed her bacon and wiped her mouth. "Yeah. Sounds weird, but that's what I'm thinking. Our results of the Fort Knox tasking took us to about that period. It could have easily been right before or after one of those two alleged meetings."

"Or in between." Marchand mused. "What if the first meeting was the request, and the next meeting, a year later, was the payoff? In the first meeting we negotiated something. We complied with the terms, and they came back a second time, a year later, to say *thanks*, and offer our quid pro quo. That would mean that Fort Knox lost some of its inventory between February of fifty-four and February of fifty-five."

Neri nodded. "Uh huh. My guess is late May or early June. I got the feeling of green grass and leaves on the trees, but it wasn't overly hot."

"Yeah." Stan agreed. "Clear skies. No haze in the air."

Neri squirted some ketchup onto one side of her plate and then subconsciously swabbed a fork-full of eggs through it. As the fork left drag marks in the ketchup, she had a fleeting vision of a sedated man being dragged to a window and eased out, making his death look like a suicide. "James Forrestal." She said as she imagined the drag marks left by the heels of his shoes on the tile floor.

"The first Secretary of Defense?" Karlsson asked as he sat down and reached for the platter of eggs.

She nodded. "Yes. Former Secretary of the Navy and then Secretary of War. Among the many changes in 1947, the President changed the cabinet post from *War* to *Defense* and he was kept in the job. Nineteen Forty-Seven." She looked at Stan.

"Roswell."

"And Aztec was the following year." She added.

Stan nodded energetically. "That's right. I forgot about Aztec!"

Karlsson slid a couple of strips of bacon onto his plate. "All right, guys. I'm familiar with the Roswell story, but what was Aztec?"

"Aztec, New Mexico in March 1948. Supposedly a large craft, maybe ninety feet across, landed or crashed and they found some... uh...occupants. The FBI was able to pass the story off as a hoax with the unwitting assistance of a couple of con artists, who got busted by the locals for trying to sell some sort of metal that they claimed had been made by aliens. With their confessions and subsequent jail terms, the entire thing got pushed under the rug as a hoax and any witnesses were publicly discredited in routine government fashion."

Marchand grunted. "Right out of the Quantico playbook." There had always been something of a professional rivalry between the Secret Service and the FBI, and Stan did little to conceal it. "When did Forrestal die?"

"May of 1949, if my memory serves me." She replied.

"What's the Forrestal connection?" Karlsson asked.

Stan reached for more bacon. "He was supposedly part of the Majestic Twelve group, or MJ-12 as they were known in some government circles. It was the group that Truman charged to take control of the whole extra-terrestrial thing and make sure that we got full advantage of any technology and could instantly control the media message whenever someone reported seeing something strange in the sky."

Nerissa continued, "Rumor has it that Forrestal didn't think an alien presence should be a secret and argued that the information should be released to the world."

Karlsson took a sip of his orange juice. "And you think he was killed for that?"

Marchand glanced at Karlsson and lifted an eyebrow. "Imagine, the US Government killing its own people to keep them quiet."

"Yeah, it's probably happened for a lot less." Karlsson replied meekly, keenly aware of the hypocritical nature of the question.

Stan continued, "The timing is about right and what we know from unpublished government reports is that Ike had some meetings take place at those bases at about the times the witnesses claimed. We also know that the US Government was beginning to consider Forrestal a security risk. In their favor, he had already expressed to friends and family that he was having mental health issues and had even contemplated suicide. That's a heck of a setup for someone who's about to embarrass the White House."

Karlsson didn't understand psychic functioning, but he certainly knew assassination technique. "Yes. All things considered; the target gave them the perfect roadmap for his own demise. That was back in the day when people believed whatever the government told them."

The group devoured the meal as they kicked around different ideas and when the discussion and the food were exhausted, Karlsson began clearing the table. Stan rose to help when he was distracted by a new text message. He looked at the screen with a frown as he read it out loud. "Groceries downstairs 16L4 33R3 41L1 3TTS"

Neri shook her head and shrugged as Karlsson's smile turned to a wide grin. "It's a safe combination."

Marchand's frown diminished somewhat. "Yeah. Left four spins to sixteen, right three spins to thirty-three. Got it. There must be a safe downstairs"

The two men had done a cursory search of the house the night before just to assure themselves that they were alone and to find any types of exits or openings that could be exploited for illegal entry. But they had not seen a safe. The basement was comprised of a finished and unfinished section and their search had focused primarily on human-sized targets and opportunities. Thus, they had not really been looking for one.

"I'd better take another look downstairs. Apparently, we have a benefactor with US Government connections."

Marchand descended the stairs from the kitchen and wandered through the entertainment area. He moved the pictures on the wall, to no avail. He went through a hollow-core door to the unfinished side where he found a workshop and several plywood panels of varying sizes that could be quickly screwed into the window frames to help stave-off damage from stormy winds. It was then that he noticed that the largest panels, which were a little bigger than the doors, were leaned up against the wall in a way that they concealed a heavy steel vault door, built into the concrete block.

"Hey Matt! I think I could use your help for a moment!" He yelled up the stairs.

Karlsson readily appeared at the foot of the stairs, instinctively ducking his head, even though the basement had eight-foot ceilings. Over the years he had banged it enough on beams that did not favor his six-foot-four-inch frame.

"What have you got?"

"Help me get these hurricane panels out of the way." Marchand said as he carefully passed some of the smaller ones over to Karlsson. He wasn't wearing gloves and detested the nuisance of splinters.

"Would you look at that!" Karlsson expressed his appreciation for the design. "They made a vault out of regular concrete block and set the door in steel. Not bad!"

Marchand took out his phone and looked again at the text message as he quickly spun the dial counterclockwise to free up the discs, slowing when he came up on number sixteen. He carefully followed the instructions to land precisely on the other numbers and then turned the adjacent handle a quarter turn to the left to retract the heavy bolts. With some effort, the door slowly opened. He flipped the light switch up and both men stared into the eight-by-eight space that had been cleverly concealed during construction to the point that if the outer wall had been paneled, searchers never would have found it.

Karlsson looked up at the ceiling. "Steel plate. Whoever built this knew what they were doing."

"Yeah." Marchand agreed. He gestured at the tarp covering the objects in the corner. "Groceries, I bet."

Karlsson nodded and carefully drew back the tarp revealing a stack of plastic rifle cases and smaller rectangular tubs. It only took a minute to open everything up and begin taking inventory. Two M-4 assault rifles with adjustable stocks and red-dot optics, two Remington 870 shotguns with twenty-inch barrels and a Remington 700 with a synthetic stock and a Leupold VX Freedom 4-12X50 CDS rifle scope.

Karlsson let out a low whistle as he gently pulled the rifle out to get a closer look. Keeping the muzzle pointed down, he lifted and retracted the bolt. Satisfied that the weapon was empty, he shouldered the rifle and gradually exerted pressure on the trigger until the distinctive click could be heard, signaling that the firing pin had been released.

"Wow. Smooth trigger: I'd guess right around a two-pound pull." He looked at the barrel. "Chambered in .30-06."

Stan opened the waterproof tubs and found a pack of five hundred rounds of 5.56MM ammunition for the M-4's, fifty rounds of 00 Buckshot for the shotguns and a variety of .30-06 caliber ammo for the sniper rifle, with different bullet weights and types. "Someone wanted us to be prepared for something."

In one of the smaller tubs, they found three Glock 19 pistols with Kydex holsters and three magazines for each gun along with three hundred rounds of Speer law enforcement ammunition. In another tub was found a half-dozen CTS flash-bangs and three tear gas grenades. Taped to the tub was a slip of paper that had the link and passcode to the house's security systems that would allow them to monitor the audio and video systems around the house and property.

The house had been built into a gently sloping hillside, on a six-acre lot that gave them 140 feet of rare drivable private beach, allowing them to launch small boats if necessary. However, larger craft would have to come down from Milwaukee or up from Waukegan to tie up there. While more visible cameras could be found on the corners of the house, covert ones had been installed in the trees surrounding the property and facing the long driveway.

Karlsson and Marchand each added the app to their cell phones and then clicked on the link to download the profile for their site. Individually, they scrolled through the cameras and then looked at the alarm points that had been established in the house. They also found that whoever set the security up for the residence added a buried sensor at the beach end of the dock, which would alarm if anyone attempted to enter or exit the dock itself.

"Nice." Karlsson admitted.

Stan concurred. "Yeah, this looks like the stuff we used when I was on the job."

Karlsson nodded thoughtfully, remembering the fate of the Chinese businessman who had originally purchased the place. Hopefully, the robust security system would keep their party safer than it had him.

Francine Dantonio relaxed on the back of the Carver C-37, quietly sipping coffee from her travel mug as her bait-less line trailed behind. Somewhere in her past she had been told that the most common technique for attracting a curious muskie following one's lure was to make wide sweeping motions in a *figure 8* shape. But one had to make sure they were using wide enough patterns since a large muskie would have trouble following shorter turns. It was all academic. She could not care less if something bit, and she felt she had paid her homage to angling science by the simple fact that she recognized that in colder water, fish are more sluggish. Therefore, she had opted for smaller baits like the rattle traps in her tackle box. "Put those down!" She commanded softly but firmly.

Her associate, a couple of years older, but organizationally subordinate to her paused and turned before touching the binoculars on the deck of the boat. "What?"

"We're supposed to be fishing, numb nuts! We're less than two hundred yards from shore so if they happen to be looking out this way, they won't see a loving couple enjoying the morning air. They'll see someone scoping out their house with binoculars."

"Oh. Yeah, sorry." He replied as he instead reached for the adjacent tackle box and rested it in his lap as he seated himself in the deck chair next to his companion.

The thirty-seven-foot Carver was comfortable and quick, with the twin Volvo diesels rated at three hundred horsepower each. The fiberglass body and *modified V* hull meant that it could get-up-and-go if the need arose. It also offered relative anonymity on the lake since the company had begun in nearby in Pulaski, in the late 1950's with Charlie Carter and George Verhagen, who were just having fun building mahogany boats for friends and family.

Through the years, the company went through some organizational changes but emerged as a great example of a dependable, mid-range boat. They didn't have the beauty of the Sea Ray, but there was nothing shabby about them either. They were known for making excellent use of all possible space on the boat and producing a finished product that could really take a pounding on fresh water. And, as most boaters knew, fresh water was much harder than salt water.

Francine brushed her hair back, momentarily revealing the vertical hairline scar on the outside of her left eye. The winds were relatively calm, but occasionally they would create a slight gust, making her beautiful brown hair something of a nuisance.

Her male associate was a newcomer to her team. Another retired military guy looking for something to do to augment his government pension. She was certain he had been great at artillery tactics, but he still had something to learn about covert operations.

"Sorry, Dale." She touched his arm. "I didn't mean to snap at you, but I've got a lot on my mind."

A lot, indeed. Officially, her man in Belize had fumbled his assignment. All he had to do was take out a local thug who had helped them bring down an airplane in a rather unorthodox fashion. That was the story, anyway. She shook her head and tugged absentmindedly on the rod to make herself look attentive.

Dale Braun had started out in the Air Defense Artillery branch with the goal of doing his time and then teaching school, thus drawing a tolerable salary while collecting his Army pension. He was in no hurry to get shot at or blown up. Unfortunately, a couple of marginal OER's indicated he was far more interested in reading about warfare than practicing it. The evaluations got him riffed early, on a reduced pension, forcing him to look for something else to live on.

"My bad, Francine. I should have known better." He opened the tackle box and rummaged around until he found a lure that looked impressive enough. The truth be told, he had only fished twice in his life and was just there to learn the ins and outs of covert surveillance. As far as he had been told, they were watching foreign agents who had somehow infiltrated the nation's impaired immigration system and were simply reporting back on their activity. He looked at his watch.

"Zero seven hundred. How long can we sit here before we look suspicious?" He asked.

Francine had been lost in thought. "Huh? Oh...uh...we'll drift for a while and then head north." She tried making figure eights with the line, just for the exercise. "We'll come back again after sundown tonight and again tomorrow morning. If they notice us we'll want them to think we're locals and are around here on a regular basis."

Dale found her attractive. Her figure was easy on the eyes and indicated that she took care of herself, and he found the droopy left eye to be cute and alluring. He tried to imagine her in a tight skirt and high heels. "Sounds good. I really appreciate you taking me on."

She smiled at him. "Yeah, no problem. You'll learn as you go." He would do, she thought, at least for the time being. She had bigger problems on her mind that she couldn't share with her new protégé. She knew far more about her targets than she could impart to the baby-faced former Army Major Dale Braun. She knew the targets weren't foreign spies, and she knew that her and Braun weren't there to simply observe and report back to the CIA or some other such agency. She also knew that when the time came, her targets were not going to be easy. While she considered her fangs to be sharp, she knew that the group she was watching had fangs too. Maybe sharper than her own.

She could not afford to let those thoughts deter her or cloud her judgment. She was, after all, Vesuvius.

CHAPTER 10

Lenny Hart scratched Alphonse on the head and smiled as the two-year old Black Labrador Retriever wagged his tale with unbridled energy. The pup was coming along nicely in his training, and they had been working with decoys every weekend to get him up to full hunting-speed in time for the fall. His cousin had a nice place on a lake out in Western Pennsylvania and the two men had talked about getting the dogs together to chase some ducks.

"Alphonse, come!" Becca snapped her fingers.

Becca, the latest addition to his stable of past and present wives, was still girlishly beautiful at forty-five and even though she didn't share his love of hunting, she didn't mind spending time in the wet weeds with her husband occasionally. "I'll take good care of him while you're gone." She said as she reached for Alphonse's collar to keep the dog from following his master to the car.

Lenny kissed her lightly. "I'll be back before you know it."

She knew that he was in some type of sensitive work for the government but was not sure what it entailed. She reckoned, considering his law enforcement background, that the occasional last-minute crisis was not out of the ordinary and should probably be expected. "I'll let Jeff and Tammy know that you got called out of town and may not get back until Saturday evening. I'll see if they want to reschedule or if they just want to entertain me by myself." She smiled stoically.

Hart nodded and waved as he climbed up into the black Chevy Suburban. With gasoline prices fluctuating every day the four-year-old beast probably wasn't the most economical choice for a vehicle, but then he wanted room for his guns and dogs. He made sure his sport coat was out of the way as he slung the shoulder belt over and clipped it into the latch between his seat and the center console and gave another quick wave to Becca who was standing in the garage, barefoot in her nightgown.

The nice two-story home off Glenkirk Road near Lake Manassas was a bit pricier than he had been used to in Central Ohio but put him in easy range of the trails that he and Alphonse loved to explore. Becca's job in accounting helped significantly on the bills and it was not too far from both their offices. Depending on the time of day and day of the week, it could take anywhere between forty-five minutes and two hours to drive I-66 into his office. Many days, he preferred instead to drive into Manassas and take the train to his stop in Crystal City.

He backed carefully down the fifty-foot driveway and into the road and thought about Paul's message the night before. "URGENT – UNITED #2100 IAD to CLE 0816 TOMORROW. TICKET AT COUNTER - CALL WHEN YOU GET TO CLE."

Paul had been uncharacteristically distracted lately and there were several indicators around the office that something was going on. His office door was shut more often than usual, and he was attending more offsite meetings than he had in previous months. If one attempted to seek information from Jillian, the office's Majordomo, she would simply stare over the top of her bifocals and redirect the conversation by asking for an update of whatever project the *asker* had been working on.

He was curious about what awaited him in Cleveland but stayed focused on his driving up Route 29 watching for his turn onto Sully Road, which would take him into the airport. The traffic was steady but not at all heavy and he reasoned that the trip should take no longer than forty-five minutes. Another fifteen minutes to park and get through the terminal, a half hour for security and five minutes to get a cup of coffee. He glanced at his watch and smiled. That would get him to his gate thirty minutes before departure. Perfect.

Two and a half hours later he was trying to figure out where to put his legs in the cramped row of coach class seats as the pilot informed everyone that they were at cruising altitude and to sit back and relax. Relax? He was as close to the guy in front of him and the woman next to him as he was with Becca every night. He hated commercial air travel but was excited about the opportunity to get out of the office on an assignment of sorts. Whatever the hubbub was about, he was certain he would learn more about it when he got to Cleveland.

The cabin attendant and his squeaky cart finally got to row eleven. "Something to drink sir?"

"Just coffee." Hart replied as he unlatched his tray table and eased it down onto his knees.

The attendant poured an ounce or two into the small Styrofoam cup and passed it to him, wrapped of course in the complimentary napkin. Looking past Hart, he asked, "Miss?"

Hart glanced at the woman in the center seat, her head was back in the seat, eyes closed and earbuds in. "Miss?" The attendant repeated.

She opened one eye. "Coffee, thanks."

She was an attractive woman, about Becca's age. Physically fit, but not dainty, as his mother might have said. There was something about her that reminded him of women he'd met in police work. The attendant passed her ration of coffee across Hart, and he instinctively raised his hand up under it in case turbulence caused the attendant to spill it.

"Thanks." She half-turned with a smile. "Three hundred bucks to get to Cleveland and they give me a seat built for a twelve-year old. She glanced over her shoulder towards the rear of the aircraft and then shook her head. "Every seat full. I remember the days when air travel was fun."

Hart chuckled. "It's been a while but I sorta remember that too. That was a long time ago."

She smiled. "It seems like every year the aisles and rows get narrower, and the seats get smaller. The staff used to be friendlier too." She grunted as she took a careful sip.

She sounded like she would be fun. After all, a little conversation might help pass the time and make the trip seem shorter. He asked, "You headed to Cleveland on business or is that home?"

She turned her head a bit more in his direction; as much as she could without straining it in the cramped surroundings. "I'm actually from Lansing Michigan, but don't get back there that often. I'm calling on a customer in Cleveland. I'm in software." She took another sip of coffee. "You?"

"Uh, retired." Being partially truthful. "I was in law enforcement for a bunch of years and decided to grab the pension and take a stab at consulting myself. Security stuff."

"Oh!" She nodded slyly. "You don't look like a cop."

The corners of his mouth turned up. She was flirting a little. "Yeah? What's a cop supposed to look like?"

She shrugged and grinned. "You know, donut in one hand and handcuffs in the other."

He nodded. "I see. And just how much experience have you had with handcuffs?"

She laughed. "Very little. And if it makes a difference, I gave up donuts long ago too."

"Gave up...too? As in..."

"Stop it! Let's not go there. This is supposed to be a family flight."

He blushed a bit, as he was prone to do at the least possible embarrassment. For just a brief moment he was able to forget that he was a devoted married man with an adorable wife at home, who was not only *smoking hot*, as the kids would say, but quite successful in business. He needed her at this point in his life, and for that reason his conscience kicked in and redirected the conversation to the economy and the latest political scandals.

It wasn't long before they could sense a power reduction in the engines and an iota of weightlessness as they slowed and started their descent into Cleveland Hopkins. The attendants moved through the cabin again, collecting trash and getting passengers to return their seatbacks and tray tables to their upright and locked positions. Lenny and his seatmate leaned over the elderly chap seated next to the window so that they could see if the ground was down there somewhere. The clouds and morning fog diffused the sunlight, making the buildings and roads in the town below look like a storybook village around someone's electric train set.

Moments later, the wheels touched down and the captain welcomed them to Cleveland and asked them to remain in their seats until the aircraft had completed all necessary docking maneuvers and the cabin attendants had released everyone from their incarceration. When the chimes signaled that it was okay to move again, everyone immediately stood and began searching the overhead compartments for their possessions.

Lenny stretched his six-foot-one frame and asked, "Did you have a bag up here that I can help you with?"

"No." She shook her head as she began to move towards the aisle so that she too could start the circulation back in her limbs. "Just my laptop. I plan on returning this afternoon. Are you in town for long?"

"Couple of days. Hopefully no more." He noticed that her eyes were on his wedding band.

"Well, it was nice chatting. I hope you have a successful visit." She said coyly.

"Ditto!" He responded. "By the way, my name is Lenny." He extended his hand.

She took it lightly and raising her gaze to meet his, gave it a shake. "Mine's Davina. But most of my friends call me Dave."

———— ◉ ————

Since Karlsson was not enamored of running without a genuine need to do so, he agreed to have Stan run with Neri on her morning jaunt. They headed towards the Chiwaukee Prairie Ramble turning west and then ultimately south to get them back to their current domicile, which in their absence had been converted to its own version of Fort Knox. They calculated that they completed more than their planned three miles in just under thirty minutes. Neither was going to win a marathon, but both felt they had gotten their cardiac workout in for the day.

Karlsson had used that time to ensure that all the items in the grocery delivery were functional and battle-worthy and that they could be strategically placed throughout the house. He had taken each firearm apart, conducted a full inspection and reassembled them before performing a function test. He was confident that they would perform as the manufacturer had promised. However, the bolt-action rifle was a different story.

Because long-range rifle shooters were all a bit different, it was necessary for each to sight in the rifle and scope to suit their own anatomical and experiential profile. The different boxes of ammunition would be ballistically similar at a hundred yards but might be way off at three hundred. The only way he would be able to collect the *dope* on each round would be to actually go to a range and fire them. In the meantime, if he was going to engage a target out in the middle of the lake, he might have to have Stan spot for him and let him know where the rounds were impacting on the target.

Neri and Stan were laughing as they came through the front door and headed straight to the kitchen to grab bottled water out of the refrigerator.

Karlsson grinned. "It looks like you two kids had an enjoyable morning while I was in here slaving away. How far did you go?"

"A little more than three miles." Neri guessed. "I could have done more, but I had to drag grandpa with me."

Stan laughed. "You wish! I was just holding back to see how much you really had in you!"

"Oh please..." her comment was noisily abbreviated by Stan's phone receiving a call.

He looked at the number and shook his head. "DC area code, but I don't recognize it. Should I?"

Karlsson nodded. "Might as well."

Marchand hit the button to activate the speaker and spoke loudly. "Pizza parlor. Will this be for pickup or delivery?"

Everyone in the room recognized Paul's voice. "We have a problem. One of our newer teammates has gone missing. His wife stated that he received an urgent text from me last night about eleven-thirty that directed him to catch a flight from Dulles to Cleveland and to contact me upon arrival for further instructions. I issued no such instructions." He paused briefly.

"We checked the manifest for the flight in question and learned that he did make the trip. However, there has been no contact with him since he left his home this morning."

Karlsson spoke first. "We're assuming foul play, or we wouldn't be having this call?"

"Subject's name is Lenny Hart, age 61, white male, former law enforcement officer. His wife said that the text he received came from my telephone and appeared genuine. There had been no recent charges to his credit card and so upon further checking, we found that his ticket was pre-paid by a gift card. He picked up the ticket at the counter and provided positive identification this morning. We're sure he was on the plane. However, we don't have any visibility into what happened when he landed in Cleveland."

"And this is important to our assignment, why?" Karlsson asked.

"We asked Mr. Hart to view one of the same targets given to your Protectee prior to her dilemma. I'm afraid this particular client has been somewhat disappointing to work with and is rapidly building a casualty list, to include one of their own."

The two men had been discussing an equitable division of labor based upon their skillsets. Stan would be the lead for all things relating to the protection of their houseguest. Karlsson on the other hand would take charge of the counterattack, if and when one was identified. "Do we have a new assignment?" Karlsson asked.

Neri shivered a bit. She knew what that meant, coming from him.

"Perhaps." Paul continued. "I have someone looking into our telecommunications security. Whoever issued last-night's instructions knew enough about our operation to find Lenny's cell phone number and to spoof my number into their phone. The number of people on the planet who could know that information can probably be counted on one hand."

Marchand thought for a moment. "Obviously, you'll have to meet with the employees, give them some sort of briefing and collect their phones. At this point, we don't know if any or all the devices have been compromised and are spewing out data and conversations everywhere. If you suspect any of the employees of being intentionally involved, you may have to require polygraphs to try to weed him or her out. Then, you'll need a tech sweep to see if your office space and network have been compromised. Start with Jillian's desk. She processes everything the Tank does and if someone wanted to get the most information from the least number of incursions, then that would be the system to hit."

Paul spoke softly, "There is also the issue of the client himself. We know who the late Colonel Babic worked for over there. But the question is whether his superior is driving this or if someone else yet to be discovered is in control. What have you folks put together from the remote viewpoint?"

Neri briefed Paul on the results of their discussions and then asked. "What about Lenny and the others? What did they come up with?"

The listeners could tell that Paul was deep in thought. "A consensus is that there is a ninth planet that is on its way back from a trip to the farthest reaches of our solar system, on a large elliptical orbit. Our own Space Force and Russian intelligence seem to want to know what will happen when it gets back. Will it affect our climate? Our gravitational forces? Tides? Will their civilization need more gold? Do they have something for us that we will need? I guess, more importantly, when amateur astronomers begin to see it coming, will their sporadic reports antagonize or disconcert the population? Will the media be responsible in their reporting?"

"And how will it affect the power brokers in government? You know this'll be exploited." Marchand had spent too many years in Washington.

"Of course." Paul answered. "In terms of strategy, I must consider team safety as one element, and the apprehension of the perpetrators as another. If you can handle the team safety component, I can pursue the investigation from here. I have an idea though, which we would have to implement before collecting everyone's devices. I'm going to assign another tasking from the same client to a viewer who isn't currently assigned to the Tank. But we'll circulate communications and email chains to support his activity in the hopes that someone will try to go after him."

"You have someone in mind?" Karlsson asked.

"I do. It will take a day or so to create the character backdrop and educate the person I intend to put into the role."

"Another psychic? They may have their own viewers on this, and they might be able to recognize the trap." Neri postulated.

"Yes." Paul said quietly. "Although he's been inactive for several years."

"As far as defense and offense goes, do you want us moving, or should we stay put?" Karlsson sought to clarify Paul's expectations.

"Stay put for now...but be ready. The signal to move will be ABRAXAS. And Matt..."

"Yes, sir?"

"If you get the signal, it would be helpful if it doesn't point back to us." After a moment, "But then again, if it goes that far, it might not make any difference."

———««»»———

Lieutenant General Nelson Scott carefully read the message a second time so that he was sure that he understood it. "TRANSACTION PARTIALLY COMPLETE – NEED ASSURANCES WE'RE NOT NEXT ON THE LIST BEFORE TAKING FURTHER ACTION."

Partially complete? What did that mean? His blood pressure was up, and he was not used to his orders not being carried out expeditiously upon command. He clumsily texted back, "PLEASE EXPLAIN"

A few moments later, the flashing ellipsis morphed into a message from the person who called himself Dave Fox. "U R SENDING A LOT OF WORK OUR WAY AND WE NEED TO KNOW WHERE IT ENDS".

"DID U ACQUIRE TARGET?" He typed

"OF COURSE." Dave replied.

"STATUS?" General Scott's heart was racing. He had gotten too comfortable with the arrangement and now he feared that he could easily lose control of the entire mission.

"RESTRAINED AND MODERATELY COMFORTABLE" The message said.

"Shit!" He screamed out loud. The guy was still alive. "WHAT DO YOU NEED TO COMPLETE THE TRANSACTION?"

"ALL OF THE NAMES NOW – WE WANT TO BE ABLE TO PRICE ACCORDINGLY AND MOVE OUR LOCATION BEFORE WE GET UNIVITED GUESTS"

Scott's mind was trying to catch up to his heart rate. "ALL WHAT NAMES?? WHAT GUESTS?"

"DON'T BE STUPID GENERAL – YOU'RE SWEEPING YOUR TRACKS. WE NEED TO BE AN EQUITY PARTNER FROM HERE ON."

Equity partner? Scott was infuriated. There weren't a dozen people that had full knowledge of the implications of Niburu. Who did these people think they were? They were just skilled labor. "EQUITY PARTNER OF WHAT? YOU HAVE NO IDEA WHAT YOU ARE DEALING WITH!"

The response was quick, "OF COURSE WE DO – WE'RE DEALING WITH A CLIENT WHO IS COMMITTING FELONIES TO COVER HIS TRACKS, AND CAN EITHER WORK WITH US OR SUCCUMB TO US. LET ME KNOW TOMORROW."

"Aaarrrghh!" The General screamed as he threw the phone across the room. It struck a lampshade on the table at the end of the couch and then bounced from the couch to the floor.

He sat down heavily in his chair and began to feverishly rub his temples. "No, no, no! These morons think there's some fucking pot of gold at the end of a rainbow. They have no idea!"

He got up and walked over to the sofa so that he could retrieve his cell phone and then returned to his desk to consider his options. After a moment he brought up a spreadsheet that contained names and contact information of high-level appointees and elected officials that were part of the Washington power elite. Finding the name that he wanted, his shaking fingers punched the number.

"Good afternoon, General. I hadn't expected to hear from you again." The voice on the other end sounded cordial but did not totally conceal the latent annoyance.

"We need to meet. Where and when?" General Scott said curtly.

"Excuse me?"

Scott repeated, "We need to meet. It's important."

"I'm really quite busy today. How about this afternoon, say six o'clock. Do you know a place called the Cardigan?"

General Scott closed his eyes. "You know I do. See you at six."

Francine Dantonio unwrapped the clove hitch that had been knotted around the dock cleat and tossed the line to Dale Braun. He stood by as she grabbed the bow rail to help pull herself up onto the deck, and then he offered his hand to help her over the glistening chrome rail.

"Thanks! Secure those lines and we'll get underway." She enjoyed being the captain and being able to use her vast vocabulary of nautical terms. It had come naturally. Her father had been a naval officer who had a passion for sailing on the weekends. Thus, she was masterfully using the nautical lexicon by the first grade and was the first girl in her class to ask her teacher for permission to use the *head*. Some of the other kids looked at her askance when they were displaying the artwork they had created, and with a wink, the teacher invited them to hang their masterpieces on the *bulkhead*.

She managed the twin Volvo Penta's like a pro and had them out of the harbor in minutes, headed south for the day's activity. "Do me a favor and grab the sat-phone."

Braun nodded and disappeared below decks for a minute, reappearing with the satellite phone. Handing it to her, he smiled just a bit.

"Thanks. Do you want to take it for a minute? Just keep us steady on one six zero for about a half hour and we'll see where we are." She smiled back.

Braun nodded and took the wheel as Francine moved aft and began punching in a sequence of numbers. It rang three times before she heard her associate pick up.

"Hey girl! How's it look over there?" Davina asked cheerfully.

"Fine. I'll turn that baby-faced grunt into a sailor if it's the last thing I do. How'd it go with your side of things?"

Davina Fox sighed, "Easier than I thought it would be. I played helpless-girl to his ex-cop mindset and told him that I'd feel so much safer if he could walk me to the rental counter. After that, it was a quick bite at one of the snack-stands where I was able to spike his tea. By the time it started to take effect I told him that I needed some air. He agreed and I just basically walked him out of there to Jerry's car, waiting in the cab line in arrivals."

Francine chuckled. "You've still got it girl! Did you get anywhere with Captain Kirk?"

"Huh uh." Fox replied. "I made the first pass at being partners, but I think you could say he was resistant to the idea. I figured I'd let him consider his position overnight and then try again tomorrow. Do you have a plan yet for your thing?"

"Not yet. We're not going to do anything that Captain Kirk doesn't pay for. Technically he only hired us for the one guy, but now it looks like there's another man and a woman there. From a distance, they all look pretty competent, and I'm not crazy about trying to isolate him from the other two. That means that when the time comes, we may have to clean house. And that's going to cost more because I guarantee it's gonna cause major problems with the locals and the feds."

"Yeah. We need to put some thought into that." Davina concurred. "What kind of payday do you anticipate?"

Francine looked at the harbor, slowly receding in the distance behind them with the gentle rumble of the diesel powerplants beneath her feet. "I really don't know. It would be nice if you could get your psychic guest to help you figure out what they've got going on down there. Whatever it is, Captain Kirk is running up a serious body count to protect it."

"Yeah." Davina replied. "I might have an idea."

———— ((O)) ————

Margarita Vallejo rolled over and looked at Marco with a smile. He kissed her lightly on the mouth and savored her scent as he recalled their first meeting, a month earlier. He, the Frenchman and the German were the latest addition to the astronomy team, and she was beginning her walking tour of the Vera C. Rubin observatory on top of the same desolate Chilean mountain that seemed so very inviting to other astronomers with other telescopes studying the same sky for different reasons.

"Formerly known as the Large Synoptic Survey Telescope, or LSST, its primary purpose was to conduct a legacy survey of space and time. Housing the 8.4-meter Simonyi Survey Telescope, it used a three-mirror anastigmat to enable wider fields of view, much larger than possible with telescopes featuring only one or two curved surfaces."

Marco Pozos smiled back, causing her to momentarily break her concentration. "The...uh... observatory, as you know, is named after Vera C. Rubin and honors her and her colleagues' legacy to probe the nature of dark matter by mapping and cataloging billions of galaxies through space and time."

"The design is unique among larger telescopes by its very wide field of view which is 3.5 degrees in diameter, or 9.6 square degrees. So, by comparison, both the Sun and the Moon, as seen from Earth, are 0.5 degrees across, or 0.2 square degrees. Think about an area of the sky that has forty moons in it. That is the size that we are talking about. The LSST also features a larger aperture, improving light gathering capability, giving it a spectacularly large light spread of 319 square meters per degree. This is more than three times the etendue of current earth-based telescopes."

Pozos found her captivating, here atop this mountain a hundred kilometers from nowhere. Located on the El Peñón peak of Cerro Pachón, a 2,682-meter-high mountain in Coquimbo Region, in northern Chile, the nearest civilization of any size was the town of La Serena, the second oldest city in the country, after Santiago. In the summertime, the beaches drew the tourists. The rest of the year, it offered sanctuary to the myriad of astronomers stationed at one of the many sites throughout the region.

La Serena also held the offices for the European Southern Observatory organization which operated the La Silla Observatory. There was AURA, Inc., the operator of Cerro Tololo, located in the Valle de Elqui, about 85 kilometers east of La Serena, and the Gemini observatories. It was also home to the Carnegie Institution for Science, which operated Las Campanas Observatory and, of course there was the Vera C. Rubin Observatory.

Pozos wasn't thinking about astronomy now. He was using his limited mathematical brain to calculate the best way to get this young lady to someplace like Club de Jazz, a trendy spot built into a neoclassical home, with live music several nights a week. The music was good, and just loud enough that you had to lean in close to your date's ear to speak. It had great food and wine and was not far from his apartment on Oscar Aldunate Street. From there, who knew where the night could lead.

"The 3.2 gigapixel primary focus camera takes approximately two hundred thousand pictures each year, which means it will process a fifteen second exposure every twenty seconds. Once the image is taken, it can be processed one of three ways: prompt, daily or annually. The *prompt* products are issued as alerts within sixty seconds of observation. They are usually of objects that have changed brightness or position relative to archived images of that particular sky position." Pozos caught her eyes moving up and down his six-foot frame and noted that her smile widened a bit as she spoke. "As you know, the primary goals of the program include the study of dark energy and dark matter by measuring weak gravitational lensing, baryon acoustic oscillations, and photometry of supernovae, all as a function of Doppler redshift; the displacement of spectrum of astronomical objects toward longer red wavelengths."

He smiled back at her, his eyes locked on hers as she ignored the other two scientists on the tour and focused on him. "The other program priority is to map as many small objects as possible in the solar system, including near-Earth asteroids and Kuiper belt objects." She gayly bobbed her head, "And, of course, to see if there is really a Planet Nine out there."

The group laughed as she concluded. "In short, we are mapping the Milky Way. Are there any questions?"

The arrogant Frenchman would not have asked anything technical as he felt he knew everything there was to know. Nevertheless, he spoke. "And the shuttles to La Serena? How often will they run?"

"Depending on the time of the year, they will run at six in the evening, midnight, six in the morning and noon. You are also welcomed to drive your own auto if you prefer. Food and other personal items can also be delivered at these times if you request."

The German nodded and continued walking to the conference area where the smell of empanadas and ceviche wafted into the narrow hallway. His stout form indicated that he was not used to missing meals and so Margarita waved everyone onward so that they could finish the briefing in the comfort of the area set up in the corner of the Control Room.

"You did very well." Pozos said to her as he casually sequestered her in another corner of the room. "You have a great talent for speaking."

"Thank you." She blushed a bit and looked away. She was probably used to receiving compliments but didn't want it to seem apparent. "Did you get settled in your apartment?"

"I'm officially in, but I am afraid I have not had time to find furniture and housewares. I have a bed and a chair. That is about it."

She enjoyed his Caribeño accent. But there was something unique about him. His scientific vocabulary seemed much more comprehensive in English than in Spanish. Perhaps it was because he had studied in the United States for so long. After all, he was there to finish his doctoral dissertation as a guest of George Washington University. "I have some things that I'm not using, plates, silverware and some other furnishings if you would like to borrow them?"

"I would appreciate that very much." He whispered as he moved closer. "You are very kind. Would you join me for dinner this evening?"

She quickly glanced at the other attendees, working their way down the serving line, and then back at him. "Well, I probably should not. But...I suppose it would be good to get to know you better." Her smile broadened. "I want very much to support your dissertation any way I can."

And now, a month later he was deeply involved with her. As deeply as they could be without letting any of their peers know that there was something going on between them. That would have been considered unprofessional, and given the covert nature of his assignment, might very well upset his boss in Washington. He had only met Lieutenant Colonel Babic twice since he had completed his training and was no more certain of his real job than Babic seemed of his. Nevertheless, he was just starting out and he did not want to do something to jeopardize his career this early.

He ran his hand up along Margarita's ribs and was about to suggest something reasonably lurid when his cell phone began to chime with a certain tone that was reserved for only one person. The boss. "Hey Bonita, why don't you make us some coffee?"

She smiled and skipped towards the kitchen located at the front of the small apartment, as he entered his password and read the brief message. "BARONOWSKI TOMORROW AT VERA."

His heart skipped a beat. It was his first message from his handler in Washington, and it drew him back into the reality that he was there for more than stars and romance.

—⟨⟨●⟩⟩—

General Scott had switched into civilian attire before having his driver drop him up the street from the Cardigan. "I'll meet you here in an hour," He barked as he jumped out of the back seat and slammed the door behind him. Because he had seen too many poorly contrived espionage movies, he walked in the opposite direction for a block before crossing the street and walking back towards the restaurant, as if that would have confused electronic trackers or skilled surveillants.

It was almost six. He was early and debated circling the block once more so that he did not look desperate. He wanted to look as if he was in control. He had to be in control. He stepped inside and allowed his eyes to adjust to the dimly lit and cozily intimate place before stepping down into the dining area. In the booth along the wall on the left side, he saw the man he had come to meet. Well-dressed, in his fifties, the gentleman had retained most of his dark hair, with the exception of a patch of white hair that ran from the frontal lobe above his left eye, backwards to his parietal area, somewhat reminiscent of a skunk.

General Scott glanced once more around the room as he approached the booth and then seated himself. No formal greetings were exchanged. "Tell me how you found those cowboys that you sent me to."

The distinguished and quietly confident man in the blue suit did not look up from his iPad. "Let Wally know what you'd like. I already ordered a Manhattan."

General Scott looked at him for a moment and then tried to catch Wally's attention. He seemed to be busy with two young, attractive women at the bar, so Scott got back up and walked over to interrupt him. "Do you have single-malt Scotch?"

Wally glanced up. "Of course. Do you have a preference?"

"Maybe a Cardhu or Glenmorangie sixteen?" Scott responded, reaching for a one-hundred-dollar bill in his pants pocket.

Wally smiled at the ladies once more and then turned to survey his collection of distilled beverages on the back bar. "Did you want that neat?"

"No. Rocks, thanks." The general replied, knowing that Wally and other Scotch purists would consider him vulgar for diluting superb scotch whiskey over ice. He was a General. He could drink it any way he bloody-well wanted.

He returned to the booth and sat down. "Let me repeat the question. How much do you know about the people you sent me to?"

The reticent power broker with the unique salt and pepper hair had been working the Washington system for more than thirty years. His positions had alternated back and forth between being the Chief of Staff for a Speaker of the House to occupying high-level civil service positions in the Executive Office of the President, that were high enough to have access, but not so high as they required an appointment that lasted only as long as the POTUS held the office. He had served democrats and republicans alike and knew how to get things done regardless of which elected neophyte was in office. He was a tenured part of the back-door government whose power didn't wax and wane every four years. It was the government that most people did not know of, and it ruled in perpetuity.

Conspiracy theorists called it the *cabal*. However, most of the senior members of the club would have claimed the overused moniker to be indicative of group paranoia. There were no membership cards, and there were no dues or meetings. From time to time, various affiliated parties did meet to discuss important issues at places like the Bohemian Grove in California or other private and well-guarded retreats around the world. But for the most part, these visits were primarily social networking. People introducing people to others of mutual interests. Spreading the pernicious power like a cancer.

The man in the blue suit exited out of the application he was using and laid the iPad face up on the table. "I sense that you are distressed about something?"

Scott was put off by the man's mid-Atlantic accent. Sometimes known as the Transatlantic accent, it was not a regional accent but a learned one. Primarily used by wealthy northeasterners who had attended snooty preparatory schools, or even snootier schools for film and stage acting.

"Distressed?" The general asked incredulously. "Of course, I'm distressed! Those pricks are trying to go rogue! They're trying to insert themselves into our business!"

The man quietly sipped his Manhattan. "Really? That doesn't seem like them. But, in response to your question, those...cowboys, as you called them, were part of the Special Operations Community and after the reduction in the hostilities in Afghanistan and Iraq, they were picked up by the Agency." He thought for a moment. "Then, primarily due to changes in the political environment it was determined that they could function more effectively if they were not part of the government. Thus, they became contractors."

"What?" The General said louder than he should have. He saw the frown across the table and lowered his voice. "What does that mean? They still have a boss somewhere, don't they?"

"In a matter of speaking." The man chortled. "It's a very lean outfit and the organization changes frequently. So, I guess you could say that their leadership are all working members. There's no office anywhere."

"There must be somebody at CIA who can get them under control?"

"Not really. The Agency is not their only customer. Obviously. Virtually every cabinet post and military department from time to time has need of specialists that can get in, do their job and get back out without leaving a trail that implicates their customer." He raised his eyebrows. "That's why you hired them."

General Scott looked at his scotch and then took a pensive swallow. "Do we know their names?"

The man in the blue suit chuckled. "We have contact information for some of the leaders, but the teams select their own people for each job. They are paid out of the Black Ops budget through one of a dozen different bank accounts. They draw money as allocated and Treasury simply keeps the accounts full and releases funds as needed."

"But...how do you know who's using them for what? What keeps someone from just removing their competition or their political opponents?" Scott was thinking quickly.

"Well, they're all former military. They've all taken oaths. They wouldn't act on their own or without orders from a senior level government official. Often the President. Thinking prudently and objectively about it, they're not nearly as politically corruptible as the FBI has become."

Scott stared down into his drink. "How much do you think they know about our project?"

The man shook his head. "I would imagine, absolutely nothing. That is, unless you read them into it."

"Huh uh." Scott rubbed his temples again. "We just provided basic intel as to where the targets would be at what time. What they looked like, the cars they drove. You know."

"Look General, you can only sit on this for a few more months anyway. Maybe six tops. The President will need to be informed much sooner than that so that we can begin to overtly put our contingency plans into effect, brief our citizens, and of course coordinate with the Russians and the Chinese."

Scott took another heavy sip of the single-malt scotch and gently set the glass down. "What would you recommend?"

"Simple." He raised his Manhattan in a toast of sorts. "Pay them whatever they want. It's not your money and in the end, it may not make any difference."

———— ((◦)) ————

Clayton Stanford and Sigurd *Siggie* Arnesen barely knew each other. They had met briefly during an operation outside of Erbil, with a mutual associate named Jerome Jones leading their specialized

MARSOC Raider team on a mission to abduct a suspected terrorist organizer. The insertion had gone as planned, but thanks to a barking dog, too many of the suspected terrorists awoke prematurely from their slumber and thus the exfil became complicated as several shots were exchanged during the brief but tumultuous firefight. Siggie had used the special auto-injector to drug their target, and he and Stanford dragged him down two flights of stairs to the waiting van before speeding into the night.

Arnesen glanced at his watch again. It was just after midnight and the lights in the two-story red brick home off Glenkirk Road were out. He double-checked the address and then compared it to the online photograph he had retrieved from the real estate site. Two car garage with white doors. Fifty-foot driveway. No cars visible. If all went according to plan there should be one white female and one Black Lab at home. No streetlights visible in the immediate area. No sidewalks. "Pull up right here." He whispered.

He had deployed with Jerry Jones a couple of times overseas in the last two years, but was surprised to get a call from him, asking him to take part in a domestic operation. He never realized that contractors supported US intelligence missions in the United States. Now he was parked in a van on a dark street getting ready to make a covert entry and perform another involuntary extraction of a suspected terrorist. His heart raced but he remembered his training years earlier at the three-week assessment and selection course in Camp LeJeune North Carolina. A week later, he was whisked away to some abandoned World War Two post in Arkansas for Phase II of the program. Considering the intensity of that training, this operation would be a piece of cake.

He had actually enjoyed the training and camaraderie. Except for the running. God how he hated running, especially with the instructors barking at them to keep up the fifteen-minute per mile pace with fifty-pound rucksacks on their backs. Nevertheless, he was serving his country and making the wolf stronger.

"Vis Gregis Est Lupus" The instructors reminded them of the Rudyard Kipling quote several times a day. "For the strength of the Pack is the Wolf, and the strength of the Wolf is the Pack."

Stanford looked at his watch. "I'll give you four minutes to get around the back and make your entry, and then I'll back down the driveway."

"Check." Siggie replied. They had driven past the house twice before and thought that another pass might only alert neighbors to suspicious activity. "Let's do it!".

He checked the front pockets of his vest to ensure that the aerosols were both there. One for the dog and one for the woman. The extraction could not have the appearance of an abduction and therefore they could not afford to leave a dead dog onsite. Or, for that matter, have one missing. The animal would wake up in a few minutes with a small headache, and then wonder where his owner was. If the police were somehow notified of something suspicious going on, there would be no evidence of violence or forcible entry. For all intents and purposes, it would look like the woman just decided to leave. He had to remember to collect her purse and some other personal effects to make it look like she might have gone to visit a friend.

Siggie quietly alighted from the vehicle and carefully worked his way around the back of the house. There was only a half moon out and very little ground light. He crept onto the back patio and listened for any sound coming from inside the home. Satisfied that all was quiet, he began to pick the lock on the back door. It was a standard residential model and took him less than thirty seconds to feel and manipulate the tumblers to their sheer points. So far so good. No barking from inside.

The door opened without a squeak, and he found himself inside the darkened kitchen. A light was on in the living room, but it had been determined earlier that it was on a timer. He tilted his head a bit to look into the darkened den adjacent to the bottom of the stairs and then quietly turned and put his left foot on the carpeted stair. As he reached his gloved hand for the stair banister he was startled by the cold metal of the silencer pressed firmly against the base of his skull behind his right ear.

The strange whisper caused his mind to race and his heart to sink. "FBI. Don't turn around. Don't flinch...as a matter of fact, don't breathe." Somewhere from inside the darkened den he heard some-one speak softly into a two-way radio. "We have this one. Wait until number two gets all the way into the driveway and then take him!"

A heavy boot caught Siggie in the back of his knee, causing him to collapse forward onto the stairs.

As he felt his hands being zip-tied behind his back he quietly risked a question. "But...how...?"

A burly SWAT agent, adorned in the standard black gear inter-rupted him. "We knew you were coming before you did."

Outside, the peaceful night was disrupted by flashing red and blue lights, and hostile men yelling at the driver of the beat-up white van to show them his hands. The sleepy neighborhood would soon be awake. As for Alphonse and Becca, they had not yet been to sleep. Temporarily stashed next door at a neighbor's house, their anxiety was only moderately quelled when the SWAT commander looked over his shoulder with a small smile. "We've got them both. We'll have you back in your home in no time."

Becca breathed a small sigh of relief and pulled Alphonse closer. With a Labrador grin so genuine it made his eyes squint, his tail wagged feverishly as if it was time to play.

CHAPTER 11

Despite his best efforts, General Scott had only managed to catch three or four hours of sleep. He was getting used to the couch in his office and the morning trips to the athletic facility and looked forward to that first cup of fresh coffee to get him motivated to face the rest of the day.

He spent most of the previous night tossing and turning and trying to determine the best course of action. The meeting with his colleague the day before steered him down the path of least resistance. "Pay them." He mimicked the man's mid-Atlantic accent. But there was no hurry. Fox had texted that he would get back in touch today and the General had every reason to believe he would.

Leaving his office lights off, he scribbled some notes on a legal pad under the soft illumination of his desk lamp. He wanted to phrase his response in a way that would make sense to a lethal blackmailer, and he needed a plan to string him along for a couple more assignments. After that, who knew? Maybe it would be time for an official statement from the White House. Maybe Fox and his team of assassins might meet with foul play themselves.

He scratched through the notes as he eliminated ideas one by one, and then frustrated, slid the three pages into the shredder behind his desk. He looked at his watch and noted that it was nearing seven o'clock when he saw the email pop up in his inbox. It was from the Director, NTIA, the head of the group that was known as providers of so-called Non-Traditional Information Analysis. He was a bit surprised as this had been Babic's project and all communications with the *psychic spook* group had heretofore gone through him.

Wondering how they got his name and contact information, he curiously clicked on the line. "RECEIVED FINAL INPUT FROM M-33. CAN FORWARD IF PROJECT IS STILL ACTIVE."

Who was M-33? This had to be connected to Babic's investigation. But he thought that they had already received a final report. Actions had been taken. The link had been closed. He typed back, "PROJECT ACTIVE – SEND REPORT"

A moment later, his email updated. "SECURE ACCESS FILE EXCHANGE – KEY: 5@^d5j7*_3eS" They were sending him an encrypted file on the DoD's SAFE system. He quickly booted the other computer on his desk and entered his passwords at the appropriate prompts.

He sipped his coffee in stony silence as he read the report summary. He couldn't believe it. They had the story almost perfectly. They knew about the return of Niburu, they knew about the need for gold for their atmosphere. They knew about the technology exchange in 1954 and they knew about what the Annunaki wanted over the next ten years. It was an impossible connection. This M-33 was incredible, whoever he or she was, a vastly superior viewer to the late S-2. Too good to stay alive.

<hr />

Marchand grabbed a cup of coffee and sluggishly joined Karlsson at the kitchen table where he had set up his laptop and built a small workstation.

"Morning." He said as he sipped his first taste of liquid energy. "What are you looking at?"

Karlsson was using his mouse to advance and reverse though recordings made by the surveillance cameras. "Maybe nothing, I hope." He found the frame he had been searching for and froze it. Then he clicked and outlined the image of the cabin cruiser out on the water and enlarged it. "See this?"

Marchand leaned in. He did not have his reading glasses but

could make out the image of the couple fishing off the back deck. "It's a boat."

"I was using the analytics feature in the software and this kicked out. They come from the north and pass south towards Chicago, and out of view, before drifting north again. Two, sometimes three times a day."

"They're fishing." Marchand said with a touch of mockery.

"I've pulled up all the data files that show when they come into view and then follow them out of view. In all that, I've never seen them catch a fish or bait a hook."

"Maybe it's just a old couple who likes to sit on the water and enjoy the air. You think something's up?" Marchand rested his coffee cup on the table and leaned closer.

"I wondered about that. This video analytic system is pretty impressive. It's the same one they use in airports that can see a thousand different people come through in five minutes and automatically alert the other cameras to follow any suspect individual as they move around the terminal. It can tell if one person sets a bag down and someone else picks it up. It can tell if one person sets a bag down and walks away from it, leaving it unattended. So, it was the system that alerted me to the regularity of their passes. I just went back in and did a manual review. It looks like the same couple every day, but the funny thing is that they just started fishing this spot the day before we got here."

"What?" The concern instantly recognizable in Marchand's voice.

"Yeah. The Secret Service or whoever was maintaining this building had the surveillance system going twenty-four hours a day. When the data fills up the server, it just records a new loop over the top of it every three weeks. That means we have about three weeks' worth of recordings on here. I was curious to see if this couple had been fishing here for a long time and it turns out, they haven't. They got here the day before us. Crazy?"

Marchand stared at the frozen image. "Can you get any closer on the people?"

"These are five mega-pixel cameras, but I flipped through a couple of these strings and the best we can do is identify a man and a woman in their forties. Hardly anything sharp enough to put on a *wanted* poster." Karlsson advanced to another set of images. "But, as they headed north last night we did manage to catch a shot of the back end of the boat. I can't be sure, but it looks like it says *Gusty Gail*. I can't make out the name of the town. You can see part of the registration, WS 51 something."

Marchand squinted and then tapped the name into his cell phone. "I think a friend of mine can run that and we can see who it belongs to. Maybe. Vessel names and hailing port are required for commercial vessels, but optional for recreational boats. We'll see what we can turn up."

Together, the two men went back through the video archive and watched the curious cabin cruiser and its occupants. Just a couple sitting on the back of their boat, fishing for something. Marchand was on his second cup of coffee. "So, do you want to swim out and tread water until they drift past, and then ask them for a ride?"

Karlsson lifted an eyebrow. "Possibly, something like that. There's a half-dozen gun ranges between here and Racine. The closest is just a couple miles from here. I was thinking about taking that .30-06 up there to get it sighted in. After that, I could head over and check out some of the marinas to see if they have a Gusty Gail berthed there. That would also give me the opportunity to rent a boat to do some fishing of my own. I could position further out in the lake and when they drift past again, see where they're going. Maybe get a closer look at the crew."

Marchand thought for a moment and then agreed. "Yeah. That makes perfect sense. If they're busy watching us, they may not notice you behind them."

Nerissa descended the stairs and frowned at the near empty carafe. "You left me a half cup? How long have you guys been up?"

"Good morning." Marchand nodded.

"I couldn't sleep." Karlsson gestured at the laptop. "I decided to come down a little after four-thirty and go through the surveillance logs to see if anything looked suspicious."

"And did it?" Nerissa brought her half-cup of coffee over to the table and sat down.

"Maybe." Karlsson answered. "There's a couple in a white cabin cruiser that drift past here a couple times a day. They give the outward appearance of fishing but aren't really serious about it. I checked the archive and found that they just started showing up here the day before we got here."

"Really?" she looked at Stan. "You think it's a coincidence?"

Marchand shrugged. "Maybe. Maybe not. We're going to get a closer look at them this evening. Regardless, if they're hostile and they got here a day before us, that would indicate that they learned our travel plans at the same time I did."

<hr/>

General Scott looked at the communications mask and checked the times during which the report had been generated. He filtered out all the calls that were to or from recognized numbers; numbers that had previously been reviewed as a part of earlier operations, other routine calls for maintenance or administrative purposes. During the period of time in which he was interested, there was only one new telephone call between Paul and someone that the system did not recognize.

The Space Force operates seventy-seven publicly acknowledged spacecraft supporting various programs such as the Global Positioning System, the Space Fence, a variety of military satellite communications constellations, an unknown number of X-37B spaceplanes, the U.S. missile warning system, the Space Surveillance Network, and the Satellite Control Network.

Of course, as most taxpayers knew, the SCN provided support for the operation, control, and maintenance of a variety of United States Department of Defense and some non-DoD satellites including telemetry and tracking. In addition, the SCN provided launch support, and early orbit support while satellites were in the initial phase or transitioning orbits and required maneuvering to their final orbit. And in their spare time, they maintained the catalog of space objects and tracked the trajectory of naturally occurring astronomical objects as well as artificial satellites in the sky. The *ephemeris*.

With these types of classified and non-classified orbiting resources, the General enjoyed limitless access to everything that was sent through the air waves. With his support from the NRO and his friends in the NSA, it was no trouble creating the ultimate spy network. Nothing anyone said on the internet or on their phones could be protected. And so, it was not difficult to find the name and contact information for a remote viewer that went by the designation M-33.

He looked that the data that he had filtered. "M…Marines… it's possible." Mark Reynolds, MAJ USMC (ret) Saigon 1975, DIA/SRI 1980, Beirut 1983, Non-Traditional Information Analysis unit report (TS/ETERNA) 1997, retired 1998, Police officer City of Plano, TX (1999 – 2015 ret). Current clearance, TS/SCI/SAP.

The General grunted, "A bit long in the tooth, perhaps, but this had to be M-33."

A quick Google search yielded the retired Major's home address. He pushed his chair back and put his feet up on the desk. A smile came to his face as he clasped his hands behind his head and leaned back in the plush leather chair. Things were coming off as planned and he chided himself for having been so diffident and skeptical of his own mission. It was going to be a beautiful day because he was so ready for his call with Dave Fox.

⸺))•((⸺

Marco Pozos was at his Summit workstation in the Control Room, trying to make some numbers jive in the complex calculation he had been running since the day before. He hated math. He hated complex spreadsheets with pivot tables even more. He just wanted to look at stars, and this week, they were really showing off. There were some things moving around out there, possibly due to some sort of transient gravitational perturbation. Whatever it was, it couldn't be seen directly from earth, yet. What could be seen were minor ripples in space time that indicated that something larger and darker might be approaching or transiting the outer reaches of the solar system. Nevertheless, it was not that far away, cosmologically speaking, somewhere past the Kuiper belt, but well-inside the Oort Cloud.

Margarita tapped on the wall of his cubicle. "Señor Pozos, you have a visitor. This is Lieutenant Colonel Baronowski from the United States Army. He is a guest of our government and would like to have a minute of your time." Her smile was seductive. "I have a presentation to prepare and must leave you two alone. Colonel, please enjoy your visit, and text me when you are ready, and I will drive you back to the city." She winked at Pozos and walked away.

"Good morning." Pozos stood and extended his hand to the Colonel as his eyes followed Margarita out of the room.

Darren Baronowski took it with a smile and as they shook, was able to pass the challenge coin to Pozos in the time-honored fashion, palm to palm.

Pozos looked down and flipped the coin over in his hand. It was the official coin of the Chief of Space Operations, US Space Force. It was the token that he had been expecting that established the bona fides of anyone purporting to be involved in the covert component of their project. He held the coin at an angle and rolled it so that he could examine the edge and read the laser-etched inscription. "Things will not calm down."

Marco looked up at Baronowski and recited the countersign, a line from a 1998 episode of a sci-fi television series called *Stargate*. "They will, in fact, calm up.".

Baronowski smiled warmly. "Great! Now that we have that settled, can we take a walk? I'm anxious to look around this place...on the outside."

Pozos nodded and led the officer down the stairs from the control room into the machine shop and then out into the cool spring morning. The seasons were reversed from the northern hemisphere, and the observatory was at an elevation of almost nine thousand feet. Thus, it was no surprise that Lieutenant Colonel Baranowski experienced slight difficulty acclimating from his regular sea-level duty station in the tropics.

"Would you like a jacket?" Marco asked.

"No, I'll be fine. But thank you." They walked a few feet further down the hill before Baranowski began. "This is all quite fascinating to me. I read something about the overall mission of this place on their website. But seeing it up close is quite exciting."

Marco nodded. As this was his first debriefing, he was not sure what to say.

"First things first." Baranowski continued. "Have you seen it yet?"

Marco Pozos shook his head. "No. We haven't seen *it*, but I have seen some indications that it is coming." He went on to explain the mathematical calculations he had been working on for the past two days that indicated something was perturbing the orbits of smaller bodies and likened it to putting one's finger in a bucket and stirring it up, and then stepping back. To the viewer who just looked in, they would see the usually calm water disrupted but would not know for certain what caused it."

"Depending on the actual orbit, it may be difficult to predict when we will be able to see it with any certainty. If you take Sedna as an example, it was discovered back in 2003 by Michael Brown from Cal Tech and Chad Trujillo. Trujillo was working right up the road here at the Gemini Observatory. Sedna is a dwarf planet about three fourths the size of Pluto and has the second longest orbital period of any confirmed object in our solar system. About eleven thousand four hundred years."

Baronowski's eyebrows raised. "And they found it at what point in its orbit?"

Pozos put his hands in his pocket as a gust of wind gave him a chill. "Sedna has a very eccentric elliptical orbit that takes it out to about 937 Astronomical Units, or AU's, back to a perihelion of about seventy-six AU's."

"Forgive me, Marco. How far is an AU?"

"Roughly the distance from the earth to the sun. Ninety-three million miles. So, if you multiply that by 937, you'll get a feel for how far out this orbit goes. The point I was trying to make is that we didn't find it until it was about eight billion miles from the sun. A little less than nine AU's. But the planet we are looking for may be five times the size of earth, so we hope to be able to see it long before it gets to the inner solar system. Well, as close as it's going to get, anyway. Even though it's considered trans-Neptunian we don't think its perihelion brings it inside of Neptune's orbit. As it completes its orbit, we don't think it will get any closer to the sun than that, so we're not likely to see a collision with anything."

Baronowski was quiet for a moment as he considered what the young scientist had shared. "All right. We haven't found it but suspect where it might eventually become visible in the sky. What about the other interests here? I assume with this set-up that most of you share resources and information rather openly. Tell me about your coworkers."

Pozos nodded as he stepped out of his astronomer's character and into his spy-brain, as he called it. "First, is Jean-Luc Dausset, PhD, astrophysicist from Paris Diderot University. Fairly full of himself. The type of guy who's surprised we would need computers to solve anything when we have him around. Not much socially. Has a place in La Serena, but he likes to take long weekends away. Not sure where. He doesn't talk a lot about his past projects, but he seems to know his stuff."

"Then, there's Henrik Neumeyer from Max Planck Institute in Heidelberg. He's a little heavy and far too sedentary if you get my drift. He had some trouble getting up and down stairs here for a while, but I think he's worked it out. I think he still harbors some resentment against Jean-Luc because he feels Paris should have become German property at the end of World War Two. I don't think he's a closet Nazi or anything, but he doesn't have a high opinion of the French. He supposedly worked a project two years ago with UCLA and Heidelberg University to find a previously unknown group of stars in a cluster. So, he has some sort of references in the field."

"They have us on twelve-hour schedules right now with four days on, three days off and then reverse it with three days on and four off. It makes sense considering it takes almost three hours to get down the mountain and back to La Serena. They have rooms for us on our rotation at El Hotel Soledad de Montaña Elqui Vicuña. It's only thirty miles away, but it could still take an hour and a half to get there. My point is that I'm just not able to see everyone that comes and goes as good as I'd like to."

"There are a few technicians here from the Astronomy Department at Universidad de Chile, as well as a couple of their IT geeks that come and go depending on what the computer is objecting to on any particular day. No one that stands out as a covert agent of sorts."

"Other visitors?" Baronowski asked.

"Hard to say. We still have contractors onsite finishing out their parts of the construction project; electrical, mechanical, network. You know, some media people. We have inspectors in from time to time, most of whom I'd guess were Chilean. But no one seems to take an interest in our work, to the degree that I'd take them for a foreign asset."

Baronowski nodded and looked out over the barren terrain. "What about the woman that brought me out here? Margarita?"

Pozos was taken a bit off guard but tried not to stumble. "Margarita? Oh, she doesn't work here, actually. She works for the parent organization but she's in public relations. She's only out here when there's something going on with the media or VIP's."

Baronowski had been a trial lawyer for a long time and knew how to interview people. His head turned and he looked Pozos squarely in the eye. "Does Margarita ever take an interest in, for example, you?"

It was almost noon when General Scott's phone chimed that he had received a text. He had done his best to get other work done, but the morning had been consumed with how best to get what he wanted out of Vesuvius. He smiled somewhat nervously as he read the brief message.

"DECISION?"

"I NEED YOUR ASSISTANCE AND THINK THAT $1,000,000 WOULD BE WORTH IT." He tapped in.

It was a minute before the reply came back. "THAT DOESN'T SPLIT EVENLY SIX WAYS. WE NEED SIX MILLION"

General Scott breathed deeply, in through his nostrils and out through his mouth. "I am coping." He said aloud. He needed to keep them on the hook, but he could not agree too quickly for fear that they would see it as a trap. At least he knew, or had a good idea now, that there were six of them. He got up and paced back and forth between the walls of his office as he steadied his breathing and then picked up his phone. "AGREED, BUT I CAN ONLY SIGN FOR $2 MILLION AT A TIME AND NEED TO MAKE UP MULTIPLE INVOICES TO COVER. CAN WE DO $2M TODAY, $2M NEXT MONDAY AND $2M THE WEEK AFTER?"

Fox had to be discussing it with his co-conspirators. General Scott waited a full minute to see the reply. "YES – CAN YOU DO ACH TRANSFER?"

"NO – ACH TRANSFER LIMITED TO $1M EACH. NEED TO DO A WIRE TO YOUR BANK – DOMESTIC IS 2-DAY WAIT... INTL CLOSER TO WEEK OR MORE"

"OK – STANDBY FOR DETAILS" Fox responded.

His pulse was pounding in his neck, but he knew he had control.

"BANK OF GEORGIA - TBILISI, WATCH FOR EMAIL FROM BANK MANAGER WITH ACCOUNT NUMBER AND PROCESS"

"WILL NEED ONE MORE ITEM AFTER YOU RECEIVE THE DEPOSIT. LIVES IN COLORADO." He tapped nervously.

"DETAILS?"

He transmitted the information he had learned about the latest remote viewer to be a thorn in his side. "REYNOLDS, MARK RETIRED USMC MAJOR – LIVES IN GRAND JUNCTION NOW." He inputted Reynolds' last known address and waited for the reply.

The response was satisfying. "$50,000 – AND WE'LL COMPLETE THE OTHER TRANSACTION AS WELL".

Finally! Lenny Hart was out of the equation. He sent back a *thumbs-up* icon and then switched the burn phone off. He had achieved his goal for the day.

Stan cleared away the lunch dishes and then sat down at the laptop to check his email. After deleting the obvious junk mail and scams, he opened the one from Grand Emperor Insurance and called out for Nerissa.

"Yes?" She finished wiping the sink and looked up.

"We have a tasking for this afternoon." He jotted Nerissa's task reference number down on a notepad and tore off the sheet. "Here. This one's yours. I've got one too."

The second she touched the paper she had a feeling. It was strong. "Looks like we have something to do today to pass the time. I'll be upstairs."

Karlsson came up from the basement with the rifle case and a small duffel bag containing ammunition. "I'll call you later and let you know if I can get a boat. It will take about an hour to get this sighted in, and I figure another hour to get through a couple of the local marinas. With any luck, you'll see me about five hundred yards out by four o'clock."

"Paul sent us some homework, so our phones will be off for the next couple of hours."

Karlsson nodded and headed towards the door. "Happy hunting. To all of us."

He locked the deadbolt behind him and then threw his gear in the back of the Honda mini-van that Marchand's friend, Dan Noble had loaned them. Noble had actually borrowed it from a friend of his that ran a delivery service in Waukegan. So, if anyone decided to run the Illinois license plates, it would not lead them back to Pleasant Prairie.

The Southern Wisconsin Gun Club off Highway K near Route 45 had been constructed on a piece of relatively flat farmland and featured fifteen one hundred-foot public lanes, three private bays for members, and a rifle bay that allowed targets to be set up from 100 yards out to 300 yards.

Matt meandered around the retail area and found a cleaning kit, a set of earmuffs and pair of plastic safety glasses and then went to the counter. "How you doing?" He asked the clerk.

"Good. You?" The clerk nodded.

"Good." Matt replied. Gun people were the same around the country. Basically, good people but they could be relatively aloof until they were satisfied that you were competent around firearms. "I've got a hunting trip coming up and I wanted to sight-in my Remington." He opened the duffel on the counter and pulled out the boxes of ammunition that had been left for him in the grocery cart. "I wanted to get something that shoots flat but still packs a punch out to three hundred."

"White tail?" The clerk asked.

"Elk. We're headed out west, and I have to learn to ride a horse again so I can keep up with the guide." They both laughed.

The clerk looked at Karlsson's collection of cartridges and nodded. "These will work. I usually recommend controlled expansion bullets that are at least a hundred seventy grain or heavier, maybe something in the one seventy-five to one eighty weight. Have you ever tried Barnes VOR-TX?"

"Huh uh." Karlsson admitted. "Do you have any in stock?"

"Absolutely." The clerk retrieved a box from behind the counter. "The 180-grain load is an excellent choice for elk, deer, bear, even moose hunting. While it's not really designed for those impossible longer-range shots, it's still great for shots out past four hundred yards."

"Give me two boxes and a lane." Karlsson smiled and reached for his wallet.

"I'll put you on lane number one on the rifle side. You're the only one out there but when you want to go downrange to change your target, be sure to flip the switch to activate the red flashing lights, just in case. That means all lanes have to cease fire while anyone is in front of the firing line. There are some sandbags out there if you need one."

"Thanks! By the way, I'd like to do some fishing while I'm in town, do you know where I can get a good deal on a boat rental?"

"Yeah. There are several marinas up the coast as you head to Milwaukee. But you might have more success looking at that VRBO app."

"Verbo?"

"Yeah. Vacation Rental By Owner. Most of the people I know rent boats that way. You can let your fingers do the walking and find what you need pretty quick."

"Thanks!" Karlsson collected his gear and wandered out to find his lane, which was not difficult since it was the first one to the left out the door. He flipped the switch and took his targets down to the one-hundred-yard mark, set them as close to eye-level as he could. He set another target at the two-hundred-yard mark and then returned to the bench.

He switched the flashing lights off and then opened his duffel. He took out the small screwdriver and the pair of binoculars he had packed and laid them on the bench. Two lanes down he noticed one of the sandbags so he brought that back to his lane and set it up on the bench.

Carefully, he extracted the rifle from its case and gave it one more look. He retracted the bolt and checked the chamber to ensure that it was empty, and then rested the stock on the sandbag. He loaded three rounds of the Barnes ammunition into the magazine and then put his eye and ear protection on. He did a final sweep down the line to make sure there was no one else down range and then seated himself at the wooden bench.

The first part of his ritual was to get comfortable with the rifle, finding a position that allowed him to firmly shoulder the thing while giving his eye the right position behind the scope. He used his left thumb to push the top round in the magazine downward so that he could close the bolt over the top of it without chambering a round. He got back into his shooting position and positioned the crosshairs of the scope on the red dot in the center of his target, and then slowly pressed the trigger until he felt it release and heard the distinctive *click*.

Satisfied, he engaged the rifle's safety and then cycled the bolt, loading a round. He steadied his breathing for a moment and concentrated on keeping the crosshairs on the red dot. When he felt he was ready, he clicked the safety off, took a deep breath and then let it halfway out. There was very little slack in the trigger, and it reached break-dawn almost immediately.

There was a loud explosion and the feeling that someone had just punched him in the shoulder. He waited just a moment and then cycled the bolt. *Boom!* The second shot had not caught him with as much a surprise and hurt less because he had instinctively held the rifle firmer against his shoulder. He cycled the action once more and took another deep breath. Exhaling to a degree of comfort, he gently pressed the trigger again. *Boom!*

He opened the bolt and shook off the sting in his poor shoulder as he reached for the binoculars. It wasn't bad. The three holes weren't perfectly centered, but they were all touching, clover-leafing, as the shooters called it. At one hundred yards, the rounds impacted about an inch and a half high, and an inch to the right.

He could live with the elevation. He checked his ballistic tables for the weight of the bullet and saw that if that particular round was sighted-in at one hundred yards, then it would drop 3.4 inches at two hundred. Thus, since it was an inch and a half high at one hundred, his rough calculations told him that it was probably dead on at one-fifty and would drop two inches at two twenty-five.

He unscrewed the cap on the scope and used his screwdriver to adjust the windage to the left, one inch at one hundred yards. He counted the clicks and repositioned the rifle on the sandbag. Taking another deep breath, he repeated the pounding cycle, firing three more rounds at the target. This time, he had all three shots touching an inch and a half over the red dot. Reloading another three rounds, he moved the scope onto the target that was positioned at two hundred yards. He held about two inches above the red dot and slowly pressed the trigger, cycled and fired again. He rubbed his shoulder once and then slid his left fist back under the buttstock. *Boom!* A smile came to his face as the binoculars confirmed three holes in the red center of the target.

He spent the remainder of his half-hour testing the other rounds in his duffel to find out where they impacted on the same target. At one hundred yards, there was not much difference among them. However, if he had to take a longer shot, even out to four hundred yards, he decided it was more prudent to stay with the Barnes.

On his way out, he thanked the clerk and bought two more boxes of the VOR-TX. The clerk seemed much more engaging, having just watched his performance on the range's camera system. "Pretty good shooting! Did you ever compete?"

"Just with myself." Karlsson laughed. "VRBO, you said?" Changing the subject.

"Yep." The clerk turned his monitor so that Karlsson could see it. "Here you go. I'm in here all the time." He opened up a page and began to flip through a variety of offerings that seemed to average about one-fifty to two hundred dollars a day.

"Stop." Karlsson moved in closer. "What's that one, right there?"

The clerk looked over the top of his glasses. "Yeah, those are nice. That's a thirty-seven-foot Carver. They're made here in Wisconsin, so we see a ton of 'em around here."

Karlsson recognized the lines, and having spent considerable time on the water in the recent past, he was getting more comfortable identifying watercraft at a distance. The couple that had been fishing near the house were on an identical boat. "Carver, huh? Thanks! I will have to check them out!"

⟫⟪⟪◉⟫⟪

Two hours later, Nerissa and Stan were guzzling water as if they had been in the desert. It had been a physically demanding session for both individually as their immediate connection to the target gradually emerged, driving them towards certain powerful gestalts. This was a target that wanted to be found, and to Nerissa it seemed as if the target was transmitting impressions as she was receiving. When Paul returned their call from a safe phone thirty miles from his office, they could hardly contain their energy.

"I guess we can break with protocol this one time, in the interest of time and personal safety. Talk me through what you have." He said.

Nerissa was the stronger psychic of the two, so she began. "We think we were on the same task, a missing person. Someone we have worked with indirectly. He was recently abducted. He is being held near a large lake, but not the one near us. He is near a large airport. There is a busy freeway system crisscrossing near him. There is…" She paused, "I see something like a phallus, something kids would draw on a wall, like graffiti, but it contains dead people. There is some sort of water source spewing from the end."

"Go on." Paul said flatly. They were passing along gestalts as they received them and there was no room for judgment or sarcasm.

Marchand joined, "There is the sound of impact wrenches and the smell of automotive fluids, not in the same room, but nearby. And I got the feeling of a cemetery with houses on one side and industrial buildings on the other. I also felt a building, perhaps a hotel that is closed temporarily, maybe for remodeling. I smelled paint. I seem to hear and feel power tools."

Paul was obviously feeling rushed. "Open your computer if you're near one. Start with Cleveland Hopkins Airport and do a map search of that area. Switch the view to aerial imagery and widen out so you can see a half-mile in any direction.

Stan saw it first. The penis spewing from the tip. "Shit! Holy Cross Cemetery, it's right off Brookpark Road, east of 140th Street." From the air, the layout of the drive around the cemetery did in fact resemble something phallic and upon closer examination, there was a pond with a fountain in the far north side near the entrance. They zoomed in and carefully examined the periphery. On the west side was a residential area, and on the east side, industrial buildings, which included an auto repair shop. Next door to the repair shop was a hotel. They gave the name and address of the hotel to Paul.

It wasn't the first time that psychics had been brought in to determine the location of kidnap victims. Perhaps the most famous case was the December 1981 kidnapping of Army General James Dozier by the Italian Red Brigades, a Marxist terrorist group. One of the Army's top remote viewers was able to name the town he was being held in and knew that he had been chained to a wall heater. The psychic was able to draw a map and described the building where the victim was being held. Unfortunately, the information did not make it up the chain of command to the right person before the General was released, but had nevertheless proved accurate on all counts.

"You guys relax for a while. I need to get this to the Bureau and see if they can check it out before anyone tries to move him."

With that, he was gone.

———— ◦))(◦ ————

After downloading the app and filtering his way through a variety of offerings, Karlsson settled on a thirty-foot Carver 300 Aft Cabin, and contacted the owner who was based close by at the Southport Marina in Kenosha. The owner had just finished washing her down and performing the regular maintenance from the last rental and was available to meet right away.

He found a parking lot near the end of 56th Street and walked into the main office. There was a forty-something looking professional chatting with a young lady near the desk who looked up with a smile. "Matt?"

The two men shook hands "Yes. You must be Tom Leach?"

Leach was dressed more like a lawyer than a sea captain in a blue pinstripe suit and white button-down dress shirt. The striped tie had been loosen and the knot hung slightly to the left. "Yes! Tell you what, I walked down from my office, so if you don't mind driving, we can head down to the slip, check her out and you can drop me back off at the office."

Karlsson shrugged, "Sounds great!"

They headed down Third Avenue and parked in another lot just south of 58th Street and walked down to the boat that was berthed in slip 203.

"Have you had much experience in boats, Matt?"

"Through the years, a little. But I just got back from a SCUBA trip in Cozumel and spent a week helping crew a forty-foot Sundancer."

"Sea Ray! Good boat!" He said as he stepped aboard and turned to assist Karlsson, who had gotten comfortable enough that he needed no assistance. "Well, let me give you a tour and you're free to ask any questions."

"You obviously know fore and aft and port and starboard, so I'll start by telling you that this is a 1994 Carver Aft Cabin. This model first came out in 1992 as the three hundred Aft Cabin. It's a really sharp little mini-yacht with a good size aft stateroom, full-service galley, V-berth up forward for your guests and tons of storage. It's got a rear cockpit and a flybridge that can be closed off with clear curtains if the weather gets raw."

Matt nodded and Leach continued, "I'm the second owner and I can tell you that this boat has been extremely well cared for and maintained. Even the upholstery looks new. She runs on twin Crusader 350XL's which are both in great condition. Crusader was a well-known engine up here, but the company was acquired by Pleasurecraft in 1998. You could spot them at a distance because all Crusader engines were blue."

"Everything onboard works, and it's got a Garmin 2010C chart plotter. There's a two-burner electric stove, and a carousel microwave oven, refrigerator, manual flush head, and the fuel tanks hold one hundred sixty-eight gallons. Paradise on the water!"

Karlsson was impressed and nodded his head. "How much does she draw?"

"A little less than three feet. So don't get too close to the shoreline unless you know what's on the bottom." He replied with a wink. "She'll do about twenty-three knots, but optimum cruise speed is closer to seventeen. I just filled her up. She runs on gas and holds one hundred sixty-eight gallons. She's got fifty-one gallons of freshwater and her holding tanks will take twenty before you have to pump her."

Karlsson smiled. "I'll take it. Let's go back to your office and we'll take care of the financial stuff."

He had been right about Leach. His office, as it turned out, was on the second floor of a legal practice, a block east of the courthouse. There was not much in the way of a contract: Bring it back the way you found it. He gave Leach a credit card which was entered into some sort of online app and after the charge had gone through, the two men shook hands.

Karlsson stopped at a grocery store to pick up coffee and deli meats to make sandwiches later if it looked like he was going to be out for a while. Then he headed back to the boat to load up and take a quick picture of his recent acquisition to text to Marchand.

He familiarized himself with the controls and went through the engine start-up procedure before casting off and cautiously backing out and getting underway. He meandered carefully around the marina and though the breakwater into the open lake and then headed south at the recommended speed of seventeen knots. By water, he would only be about seven or eight miles north of the residence, so at that speed, he should be in visual range in no more than twenty minutes.

Navigation was easy, land to the right and lake to the left. He watched the shoreline and changed course just enough that his path took him a bit further out, into the lake. There were only a couple other boats visible on the horizon, but neither were the Carver he wanted. When he spotted the house and its substantial dock, he estimated that he was about six hundred yards from shore.

He stopped the engines and cast an empty hook into the water before sticking two fishing poles in the rod holders on the stern. And with that, he went below to find the makings of a good sandwich to go with the coffee that had finished brewing. He took his coffee and sandwich up to the fly bridge and stretched out on the deck such that he could barely see over the short bulkhead, but it would be difficult for other boaters to see him. The added elevation made the perch a perfect choice for scanning the horizon for boats coming and going.

It was about 4:30 when he noticed the bow wake coming up from the south. What caught his attention was how the vessel slowed as it got to about a half mile from the beach house. The wake subsided and the boat seemed to coast and then drift through its usual spot, about two hundred yards offshore. Karlsson slid down a bit more and reached for the binoculars. It was still somewhat overcast, but the sun was in the west now, so he wanted to make sure that the lenses did not give away his position with a flare. The man and the woman on the back deck seemed innocent enough. Perhaps too innocent. They practically ignored his presence as they went through the motions of tossing their lines off the back and taking their seats, as they had every day that week. One might have assumed that they would have been at least moderately interested in another boater in their general area. Perhaps, even offering a friendly wave.

The boats drifted quietly for about a half hour before the couple decided to move on. They moved slowly northward for about a half mile before opening the engines up to a respectable cruising speed. Karlsson started his engines and then made his way down to secure his decoy fishing poles. If they were watching with binoculars, he did not want to appear to be in any hurry. He came about and started out slowly, tracking them as they passed his harbor in

Kenosha. But he stayed well back, allowing them to get almost out of view, until a half-hour later, he saw them change course to port and head into the Reefpoint Marina, near Racine.

It was a much larger marina than the one from which he had rented his boat. Located about twenty miles south of Milwaukee it seemed to cater to a variety of boat types and sizes and when he pulled up their website, he could see that they offered every amenity that a long-term or transient boater would want; food, beverage, laundry. Their office was open until nine, but if someone needed assistance after that, their uniformed security patrol monitored channel nine and would be happy to lend a hand or provide information.

The couple's Carver entered the harbor where the Root River dumped into Lake Michigan and followed the breakwater northwest to a slip in that pocket managed by the Racine Yacht Club. He stayed offshore about two hundred yards and paralleled them until he saw them dock and tie up. They were too far away for him to get pictures with his iPhone, but from what he could tell through the binoculars, they got into a silver mini-SUV, and then left the parking lot turning West on to Barker Street.

"What the hell." He whispered. He was in a rented boat and could always claim that he was lost. He turned his boat around and found the entrance to the marina and cruised slowly enough on in so as to courteously follow the *No Wake* rules. He could see Gusty Gail tied up in a slip towards the end and looked casually around to see if anyone was watching his approach. He backed into a slip two places down and left the engines idling as he quickly tied off and jumped up onto the pier.

Seconds later he ducked into the cabin of Gusty Gail and made a cursory search to see if anything jumped out at him as being an indicator of the owner's lifestyle or character. Or, more importantly, reveal any reason they might have had to want to watch Stan, Nerissa, and him. There was nothing. Literally nothing. There were no clothes, magazines, pictures, or anything that would lead anyone to believe that this couple spent any appreciable part of their marriage together here. He opened the refrigerator. Empty. Below decks, the berth appeared tidy, but it was evident, no one had slept in it. He opened the tackle box that was stowed next to one of the aft deck chairs. It contained extra line, bobbers, tools, and a variety of lures that were still in the plastic boxes that they had come from the store in. The only thing missing was the smell of fish. On the deck, next to the tackle box he found a lens cap for a pair of binoculars. Evidently, someone had hastily packed the binoculars, but had missed a cap.

He had seen enough. It was a rented boat, just like his.

CHAPTER 13

Lenny Hart turned in his sleep, but the handcuff on his right wrist was beginning to chafe and it immediately woke him up. He lay quietly for a minute, listening to the sounds of his environment. In the distance, he could hear cars on the freeway, and every few minutes he could hear large jets landing and taking off from an airport. The windows had been covered up and they had taken his watch, so he had no real reference as to what time it was. The only light in the room came from the bathroom and was on all the time. Someone had tampered with the switch so that it could not be turned off, and the door had been removed to permit him to drag the tool chest into the toilet.

He once again examined the steel cable that connected one of his cuffs to the large Knack jobsite toolbox. The monstrous steel container was easily four feet wide and three feet tall and felt like it weighed a thousand pounds. It was a simple cable that could be found in any bicycle shop; a quarter inch thick with loops on either end to run through the bicycle and attach a padlock. One loop had been bolted into the end of the large steel tool chest, with the other connected to the free cuff. The toolbox was on casters, so that he could drag it from his bed to the bathroom and back but would have a tough time getting out the door and sprinting to freedom.

His minder, a bearded and sturdy man in his thirties who had introduced himself as *Jerry*, dropped in from time to time to bring food and watch TV, before disappearing and reappearing according to no particular schedule. Hart reasoned that Jerry was close by though as he did not hear a car engine start or stop consistent with his appearances. But instead of making himself crazy with the myriad questions running through his mind, he forced himself to do quite the opposite. He was a psychic, supposedly. He should be able to communicate with others not in his time and space. Thus, he focused to the best of his ability on clearing his mind and engaging the universe to transmit those smells, sights and sounds that he was experiencing, to anyone who was listening. He was not sure that his messaging was going anywhere, but chained to a steel tool locker in a seedy, blacked-out hotel room, what else did he have to do?

He heard the footsteps approaching before the key went into the lock. Although he was on his side, facing away from the door, he could still tell that it was dark outside. When the door opened, no substantial light came in. Plus, the sounds of the construction workers had subsided several hours earlier. He could hear the door close and then heard his new roommate pull a chair out from the table and seat himself. He heard the *pfft* of a pop-top as some sort of carbonated beverage was opened. He pretended to be asleep so effectively that he actually started to relax. His breathing deepened and he started to feel himself drifting off into another world.

It could not have been more than a few minutes later when the simultaneous noises shocked his senses. They seemed to occur almost instantaneously, but the first noise was the sound of breaking glass, accompanied by a blast at the door, sending splinters across the room. Then there was a light *tink* sound that he knew from his years in law enforcement was the spoon flying off a distraction device. He readied himself for the blast, but the flashbang was still deafening, as intended, and the resultant concussive effects were painful.

Jerome Jones, perhaps through instinct, perhaps through his years of training, immediately reached for the Sig Sauer pistol on his hip and realized all too late what a mistake that had been. As he fought to shake off the effects of the explosion he drew his pistol the way he had practiced countless times before, not realizing that his chest was being carved up by a dozen 9mm bullets that seemed to follow the little red laser dots that danced around his torso. As the finality and hollowness of death consumed him, the Iraq War veteran and Silver Star recipient's mind raced through the events of his life and left him with a fading question that would accompany him into eternity. "What just happened?"

———◦((◦))◦———

When Karlsson emerged from his room, he was still drying his hair from the steamy shower that washed away the previous day's activity. The smell of coffee lured him to the kitchen, and he could see Marchand on the deck having his usual morning call with either Tricia or Paul. Behind him, he could hear Nerissa bounding down the stairs and when he turned, he saw she was ready for a run.

"Good morning!" She grinned. "It's going to be a beautiful day!"

"Coming from a psychic," Karlsson smiled, "I'll take that as a guarantee."

Marchand finished his call and was ginning ear to ear when he came in. "They got him! I should say, we got him! The FBI raided the hotel in Cleveland about one this morning and found our guy alive and healthy! Paul extends his sincere gratitude to all of us!"

Neri looked at Karlsson and winked.

Karlsson bowed slightly to indicate that he recognized, at least in this particular case, her psychic performance had been spot on. "Well done!"

Marchand walked around the table and gave her a fist-bump as he made his way to the coffee pot. "Lenny Hart is the guy's name. FBI SWAT got him out of there and he was back home in Virginia by zero six hundred today. The downside is that the only suspect they found was killed during the rescue. But, they got a warrant and have agents going through the rooms to see what they can find. I can't believe how close we got on this one. Hotel under renovation, next door to an automotive shop. And of course, the cemetery. I can't believe it."

Nerissa agreed. "It reminds me of the *out-bounder* experiments they did at SRI back in the seventies. They'd send one of the researchers out to a location somewhere to just stand around and take in the sights and then let the viewers try to receive inputs and determine where he or she was. The viewers would sketch out what they thought the outbounder was seeing or experiencing. Some of those early tests were so accurate that they were able to successfully demonstrate it to their Agency clients and teach them how to do it in a matter of hours. Even the skeptics."

"Congratulations, to both of you!" Karlsson repeated. "I suppose I should tell you about my day." Over the next few minutes, he talked about the nautical surveillance he had been able to pull off and what his plans were for the day.

"I'd like to take the van up and park on Barker Street this afternoon and wait for them. They seem to be pretty regular in their timetable, so that would put them offshore here around four, and would get them into the dock in Racine around four-thirty. I'll wait for them to drive past and just tag along."

Marchand nodded. "Yeah, we were able to trace the boat's registration back to a local guy, some IT geek at a Milwaukee company, but he rents it out by the day or week on a credit card and driver's license. I don't think we should contact him directly just yet until we see if he plays more of a role in this."

"Probably not." Karlsson concurred. "If we know who he is we can always find him later if we need him. I took a quick peak on Gusty Gail after they left, but it was clean. Except for a lens cap I found on the aft deck. It looked like it came off of a pair of ten by fifties."

Marchand grinned. "Interesting. They must've been in a hurry to get cleaned up."

Davina chose her words carefully since they were going out over a public satellite phone. "The Feebies hit the room about zero one hundred. We lost Jerry, and they got our prize."

Francine closed her eyes and tried to breath normally. "Damage?"

"Well, there was nothing at the site to connect them to us, but it's only a matter of time before they run Jerry's prints and find his military and contractor records. From there, their interviews could get them closer to some of the other contractors. Guys talk. You know." Davina was more pensive that she had been in the recent past and verbalized her thoughts as safely as she could.

"Still, it's hardly likely that the General will know about the Bureau raid. He didn't know where we were keeping him. And, he wouldn't have known about the grab on the wife, since that was our idea and not his. We already have the Colorado deal on the table. My thought is to string him along for a few more days until some, or all his money hits our account."

"Any idea how they knew where we were?" Francine asked.

"Not a clue."

Francine nodded at the pristine lake as the Carver gently bobbed up and down in the gentle morning waves. "What are you thinking?"

Davina exhaled through tight lips. "It's your show, but I'd say do your regular thing today and then pull out tonight and head to Colorado. We should start getting set up for that one. After he sterilizes the boat and your car, send your protégé out here. With Jerry gone, I'm going to need some assistance, and he probably wouldn't be of any use to you out there anyway, since he hasn't been fully read in. When we're finished out west, we can come back and take care of Wisconsin."

Francine quickly considered a variety of alternatives before offering her concurrence. "Agreed."

After she disconnected the satellite call, she grabbed her burn phone and sent the General a quick message. "PROBLEM HAS BEEN HANDLED. SEND PAYMENT. NEW CONTRACT NOW IN WORKS."

She would watch her account. If he sent the money, she would know that her plan was working. Still, it would have been nice to know what the arrogant ass was up to.

Karlsson found a parking lot off Hoffert drive, which was adjacent northwest of the yacht club and provided him a clear view of the exit from the club's lot. He pulled the van into a space and jumped into the back to send Marchand a text to let him know that he was in position. He had timed his arrival perfectly as Marchand's response was almost immediate.

"MA AND PA JUST LEFT HERE - HEADED YOUR WAY"

He would not be able to see the Carver enter the marina or dock, but he did have an eye on their Silver Nissan Rogue about three hundred yards away and would have a clear line of sight to them as they entered the vehicle. And as predicted, a little more than thirty minutes later, he saw them as they walked up to the car. But then, they shook hands and the male half of the duo turned around to head back towards the boat leaving his female partner to drive away alone.

Karlsson jumped into the driver's seat and followed at a reasonable distance as she turned south on Main Street and crossed over the Root River. A few minutes later she turned west on State Street, and then went around the traffic circle, heading west on Spring Street. She kept up with the pace of traffic and did not appear to be watching for a tail.

When she got to Green Bay, she turned south again and then made the turn onto Washington before pulling into a hotel parking lot, and parking in an open space near the entrance. The hotel did not appear to be that busy, so Karlsson drove past and parked in the corner of the lot, pulling face-in. He jumped into the back again and watched as she entered the lobby before sending a quick text to Marchand. "MA AT HOTEL ON WASHINGTON – PA STILL ON BOAT".

As he had driven past the Nissan, he had seen the bar code on the driver's side rear window and guessed that it was probably a rental. That would make sense. Rented room, rented boat, rented car. His curiosity was piqued, and he felt more alive than he had in months. The job was evolving, he was physically stimulated and psychologically energized with a sense of worth that he thought he had permanently lost when he retired. Well, with his most recent retirement, anyway.

Twenty minutes later, a taxicab rolled into the lot and stopped in the driveway in front of the portico and the baby-faced man they had been referring to as *Pa*, got out and dashed inside. On closer inspection he looked like he was in his early forties, clean-cut and in reasonably good shape. Nevertheless, there was something about his gate that implied a sense of urgency, as if he was running late for something. Ten minutes later, he emerged from the hotel, with Ma, and they loaded two large suitcases and a garment bag into the back seat of the Rogue.

The couple headed North on I-94 and took the exit for General Mitchell Field, Milwaukee's international airport. As the traffic had picked up, Karlsson felt more comfortable following a little closer, and he stayed two cars back from them as they drove into the *Ticketing/Check-In* Lane. The Nissan slowed and pulled over under a black sign with white lettering listing several carriers. Karlsson put his flashers on and pulled over behind them. He craned his head as if he was looking for someone on the sidewalk but watched as the woman got out and grabbed her bag out of the back seat. She said something to the driver and then slammed the door shut and stepped quickly inside. Pa immediately moved into the traffic lane, but instead of exiting the airport, took the freeway loop around and ended up back at the rental car return entrance to the garage.

Karlsson watched as Pa pulled up into a row of returning cars that were being checked-in by the agency staff. He collected his suitcase and wardrobe bag back out of the back seat and waited for the clerk to hand him a receipt. He did not appear to be in nearly as big a hurry as he had been earlier and took his time heading back towards the terminal. But instead of going inside, he took a place in a queue that was reserved for guests of the Airport Four Points Sheraton. He was waiting for the shuttle.

Karlsson figured that the shuttle would have to make at least two other stops to pick up passengers along the Arrivals Lane, and that should give him some time. On that hunch, he found the exit, paid his ticket and then sped around the loop to get to the Sheraton before the shuttle bus did. He pulled into an empty space and then waited for the shuttle to arrive. When he saw it roll in, he jumped out and simply got in line with the five other people who disembarked to go inside and register at the hotel's front desk.

There was a young couple between Karlsson and his target, but the line was so tightly spaced that when it was Pa's turn at the counter, Karlsson was close enough that he could hear him tell the clerk, "Hi, my name is Braun, B-R-A-U-N, first name is Dale. I made a reservation about a half hour ago."

"Yes, Mr. Braun. We have it right here. We have you on the third floor. Will you be needing one key or two?"

"One's fine." He replied. "Can I get a wake-up call for five tomorrow morning?"

"Absolutely! I'm making a note of it right here." The clerk said with a smile. She slid his key across the counter to him and said, "The elevators are right over there. Please enjoy your stay!"

Karlsson had a name at least and considered that a small win for the time being. He did not want to risk being recognized within the confines of the elevator, so he made his way to the cocktail lounge and took a seat at the bar before calling Stan.

"Female subject unidentified, but on a plane headed somewhere in a hurry. Possibly Southwest." He turned his chair a few degrees so that he could see the door to the lounge. "Male subject is Braun comma Dale. B-R-A-U-N. Appears to be in his forties, current residence is the Airport Sheraton Four Points."

"Great work! It looks like they're breaking camp but headed different directions?"

"Yeah. He left a wake-up call for oh-five hundred. I was thinking about hanging out here for a few minutes to see if he comes down for dinner or drinks. He already dropped his rental car so if he leaves he'll have to walk or take a cab."

It was then that Karlsson caught a glimpse of Dale Braun walking past the doorway towards the restaurant, and then back again. He stuck his head in the lounge and walked towards the bar.

"I'll be damned. Tally-ho, mom, the prodigal son is returning." He said softly and then raised his voice a bit. "No, tell him that I have an early flight out tomorrow morning and will be there as soon as I can. Love you too!" Karlsson hung up as the bartender materialized behind the counter. Braun had pulled out a stool about three away and was looking at the inventory on the back counter.

"I'll just take your house cabernet." He said as the bartender greeted him.

"And you sir?" The bartender must have worn the name tag for a reason.

"Hi Jeff." Karlsson replied. "I'll take a light beer. Whatever you have on draught."

"Right away gentlemen."

Braun nodded at him and Karlsson nodded back, noticing the tattoo on Braun's right forearm, of crossed cannons with a missile superimposed over them. "Army?"

"Yeah, Air Defense Artillery. You?"

"Ah, a red-striper." He smiled "Yeah, Infantry, twenty-two years."

"Powder blue." Braun laughed.

"Infantry blue." Karlsson jokingly corrected. And the ice was broken. For the next hour and three drinks the two men held an in-depth discussion about the history of Army branch insignia, a tradition that began prior to the civil war. Colored piping on the uniforms of foot soldiers and lace for cavalry units changed throughout the years and evolved along with the dress uniforms themselves, with the colors of rank epaulets denoting an individual's branch. Yellow for cavalry officers, red for artillery, light blue for infantry, and so on. As specialty branches were added, so were additional color schemes to remain current. One couldn't have an army that didn't reflect the fashion palette of the day.

There were several toasts throughout the conversation to different units, different leaders, and different battles. Braun knew his military history, but eventually admitted that he missed the comradery.

"What do you do now?" Braun asked after a pause.

"Raise horses." Karlsson answered truthfully. "You?"

"I taught school for a while and then got back into contract work for DoD."

"Really? I heard about some of that. I had some friends that went back over on State Department contracts. The money was better, but they said it still sucked."

"Embrace the suck!" Braun lifted his glass as Karlsson joined him.

"Embrace the suck!" Karlsson looked at his watch. "Time to call the wife. But listen, I have to drop my rental car at around 0600. I don't know what time you're out of here, but if you like, I can give you a lift."

Braun stood and stretched. "Thanks, I appreciate it. See you in the lobby around oh five forty-five."

Karlsson watched him leave and thought that he kind-of liked the guy. But it wouldn't stop him from doing what he had to do when the time came.

⟫⟪⟨⦿⟩⟫⟪

It was just after six and General Scott frowned at the couch across the room from his desk. It was time to go home. At least for an evening. He was physically and emotionally exhausted after having spent the better part of his day moving funds out of one of his covert accounts into a bank in Tbilisi according to the instructions supplied by yet another person whom he had never met, but had been forced to do business with. A foreigner no less!

He would have to act quickly because sooner or later, the audit team was going to want to know where the two million went, and for what reason. He was walking a tightrope of time and there were too many uncontrollable elements dependent on each other to make the entire plan fit together. Baronowski's visit to Chile alleviated some of his concerns, but told him that he did not have much longer. Their communications were line-of-sight, and it was going to be visible any day now.

He opened his desk and looked at the piece of sheet music, ironically titled *Chatting With the Cosmos*, by someone named

Barclay, penned almost a year earlier. When he first came across the piece, he tried to play a few passages on his wife's piano. The song sounded like discordant rubbish. It wouldn't make it in today's hip-hop environment and it certainly was not a classic, by any definition. It seemed like the composition was a mishmash of notes strung together in no particular order with no thought given to harmonics. Played correctly, the chords were not majors, not minors, and not even diminished. The tonality was below juvenile and was painful to listen to. Certainly, there were no lyrics. It was an instrumental piece only. But it took an autistic savant to introduce him to the fundamentals.

Fundamentals, as they existed in musical theory; the harmonic component of a complex wave that had the lowest frequency and often the greatest amplitude. The tonic, and sometimes the root of a chord. It took a thirteen-year-old boy to remind the scientists that all musical notes have a special frequency. Unique vibrations, that could be measured in *hertz*, with each Hz indicating one cycle, or vibration per second. Thus, twenty Hz would mean twenty vibrations per second. As it turned out, the normal human ear could only hear frequencies from 20 Hz to about 20,000 Hz, even though the lowest semi-tone in the chromatic scale was 16.35 Hz. It was the lowest C, referenced as C-zero by musical theorists.

Most people who had studied music at some point in their lives were more familiar with C-4, which was middle C on the piano, and vibrated at 261.63 Hz. Thus, a C-major chord which would consist of C, E and G, would have three frequencies associated with it, played at once. Played individually, the three notes would be considered an arpeggio and would have a different interpretive meaning to the ear. Played in a selection of music here on earth, the sounds would be easily recognizable. However, since space was a vacuum, there was no sound. Sound as humans knew it, required a medium through which to travel. Audible sound required the presence of molecules or particles to push against to travel from one place to another. And as SCUBA divers could attest, the denser the better. Sound traveled much further under water than it did through air.

And so, the relationship between *pitch equaling rhythm* became increasingly significant.

Mathematically considered, Middle C's resonation at 261.63 cycles per second, could be equated to beating 15,697.8 cycles per minute. If one could electronically slow that pulse down by a half then they would hear the audible tone drop accordingly. In fact, a complete octave. Slow it by another half and the tone drops another octave. Then by yet another half and it drops again. If one continued to reduce the speed of the pulsing, at some point, instead of the audible tone the human ear would begin to perceive rapid tapping at equidistantly spaced intervals. Slow it once more in half to about 2 Hz and they would hear the tapping slow consistently, more akin to a pulse that resembles a rock band's bass drum beating quickly.

Taking the concept the other direction, if one began with a drum beat at 168 beats per minute, and gradually increased the tempo of the pulse, at some point human ears would quit perceiving it as a quickening pulse and begin to hear it as a solid tone, increasing in pitch. The same relationship exists with chords, which are multiple notes played at the same time. Two different pulses sped up gradually become two tones that were either in symphony or cacophony to the human ear.

It was not a new science. In Europe, people had been studying vibrations and sound since the Middle Ages and in the Baroque period musicians of the day had agreed that the note A, used as concert pitch for tuning purposes, should be 432 Hz. It wasn't until 1939 that a number of interested parties decided that the concert A should be officially adopted to be 440 Hz. Among the people who pushed this change were Joseph Goebbels, the chief propagandist for the Nazi party, along with some unlikely partners such as the Rockefellers and the Rothschilds, which later resulted in a cottage industry of conspiracy theories. Some people thought that Goebbels was trying to use the frequency to control people's thoughts. Others did not think he was that smart.

The Ancient Indian Rishis knew that 7.83 Hz was the correct

frequency for OM chants. In fact, chakras were referenced in the oldest written Indian tradition, the Vedas, which dated from 1500 BCE to 500 BCE and talked about healing frequencies that affected different parts of the body. It was possible that the chakras were originally discovered by the ancient Brahmins years before. The chakras were passed down through time and were gradually considered as psychic centers of energy in the Yoga Upanishads by 600 BCE and were still used in Yoga schools around the world in modern day.

But the ancients and modern practitioners alike attributed certain frequencies to the activation of the different chakras throughout the human body. While the root chakra was believed to be focused at 432 Hz, the Sacral chakra could be activated at 480 Hz, the Solar Plexus at 528 Hz, and so on. As Einstein said, "Everything is vibration".

Through this time, it was also generally accepted that 8Hz was the fundamental *beat* of our planet. The so-called heartbeat of the Earth was better known in scientific communities as Schumann Resonance, so named for physicist Winfried Otto Schumann, who documented it mathematically in 1952. Schumann recognized a global electromagnetic resonance, which was discovered in electrical discharges of lightning within the cavity existing between the Earth's surface and the ionosphere. He found that this cavity resonated with electromagnetic waves in the extremely low frequencies of approximately 7.86Hz to 8Hz. And for many years this resonant frequency hovered at a steady 7.83 Hz with only slight variations until June 2014 when technicians at the Russian Space Observing System showed a sudden spike in activity to around 8.5 Hz.

Research indicated that emerging resonances were also correlated to human brainwave activity. In neurofeedback, the spectrum between 12-15 Hz was known as Sensory-Motor Rhythm frequency, and this SMR was recognized as an ideal state of *awakened calm*. Within this range, human thought processes were thought to be clearer and more focused and were still in a conscious state. Because researchers were seeing occasional spikes in Schumann

Resonance to over 12.6 Hz, they speculated that the Earth was shifting its vibrational frequency and perhaps so were humans, leading to speculation that the human race itself was spiritually awakening.

Thus, it became apparent that everything around us was vibrating. And as Zecharia Sitchin had pointed out, whether one agreed with his premise or not, sometime about six thousand years earlier, *sky people* came down from the heavens and imparted highly technical wisdom to the ancient Sumerians. They taught them how frequency could reveal mechanical movements observable throughout the universe, and how certain harmonics contained keys and codes to unlock the very process of creation, and how one geometric system revealed the very matrix of our existence. When the Annunaki had visited Earth four hundred thousand years earlier, mankind was not ready for all that. But the fusing of technology with spiritualism had allowed an enlightened few to understand that we were not alone and that others in the universe were trying to communicate with us.

While it was true that one could not transmit Barclay's musical score through the emptiness of space, it was however possible to break each note down into its individual frequency and send it out as independent pulsed packets. When they had explained it to General Scott, they described it like advanced channel-hopping.

"It's like the SINCGARS system on steroids." The young Army captain told him. "The Exelis Single Channel Ground and Airborne Radio System RT-1523 is the most widely used Combat Net Radio in the world. The SINCGARS operates on any of 2,320 channels between 30 and 88 megahertz and accepts either digital or analog inputs. It then superimposes the signal onto a radio frequency carrier wave. The input changes frequencies about a hundred times per second over portions of the tactical frequency range. Channel-hopping, as they call it."

"Thus, individual musical notes become pulsed transmission on their own different frequencies. It's channel-hopping on a much faster and more complicated pace than the US Army ever imagined. And it's not likely to be picked up by a Ham radio operator, simply because the individual pulses last less than a second and jump from frequency to frequency faster than most scanners could pick up."

General Scott looked at the *Music Note to Frequency* chart on his desk. "So, if I want to send a C- major chord out into the cosmos, I would send C, E, G and C as a blip of 261.63 Hz, 329.63 Hz, 392.00 Hz and the high C as 523.25 Hz?"

"At the same time." The captain replied. "If you send them one after the other, it would be an arpeggio. Quarter notes, half notes, sixteenth notes are all determined by the length of the pulse. Assuming that someone out there has the capability to receive these frequencies."

He replaced the sheet music in his desk drawer and then locked it. He needed to hear from St. Paul Island. The abandoned LORAN-C Station was being used as a listening post, with a double secret mission. The team of Coast Guard and civilian scientists were supposedly there to study migratory patterns of birds and seals to see if there was a correlation to climate change. However, when presented to the congressional budget office for funding as a Black Operation, overseers were told that their location in the Bering Sea made it an optimum position from which to observe and record Russian communications and movements in the area. The reality was that Tom Baranowski, Darren's brother, was listening for a symphony. Either one originating in the cosmos, or heaven forbid, one coming from somewhere in Russia that was intended for a distant audience.

The Russians knew the secret too.

CHAPTER 14

Marchand checked his watch as Karlsson pulled the van into the hotel parking lot. "Zero five forty. We have about five minutes."

"Yeah. Let me pull past the entrance so that he has to approach from the rear." Karlsson went to the corner of the parking lot and turned the van around. "Jump in back in case he's waiting in the lobby."

Marchand moved into the back and quickly checked the tools he had brought with him. Duct tape, two zip ties, wire cutters and a paper bag. He was prepared.

Karlsson looked in towards the lobby as he drove slowly past the portico and then stopped. He exited and walked around the front of the van so that he would be able to see Braun approaching, and then unlocked the sliding door on the side of the van and let it open a few inches. He started towards the entrance when he saw his drinking buddy from the previous night coming out with his luggage and a smile.

"Hey! You made it!" Karlsson smiled back. "Let me take one of those." He gestured at the wardrobe that Braun was trying to drape over an arm.

"Thanks." Braun replied and passed the floppy bag to Karlsson.

The overcast dawn light combined with the tinted windows on the van concealed Marchand's presence adequately. Karlsson gestured, tossing the wardrobe bag over his right shoulder. "Here you go. You can throw that in the back."

Karlsson reached for the door with his left hand and when Braun got closer, he punched him in the side of the neck, stunning his brachial plexus nerve network, causing his legs to buckle involuntarily. Marchand moved with lightning speed and grabbed the semi-conscious Major by the lapels and dragged him into the van. He rolled him onto his stomach and applied the zip ties to his wrists, linking them together like handcuffs. It only took five seconds. Karlsson tossed the wardrobe bag back on top of them and slammed the door shut. He walked back around the front of the van and once he was in the driver's seat, put the transmission in gear, and they drove casually off the lot as if nothing had happened.

It was dark in the back, but Marchand slid the paper grocery bag over Braun's head anyway to make sure that he could not tell where they were going.

Braun grunted. "What the fuck is going on?"

Marchand replied calmly. "You can tell us what we want to know right now, and we'll drop you at the airport, cut you loose, and you'll have time to catch your plane. If you choose not to tell us what we need to know, you'll be taken to a place where the information will be extracted using less comfortable techniques."

"You're making a mistake." Braun tried to sit up, but Marchand drove a knee into his side and forced him back down.

"We hear that a lot." Marchand shook his head. "Let's not make this take any longer than necessary. Who are you working for and why are you watching us?"

After an awkward period of quiet, Marchand spoke softly. "Look, Dale, you really don't strike me as the tough-guy type. You're not going to enjoy sitting still while my friend practices shit on you that he learned in places that I can't pronounce. Just tell us what you can and then we'll drop you at the airport."

"I'm a contractor for the Defense Department. You already know that."

"Specifically, which part of the DoD? Give me the name of the person who hired you?"

"Uhmm...the woman who hired me was Davina Fox, but I work for a woman named Francine Dantonio. I'm not sure which of them is really in charge. They kinda share responsibilities, but I think Francine might be senior."

"Was that the woman you dropped off at Southwest yesterday afternoon?"

"Yes."

"Where is she headed?"

"Colorado."

"Is that where you're going as well?"

"No. I'm supposed to go back to DC, well, to Virginia to meet Davina." His voice dissolved to a whisper. Marchand had interviewed thousands of suspects in his career, and he felt this one was being honest.

"And what is it they hired you to do?"

"To help support Homeland Security by doing surveillance on terrorists and foreign agents."

"Are we terrorists or foreign agents, Dale?" Marchand asked somewhat mockingly.

"Both. We were to watch to see if your numbers grew. If you were using the house to hide other people involved in any type of conspiracy. We were drifting past several times a day to get you comfortable seeing the boat and to basically do a headcount of people staying there."

It sounded like a strange assignment, but Marchand felt that Braun was being forthcoming with what he knew. "What's in Colorado?"

"I don't know. Another surveillance. We just got it in a couple days ago. They said to drop this for now...that...we'd come back here later."

"What are you going to do when you get back to Washington, Dale?"

"Not a fucking thing! I didn't sign up for this! I'm going back to teaching."

Karlsson rolled up at the end of the Ticketing/Check-In Lane that he had briefly visited the previous day. He pulled all the way to the end of the line so that Braun would have a brisk walk back to his gate. Marchand sat his prisoner upright, with the bag still on his head.

"You're at the Departures area for your flight. I'm going to put your gear out on the curb and then I'm going to free your hands and help you out. Once you're outside you can take the bag off your head and be on your way. You might be tempted to get a license plate number or a description of the van, but I would urge you not to, because your boss may ask you if anything unusual happened this morning. It's up to you as to what you tell them, but if I were you, I'd think up something pretty benign because they are not nice people. If they think you've been compromised you might very well be their next target."

Karlsson looked around and then nodded at Stan, who opened the side door and put Braun's luggage out on the sidewalk. He quickly snipped the zip-ties and helped him onto the sidewalk. "Take care of yourself, Army!"

———◈———

By seven-thirty the sky was beginning to clear and Karlsson and Marchand were back at the house in Pleasant Prairie starting breakfast. At Neri's urging they had agreed to try something a bit healthier than their usual fare and were making egg-white omelets with green pepper and onions. Everyone agreed that it was a moderately tasty substitute for the more traditional cholesterol-laden breakfast and after they had taken the plates to the sink, Marchand dialed the number Paul had covertly provided the day before, and put his phone in the middle of the table for all to hear the conversation.

Paul was satisfied that their work had yielded the names of the two women in leadership positions but was nearly childlike with exuberance when they mentioned that Francine Dantonio had booked a flight for Colorado. Certainly, a rarity for his normally subdued character, he proclaimed, "We've got her!"

"That's exactly what we wanted to hear. I will provide confirmation to our team standing-by there. They have been expecting her since your report yesterday." He said more calmly. "Maybe this will get us one step closer to the top of her organization."

"You have doubts that the General is at the top of the organization?" Karlsson asked.

"That's where the signs point." He mused, "But, this is Washington. The person seen giving all the orders isn't always the one calling the shots. It will be interesting to see with which agencies these ladies and their colleagues have been associated in the recent past. My guess is that they have accepted work from other intelligence agencies and may be pawns in an even larger scheme."

Marchand asked, "Should I try to run the names through my sources?"

"No. Allow me try a back-channel approach and see what I can find out locally." Paul replied. "There are certain agencies that do a great job of covering their tracks, and with the General's demonstrated prowess in intercepting communications I am concerned that official database searches might tip our hand."

After a suitable pause in the conversation, Nerissa injected, "How are my mother and son?"

Paul's confidence was obvious. "Both are fine. We have people close by and are watching for any signs that their security might be at risk. Your mother seemed to regard the special protection as nothing more than the flavor-of-the-month. She's been in the business for so long that when we approached her she was not surprised. She claimed that after your visit last week that she knew something was up. And we still think that the General believes you to be dead."

There was a short pause. "Hunter and his wife, on the other hand, were not nearly as comfortable having someone else around, no matter the purpose. We explained that you were safe, on official business and that this was just a formality. But I sensed that he was reluctantly playing along because he thought that is what you would want."

"That's my boy." She nodded and looked out the window towards the lake.

⋯⟨◉⟩⋯

While the expats assigned as permanent staff at the Observatory preferred the conveniences offered by the metropolitan area of La Serena for their permanent habitation and recreation, they tended to utilize the Hotel Soledad de Montaña down the hill to catch some sleep and a shower between their shifts. The thirty-five-mile bus trip to the local Vicuña hotel often took an hour and a half down the unpaved roads laden with dangerous switchbacks, but provided scientists and technicians additional time to collaborate on aspects of their various assignments if they were so disposed.

However, today was the start of Marco's four-day weekend, so to speak, and Margarita had invited him to lunch on the beach at the Restaurant Bakulic, a trendy spot with fantastic seafood, excellent service, and a magnificent view of the South Pacific Ocean. The exposed beams and rafters lent a *local* feel to the place, but the cuisine was modern and most enjoyable. She was expected back at her office in AURA, the Association of Universities for Research in Astronomy, after lunch, but it was guaranteed that she would be his for the rest of the weekend.

It was an important job for her. AURA was a consortium of fifty US and international affiliates, which operated astronomical observatories for the National Science Foundation and NASA around the world. Their principal role was to advance innovative astronomical research among public observatories in an open and cooperative environment of shared science. However, considering their funding and how that scientific information was stored and shared, she knew that she was being used as a pawn in a much deeper game.

The data that was produced every night at VRO was transported from the camera to the control room on the summit, down to the LSST Base Facility in La Serena, and from there over fiber-optic cables to Santiago and ultimately, to the LSST Data Facility at the National Center for Supercomputing Applications in the United States. It was a tremendous amount of information to process as the team generated more than ten million alerts each night.

The NCSA itself was a state-federal partnership created to develop and deploy national-scale computer infrastructure that advanced scientific research and operated as a unit of the University of Illinois Urbana-Champaign. It was created in 1984 through a ten-page proposal that led to funding from the National Science Foundation to establish supercomputing centers. Of course, the significant role played by the U.S. Government in funding the center was evident, so even though the organization was overtly invested in the scientific community, the United States Government had its hands all over it.

Pozos looked across the table at Margarita and smiled. He could not wait to get her alone as soon as she left work. As usual, she was seductively dressed, today in a white print blouse with a dark blue skirt and high heels. It was in the mid-sixties, but she did not seem to mind as they enjoyed their grilled Albacore on the patio overlooking the beach. Everything she did excited him, including the simple act of raising the fork to her mouth and taking a bite.

"You are staring at me!" She said coyly. "Are you amused by me eating?"

"Something like that." He grinned. "You are the most beautiful woman I have ever met, and I enjoy watching every inch of you, every second."

She was twenty-five and quite fit. Her ritual of running four miles every morning kept her trim and lithe, but nature gave her enough curve that she was attractive at any distance, from any angle. Her long dark hair had a subtle wave that gave it character and her tanned skin and brilliant smile made her a perfect fit for the public relations role that one of her professors at the Universidad de Santiago had helped her obtain. In addition to the phenomenal Communications program, the school also boasted one of the biggest planetariums in the world, with a dome that was more than seventy feet in diameter.

"Is sex all you ever think about?" She chided insincerely.

"When I'm with you." He answered. "And when I'm thinking about being with you."

She laughed. "Okay. You have passed the test." She dabbed a piece of Albacore in some sauce. "So, how are things with Jean-Luc? That man is a constant source of aggravation."

Pozos chuckled and shrugged. "We get along, but I try not to spend any more time with him than I have to. He's such an arrogant prick. What's he doing to aggravate you?"

"Always a new demand. He wants additional money. He does not like his apartment. He does not like the food we bring to the site. He thinks he should be treated better than you and Henrik, even though you all do the same job."

Pozos took a sip of his beer. "Why would he think that you can get him more money? He is here on a university grant, just like the rest of us."

She shook her head and frowned. "I don't know. Maybe he is trying to get hired by AURA. I think he may be meeting, or even interviewing with other observatories. He never seems to be in his apartment here, so I wonder what he does."

"Maybe he has a girlfriend?"

She scowled. "Him? Not likely. What woman could be happy with a man who loves himself more than her?"

"Wait a minute. How do you know he's not in his apartment on weekends?" Pozos asked with mock jealousy.

The question seemed to catch her off guard. "Well, someone tried to deliver some papers there last weekend and it looked like he hadn't been home in a few days."

"Ah. Well, you better not be delivering anything else over there!"

She looked at him for a moment before she realized he was joking with her. "I see. But I am curious though. Does he ever mention anything to you about his activities?"

Pozos shrugged. "No. But then, I never asked."

"You are all such quiet people." She smiled. "To be honest, I do not know that much about you, either. We have rarely talked about your family. Your mother, father...sisters?"

He was certainly captivated by her. Enough that it took him a minute to realize that her questions were beginning to take the shape more of an interview than an intimate lunch. He suddenly remembered Baranowski's curiosity about her, and it took him a moment to lapse back into his spy-brain and recite the cover story that had been arranged for him back at The Farm in Williamsburg. For simplicity, they kept his new past to be as close as possible to the real one, but switched his father's occupation from Air Force to IBM to avoid any connection to the government.

"Really? I thought we had." He took another sip of beer and the-atrically locked eyes with her. "My dad is gone now. For almost forty years, he worked for IBM, where he met my mother. We moved around a lot, mostly in Latin America. Mom lives in Miami now. No brothers or sisters, but I have a cousin in Atlanta. I haven't seen him since my first year of college."

"What does he do?" She asked with almost genuine curiosity.

"He's a high school music teacher, and then plays in a band on the weekends."

"That's it? Twenty-five years of history in one paragraph?" She grinned.

Pozos shrugged again. "Not much to tell. I played football in high school for a couple of years but got hooked on astronomy. I've wanted to be a professional stargazer ever since then. Never been married. Never engaged. Lost my virginity in my first year of college to a girl I met at a party. We went out twice and realized that we were seriously not meant to be together."

Margarita blushed. "That is more than enough. I am sorry I asked."

"What about you?" He asked her.

"Me?"

"You! I've told you all about myself. Why don't you tell me something about you that I don't already know."

"I was born in Santiago and lived there most of my life. My father was a teacher who lived through both Allende and Pinochet and was able to raise us properly. I have two brothers and two sisters, and I am the one in the middle, as they say."

"I already knew that. Tell me something else."

"I had a large family and many friends, but somehow I always felt alone. Different. I loved them all but felt that I was destined to leave here and do other things. My brothers and sisters were all content to stay in Santiago and they each found worthwhile jobs and *cónyuges*, but I wanted something different."

"You wanted to make your own way. That is admirable and courageous." Pozos wanted to be supportive no matter what she said. He would say or do nothing to jeopardize the evening yet to come.

She tilted her head. "Perhaps, but it can leave you feeling very alone. Like a tiny Quasar spinning in the void of space."

"You mean pulsar, don't you?"

"What?"

"Pulsars are dead stars that are rapidly spinning and blowing off neutrons, Quasars are at the center of active galaxies and are about the brightest objects in the universe."

"Oh, yes." She blushed again. "It has been a while since my last astronomy exam."

They both laughed as they chatted their way through the remainder of lunch before she dropped him at his apartment with a brief kiss. "I will work till about five thirty and then stop at home for a shower and to pick up some things. See you about six-thirty?"

"Looking forward to it." He smiled as he gently closed the door of her Chinese-built Chery *Tiggo 3*.

He watched her drive away and as he turned to go into his apartment building, he could not help but think it unusual for a Communications major with a minor in Astronomy to confuse Quasar and Pulsar. Pulsar, after all, meant *Pulsating Star*. How could anyone in the business get those two terms confused? Maybe Baranowski's visit had made him a bit paranoid. On the other hand, maybe it had awakened him to the reality that foreign interests might very well be trying to determine what he was up to, much the same as he had been working to identify his opposition. As he had learned at The Farm, the Honey Pot Trap was nothing new.

During the cold war female Soviet KGB agents were used to spy on foreign officials by seducing them and involving their targets in false relationships. The so-called *Mozhno girls* were allowed to operate outside of traditional espionage protocols and regulations. The term Mozhno itself meant; *it is permitted*. It was used many times by governments around the world, and then with private investigators attempting to set up unsuspecting spouses to determine infidelity in a relationship.

As recently as 2009, British MI-5 was concerned enough about the practice that it circulated a briefing to hundreds of its financial institutions titled, *The Threat from Chinese Espionage*, as a warning that Chinese intelligence services were attempting to blackmail western business leaders through threatened exposure of their illicit romantic liaisons. With these practices, they hoped to pressure key executives into cooperating with them in business deals which otherwise might have been avoided. With that in mind, Pozos wondered if it was prudent to question Margarita Vallejos' intent?

It was a ridiculous thought. Given his limited knowledge of intelligence operations, Pozos could not guess whose interests she might be representing if she was anything other than who she presented herself to be. It was already understood that all of the data from the VRO was sent through Santiago, so the Chileans could certainly tap into it in their hub site if they were curious. The Chinese and the Russians already had access to the data through the NCSA at the University of Illinois. What could they hope to gain by having an asset inside the VRO on the summit?

As he climbed the stairs to his second-floor apartment, he pushed all those thoughts aside. He was getting laid tonight!

With a complement of eighty-five officers and more than five hundred enlisted personnel, the 23,000-acre Coast Guard Air Station in Kodiak, Alaska was the largest USCG station in the Pacific region. Sharing an airport with Kodiak's Benny Benson State Airport, the unit operated a number of MH-60 Jayhawk and MH-65 Dolphin helicopters as well as several HC-130 fixed-wing aircraft and was tasked primarily with search and rescue response to a four-million-square-mile slice of the Pacific Ocean, Gulf of Alaska, and Bering Sea. They were also tasked with logistical support for various Coast Guard units deployed to permanent remote stations that might only be accessible by air. Including Saint Paul Island.

Baranowski took a twenty-one-hour Delta flight from Santiago to Anchorage via Atlanta and Seattle and then took a cab to Elmendorf AFB to avail himself of the Coast Guard's hospitality for a quick hop to Kodiak Island to pick up another passenger and then make the final two-hour ride into the small airport on Saint Paul Island, Alaska. As it turned out, the additional passenger on the no-frills flight was a Navy SEAL Lieutenant who was scouting-out potential training locations for the units that were assigned to the Naval Special Warfare Cold Weather Detachment on Kodiak Island. He was amiable, but none too chatty throughout the journey. Neither was LTC Baranowski who was exhausted and needed a shower and a shave.

The lumbering aircraft touched down amid heavy fog on the island's only runway, and Baranowski felt he could finally breath again. It was a strange phobia indeed for an educated man to have, who worked on an island, to be afraid of flying over the water. Especially water that one could not see due to the fog. Nevertheless, as the aircraft rolled to a stop, he immediately stretched and twisted to assure himself that blood was reaching everywhere it needed to go.

Saint Paul Island was the largest of the four Pribilof Islands, discovered by Russian ship captain Gavriil Pribylov in 1787. Its forty-four square miles were home to four hundred eighty people, on a good day. In truth though, Pribylov did not actually discover the islands himself. He had been directed to their location by the son of an indigenous Aleut chief who was showing him where a multitude of fur seals could be found. And, at the time, the then-uninhabited islands were known to the Aleuts as *Amiq,* which literally translated, meant something to the effect of *Land of mother's brother,* or *related land.*

Three years after discovery of the low-lying volcanic island in the middle of nowhere, the Russian merchant vessel *John the Baptist* became shipwrecked off the shore. The crew were listed as missing until 1793, when the survivors were rescued by another Russian explorer, Gerasim Izmailov. From then on, the Aleuts were conscripted into involuntary servitude to trap seals for the Russians. They were denied a return ticket to their homeland, kept in inhumane conditions, beaten regularly and were even told by their Russian captors who they could marry. All until March 30, 1867, when William H. Seward bought the surrounding area from the Russians for 7.2 million dollars.

Some would argue that the Aleuts were treated no better by the American government than they had been by the Russians. At first, the Aleuts were paid competitive wages by US companies, at a rate comparable to other industrial workers in America at the time. However, after forty years, the fur seal populations became depleted, and the Aleuts began to experience a severe decline in their income and living conditions. The U.S. government took over the industry in 1910, and some Aleuts claimed they lost the few rights they had held as Russian subjects, returning to an environment where their culture, language, religion, and everyday freedoms were adversely impacted.

This state of perceived servitude to the U.S. government reached its apex in 1942. As was the case with Japanese Americans in the rest of the United States, the Pribilof Aleuts were evacuated and interned in dilapidated locations like fish canneries throughout southeastern Alaska until the end of World War II. Not because they were thought to be subversive, but rather because their homes were in a Japanese-occupied war zone. Many Aleuts died in the substandard conditions, lacking adequate food and shelter.

With the Civil Liberties Act of 1988, Congress authorized repararations to Japanese Americans, and issued a formal apology. The Aleuts were added, seemingly as an after-thought, with each Aleut survivor or their descendants receiving $12,000, with an additional $5-million trust fund set up under the Interior Department to help restore their culture and commerce. Another $1.4 million was earmarked for rebuilding churches in six villages that had been damaged by the Japanese army. There was an additional $15 million awarded as compensation for Attu Island, which had been occupied by the military after the war and remained closed to its former inhabitants. The Attuan residents, seized by Japanese troops in June 1942, and taken to POW camps in Japan, were resettled after the war in Atka, more than five hundred miles from their home.

Despite its size, the quiet island where everyone knew everyone, now built its meager economy on fishing, but still managed to make the headlines from time to time. In July 2001 an indignant man came all the way from Anchorage to kill a Coast Guard Officer whom he believed was having a romantic relationship with his estranged wife. She lived on the island with her two children, along with some of her other friends and relatives. After a night of binge drinking, he forced one of her friends to drive him to the Coast Guard Station and wait outside while he went in and shot Chief Warrant Officer Timothy Harris, the station's Commanding Officer. The drunken malcontent was later convicted of murder and sentenced to a term that would keep him locked up for more years than he could count.

Then, in June 2006 a C-130 from Kodiak, carrying nine crew members and a fuel truck, was attempting to land, but fish-tailed twice, causing the right wing to strike the runway surface. The wingtip was sheared off as well as the number-four engine's propeller. Unable to stop within the remaining distance, the aircraft over-ran the runway and came to rest in the grass. All nine occupants escaped injury, but the aircraft was damaged beyond repair: *TFU'd* in the Coast Guard vernacular of the day.

Often called the *Galapagos of the North* due to the migratory patterns of more than two hundred species of birds and a half-million seals, its location in the Bering Sea made it cool year-around. Temperatures seemed to average between lows in the teens to highs in the mid-sixties with a couple inches of precipitation each month. There were no hotels or restaurants to speak of on the island so the visiting ornithologists who made the long trip were forced to buy food from the local store at significantly higher prices than they would pay in the lower forty-eight. Needless to say, no one was going to build a golf course on that cold basalt ground.

The whine of the C-130's engines began to diminish as the crew chief slid the hatch up on the port side. "All ashore that's going ashore." He joked with a grin. "Don't forget your sunscreen!"

Darren's older brother Tom was waiting on the tarmac near the Operations building, smartly attired in his crisp blue ODU's. The Operational Dress Uniform was the Coast Guard's equivalent to the other services' Battle Dress Uniform, BDU's or *Utilities*, as they had previously been called in the Marine Corps. Despite his actual civilian grade within the intelligence community, to maintain consistency with his cover, he was wearing rank insignia of a CWO3. It was therefore in keeping with military protocol that he saluted when his brother and the Navy Lieutenant approached.

"Good morning, gentlemen!" He dropped his salute and reached to shake hands with his brother first. "Welcome to our Bering Sea paradise, Colonel!"

After shaking hands with LTC Baranowski, he moved to the SEAL and after a firm handshake handed him the keys to the six-year-old Chevy Silverado, which was showing signs of rust around the wheel wells. "Sorry L-T, this is the best I could scrounge up on short notice, but the tank is full and there are some maps on the seat. If you'll drop us at the station, it's yours for the remainder of your visit."

"Thank you." The SEAL replied with a practiced smile. He was obviously an adherent of former CENTCOM-leader-turned-SECDEF James Mattis' philosophy: *Be polite, be professional, but have a plan to kill everybody you meet.*

The men started walking towards the four-door pickup truck.

"You and the C-130 crew will be bunking with us tonight. I guess you're scheduled for an oh-seven hundred departure tomorrow." He gestured towards the CG station. "Enjoy the island; it's tough to get lost here. You can't miss us!"

Tom Baranowski tossed their gear in the bed of the truck and climbed into the driver's seat. During the three-minute drive to the old LORAN-C Station, he kept the conversation to weather patterns and ocean currents, along with a bit of the island's history. When he pulled into the gravel drive, he put the truck in park and left the engine running. "Dinner will be at 1800. No need to dress up, it'll be nothing fancy!"

The Baranowski brothers watched the Chevy turn around and head down the road and then entered the double door vestibule. Even though it had been many years since smoking had been permitted in government buildings, one could still pick up the odor of stale tobacco in the air. The rugs bearing the Coast Guard's LORAN-C Station logo, were relatively clean but well-worn and slightly askew.

"The galley is here on your left, Colonel, and your quarters are down this hall on your right." They moved past the pool table that was situated in the crossroads of two different hallways to a steel door with an electronic keypad. As Tom entered a string of numbers into the pad he explained, "Back in the Station's LORAN days, this used to be the non-Rate wing."

He pulled the steel door open and said, "Watch your step." As they moved up four stairs and down a narrow hallway, they noted a totally different smell. It was one of sanitized environmental control, that the LTC associated with other data centers that he had frequented.

As if he was giving a tour to a VIP officer, Tom continued, "In the Coast Guard, the non-Rates were E-1's through E-3's who were just starting out and had not yet attended a formal resident training program or an on-the-job-training program for any particular occupational specialty." He lowered his voice a bit. "Because this is a classified facility, there's no one here that's non-rated, so we converted the space to house the SCIF. But since we don't get that many visitors, we billet flight crews, staff, and other honored guests in staterooms down the officers' wing, which is where you'll be tonight. Of course, visitors only have access to the non-classified part of the facility and would need to be escorted down here." He winked.

Once they were towards the rear of the wing, Tom opened the door to his office and let his younger brother walk through. "Coffee?"

"No, thanks." Darren looked around. "Cozy place you have here."

"It'll do." Tom smiled and gave his brother a big hug. Something that could not be done in public by two officers in uniform. "Damn, it's good to see you. I can't believe, with our fucking seniority, we both got stuck on an island in the same ocean, but you're getting sunburned while I'm freezing my ass off every day."

Darren slapped his brother on the back. "Yes, the benefits of a formal legal education!"

Tom gestured for his brother to have a seat and then rotated a switch on the black box beside his computer screen. As he adjusted the volume of the white-noise generator he spoke quietly. "The windows have been blocked up, but protocol says we still have to use the transducers and noise in case someone out there is trying to listen."

"I noticed you didn't flash the blue light." Darren nodded, referencing a requirement to visually notify staff in a Sensitive Compartmented Information Facility that a non-cleared guest was in the area and that all information should be safeguarded appropriately.

"Naw, you're about as read-in as you can get." Tom smiled. "What brings you all the way up here? Not that I'm not happy to see you."

"Leadership is coming unhinged in eager anticipation of the up-coming event and wanted a face-to-face meeting with you to get your perceptions. Anything you might be sensing that you haven't put into official reports."

Tom swiveled in his chair and typed a password into his desktop computer. "Nothing. If the Russians or anyone else for that matter are sending anything, we're not picking it up. I think they're waiting, just like us, before they unzip their fly and make us all aware of their intent. They know we're on it and we know they're on it, so it's sorta like two gunslingers on the street at sundown...neither of us wants to flinch first."

"If you do hear something, what are your instructions?"

"Simple. We send the confirmation signal to the General and then I hit the send packet on the pre-recorded composition." Tom opened the file and played the audible version of the music. The notes that would be sent into the vacuum of space would be slowed down dramatically in the form of individual pulses, each on different frequencies, unrecognizable to the human ear.

"That's horrendous!" Darren frowned. "What the hell does it mean?"

"No idea." Tom replied. "It's what they sent me. It's what we're listening for. We were never told which experts came up with it, or why they thought some alien life form would know what it all means." He closed the file. "We're not even supposed to wash it through our own software. We have orders to send as-is, and that's what we'll do."

The younger Baranowski quietly stood and put his hands in his pockets. His backside hurt from too many hours on airplanes. Since there was no window in the office, he stared instead at the presentation plaque on the wall, a metal etching of the USCG Cutter Spar, hull number 206, with an engraved plate underneath that read, *Thanks for your hospitality and support June 2003.*

"Well, if you ask me, they're keeping this thing entirely too bottled up. If there really is someone out there, they're going to get closer and realize that none of us get along with each other and we're all killing each other to get ahead." Darren shook his head. "If they believe us to be nothing more than a war-like planet consisting of unruly tribes, eager to expand our turf at the cost of incessant violence, there may not be any peaceful exchange of information.

They may fly by and tell us to fuck off."

Tom closed-out his desktop file. "Or worse. They may come to think that we need adult supervision and decide to return us to being the slaves we were twelve thousand years ago."

———»《◉》«———

Dr. Peter Newell had been a fixture in Washington for more than thirty years. A product of a wealthy and learned New England family, he had received his law degree from Harvard before venturing on for a doctorate in Economics from Princeton. His undergraduate science degree, courtesy of the US Military Academy at West Point, had initially required an obligatory service period of eight years, but with daddy's help, his career path had been streamlined to include four years of active duty and four years in a reserve component, which gave him ample time to pursue his academic interests and stay out of actual combat.

His family had convinced him that he was a strategist. His job was to guide the nation and the world, not to engage the enemy in face-to-face battles of mere tactical importance. His family affiliations had granted him significant positions of trust and power in both The White House and Congress, but his own prowess of negotiation and flawless intuition had enabled him to remain in key slots no matter which political party was in power. While some considered him an arrogant narcissist, they dared not mention it since his social and professional connections were ubiquitous and their range limitless. Politicians and other elitists needed him and could not afford to be in disfavor.

He had money. Family money, and of course, government money. In his current position as the Director of Government Affairs for the National Science Foundation, he controlled the purse strings for the money coming out of government and going into sponsored projects. Billions. If he wanted something done, it got done.

The National Science Foundation was a *supposedly* independent agency of the United States government supporting research and education in the non-medical fields of science and engineering. Medical money went to the National Institutes of Health, which had unfortunately become just as politicized by self-serving bureaucrats racing to be in front of the camera as every sniffle garnered a headline. Nevertheless, the NSF managed an 8.5-billion-dollar budget of its own and funded more than a fourth of the basic research conducted by American universities.

The NSF's director and deputy director were appointed by the President of the United States and confirmed by the United States Senate. However, the remainder of the leadership did not require confirmation of any kind. And, while the director and deputy director may have been responsible for administration, planning, budgeting of the foundation, they, like other Cabinet appointees, relied heavily on professionals who knew the system. Professionals who could get things done.

CHAPTER 15

Francine Dantonio did not go back to her hotel room. Once she had received the ABORT-5 message, she knew there was a serious problem and that she needed to pull her team away and sanitize everything they could as quickly as they could. That meant dropping the rental cars, tossing the burn phones, abandoning certain restricted equipment, and going different directions. In her twenty-plus years in special operations, she had aborted missions many times. A level one or two signal meant *close it up and make your way back in an orderly fashion*. A three was considered urgent, but a five meant that the operation and team were compromised and in lethal jeopardy.

There would be time to ask questions later. However, in the interim, they had to flee the area without leaving a footprint. After alerting her two teammates, she did her best to wipe her fingerprints off of the surfaces of the car: steering wheel, door handles, switches. There could ultimately be an audit trail of the transaction, and there was also the problem of her personal belongings in her hotel room, that might tie an investigator back to her. But the items in the hotel were all purchased for the trip, the name on her luggage tag matched her false driver's license and credit card and would lead someone away from her, at least for a few hours. Her fingerprints and DNA though would be all over the place and it would not take federal agents long to make the connection. She had done the best she could by calling the hotel desk and requesting maid service as soon as possible. If the room was properly cleaned and disinfected, that might at least provide her some options for a minor legal defense down the road if it came to that.

For the time being though, a new car from a different agency was her best bet.

It was almost five hours later when she reached the outskirts of Salt Lake City and felt comfortable enough to contact Davina on her new burn phone. "Okay, what-the-fuck?"

"I met with grandfather last night. We were set up. Well, to be more accurate, I should say that the General was set up."

"How?" Francine asked succinctly.

"I don't know. I'm guessing that the General has a leak in his organization." Davina speculated. "I think he's been under some stress. Of course, we caused some of that. Or it could be he's just getting sloppy."

"We need to find out how badly we've been compromised."

Davina bit her lip. "Well, about that. Grandfather says we need to do something about the General."

The connection was quiet for a moment as Francine considered the gravity of what her partner had just said. "Does that mean what I think it means?"

"I'm afraid it does." Davina confirmed.

"This scares me a bit. Did he give you an indication of how fast this has to happen?"

"He didn't specify a date, but I'm thinking that it has to be soon."

Francine watched the traffic zipping northbound on Interstate 15. It was just after six o'clock and people were already eager to start their day. "We've got the first two million in the account. If he's not already aware of this falling apart, we'll have another two million this coming Monday...two more days. I'm starting your way and should be back there tomorrow night. Assuming the transfer takes place Monday as arranged, let's plan a party for him Monday night. If we have to move sooner, we will."

⸻ ◦《◉》◦ ⸻

Lenny Hart gingerly rubbed his wrist. The marks left by the

handcuff were receding and the pain was now down to a level of mild irritation. "Thanks again for sending the feds to bail me out of there."

Paul nodded. "It was because of your employment here that you were abducted. Thus, it is I who owes you a debt of gratitude. In the meantime, however, we need to know as much as we can about your abductors so that we can begin to backtrack their leadership." Paul spread a series of photographs out on his desk and turned them around so that Hart could see them.

"This is a gentleman named Dale Braun, a retired Army Major." He said pushing it closer to Hart with his index finger. "Does he look familiar?"

Hart shook his head. "Huh uh."

Paul then nudged the next photo an inch closer. "Francine Dantonio, also ex-Army and later CIA. How about her?"

Hark shook his head again. "Nope. She doesn't look familiar either.

Paul slid the third photo across but was cut-off as Lenny smacked his hand down. "That's her. The woman on the plane!"

"Davina Foxwell. Sometimes goes by the nickname of *Dave* and has been using the abbreviated surname of Fox in most meetings and correspondence since retiring from the US Army Criminal Investigations Division four years ago."

Paul opened a dark brown file folder and withdrew an eight-by-ten color photo of an African American male, obviously taken postmortem. "You were a police officer for many years, so I assume that you've seen autopsy photos before." He oriented the photograph in front of Hart. "Jerome Demetrius Jones, also known as Jerry. Forty-one years old, retired Sergeant First Class, US Army. Three tours overseas, Silver Star recipient his third time out. Bronze Star and Purple Heart on his first tour."

Hart nodded. "That's Jerry, all right, but he's looked better. He's the guy who dosed me when Francine got me outside the terminal. Hit me in the shoulder with some kind of injection. I was woozy before, but that took the fight right out of me."

Paul pushed the other two photographs towards Lenny. They were colored *booking* photos provided by the FBI. "Clayton Stanford and this is Sigurd Arnesen, sometimes known as *Siggie*. The men who attempted to abduct your wife."

Hart carefully examined the faces, hatred visible in his eyes. He was personally offended and wanted to see them punished severely. He fantasized about what he would do to them if given the opportunity. "Never seen either one of them before."

Paul collected the photos and stacked them on the corner of his desk. "Each and every one of the operators we have identified had an honorable, unblemished, and highly decorated career in the military. No misfits. No *Section 8's*. There is nothing in any of their backgrounds to make anyone believe that they could become rogue mercenaries. Stanford and Arnesen were MARSOC, Marine special forces. Both highly decorated combat veterans."

Hart did not care about their contributions or professionalism. To him, they were vermin. "What ties them all together?"

"We're still checking. They were all employed by a contractor group that does covert operations for a number of federal agencies. They seem to be well-funded and equipped. Considering the nature of their work, and what we found out by debriefing their people is that they believe they are supporting Homeland Security in some sort of anti-terrorism capacity. They think they are the good guys."

"How can that be?" Hart asked.

"Someone with high-level access has recruited and trained military personnel to serve in an anti-terrorism capacity, but through a privatized agency. The State Department and other agencies have been doing it for years. It affords the agency the cover of deniability. It keeps information out of the hands of the public. It prevents someone from getting ahold of something that could be disclosed through the Freedom of Information Act."

Paul placed his hands in his lap and spoke softly. "Much of what we do here has been privatized. Our work started in academia and research and eventually found its way to the CIA. Several years ago, it became obvious that we needed to return it to the private sector so that we could restrict knowledge of it."

"I understand that." Hart acknowledged. "But how do you take career soldiers and Marines, professionals of the highest caliber, and get them to abduct or murder US citizens?"

"Easy." Paul pursed his lips. "They tell the operatives that they are investigating or intercepting foreign agents or terrorists. The individuals involved in the operations think they are working for the United States government. But, in reality, they are being lied to by their superiors. Have you ever heard of the *false-flag* operation?"

"Exactly. What we are finding is that these people thought they were working on behalf of the United States Government. But they weren't. Somewhere in Washington is a puppet-master who has been pulling strings for his or her own personal benefit."

Hart tried to clear the fog of revenge out of his head. "The two individuals the Bureau busted at my house; they thought they were going after some sort of terrorist?"

"That is what they told the arresting agents. They have agreed to sit for polygraphs, but I don't know if the Bureau has administered them yet." When Hart did not respond, he continued. "I can imagine how you feel right now, but I must ask you to put aside your feelings of animosity until we sort through all this. I need you here and I need you to have a clear mind."

Hart nodded. "Whatever you need."

————))(((◦))(((————

Darren Baranowski popped his jaw and tried to equalize the pressure in his ears as the wide-body jet lined up for the approach to Daniel K. Inouye airport in Honolulu. The weather was clear, and the sun was out, and he felt like he needed thirty hours of sleep. It seemed like it took forever to find the gate, roll-up the jetway, and open the hatch, allowing the travelers, who had been unpleasantly entombed in coach seats during the four-hour delay and the six-and-a-half-hour flight from Seattle, to finally get out of their confinement and begin enjoying Hawaii.

Fort Shafter, while only eleven and a half miles away, was usually a thirty-minute drive once one had collected one's luggage. While in the baggage claim area he turned his phone back on and began sifting through the multitude of emails that had come in during the last thirty-six hours and tried to prioritize them in his mind. Obviously, the junk mail could be deleted immediately, but there were a few from his commander, and naturally one from a neurotic and insecure General from the Space Force.

Once he had located his bag, he stepped outside into the warm tropical early morning darkness, a far cry from what he had experienced in the last few days from the top of an arid mountain in Chile, to the incessant cold of an island in the Bering Sea. If he didn't catch a cold because of the severe climatic changes, it would be a miracle.

By the time the military flight had gotten him back to Kodiak and from there to Anchorage to catch the connection to Seattle, his exhaustion had become exacerbated by the revelation that the flight was going to be delayed for a few minutes while they replaced some sort of equipment that was deemed necessary to keep them airborne. A few minutes turned into a few hours. It was now well after midnight, but he was nevertheless delighted to be home. He waited next to the terminal for some tourists to pass by and then made the call.

When the General answered, some forty-eight hundred miles away, he tried to be as cordial as he could, but was simply too tired to make it work. "I'm back in Honolulu. I'm afraid we don't have a lot to report, but I can tell you that no one has seen what we're looking for. Both staffers are extremely well-acquainted with the protocols to report it when they find it."

The General was quiet for a moment as he digested the brief report. "Anything unusual?"

"Such as?" Lieutenant Colonel Baranowski was not in a mood to play guessing games.

"Is anyone taking an interest in their work? Asking unusual questions of them? Following them around?"

Baranowski was at his wits end. "No, sir."

"You're certain?"

"May I remind the General that I spent my first two tours in the Military Intelligence branch before transferring to the Judge Advocate General's Office? I think I can debrief an operative."

General Scott paused at the insubordinate tone, but then continued on. "Yes, of course. Did either of them give any indication whatsoever of when they think this thing might become visible?"

"No. None. There's no traffic at Saint Paul Island, and our guy in Chile says that there's some sort of disruption, he called it a perturbation, of objects out past Neptune that would indicate that something large is out there, and might be getting closer, but so far nothing. It could be weeks or months. Maybe longer."

"Okay. Get some sleep. We'll talk tomorrow." He said in a dreary monotone and then rang off.

Baranowski started towards the taxicab line and then stopped. Resting atop one of the trash cans on the sidewalk, was a discarded copy of the day's newspaper, opened to the second page. He read the first few paragraphs of the story relating to the Subaru Telescope on top of Maunakea, a dormant volcano on the big island of Hawaii. The summit was close to fourteen thousand feet in the air, requiring visitors to go on nasal cannula oxygen for their tours, but its location made it perfect for looking at the universe. The article listed some of the accomplishments of the telescope and team and then mentioned something that caught his eye. "Scientists now think that they will find a new planet in the next few months."

He slid the newspaper into the trash receptacle. "Well, shit. So much for secrecy. Everyone's going to have a piece of this."

⸻))•((⸻

It was a cool morning in Pleasant Prairie and the damp air was carrying the first scent of autumn leaves. Rain had passed through the area sometime during the night and the patio and dock still offered reflections of pooling in the dawn light. Karlsson sat in one of the deck chairs and sipped his coffee, looking out across the water. There were no boats to be seen anywhere on the horizon, but he had a feeling. He could sense that something was in the offing but did not want to make his paranoia known to Stan and Neri yet for fear that they might think he was suddenly becoming psychic himself.

It was more the byproduct of forty years in the business. Call it intuition or call it empiricism, Karlsson had a keen sense of awareness when the potential for violence loomed on the breathtaking magenta horizon. Some called it the *gift of fear*, including author Gavin deBecker, who in 1997 explored trends and patterns in a multitude of targeted attacks and taught the reader to trust their instincts by evaluating pre-incident indicators of violence. DeBecker's research was applicable to a variety of occupations and personal situations, but it nevertheless taught the reader to understand why the hair on the back of their neck occasionally stood up, and why they should listen to the signals.

He tossed the remnants of his coffee out and went back inside to have another look at the surveillance footage. The cameras at the rear of the house gave up nothing. There was very little marine traffic over the preceding two days, and they were confident that they had sorted out the couple on the Carver. Dale Braun was back in the DC area and under FBI surveillance. Francine Dantonio had fallen off the radar screen somewhere near Grand Junction, Colorado, but the feds were looking for her to pop up in an airport or train station. Her associate, Davina was also being watched, but it was obvious that she was quite skilled at countering surveillance. Her cell phone had been continually charging in her Georgetown apartment, however, the apartment had been empty for several days. Wherever she was sleeping, it wasn't her apartment or any of the DC-area hotels.

The Pentagon Police were also included in the project, to a

minor degree, in that they were supplying General Scott's access card records to the FBI, thanks to a FISA warrant. The FISA Court was a wonderful tool for certain elements of law enforcement, including the Bureau and the DEA. However, there had been questions of abuse arising over the level of actual *probable cause* that needed to be demonstrated prior to receiving this innovated information weapon, as rumors of illegal wiretaps emerged following presidential elections. The Justice Department claimed it had good control over the process. The Congress disagreed as warrant-after-warrant were overturned on technical grounds. However, neither Scott nor his superior, the Chief of Space Operations, knew that his activity was of interest.

Karlsson moved back in the file archives and switched to the cameras that captured the driveway and the public street just beyond. He looked at the street view for day-one of their stay and tried to see a trend or pattern of activity. Nothing. There was a white cargo van, northbound, that passed by once at eight-fifteen in the morning and again at two in the afternoon. Probably a local delivery service.

He moved on to day two and likewise, could find nothing that indicated a hostile surveillance. Then day three and day four. Nothing, until the northbound blue Toyota drove slightly off the right side of the street around two fifteen. He remembered a driver safety course he had taken years earlier, and the instructor's words. "You will drive where you are looking."

He immediately went back to day-one of his file and realized that both times the delivery van had passed their driveway, it veered slightly off the roadway on the right side. He, or she, was looking at their house. Maybe just checking address numbers on the mailboxes? He advanced to day two. As he moved quickly through the video, he paused at the silver Hyundai that drove northbound at nine o'clock. It too veered slightly to the right when passing the house.

On day three, it was a black Ford pickup, once at eight-thirty and again at four in the afternoon. Then of course, the Toyota on day four. That was it. That was the behavioral signature he had been looking for.

The Defense Department had been investigating behavioral signature in asymmetric warfare since 2007. Falling back on psychological theory from the early nineteen-hundreds, they tied certain signatures, or schemas, to people through repetitive use or display. In one case, they identified a terrorist in a hotel room by the way he tied his drink straws into a knot. Every morning, room service workers picked up his tray from the previous evening and found a single straw tied into a knot and dropped in the empty glass.

Another time, it was a cigarette butt; the repetitive practice the suspect displayed of tearing the paper off, down to the filter, before leaving it in the ashtray. It was a signature. Something that the person did sub-consciously that set them apart from others. A uniqueness that could help isolate and identify them from other suspects.

Marchand joined him at the table. "You look deep in thought. What's up?"

"I'm still putting it together." Karlsson responded as he made some notes on a pad. "I think Dale and Francine were only part of the surveillance. They might even have been the decoys we were supposed to see."

"What?" Marchand leaned over.

"I'm looking at the video on the front of the house for the period we've been here. No one-single car has buzzed us on more than one day. But look at this." He clicked through the various video files and walked Stan through his thoughts."

"The first day, it's the white van. Notice how he drives slightly off the roadway right here? He's looking to his right. Watch as he goes down the street, he makes the next left turn and rides his brakes through the turn."

"Day two...the silver Hyundai. It veers off the road to the right, in front of our house, turns left on the next street north of us and rides his brakes through the turn."

Karlsson clicked on the next file. "Black Ford pickup truck. Veers to the right here, and makes the next turn left, riding his brakes through the turn. And this one, the blue Toyota. Same thing."

Stan stared at the screen for a moment. "Same driver every day, different car."

Karlsson moved back to the day-two file. "Fuck. Look at this!" He used his mouse to draw a mask around the area of the silver Hyundai's license plate, and enlarge it, and then compared it to his notes.

Marchand frowned. "Fuck is right. All four vehicles have the same license plate."

"It looks like a Wisconsin Dealer's plate, but I can't make out the numbers." Karlsson squinted at the laptop screen.

Marchand adjusted the screen to see if it improved his view. "Someone owns a used-car lot and is using the inventory to drive past here every day?"

"Usually twice." Karlsson added. "I think it's time to play offense again. We might have a few minutes before he makes his regular morning pass. I'm taking the van up the street and sitting around the corner where he makes his left turn. When I see those plates go by on the vehicle-du jour, I'll tail him and see where he goes."

Karlsson grabbed a few items from his bedroom, including a set of binoculars and the 9mm Glock and snatched the keys off the counter. "I'll sit for a while and if he doesn't turn up, I'll be back for lunch." He smiled mischievously and headed to the garage.

He offered a quick wave to Neri as she reached the bottom of the stairs. "There's a quiche in the oven. I'm off for some early morning hunting."

She waved back with a curious look and then glanced at Stan who nodded back. "Get your coffee. I'll explain."

Moments later, Karlsson was down the street, around the corner, and parked off the roadway on 116th Street so that he could see vehicles westbound from the intersection where the suspect vehicles had all turned. It wasn't perfect, but on short notice, it was the best he could put together. He switched the ignition off and moved to the back seat so that he could relax with his back up against the passenger side frame.

About ten minutes later, his initiative was rewarded as a north-bound Honda CRV turned the corner and headed west. It seemed reasonably clean, but the only thing he cared about was the Wisconsin auto dealer's license plate. All things considered; it was a perfect car for surveillance work as it had been one of the top selling vehicles in the US for the past few years. The male driver appeared to be in his middle to late thirties with brown hair, cut short. Clean shaven, he wore aviator sunglasses and a Green Bay Packers wind breaker. He pulled off the roadway about a hundred feet in front of the van, and appeared to make some notes, his foot still riding the brakes.

A few seconds later, he was off again headed west. Since there was little traffic, Karlsson allowed the CRV to get several hundred yards away before he put the transmission in gear and pulled into the roadway. As he crossed over Sheridan Road he noticed the traffic starting to pick up so he decreased the separation distance just enough that he could make it through traffic lights with the suspect vehicle, but not so close as to call attention to his presence.

At Green Bay Road, the white CRV turned north for a few blocks before turning right again on 104th Street for a moment, and then made an immediate right into Marquette Used Cars. Karlsson drove past the car lot about five hundred feet and turned north onto Old Green Bay Road, where he could turn around and watch and wait. In minutes, he saw his quarry emerge from the small office and get into a late model Dodge Challenger, styled in the most sickening color of purple he had ever seen. The car turned west on 104th and accelerated. Karlsson followed.

Just past the entrance to Bristol Park, near the end of 104th, the Challenger turned north on a small road and then into the driveway of a modest red-brick split-level home with a gravel driveway and a two-car garage. Karlsson drove past and found that the road dead-ended into some sort of agricultural facility where he was able to turn around.

It was the first opportunity he'd had to text Marchand. "TAILED WHITE MALE, 30ISH TO HOUSE." He provided the address and the license plate number of the visually revolting Challenger. "TIME FOR A CHAT".

Karlsson saw an immediate thumbs-up icon as a reply and slowly returned in the direction of the suspect's house. He pulled into the driveway and parked about five feet behind the Challenger, making a quick glance around to see how private the property was. The place looked reasonably secluded with the agricultural facility a quarter mile away on one side of the woods and the nearest house about as far in the other direction. The garage door was down so he could not tell if there were other vehicles, or people, present.

The concrete in the sidewalk needed repair, perhaps from the frequent use of salt to dissolve ice over the course of many Wisconsin winters. The house itself appeared to be about forty years old and had been cared for through the years. The roof was new, but the windows looked as if they would need replaced soon. The doorbell looked tarnished and questionable, so Karlsson knocked on the door.

He could hear footsteps coming from inside before the door opened. The thirty-something lad appeared to be about five foot ten and a hundred eighty pounds. The Green Bay windbreaker was wrinkled and seemed to have shifted to his right side where a slight bulge indicated a cell phone or firearm.

"Yeah?"

Karlsson offered his warmest smile. "Hi! I'm Fred McGee, with the Wisconsin Department of Traffic Safety. Our toll cameras recorded your vehicle going through several toll booths without paying and you haven't responded to the numerous notices to pay up."

The young fellow squinted, "What the fuck are you talking about?"

Karlsson grinned and shrugged, and then turned quickly and threw himself against the door, sending the surprised lad reeling backwards. Karlsson immediately darted inside after him, kicking the front door shut as he blazed past. The young man tried to brace his fall with his hands and was in the process of pushing himself back upright when Karlsson stomped down hard on his crotch. As the unknown gent doubled up in pain, Karlsson then kicked him hard in the side of the leg, aiming for his common peroneal nerve, before rolling him over and dropping down on him with a knee in his back, wedging his arm up behind him.

He immediately found the Springfield 9mm in the fellow's nice little Kydex IWB holster and quickly drew it, cycling the slide one-handed, dragging it across the man's shoulder. A round ejected indicating that he had been carrying it with a round chambered, ready for use. As he forced the barrel into the base of the man's skull, he whispered. "It's good you know something about guns. This is a Springfield XD-M with a four point two-five-pound trigger. My finger is now applying about two pounds of pressure. Whatever you do, don't try to get up."

"What...?"

"Are we alone?" He whispered, ignoring the man's attempt to speak.

"Are you crazy? I'm a fucking cop!"

"I'll ask again and then I will hurt you. Are we alone?"

There was a pause as the surprised young man considered his options. "Yes. My wife and daughter went to the mall in Kenosha."

Karlsson quickly glanced around the room and noted a picture of the mystery man and a young woman in a frame on the Wurlitzer spinet piano. He didn't see any children's toys but that did not mean that there wasn't a child living there. He leaned a bit closer. "You don't want them to walk through that door and find you in a pool of your own blood. I promise you, it's a sight they'll never be able to erase."

"What do you want?" The anger evident in his voice.

"Why are you driving past our house every day?"

"You're making a big mistake!"

Karlsson glanced around again to check his surroundings and prevent tunnel vision and then reached down and pinched the fleshy part of the lad's inner thigh. After eliciting a small scream from his target, he whispered, "This is mild pain. It's a nuisance but leaves no permanent disfigurement. If you don't wise up and tell me what I need to know, the neighbors will report hearing louder screams before the gunshot. Investigators will determine that you were tortured before your death."

"I'm a part-time P.I.... an investigator. I was hired to see if a guy's wife was cheating on him with you."

"Name of the guy who hired you."

"It's confidential. I...aaaghhh!" Karlsson pinched another inch of flesh.

"Last chance to get it right. The next thing you feel will be my blade lacerating your nut sack."

The sudden creak of the floorboards caused Karlsson to glance up and he saw a well-built man in the long sleeve polo shirt approaching with a full-size revolver in his hand. The man had the look of a pro. It was too bad. He'd asked if they were alone. The fellow on the floor had referenced a missing wife and child, but nothing about a very large guy, armed, wearing *5-11* tactical pants and a uniform shirt. Karlsson couldn't waste time with idle verbose warnings to *drop the weapon* or perhaps something catchier that a storybook hero might have used in an action movie.

Karlsson fired twice in rapid succession, putting two rounds in the center of large man's chest about an inch apart. There was a look of shock and bewilderment on his contorted face as his legs collapsed. His eyes rolled up as life left him and he slumped over on his side. Karlsson sensed that the man under his knee was starting to squirm, so he put the hot barrel of the Springfield back into his neck. "Last chance." You can die brave like that gentleman or live to tell whatever story you want."

Karlsson was thinking quickly but was now committed to a course of action and had to play it out. "What's your name?"

"Phil Gasparro."

"What do you do, Phil Gasparro?"

"I told you, I'm a private investigator."

"Yes you did. What, exactly, were you supposed to be looking for on your daily passes?"

"I was supposed to report on vehicles. How many, you know,

get the license numbers. They wanted to know about activity, but from where the house is located, it was difficult to see anything but the driveway."

"Who paid you to watch us?"

"It...it was a referral from a friend in Washington."

Karlsson leaned in and forced his knee harder into the man's back as he reached down with his left hand and retracted the clip knife from his back pocket. With a quick flip, the blade opened with a distinctive *click*, and he shoved the point just deep enough in that it pierced the jeans and came to rest on flesh. It wasn't surgical precision, but it was close.

"I have no time for games, Phil. Don't make me beg."

"It's a referral from an associate. His name is Skip Malcolm. He's a retired FBI agent and every once in a while he sends me a case."

"Where do you know Malcolm from?"

"He was my CO, my commanding officer, when I was in the Army."

"And he just happened to get wind of a salacious liaison off Lakeshore Drive in Pleasant Prairie? All the way from Washington?"

There was another moment of silence. Karlsson was about to apply enough pressure on the knife to break the skin, when Gasparro finally offered, "I think it's from the guy they call *The Professor*."

"Right. And I'm Gilligan!"

"No! No, that's what Captain Malcolm, uh, Skip calls him. He has something to do with universities. I don't know his real name. We just call him The Professor. Malcolm probably knows him, so go ask him."

"Who's the dead guy here?"

"Ted. Ted Biechler."

"And what's Ted's story?"

"He's...was a guy I worked with on the police department."

"Which department?"

"Kenosha. We're actually reserve officers. We volunteer there. We, uh...own a car lot together."

Karlsson was trying to unravel the myriad of questions that

were pulsing though his brain. "Do you know who owns the house that you were watching?"

"I was told that you did. Aren't you Moffitt?"

Karlsson could not tell if Gasparro was just stalling for time, hoping that someone had heard the shots, or if he was being truthful. "There is no one named Moffitt on either side of us. The United States Government owns that house."

"You're full of shit!"

"I beg to differ, but it's immaterial at this point." It was now an official mess. There was a dead police officer, and another one who would soon alert authorities to the tall skinny guy who had invaded his home and threatened him at gunpoint. It looked like he was going to have to take a prisoner and hand him off to someone official, as soon as Washington figured out who that would be.

"Do you or Ted have handcuffs?" Karlsson asked, looking at the Smith and Wesson revolver laying on the floor between them.

"Yeah, Ted probably does." Gasparro shifted.

"Don't move. Keep your hands where I can see them!"

Karlsson got up off the demoralized volunteer cop and picked up the revolver to make sure it was out of play in case another scuffle ensued. He shoved the Springfield into his waistband and then checked the loads to make sure the revolver was loaded. Keeping Gasparro in his view, he patted the lifeless Ted's pockets and found his handcuffs. They seemed to be stuck on something in his pocket. He risked a glance down to see what was keeping them from coming out and then noticed the movement out of the corner of his eye. By the time he had looked back up, Gasparro's hand had gone to his ankle and was reaching for the hideout gun. It looked to be a smaller Glock, perhaps a single stack 9mm or even a .380. It didn't matter. There was no time for formalities or pleasantries. He simply raised the revolver and fired. Both shots struck the center of Gasparro's chest, and he collapsed as if a switch had been turned off.

It was no longer a question of ethics or empathy. Despite its simplicity, it was the only plan he could concoct that would pass a cursory forensic examination later in the day. He used his handkerchief to wipe his prints off the revolver and stuck it back in Ted's hand. He did the same with the Springfield and put it back in Gasparro's and then checked to see that both of the shell casings from the Springfield had ejected freely where they should have. He resecured the small Glock in Gasparro's ankle holster. The detectives would gather around, take pictures and measurements, and get the initial impression that the larger Ted knocked Gasparro to the ground at which point both men went for their guns. Both men hit their targets. The splatter patterns and trajectory angles would probably bear that out. If they did gunshot residue testing on the two men's hands, they might conclude that neither fired a weapon. But then, maybe Paul could work with the local FBI office to help sell the story, if it went that far.

He examined the front door and then looked around the room once again. Other than the two dead men in the middle of a crime scene that didn't look nearly as staged as it was, nothing else was amiss. There were no marks on the door to indicate a forced entry, and from what he could tell, no cameras that might have recorded his arrival. No footprints in the blood. There were no curious crowds collecting on the front lawn, and no sirens in the distance. It would have to do. He pulled the door shut behind him and then pocketed his handkerchief. It was a shame that Gasparro's wife and daughter would walk in and find them there, just as he had warned. But there was nothing that could be done about that now. Yes, it was now an official mess indeed.

Francine drove Interstate 80 hard, all the way to Lincoln, Nebraska, more than 880 miles in twelve hours, stopping only for gasoline. Her choice of routes enabled her to avoid any State Police checkpoints on Interstate 70 coming out of Grand Junction and the likely airports the feds might watch in Grand Junction, Denver, and Salt Lake. She had no idea if agents were waiting for her anywhere, but with an ABORT-5 signal she was not willing to take any chances. Once in Lincoln, she headed straight to the Duncan Aviation FBO to grab a chartered flight into Manassas, which she had arranged the day before. Money was no object.

She found Davina waiting for her outside the terminal building in a silver Jeep Grand Cherokee, and they were quickly on their way up Wakeman Drive to Gateway Boulevard towards the hotel near the Manassas National Battlefield.

So named for the Battles of First and Second Manassas, or Bull Run, depending on the political perspective of the person telling the story, it was the place where Confederate General Thomas J. Jackson was given the nickname *Stonewall*, after capturing the Union Army supply depot at Manassas Junction. The first battle being fought on July 21, 1861, it was considered the first significant battle of the American Civil War. And despite the disorganized and undisciplined prosecution, on both sides of the battlefield, there were many lessons learned about how to wage war in that day and age. By the time it was over May 26, 1865, there were an estimated million and a half casualties on both sides.

Davina checked her rear view and side mirrors. "Tired?"

"Oh yeah." Francine replied as she adjusted her seat to give herself more leg room. "What's the latest?"

Davina glanced at her with a small grin. "The good news is that the General's money hit our account this morning as planned. I moved it to the Cayman's and closed out the Tbilisi account. If he gives up the account number to anyone, they won't find it."

Francine grimaced. "And? The bad news?"

Davina checked her side mirror as she changed lanes. "Well, for one thing, there's nothing more from Grandfather. We still have to plan something for the General tonight."

"We can't have another car accident. They're still fishing around with Babic's."

"Yeah, and we can't spike his drink. I think he's probably suspicious of that technique by now as well." She looked at her partner. "You said for *one thing*. What's the other?"

Davina went around the slower car and merged back into her lane. "You can't go home. I think the feds are on us. Probably the FBI. I pulled another ID set out and got us a room. As long as they don't compare notes with the CIA, our new IDs should be good for a while."

"Can't grandfather help get them off our backs?"

"Doubtful." She turned briefly to her right before returning her eyes to the road. "I'm betting that he doesn't know, and I don't think we want to tell him."

"What do you mean?" Francine asked.

"If the feds are onto the General, it is probably a classified op that is closely safeguarded. They would likely only read-in the agents that were directly involved in the surveillance. Grandfather was only aware of the trap waiting for us in Grand Junction. If he thought that any of us were being watched on a larger scale, he would have told us, or broken off contact already. The fact that he's still giving us stuff to do makes me think that he is unaware of any major investigation."

"So, he wants the General out of the way just in case?"

Davina nodded. "Uh huh. That, or Gramps truly thinks he's becoming reckless and straying from the plan. Whatever his plan is."

"I wish we knew more. This is getting intense, and I think there's a lot more on the table than a few million bucks."

Davina backed the Cherokee into a parking space near the lobby of the hotel. "Our room is on the second floor, right up there." She pointed at the window. I know you're tired, but I thought maybe we'd just share a room. You know, until we have a better understanding of what's going on."

Francine looked at her with a knowing smile and touched her lightly on the cheek. "Perfect. It will be good to catch up."

CHAPTER 16

Former Army Captain and retired FBI Special Agent Trevor Malcolm eased himself into the chair and asked Jimmy, his barber for the past twenty years, to trim the sides.

Jimmy lifted the flowing gray locks on the sides of his customer's bald head with his index finger. "You want 'em high and tight, Skip, or just regulation?"

"Oh, just regulation. I've been playing the part of the aging hipster for too long. I have a meeting with a big client today and he's a bit conservative, so I thought I'd look more like what he expects."

"As you wish." Jimmy smiled and grabbed a water bottle to spray his favorite customer's hair down before going after it with the shears. "Got any new stories for us today?"

"Ah, Jimmy, you know. I was a cyber-geek for twenty-five years. I never ran down spies or got in shoot-outs with bank robbers. As a matter of fact, other than regular qualifications, I never had my gun outta da holster." He said trying to mimic a Chicago accent that, in his mind, Elliot Ness might have had.

"What are you working on now?" He asked, comb and clippers working in unison.

Malcolm's mind drifted. "Nothing much. Just chasing cheating spouses. In cyber-world anyway." Despite his outward calm, he was concerned that he hadn't heard back from his investigator in Wisconsin. It was unusual in that, until yesterday, he had received a report every afternoon at five o'clock. When he didn't receive his daily briefing on time, he sent an email that went unanswered, and left a voice message that had been yet unreturned.

The purpose of the day's meeting in Alexandria was to brief

Dr. Newell on the investigation's progress. Moffitt, the tall skinny man in his sixties, was up for a tenured position at one of the most prestigious universities in the country and the rumors that he was having an affair with another professor's wife had to be put to bed. No pun intended. It was important that they knew all the people with whom Professor Moffitt had been in contact so that there were no surprises when announcements were made publicly. They were already aware that Moffitt had somehow obtained a false passport under the name of Karlsson and had taken an attractive young lady to Mexico for dubious purposes. But when Malcolm had attempted to make contact with the target and his trophy girlfriend at the Coco Bongo in Cancun, he had apparently spooked them somehow and the couple gave him and his associate the slip. Pretty good intuition for a professor of history, he mused.

Jimmy had just put the finishing touches on his masterpiece and was brushing Malcom's shoulders off with a small whisk broom when his customer's cell phone rang.

Malcolm glanced at the caller ID and said, "Sorry Jimmy, I need to take this."

"It's about time! I thought you were ignoring me." Malcolm said, somewhat anxious.

The line was quiet for a moment, and then an unidentified female voice asked, "Is this Mr. Malcolm?"

"Yes. This is Skip Malcolm. Who's this" He looked again at the phone to see that it was Gasparro's caller ID.

"This is Special Agent Tina Cowels with Wisconsin DCI, the Division of Criminal Investigation. We're investigating a double homicide that occurred in the last twenty-four hours and one of the victims had your name and number in his phone. It looks like you were speaking regularly?"

"Phil Gasparro?" The retired FBI agent had already put it together considering the investigator was using Gasparro's phone to call him.

"Correct. May I ask what your relationship was to the victim?"

"Yes. I'm a retired FBI agent and run a private security firm out of the DC area. I was using him on a case out your way. What happened?"

The DCI agent thought for a moment. "We're still investigating, and this is obviously not for publication, but it appears that he had some sort of altercation with his partner, and they shot each other. What type of case was he working on for you?"

Malcolm stared at the floor and shook his head in disbelief. He had lost friends and associates before so he should not have felt so affected. "Oh, it was nothing really. It was a part of a vetting for a university professor who's up for tenure and a promotion. Gasparro was doing activity checks, maybe a little surveillance, to see who the professor was entertaining."

"Is that a common thing?" The DCI Agent asked.

"I suppose. We get these types of cases from time to time. Organizations want to make sure that they're not about to get blind-sided by something after they come out with a public announcement. You know, woke-ism and all that. Companies, or in this case universities, are afraid that they'll bring someone into a high-profile position and then find out that when they were younger, they were part of a radical group, or robbed a liquor store or something."

Agent Cowels made some notes and then asked, "Can I get the name and address of the person Gasparro was investigating?"

"You think there's a connection?"

"No. Not really. But you know the game. We have to follow up on every lead. I promise to be discreet."

Malcolm gave the agent the information she requested and after hanging up thought through the discussion he'd had with Dr. Newell the week before. Even though most of his years at the Bureau had been behind a monitor, he could not help but think that Newell hadn't been completely truthful about his request. This seemed like a relatively minor case that someone of Newell's stature would never have dirtied his hands over. He knew there had to be more to the story. Was it Newell's wife that Moffitt was having the affair with? He shrugged it off as he reached for two twenty-dollar-bills in his pocket. "Here you go Jimmy. Keep the change!"

He turned to leave and thought about the obvious statistics. Somewhere in the world friends had disputes every day and sometimes, they killed each other. Apparently Wisconsin was one of those places.

———— ((())) ————

Marco Pozos rolled over in bed when he heard the shower start to flow. It had been a wonderful evening of music and love. He was content. He liked having Margarita there and the sounds of her bumping around in the bathroom made him feel somehow complete, like a couple should. He found his shorts on the floor and stepped into them and then wandered out into the kitchen to start the coffee. He carefully measured the scoops, and then added water to the tank and then hit the start button. In a few minutes he could look forward to his addictive drug of choice.

It was only by chance that he happened to notice that her laptop, resting on the kitchen table was open to her documents. What caught his attention was that her screen saver usually kicked in within a few minutes of inactivity. The fact that it was still open to a document meant that she had been working on something before jumping into the shower. A part of his brain told him that whatever it was, it was none of his business. On the other hand, he was supposed to be a covert agent on assignment and thus be fully aware of his environment. Besides, he was childishly curious.

The document file title was *Diario*, and at first glance, seemed to be fifty-three pages in length. He took note of where the cursor was, so that he could return there prior to getting back to his coffee, and his eyes quickly jumped across the page to where he saw his name.

A hollowness in his stomach crept its way up his throat as he read, "Subject Pozos was isolated and interviewed at which point it was determined that neither him nor anyone else on the team has found X yet but have seen disruptions in some of the astral bodies that could indicate its presence. His only external contact observed thus far has been a US Army Lieutenant Colonel named Baranowski, who made a special trip to see him. They spoke privately, outdoors for about fifteen minutes, but subject has not referenced their conversation in social situations before."

His heart sank. In her fifty-three-page diary, she had reported on all of the scientists employed at VRO but had paid special attention to him and Jean Luc. He returned the cursor to where he had first found it and quickly checked her outbound emails. The majority of them went back and forth to AURA, her employer. Her supposed employer, anyway. It would take more time than he had to go through each one of them individually, so he backed out and returned the screen to the page she had been on in her Diario. Then, as an afterthought, he locked the screen. It would be poor tradecraft indeed if she came out of the bathroom and found her screen not locked.

⸻))(()((⸻

Neri was in the shower and Marchand and Karlsson were having a cup of coffee at the kitchen table when the chime alerted them that a car had turned into their driveway. Marchand looked up at the monitor on the counter and said, "I've got it."

The woman was about five-foot-six and solidly built, wearing a dark pantsuit that would have screamed *law enforcement* even if she hadn't gotten out of the black Dodge Charger with the cheap wheel covers and ram bumper. He was still in his sweats and University of Cincinnati t-shirt and was smiling as he opened the door to greet her. She was, after all, sort of expected.

"Dr. Moffitt?" She asked as she presented her badge and credentials. "I'm Tina Cowels, with the Wisconsin Division of Criminal Investigation."

"I think you have the wrong house." Stan replied, still smiling.

"Really?" She opened her notebook and looked at the address she had received from Skip Malcolm. "This is the address I was given." She continued unabated as she slid a color photograph from the slot in her notebook. "Do you know a Philip Gasparro?" She held the driver's license scan up for him to see.

"No." He responded truthfully, aware that she was studying his reaction.

"You haven't seen him in the neighborhood?"

"Not at all. But again, my name isn't Moffitt. There are no Moffitts here, anywhere in the neighborhood as far as I know."

"I see. May I get your name, sir?"

"Yeah, sure. It's Stan Gable. Stanley, actually."

"Mr. Gable, I apologize for the inconvenience, but could I see some ID?"

Stan grinned a bit more. "Certainly. Just a minute." He closed the door just enough to let her know she was not invited in, but not enough to make it look like he was hiding something. He went into his bedroom, retrieved the Gable passport from the top dresser drawer and grabbed his reading glasses.

"Here you go." He said has he handed it to her, opened to the page with his photo.

She flipped through it and smiled back. "Just getting back from Mexico?" She returned the passport to him open to the page with the Customs stamp.

"Yes. I did some diving down around Cozumel and Cancun."

"Thank you, sir." She pulled another photograph out of her notebook. "Have you seen this man in the neighborhood?"

Marchand pulled his reading glasses down and fought to keep a reaction from being visible. "Uh, no. Who is he?"

"No idea." She said, replacing the photo in her notebook. "A private investigator was supposedly following this guy. We found it with some of his personal effects."

Marchand winced a bit. "Personal effects? That makes it sound like he's not with us anymore."

"You could say that." She flipped a page in her notebook and asked, "Just what is United Sterling Steel Structures, Incorporated?"

Stan's grin widened. "You do your homework, Detective. That's the company I work for. They own this property." She had checked with the county records office to see who the property was deeded to before she made the trip. "It's a play on words; Sterling Steel, like sterling silver. It's supposed to make you think our products are all as valuable as silver." It was actually the brainchild of someone at the US Secret Service's Asset Forfeiture Division who had no creative instincts whatsoever. Same initials. Nevertheless, it would not have been prudent for the Secret Service to run a covert safe house when the property records were visible for everyone to see.

"It's Special Agent. Well, sorry to have troubled you." She gave him her card. "Here, if you see this guy around town, please give me a call." She turned and walked away, her jacket flaring over her belt, which was laden with the standard issue of gun, extra magazines, handcuffs, pepper spray and heaven knew what else.

Marchand waved as he closed the door and then returned to the kitchen.

He handed Karlsson her business card. "Here, Dr. Moffitt. Apparently the guy you killed yesterday had a picture of you with the name *Moffitt* written on the back."

"That's what Gasparro called me. I've never used that name before anywhere. How did he get a picture of me? We haven't been in town that long."

"It wasn't a recent shot. You looked younger, and it was taken in the desert. As a matter of fact, it looked like it was in front of a fucking whale."

Karlsson was stunned. He went into his browser and pulled up a photograph of Ethyl the Whale, an eighty-two-foot full size sculpture of a blue whale, which was made entirely from recycled plastics. Created by two artists in San Francisco to bring awareness to the impact of discarded plastics on the environment, it was moved to Santa Fe Community College in 2019.

"That photo had to be taken five years ago. Aaron Capaz, my

veterinarian's son, took me there one afternoon. He was a student who worked for me on the ranch part-time. How the hell did they get that shot?"

"And why would they think you're a Dr. Moffitt?" Marchand thought out loud.

A momentary wave of guilt swept over Karlsson. "Gasparro was telling me the truth. He really thought I was having an affair with some guy's wife. He said he got the case from an associate in Washington. A retired FBI agent, named Malcolm. I think he called him Skip."

"That should be easy enough to find. Just a minute." Stan rang Dan Noble, the former Secret Service agent who had been so helpful in providing the van for their use. He gestured at Karlsson when he heard it ringing.

"Hi Dan, it's Stan. Listen, do you still have that directory for the FBI Special Agents Association?"

"Yeah. Hold on just a minute." Karlsson could hear the vibrant baritone voice through the phone's earpiece. There was a pause in the conversation and then he returned, "Who are you trying to find?"

"Someone out in the DC area named Skip Malcolm. I think Skip is probably a nickname."

"Malcolm, hmmm...here it is, I think. There's a Trevor *Skip* Malcolm on Kelley Drive in Fairfax, Virginia. Want that one?"

"Yeah, please." Stan replied and grabbed a pen off the kitchen counter. He carefully copied the address, telephone number and email for the retired agent. "Thanks, brother! I owe ya!"

Marchand looked at Karlsson, "Let's pass this along to Paul and see what he'd like us to do. One of us needs to stay here with Neri, but with the locals looking for an old philanderer named Moffitt, I think it's time you could use a change of scenery."

Karlsson nodded, deep in thought. For some reason, that name sounded familiar. "Agreed. I'll start packing."

Trevor Malcolm had taken the Metro's Yellow Line and gotten off at the Eisenhower Avenue Station. That time of day, it was much easier than trying to drive and find a place to park near the National Science Foundation building in Hoffman Town Center. He entered the main lobby and let the security officer know who he was and who he was there to see. The guard made a quick phone call, checked his driver's license, and then handed him a Visitor badge. "Yes, sir. Please have a seat over there and someone will be down for you in a minute."

Malcolm chose not to sit as it usually wrinkled his clothes, and he wanted to look crisp for the Professor. He wandered around the lobby and marveled at the architecture of the single atrium space that processed guests for the two interconnected office towers. The first tower was nineteen stories tall and the other fourteen. The building also featured an underground parking facility that accommodated three hundred eighty cars. The impressive, curved facades on the south sides of the buildings were aesthetically pleasing and defined the neighborhood for blocks around. Very impressive indeed for a government building, but then it wasn't their money anyway.

It was not long before he heard the clip-clop of high heels on the granite floor and turned to see the attractive thirty-year old in the dark gray pencil skirt. "Hello, Mr. Malcolm. I'm Jeanine. Doctor Newell asked me to show you to the conference room. Would you follow me?"

They took the elevator to the ninth floor and then turned left down a hallway that seemed busy with people of all ages, dressed from business-formal to gruffy-grubby, rushing to and fro like characters in a fifties-era Broadway play. Jeanine paused at the door to a small conference room that had seats for ten people. "If you'll make yourself comfortable, Dr. Newell will be along in a minute. There's water and coffee on the counter there. Please help yourself."

She smiled and headed down the hall to join the rest of the busy bees. Malcolm chuckled. He was glad he was retired and no longer had to live like that. He grabbed a bottle of water off the counter and then took a look out the windows at the traffic below. People walking, driving, biking their way through life, oblivious to everything around them. Immersed only in their own problems, victories, and failures. The bottle crackled as Malcolm unscrewed the cap and took a swig. He was replacing the cap when he heard the door close. He turned and looked at the successful bureaucrat, immaculately attired in his customary blue pinstripe suit, clean-shaven and hair combed, proudly accentuating the white strip running front to back.

"Mr. Malcolm." He smiled artificially as he extended his hand.

"Dr. Newell. Nice to see you again." Malcolm replied, remaining standing until Newell indicated that it was appropriate to sit.

Newell crossed his legs at the knees and folded his hands in his lap. It was a practiced pose. A poker pose, someone might even say. It was the posture of a person who did not want to give anything away to his opponents at the poker table, or the negotiations table for that matter. "Your message said that it was urgent that we meet. What did you develop that you did not feel comfortable sharing on the phone?"

"It's about the case in Wisconsin."

"Yes?" Newell replied without any obvious interest.

"Please tell me again what the predication and nexus was for this investigation." Malcolm watched his client carefully.

Newell was unaffected by the question and answered in a monotone. "As I explained, the individual I asked you to investigate is a professor who is up for a significant promotion that would elevate his, and the university's, media profile."

"Yes, but which university?" Malcolm studied Newell's behavior and detected the slightest shift in his posture. The retired agent was building a mental library of *timing and clusters*.

CIA polygraphers years earlier had established that there were certain behaviors, or tells, that humans of all cultures and civilizations gave off when they were uncomfortable or deceptive about a particular interview question. Anyone could learn to lie convincingly, but even the most skillful liars often forgot about what happened to their bodies three to four seconds after the lie. Once the lie was out of their mouth, they suddenly felt that they could relax, or even prepare themselves for the next lie. The key for the interviewer was to simply ask the questions and see which ones achieved a physiological response two or three seconds after the answer. Malcolm was looking for clusters of activity within that time zone.

"Why is that germane to the investigation?" Newell was attempting to retain control of the interview and stall for time while avoiding having to answer.

"Because the investigator I hired out there was killed in a shooting yesterday."

Newell was motionless. He wanted to react but dared not. Malcolm was nothing more than hired help and he was not ready to take any new players on his team. "Excuse me?"

No indication of empathy. Just another attempt to delay answering the question. "My investigator was killed in a shooting and local detectives would like to know if it was connected to my case or not. Before I speak further with them, I wanted to get a better understanding of what this case is about and why a senior executive at the National Science Foundation would care about a particular university's public relations problems."

"What have you told them so far?" Newell asked, with only mild interest showing through.

Malcolm was silent. His questions had been met not with answers, but with other questions. He was waiting for it. He stared at Newell across the table, without expression. The silence was growing awkward and then he saw it. Newell shifted in his seat again and then tugged at his sleeve as if to straighten it. It was quiet in the room for a few more seconds before Newell repeated himself. "I asked you what you have told them thus far."

"I know what you asked, Dr. Newell. I'm waiting for an answer to my question before I begin answering yours."

Newell was motionless in his chair, but his face began to redden. He was not used to being spoken to by subordinates in this fashion. "I believe it was Yale."

Malcolm had been ready. "It was not. I checked there and they have no professors named Moffitt. In any department."

"Then it must have been Harvard."

Malcolm hated being lied to. His concerns about the relevance of his case to the death of Phil Gasparro had been building logarithmically since he had gotten off the Metro. The more he shared space with Newell, the creepier the vibes he got from him. "Maybe it was Topeka State? Regardless, how does a minor vetting for some college professor get the attention of the Director of Government Affairs of the NSF? Who is this guy Moffitt? Really?"

Newell rose. "I think we are finished here, Mr. Malcolm. Please submit your invoice to my office and it will be processed in accordance with our contract." He turned to leave but stopped by the door as Malcolm offered a parting comment.

"You know, Dr. Newell, under the laws of the State of Virginia, our agreement is considered confidential unless I am required by subpoena or other court order to provide complete details of my investigation to law enforcement."

⸺⸺((◐))⸺⸺

Founded in 1731, the town of Woodbridge began as a village made up of plantations and through the years morphed into farms and industrial complexes. Comfortably nestled at the end of the Occoquan River where it dumped into Belmont Bay and Powell's Creek, it was an area steeped in history.

Known as the Occoquan Creek throughout most of the nineteen hundreds, the Occoquan River is a tributary of the Potomac River in Northern Virginia, where it serves as an official border between Fairfax and Prince William counties. During the 1800's, geographers would say that it was the border between the American North and American South.

The Occoquan has three dams along its length. The first is located in the actual town of Occoquan, a reservoir belonging to the

Fairfax County Water Authority, and further North is Lake Jackson. The dam that created Lake Jackson served as a hydroelectric facility but had ceased operations many years earlier. The third dam, up Broad Run near its confluence with Cedar Run, formed Lake Manassas. As expected, local residents and tourists enjoyed a variety of water sports around the area, throughout most of the year. Many of them had boats.

General Scott's luxurious house was built years after the Civil War but still had the stately look of antebellum. The gravel driveway went around the house to a two-car coach house at the rear of the three-story brick structure, and white columns supported the two-story high portico.

Francine and Davina arrived in their rental car; a model they selected specifically for its plainness. It looked like every other vehicle in the US Government motor pool. Francine parked on the side of the house, so as not to block the black Honda Civic that presumably belonged to Luisa, General Scott's housekeeper. They had found that their Class B service uniforms still fit and that their hair still more or less complied with regulations. Thus, a ruse was selected that would guarantee them admittance, with a minimum of collateral violence. They did not want to hurt the housekeeper if they did not have to. Neither did they want to make her suspicious or give her a reason to remember them. Two female Army troops in uniforms and berets looked pretty much like all the others. Likewise, if neighbors were interviewed later, they would remember two women in uniform getting out of an official looking car, who left quietly sometime later.

Francine knocked on the door and waited for Luisa to greet them. Francine still had her CID badge that she waved at the unsuspecting woman with a warm smile. "Hi Luisa. General Scott asked us to come by and take a look at his internet and phones. I'm afraid there's been a bit of a concern about Russian and Chinese eavesdropping, and he doesn't want to take any chances."

Not understanding anything about espionage, but being basically intimidated by anyone in law enforcement, she quickly admitted them. Once inside, the ladies sat their official-looking equipment cases on the floor and Davina kept the charade going. "May we see your cell phone? We need to run a quick check on it to see if you might have downloaded a virus."

The anxious housekeeper complied while Davina opened her kit and took out a piece of complex-looking electronic equipment. "I don't think there's anything wrong, but we'll need you to leave your phone with us and we'll give you another one to use until tomorrow."

While Francine took the nervous housekeeper into the other room to explain the nuances of electronic eavesdropping, Davina used Luisa's phone to text the General. "THERE IS A LEAK IN THE CEILING OVER YOUR DESK IN THE DEN. PLEASE COME HOME. I NEED TO LEAVE AND DO NOT KNOW WHO TO CALL."

"WHAT KIND OF LEAK?" Was the General's response a moment later.

"I DON'T KNOW – THE CEILING LOOKS WET AND THERE IS WATER DROPPING DOWN."

"THERE IS A MAGNETIC BUSINESS CARD ON THE FRIDGE THAT HAS THE NAME OF A PLUMBER." He texted back.

"I AM SORRY – I HAVE TO LEAVE FOR AN APPOINTMENT."

Francine was sure that the General would be livid, but as materialistic as the old goat was, she knew he would be barreling out of the Pentagon just as fast as he could. This late in the afternoon, he would be driving himself since he wouldn't want to return to the District with all the traffic. Otherwise, there would be the complication of what to do with his driver.

Francine came back around the corner into the living room with Luisa trailing slightly behind. "Luisa wants to know if it's okay with the General if we send her home now."

"Absolutely!" Davina held the phone up for her to see. "I'm on with him right now."

"See?" Francine said as she handed Luisa the two crisp one-hundred-dollar bills. "It is quite all right. We will be sure to leave your phone on the kitchen counter so that you can pick it up in the morning. He wanted you to have this for your time today."

"Gracias. But, what of the phone that you have given me?" She asked.

Davina waved with a smile. "Just give it to the General when you see him tomorrow."

With that, she was gone. The black Honda turned around and headed back down the driveway.

"What do you think?" Francine asked. "Ten minutes to close out his work. Twenty minutes to get to his car. At this hour, a good forty-five minutes to get here. Fifty bucks says he'll roll down the driveway at five fifteen."

Davina thought about it for a moment. "He likes his stuff, but he's not going to break any records getting here. He may even try to get a plumber on stand-by while he's driving. I'm thinking closer to five thirty. I'll take the *over.*"

"You're probably right, but we have to plan for the narrowest window. We've got an hour. Maybe a couple minutes more."

Davina looked around the house as the ladies donned their nitrile gloves. In the back yard, near the river's edge was an old, flat-bottom rowboat that had to be fifty years old. They could see the arms of the heavy wooden oars sticking out above the bow. "Look at that, would ya."

Francine came around the corner. "Ah geez. More fucking boats. Which one of us is going to get wet?"

"What time does it get dark tonight?"

"Probably around six thirty."

"So, one way or the other, we have to wait till about seven to load his big ass in there?"

"Probably. Let's see what's in the garage."

They went through the kitchen and out across the gravel driveway on the side of the house. They opened the garage door and then flipped on the light. Davina exclaimed, "Wow! Look at that!"

The General's two-car garage was a bit dusty, but was temperature controlled and spacious enough to house the red 1973 Ferrari Berlinetta Boxer and the orange 1973 Lamborghini Miura. The year of manufacture was obvious as he had purchased Historical Vehicle plates FB 1973 and LM 1973, respectively. "Gee," Davina said sarcastically, "I wonder what year he was born?"

Francine looked over Davina's shoulder at the two classic cars. "Yeah! The old fart liked his sports cars! I wonder where he got the money to buy them. And this house!"

They stepped into the vintage garage and found the things they would have expected to find. Garden supplies, lawn care equipment, automotive tools. And a medium-sized dolly. The stainless-steel handtruck would easily handle two hundred pounds. "Well." Davina said, perhaps a bit calmer than a psychologist might have anticipated given the circumstances, "I think we know how to get him in the boat."

There were some other preparations the ladies had to make inside the house, after which they found his bar, poured some drinks, and waited for him. They were silent, for the most part. They were friends and comrades, sometimes more. But always professionals. For the rest of the evening, they were two pros who had agreed on a course of conduct, a tactical plan, and were just waiting for the time to implement it.

The sun began to recede in the west and parts of the house became dark. It was almost six o'clock when the timer in the den clicked the light on and they heard the tires on the gravel out front.

"To absent friends" Francine raised her glass in a toast.

"Absent friends." Davina nodded, and both women downed their drinks.

For all his paranoia and materialistic concerns, the General was not nearly as tactically proficient as he might have thought. He used his key to come through the front door and then went immediately upstairs. The ladies could hear the toilet flush, and then when he returned downstairs a few minutes later, he was wearing jeans and an old t-shirt. He went straight to the den to have a look at the ceiling and noticed that there was nothing wrong. No leak of any kind.

A moment later, Luisa's cell phone, on the sofa beside Davina, lit up. "I JUST GOT HOME – WHERE IS THE LEAK???"

Davina was feeling playful, "LO SIENTO MUCHO SENOR JEFE – ESTA EN LA OTRA QUARTO"

"WHICH ROOM?" He typed before he realized there was something wrong.

"Luisa? Where are you?" He yelled from the den.

"Luisa went home, Captain Kirk. We're in your living room. Come on in." Davina said it as smoothly as she could.

The General walked slowly into the room and looked at the two women, relaxing on his two opposing sofas. "Do I know you? What are you doing here?"

Davina opened the conversation, simply because she had a history of sorts with General Scott. Virtually, anyway. "Get yourself a drink, and sit down, General. We've got some news from Grandfather that you probably need to hear."

"Grandfather?" He asked as he moved towards the bar.

"Yeah." Francine explained. "That's our nickname for Newell. You might call him something else."

"Your selection of bourbons is exceptional, by the way!" Davina added. "I hope you don't mind that we helped ourselves."

"Not at all." The General replied as he lifted the towel on the second shelf to find that the .45 caliber Kimber 1911 that he usually kept there was now absent. He found a glass and dropped a handful of ice cubes in before covering them with a couple of ounces of Woodford Reserve. "So, then, what is the information that Dr. Newell wished you to convey to me this evening?"

"It's more like an exchange." Francine said. "We need to develop a status report of the entire operation and find out if we are progressing according to plan."

"You'll have to excuse me ladies, but I was not aware that you had been read-in to the project. My understanding was that you were involved in the pre-operational side of the project only." The General seated himself in a leather chair at the end of the coffee table between the two couches, his back to the bar.

"Well, General, things change. Times change. Dr. Newell thinks that he is going to need us a little more frequently moving forward and he wants us to assure him that everyone is on the same page." Francine spoke as Davina got up to pour herself another drink.

"And he has entrusted you two with that responsibility?" He said sarcastically, sipping the bourbon.

"General, sir," There was still a feeling of deference since both women were in military uniforms, "You've no idea what we've been entrusted with. Our responsibilities are without parallel at this point."

Davina clinked some ice cubes into her glass, and then noisily gurgled a couple of fingers of bourbon into her glass as well. When she came around the bar, behind the general, her hands were empty, but she was reaching into her back pocket.

Francine saw her friend coming up behind the General and figured that it was time. "General Scott, you and I have had some fun on this project and managed to get some work done in the meantime. But I'm afraid that we're going to have to get serious for just a moment."

Scott looked at her sternly. "Listen, I told you before..."

In a flash Davina had slipped the dark plastic bag over his head as Francine moved forward and shoved the auto-injector into his upper thigh. She tossed it onto the table and then jumped onto his lap to help secure his hands until he quit struggling. When the fight had left him, Davina pulled the bag off his head. "General! Can you hear me?"

The sodium-thiopental concoction was working its way through his system. The General offered a frown and then licked his lips. "Yes."

"Why did you have us kill all those people?" Francine whispered.

There was a moment when they were not sure if the drug would work or not. Then, "They had to. They had to go. They were on to Niburu."

The women looked at each other. "They were on to who? Who is Niburu?"

"It's the ninth planet. Planet X. The one that's coming back."

"Back from where?"

"From out there, somewhere. It's been on an orbit for fifteen thousand years. It's the Anunnaki. They are coming back."

"The Annu what?" Francine asked, genuinely confused.

"The Anunnaki. They are the race of extra-terrestrial beings that colonized earth a half million years ago. They're coming back for the rest of their gold so that they can purify their atmosphere."

"Gold? What are you talking about?" Davina jumped in before Francine could wave her off.

"They created man. He was used to help them mine gold. Their atmosphere ran out of certain minerals that they needed to protect their climate. Gold. They tried to mine it on Mars for a few years, but they depleted the source. Then they came here and found it in abundance. They created mankind to help them mine it and then they took it back with them."

Francine looked at Davina. "How much of that shit did you give him?"

Davina shrugged. "Whatever was in the auto-injector."

"He's fucking fried. What the hell is a Niburu, and what's this shit about us giving gold to aliens for their atmosphere?"

Scott licked his lips again. "It's a large planet that orbits almost out to the Oort cloud. It's about nine times the size of Earth, but never gets closer to the Sun than Neptune's orbit. They have an advanced, complex atmosphere that allows them to trap heat and light. But they needed gold. Eisenhower arranged to give them some out of Fort Knox, back in the nineteen fifties. In exchange, they gave us certain technologies to work on. They helped us along with ideas, that our own scientists later developed. The agreement for when they returned, was to provide them more gold in exchange for more technology."

"Eisenhower? President Eisenhower?"

"Yes."

"How is that possible? How could Ike have done that without it leaking out to the press?"

"It was a different era. People trusted the government. Most people, anyway."

"He had to have had help. Who else knew about this arrangement?"

"The MJ-12 group. Majestic Twelve. The scientists that Truman assembled to deal with the alien artifacts we recovered at Roswell."

"Roswell? The flying saucer story? That really happened?"

General Scott nodded. "Yes, of course."

"And everyone kept that quiet?"

"Everyone except for Forrestal."

"Who?"

"Secretary of Defense James Forrestal. He wanted to go public, so they had him committed to the psych ward at Bethesda. Then his brother pressured the Navy to get him out of there, but they could not allow that. They made the decision to stage his suicide. They threw him out a window."

Francine leaned closer to his ear. "What's your end? What did you expect to get out of this? Some of the gold?"

"More." He said reluctantly.

"More than gold? What?" Francine pressed.

"The one who maintains contact with their representatives, the Annunaki's representatives, becomes Earth's representative. I would be..." He was starting to doze off. "I would be the leader."

"The leader of what?" Francine raised her voice.

"Of Earth."

CHAPTER 17

What began as a preliminary reconnaissance quickly evolved into a spontaneous information collection exercise. During the twelve-hour drive towards Washington, Paul had been able to update Karlsson with some useful intelligence including General Scott's home address, and the fact that he had left work early the day before.

Karlsson found a nice hotel and after a couple of hours of sleep and a hot shower, was ready to pay a visit to the General who had been awarded public-enemy-number-one status with their agency. The FBI was also looking deeply, but quietly, into the General's business dealings to determine how an individual making seventeen thousand dollars a month in pay and benefits, could spend more than twenty-five and still be able to throw money into a 401K. Aside from two lavish residences, he had a modest car collection that included a Mercedes, Ferrari and Lamborghini licensed in Virginia, and another Mercedes and a Bentley, licensed in Florida. And, as near as they could tell, a wife who was unemployed, descended from poverty, but who very much enjoyed country club living.

Karlsson had plugged the General's address into the GPS on his phone and was running that through the *carplay* system on his dash but was still concerned that he might miss the driveway. The General's property and his two closest neighbors' lots were actually a bit more secluded, near the shoreline, than the condos and houses that had sprouted up around them in the preceding ten years. The General's neighbors enjoyed three-acre lots, while the newcomers, closer to the highway, were on postage stamps.

He needn't have worried. It was immediately apparent which

house belonged to the General. It was the one with the TV camera trucks blocking the approach to the driveway, concealing the yellow crime scene tape that had been strung across the front of the property by the police.

Karlsson drove on down the street and found a place to park. He had earned a living as a photographer for a while, in between stints of government service, and with that came opportunities to work as a stringer for a couple of magazines. Thus, he felt comfortable walking back with his notepad, and blending into the crews that were waiting for snippets of information from the police leadership at the scene. Usually, on the local news scene, everyone knew everyone and so outsiders might find the groups somewhat cliquish. On the other hand, someone from out of town who just happened upon a story and was no threat to anyone else might have an easier time integrating into the mix of personalities and agendas.

Karlsson knew better than to approach the talent, the pretty people who stood in front of the camera. At this level, they were all working to get out of affiliate stations and into a network spot somewhere. They were so fixated on their own careers that they usually could not see past the camera at the lives they often disrupted with their intrusive plotting and manipulation. As long as they got their air. Karlsson spotted a camera operator, leaning against one of the trucks, bearded, sandaled, and quietly smoking a cigarette, away from the others. He nodded when the young man looked up.

"Hey!"

"Hey." The operator replied.

Karlsson played a gamble. "This is gonna suck. I came all the way out here from Santa Fe to interview this guy about the Space Force base they want to put just outside of town. It looks like I mighta missed my chance!"

He laughed. "I think so. You're a day late...at least a few hours."

"So? Somebody whacked him, or what?" Karlsson asked.

"No. Nothing like that. The old guy was drinking out in the middle of the bay, and fell in. They found a mostly empty bottle of bourbon in the boat, and they found him snagged on a rock along the shoreline. They didn't find a suicide note, so I think they're just going through the motions."

Karlsson looked at the cruiser parked across the driveway with the liberal amount of crime scene tape surrounding the property line. "But all the cops! Geez! Don't you think something's up to have this kind of a presence?"

"Not out here. This is Washington. The guy was some general in the Pentagon. He was some heavy hitter with the Space Force... as if that's a thing. The cops all treat generals like they're some kind of royalty. I guarantee you, there'll be a dozen people drown in the Chesapeake this month and none of them will get a second look. Sometimes they have two a day, and if they're not next to each other, no one cares."

"How'd they find him?" Karlsson asked innocently.

He took a drag of his cigarette. "Fishermen called in that they found a human body hung up on rocks near the shoreline a little south of here, and the marine patrol found a wooden flat-bottom boat floating in Belmont Bay. They plucked him out of the water and figured out who he was."

"Was he in uniform?"

"Naw...jeans and a t-shirt. And, of course, the bourbon."

"Wow. Awful! How long has everyone been here?"

"Since around eight thirty this morning. The housekeeper said he wasn't in his bed last night and that he was supposed to trade cell phones with her, or something like that. She called the police; they called the fire department and we've been here as long as they have. There's supposed to be another press conference in a half hour. We're all waiting for that, and then I think everyone will break it down and head back to the barn."

Karlsson was in the process of thanking the young man for his time and patience when he noticed two men in suits coming out of the house next door. If a hundred yards away could be considered next door. "Local cops?" He asked.

"Yeah. Detectives. I've seen them around before on other scenes."

"Thanks!"

Karlsson waited for them to get back to the General's property before making his move. He wandered over, notebook in hand and knocked on the door. A woman in her early forties answered. "Yes."

"Sorry to trouble you again, Ma'am, but they need Captain Hardy back at the other house."

"Who?"

"Captain Hardy...he's running the investigation. They said he was over here."

She frowned. "No, uh, I...I don't think so. There were some officers here, but they just left. I didn't catch their names."

"Oh. Sorry for the trouble. Did they ask about the car that was there in the afternoon?" Karlsson was guessing, but thought that he had nothing to lose, and it would at least open the door for conversation.

"The black Civic? That's Luisa's, the General's housekeeper. Yeah, she left about four. Don't know about the other car."

"The other car?" Karlsson asked, as if an afterthought.

"They came in about three thirty, maybe three forty-five. Two females, but I couldn't tell if they were officers or not."

"Police officers?"

"No, Army. I couldn't tell from this distance if they were enlisted or officers. They were in their uniforms."

"Oh. What time did they leave?" Karlsson's gamble was paying off.

"No idea. My husband and I went out to dinner last night. We didn't get back till after nine and by then, the car was gone."

"What kind of car?"

"You know, I couldn't tell you. It was white or light beige...a small four-door...maybe Japanese...or Korean...sorry."

"No worries, Ma'am. Thank you for your time!"

When he was back in his car, he dialed the latest number Paul had provided. "I'm afraid we won't get the opportunity to talk with the General. They fished him out of the Potomac this morning. Apparently he was having a cocktail last night on his nine-foot rowboat and fell in. Police have the boat, the bourbon, and the body and there's a media circus in front of his house."

"Given the surrounding circumstances, I think it's fair to suspect that he didn't just go rowing in the middle of the Bay for the exercise." Paul said calmly.

"No sir. As a matter of fact, I can't forget how William Colby bought it when he was head of CIA. Not far from here on the other shore of the bay in the Wicomico River, in April of ninety-six, if my memory is correct. Colby's canoe was found on a sandbar one Sunday a quarter mile from his home. They found his body a few days later, not far away, face down in the swamp. The instance before that was in September 1978, a fellow named John Paisley, who was a former Deputy Director, was sailing his sloop about fifteen miles from where Colby was found. He'd retired four years earlier, but supposedly weighted himself down with a couple of dive belts and then shot himself in the head. The coroner couldn't tell if it was murder or suicide."

"And your point?" Paul asked.

"My point is that the neighbor saw two females get out of an unmarked car yesterday afternoon, at about the time his access badge shows him checking out of the Pentagon. I'm not an investigator, but if I was, I would take pictures of Foxwell and Dantonio over to that neighbor to see if she recognized them. This certainly looks like their handy work, and it might be worth a favor with your FBI friends."

LTC Darren Baranowski was in his quarters at Fort Shafter, enjoying his first cup of coffee of the day. He was gradually recovering from the whirlwind trip he had just made that took him almost pole-to-pole in less than a week. When his phone rang and he saw the 703-area code, he wanted to let it go to voice mail. It was not a number he recognized, and he certainly had no patience with telemarketers, either legitimate or otherwise. But for some reason, he accepted the call. "Hello?"

"Am I speaking with Lieutenant Colonel Darren Baranowski?"

"It depends. Who gave you my number?" The question was a quick way to deduce if the person on the other end was actually human, or a bot programmed with artificial intelligence.

Peter Newell casually replied, "Things will not calm down."

Baranowski was taken aback but responded in kind. "They will in fact, calm up."

"My name is Dr. Peter Newell. It is with regret that I inform you of the loss of your associate, Lieutenant General Nelson Scott. Apparently he was boating near his home yesterday and suffered an accident. His body was recovered nearby, earlier this morning. I wanted to let you know that General Scott's position as leader of my project, will not be backfilled. There is not sufficient time to recruit a suitable replacement so you will now be reporting directly to me."

Baranowski was silent for a moment, perhaps out of respect to his friend, but also to mentally process what was happening. He long suspected that Scott had not been the overall project leader, only that he had been the key executive overtly making decisions. He would certainly have to use his resources to find out who this Newell character was, but in the interim, he accepted what he had just been told. "I see. The General will be missed by many. What can I do for you moving forward?"

Ten minutes later, Marco Pozos received a similar message. Unlike Baranowski though, he was new to the process of intelligence operations and had absolutely no network or experience with which to gauge what was happening. "I'm sorry sir. I only met the General once when I was coming through training. What changes should I be aware of?"

"Your mission has not changed. Only your reporting relationship. You can remove General Scott's contact information and replace it with mine."

"What about Jean Luc and Margarita?"

Newell replied quickly, "Ignore them. Focus on the perturbation and just be the first one to find it. There's little to be gained by letting the opposition know that we are on to them."

The truth was that Scott had never shared that level of detail with Newell. Thus, Peter Newell did not have any idea who those people were.

━━━━━━━●(()●━━━━━━━

As soon as they had driven away from the area the night before, Francine Dantonio had let her client know that they had successfully completed their mission. As opposed to any type of congratulatory remarks or indications of appreciation, Newell had only texted, "COMPLETE WISCONSIN ASSIGNMENT IMMEDIATELY".

After a brief discussion with her partner, Francine decided that she needed to stay close to Newell now that he appeared to be the real heir-apparent; the next in line for being king of the world. And so, it made sense to get Davina to Pleasant Prairie as soon as possible, to take care of the target identified as Matthias Karlsson. They had been given a physical description of him, and a photograph taken five years earlier at some community college in the Southwest. They would have made their move earlier, but the target had shown up at the property with another man and a woman. This target was different. He was not a part of the Space Force, or of the late General Scott's network in any way. Scott had simply been told by Newell to take him out without explanation. Thus, Davina was on a chartered flight out of Manassas by eleven that night and two hours later was driving the streets of Pleasant Prairie.

After discussing the uniqueness of the location with Francine, and driving past the house twice herself, she realized that surveillance was going to be problematic and that she first needed to find out if her target was even in the residence. Once she ascertained that, then she could move to the operational phase and decide best how to complete her assignment. The pretext came to her suddenly while she was having breakfast in a diner up the street. After she had paid her tab she was walking out and saw the cork board near the entrance with a variety of business cards tacked up. Insurance agents, plumbers, electricians, professional resume writers. She looked at them all and then pulled three off belonging to Polly Weaver of Prairie Partners Realty. That would give her the justification she needed to be knocking on doors in the area.

She had rented a van that seemed appropriate to a soccer-mom-real estate agent's role and drove down the driveway like she had every right to. Stan Marchand was already up and walking towards the door when he heard the driveway alarm chime.

"May I help you?" He said with his trademark smile.

Davina handed him one of Polly's business cards. "Good afternoon! I'm working in the neighborhood and just wanted to stop in and tell you that I thought this is such a beautiful home. If you would be interested in selling, I'm sure I could find a client who would pay top dollar."

"Thanks, but no. We're very happy here right now. However, if we change our mind, we'll be sure to let you know." With that Stan gently closed the door before she could finish asking her next question. He was somewhat impressed with himself, and still smiling, he flipped through the photos in his phone that he had received from Paul after the FBI raids. He stopped with a grin when he found the one he wanted. He hit the forward icon and sent the picture to Paul, "ITS DAVINA FOXWELL FOR SURE...SENDING YOU SCREEN CAPTURES FROM OUR VIDEO SYSTEM."

Davina returned to her van. She had hoped that she could talk her way inside for a tour of the house, but regardless, she recognized that the man who answered the door was nowhere close to being the six-foot-four guy she was looking for.

However, unbeknownst to both Davina Foxwell and Stan Marchand, DCI Special Agent Tina Cowels had been parked in a surveillance van down the street, satisfying her curiosity about the house and its occupants, since learning from a friend in the Intelligence Unit at the Milwaukee Police Department, that the house was confidentially owned by the US Secret Service. She did not know what she had, but her instincts told her not to let the lead in her first double murder case go to waste.

As she saw Davina's soccer van drive out of the property, the DCI agent radioed ahead to have a couple of marked police cruisers begin flanking her, before asking her partner pull out behind and start following her. But, Davina, having been well trained herself, almost immediately noticed the van enter the roadway and begin keeping pace behind her. Remembering her surveillance recognition training from years before, she made a few turns up and down side streets to confirm her suspicions, but by then the police cruisers were on top of her. Suddenly realizing that the target's house must have been under surveillance, she made the decision to pull over and attempt bluff her way through the traffic stop. She was angry with herself for not having noticed the van on her previous forays, but the rules and the plan had now changed.

One of the police cruisers cut in front of her at an angle and forced her to stop, while the other car came up close behind her and pulled in at a reverse angle to allow the driver to shoot over the left front corner of the car if necessary. It was a tactical stop. She rolled her window down about four inches and then placed both of her hands on the steering wheel as she watched the van ease to a stop behind the cruiser in the rear. She studied the approach of the female detective who exited the passenger side of the van and moved steadily up along on Davina's driver's side. The detective's right arm and hand were mostly concealed from view, but it looked like she had her firearm out with the slide pressed along the outside of her right thigh.

"Good afternoon, Ma'am. May I see your driver's license and proof of insurance?"

Davina was still considering her options but offered the appearance of cordiality. "Certainly, but may I ask what I did?"

"Your license plates are expired, and when we ran them in the system they came back as being on a stolen vehicle."

Davina was momentarily confused. "It's a rental...there must be some mistake."

"No mistake, Ma'am. Please step out of the vehicle." Cowel's voice was distinct and slightly louder than before.

"Listen, officer. I am on official US Government business. I can provide..."

"Ma'am!" Cowel's voice was suddenly loud and overpowering. "Please step out of the vehicle. Now!"

Davina looked around and evaluated each option. There were two uniformed officers, both wearing bulletproof vests. The plain-clothes officer asking the questions was probably wearing one as well. Using her rearview mirror, she looked at the van behind the cruiser and saw the driver standing behind the open door. Four people with body armor, at least two with their guns drawn and at the *low-ready* position. If she complied and surrendered now, she could refuse to answer questions and contact someone in Washington to come bail her out. If she tried to shoot it out, the odds were against her, and even if she was victorious, it would only buy her minutes. With the curb on her right and police cars to the front and rear, driving off was probably not an option.

"All right. I'm getting out." She released her seat belt and reached for the door handle.

⸺◈⸺

Matt Karlsson savored the Bulleit Old Fashioned, which Wally had created using the energy and flair of a true artisan, impeccably slicing oranges and spearing cherries as if each action was a masterpiece of motion. He nodded his approval. "This is good! Your own recipe?"

"Absolutely!" The tall, dark bartender replied. "I make my own simple syrup and use fresh oranges to flavor it."

The FISA warrants had gotten FBI investigators access to the phone records of recently deceased senior members of the Space Force. Namely, the late Lieutenant General Nelson Scott, and the even later Lieutenant Colonel Jonathan Babic. Even though the two men had never socialized with each other, agents found it interesting that GPS data from their cell phones indicated that prior to their respective demises both men seemed to enjoy late-night rendezvouses at a Georgetown establishment known as the Cardigan on Q Street. As did a number of Senators, Congressmembers, and other high-ranking government officials. Even further intriguing was its ownership; a private corporation that was reasonably well shrouded from the public eye by a number of legal filings.

With time on his hands, that alone gave Karlsson enough reason to have a drink there. But when Paul passed along the results of Neri's latest viewing, something featuring a large Q, he felt that it was as good a place as any to sniff around. "This is fantastic." Karlsson looked around the bar and restaurant. It was early, and a Tuesday, so he had not expected the venue to be standing room only. Behind the bar on the right were some photographs of men in uniform. "Ex-Army?" Karlsson asked.

Wally smiled and rolled up his right sleeve to display the tattoo of his unit's famed logo. "Hundred and first, Air Assault. I was a Screamin' Eagle! You?"

Karlsson lifted his glass, "Thanks for your service. Tenth Mountain, retired."

Wally leaned over and they shook hands. "Glad to have you with us." He looked at the photos and pulled the one down that had been closest. "This is me and a couple friends...and my younger brother Rafael. He joined our unit a year after me and then went spook."

"Spook?" Karlsson smiled.

"Yeah. CIA. He did that for a while and then moved south to do boat charters for the rich."

Karlsson took a more intense look at some of the trinkets and memories behind the bar and then saw the blue circular cloth path with the name of the familiar-looking dive site. "You dove the Blue Hole? Belize?"

"Yeah, with Rafael. We were down there on vacation, and he got hooked on the place. We both chipped in on a boat, and I came home to be the silent partner, and he stayed."

"Oh!" Karlsson grinned, "So when you said he went *south*, he really went south. I hear it's nice there. Do you get back often?"

"Not so much. Rafael sold the boat and moved back last spring, but he still gets down there a couple times a year. Matter of fact, he just got back from there."

"I've always thought about diving there, but just never got the chance."

"He'll sure talk you into it. He's supposed to be in tonight to pick up some mail. If you're still here, he'll tell you whatever you want to know."

Karlsson had finished his first Old Fashioned and was watching Wally make the second when the younger Hispanic male took the seat next to his. The bartender looked over his shoulder with a big smile. Hey Bro! You made it!"

The two men made small talk before Wally introduced them. "This is Matt, ex Tenth Mountain troop. Matt, this is my brother Rafael."

Karlsson and Rafael shook hands as Wally put the finishing touches on his Old Fashioned. As he sat it down on the cocktail napkin, he looked at his brother. "Matt was asking about diving the Blue Hole and I told him that you're the resident expert."

Rafael was caught off guard, but quickly answered. "Yeah, I ran charters out of the mainland for a year and took a lot of divers to the Hole. You've never been?"

Karlsson shook his head. "Huh uh. I've done some reefs and a few shallow wrecks, but I'm a little uneasy in places where I can't see the bottom. Also, I hear that it's a breeding ground for sharks."

He laughed. "Yeah. There are lots of nurse and reef sharks, some blacktips, well, and the occasional hammerhead. Usually though, they'll keep away from you. At least during the day."

He looked at Wally, "Just a beer tonight. Thanks!"

Wally grabbed a glass and filled it up, pausing to allow some of the foam to dissipate. He sat the glass on the bar and then reached underneath to grab a small stack of mail. "Nothing much. It looks like mostly bills and advertisements."

"Gracias Wilfredo!"

"De nada, hermano!"

"Wilfredo?"

The amiable bartender answered with a wink, "Wally is easier for the Anglo's to remember!"

Karlsson grinned and without appearing nosey, casually glanced over as the young man flipped through the envelopes. In the center of the stack was one that had his name, but no return address or postage stamp. He quickly folded it and slid it into his pocket. Karlsson lifted his Old Fashioned and smiled, "Another excellent composition."

"Thank you." Wally answered respectfully. "Two years of chemistry at William & Mary. I was going to try to be a scientist until the Gulf War started, and then decided to enlist. When I got out, the only chemistry that seemed to excite me was what I do now." He laughed. "Rafael followed in my footsteps, and got further into the program, but eventually enlisted as well."

Karlsson was thoughtful, "You went from almost-chemist to boat charter skipper?"

"Not directly." Rafael sipped his beer. "I had a stop with the government first and then got fed up with the politics. Chartering just seemed like a more beneficial long-term goal."

"You ever miss it?" Karlsson asked matter-of-factly.

Rafael shrugged. "Sometimes, but not often! If I miss it too much, there's always contract work available for anyone that still has a clearance."

Karlsson nodded. "Yeah, so I hear. My trouble is that I'm too damn old and I've gotten used to being retired. And I'm pretty sure my clearance expired twenty years ago."

"You're never too old. And, if you have an interest, I could have someone give you a call to see what kind of work is available." He took another sip of his beer. "What did you do in the Tenth Mountain?"

Karlsson shrugged. "Climbed mountains and killed perfect strangers."

"Nobody's perfect." Wally interjected with a smile.

⎯⎯⎯)(◉)(⎯⎯⎯

Stan and Nerissa had been in the family room of the spacious beach home, watching the news and going over her remote viewing notes for the day when the driveway chime sounded again. Marchand gestured for her to remain seated as he went to the door. Now that he had identified Davina Foxwell, he was going to be more hyper-alert for trouble than he had been in the past week. He stuck the Glock in his pants in the small of his back and pulled the t-shirt over to conceal it. He looked through the peephole in the door first and then frowned briefly before forcing himself to display his best smile. "Special Agent Cowels! Welcome back!"

She dispensed with the pleasantries and looked past him into the house. "Sorry to trouble you again, but I wonder if I could ask you about the visitor you just had."

"The visitor?" Stan feigned surprise as he suddenly realized that she had been watching the house. "The realtor?"

"Excuse me?" Cowels looked surprised. "Realtor?"

"Yes. The lady said she was a realtor and she wanted to know if we would consider selling our home."

"Uh huh." Cowels was not impressed. "Mr. Gabel, we've taken her into custody for driving on expired license plates. Even though she doesn't have any ID, she told us that she was some sort of federal officer. And I thought, that since you're staying in a house owned by the Secret Service, that maybe you'd want to cooperate and tell me what the fuck is going on."

There was an awkward silence before Marchand replied. "Possibly. Would you give me a moment to check with my supervisor?" He smiled sincerely as he closed the door. He dialed Paul's new number, the number that changed every day now since communications were not to be trusted.

"Yes." Paul said from somewhere near the beltway.

"Sorry to bother you, sir, but there's been a recent development that I think you need to be made aware of."

Marchand detailed the recent visits of Davina Foxwell and Special Agent Cowels and then asked, "I think we can learn something from Foxwell before she lawyers-up. But we'll need to come clean with Cowels. At least partially."

It seemed as though he had anticipated such an eventuality. "I'll send you the contact info for an FBI Supervisory Special Agent that can provide verification of your status. Once Cowels believes us to all be on the same side, then you can ask to interview Ms. Foxwell."

Marchand nodded absentmindedly at the phone, "Yeah, okay. What have we got to lose?"

He opened the door. Cowels had not moved. "Well, Special Agent Cowels, I have great news. May I have your email address please? My boss would like to send you the contact information for an FBI Supervisor in Washington who might be able to explain some of this. The downside is that you may be required to sign an SF-312, a Non-Disclosure Agreement."

Cowels looked at him for a moment and then acquiesced. "Here. It's on the card I gave you yesterday. But since you've misplaced that one, I'll give you another."

Marchand forwarded Paul's text, which had the phone and email of the FBI Agent who had been leading the tactical team that had rescued Lenny Hart and his wife. It took a moment before she saw it come across her phone and then she nodded and walked into the front yard of the house to make the call. He studied her body language and determined that she must have gotten through to the agent as planned because there were some non-verbal signals of tension and frustration apparent in her mannerisms. When she finished with the FBI, she disconnected and then made another call, most likely to her supervisor, to explain what kind of deal was being proposed.

At the conclusion of her second call, she holstered her phone and then stood hands-on-hips, shaking her head for a moment before returning to the front porch. "I'm told that in exchange for allowing you to question Ms. Foxwell, that you will help me clear two suspicious deaths?"

"I think I can help." It was non-committal, but it was the best he could do.

"Put your shoes on and come with me." She turned and walked to her car.

"You are distracted." Margarita observed. "You have been distant all day."

"What?" Marco looked up from his dinner. She had prepared an excellent Sea Bass with an Asian dill sauce, but he hardly touched it. He was deep in thought.

"What are you thinking about? Is everything okay?"

He had limited experience in espionage. And only slightly more experience with women. He was in love with her, and he believed she was honestly in love with him. How could he be so wrong about something like that? She was right; he had been distracted, ever since getting the call from Newell. The trip from Baranowski seemed sudden, and not well thought out. And now this.

"Are you getting what you want out of us? Out of our relationship?" He asked, looking into her eyes.

She looked surprised. "What do you mean?"

He pushed his plate aside. "I love you. You have said that you love me as well."

"Yes, of course." She reached for his hand, and he pulled back slightly.

"I need to know if this is real, or...or something else?"

"Something else? Have you lost your mind?" Genuine concern evident on her face.

"Perhaps. I have been under some stress, and I need to know where we stand. Really." Marco was ready to risk his brief career to push for the truth.

"How can you ask that? I have always been honest with you." The edge shown through in her voice. "You think I have been with someone else? Another man?"

He shook his head. He knew he was venturing further out on a limb that he ever had in his life. There was much at stake at VRO. He was on the playing field of a global game that would not tolerate failure of any kind. If she was someone's asset and he confronted her, that could very well end the operation. "This morning when you were in the shower, you left your laptop open to your Diario. You are keeping files on us. You were asking questions about Jean Luc. Who are you working for besides AURA?"

She closed her eyes. On one hand, she knew it had been wrong of him to read her private notes. But on the other hand, she knew it had been wrong of her to be studying him and keeping a running journal of their work without his knowledge. She went to her purse and removed the letter. It was from a well-known publishing house that specialized in non-fiction and academic work.

Marco read the top line, "It is with the warmest congratulations that we write to inform you that the committee has agreed to publish your book tentatively titled, *Finding the Ninth Planet*." He looked at her. "What is this?"

"I haven't told anyone yet. Certainly, I cannot tell AURA...I would lose my job. I have been working on a book about the VRO and how it discovered the Ninth Planet."

Pozos looked at the letterhead again and then back at Margarita. "You're writing a book?"

She nodded her head, her eyes down in embarrassment. "I was going to tell you, but I did not find out until this week that the publishers had approved my outline and asked for an update on my manuscript." She took a sip of her wine. "Believe me, I wanted it to be a testament to the work that you and the others had done to get the observatory up and online. I am so proud of you...so happy to be in love with you. If you look at the entire outline you will see that everything was done with respect. Even the publisher is well-respected in the academic community. They are endorsed by the National Science Foundation themselves."

———◦《◦》◦———

Peter Newell kept a luxury apartment at The Acadia at Metropolitan Park in Arlington for those evenings when he had an early flight out of Reagan National or was too tired to make the journey back to Caddington, his 250-acre horse farm near Catlett, Virginia. So named after Caddington Meadows, a rolling estate in Bedfordshire, England, that had been owned by a family member until 1968 when it was destroyed by fire and subsequently sold to a developer. The magnificent estate off Dumfries Road was more than an hour away during regular traffic, and on days when traffic was miserable, it could take twice as long.

The estate property consisted of an impeccably outfitted compound, perfect for secluded, secure living or posh entertainment if Newell was feeling up to it. It was surrounded by lush green fields and woodlands with manicured trails for hiking or horseback riding. The main house itself was over seven thousand square feet, with an adjacent brick carriage house, which had been converted to an environmentally stable six-car garage that had an executive office on the second level. A few hundred yards away, there was a two-bedroom guest house, and naturally, there were equipment barns, two fountains, and a covered bridge that reached over the small creek that ran between the main highway and the house.

On the other hand, the Arlington apartment suited him often during the week, even though it was only slightly larger than seven hundred square feet. It gave him privacy and proximity to the airport and his office, and since several congressmen kept apartments there, the staff was quite used to dealing with Prima Donnas of his stature. The problem was that The Acadia was listed in his personnel profile and a significant number of bios throughout the professional community as being his permanent address. He had not wanted to call attention to Caddington, or the means by which he acquired it, so as a result, he was able to save it for use as a personal hideaway.

When the FBI Agent who visited him that day explained that they had found information in General Scott's papers to indicate that he had retained someone to come after Newell, the Deputy Director grew concerned enough to heed their advice and spend a couple of days away from the city at his country estate. At least until the Bureau could piece it all together and determine if there existed a credible threat. They offered to send an agent along with him to provide security, but he declined. He had his own security and did not want the FBI sniffing around his property this close to the conclusion of the project.

He made a quick call to his rising star. "I need you and some of your team at my country estate for a couple of days. The FBI was in today and said that General Scott had not only left some papers that implicated me in nefarious activity, but also suggested he had taken steps to assassinate me."

Francine was eager to remain as close as possible to her new meal ticket but was growing concerned at her own security as she had lost two of her men to the FBI during the attempt on Lenny Hart's wife, and of course poor Jerry, who was shot to pieces in the Cleveland hotel room. Dale Braun had suddenly lost interest and wanted to move on, but he might do in a pinch. Now Davina was suspiciously overdue in reporting on her activity in Wisconsin. But there was always Rafael. "No problem, sir. We'll head that way in a half hour."

Just back from the sabotage case in Belize, rather than kill him as Scott had requested, she erred on the side of sanity and told Rafael to get away from there as soon as possible. He was, after all, qualified help and she could not afford to lose more of her people than events were already claiming. She sent him a text, "LOCATION AND AVAILABILITY?"

A moment later, he responded, "CARDIGAN AND REASONABLY TACTICAL".

She was walking as she texted, and almost fell over a chair. "SENDING YOU ADDRESS IN CATLETT. SECURITY DETAIL FOR GRANDFATHER. GRAB KIT AND MEET ME THERE ASAP."

Luckily, Wally was tied up with a customer at the other end of the bar and could not see Karlsson looking at Rafael's phone. The young man hastily signaled his brother and left a twenty-dollar-bill on the counter before grabbing his mail and heading for the door.

A few minutes later Wally made his way back to Karlsson's end of the bar. "One more?"

"No but thank you! It's getting late and I should probably get going. Your brother seemed like a nice guy. Pity he had to light out."

"That's the way he is sometimes. Always in a hurry."

The two men shook hands and Karlsson pushed his barstool in. Outside on the sidewalk, he sent a text to Paul. "THANK THE FBI — THEY'RE HEADED TO THE CATLETT PROPERTY."

CHAPTER 18

Davina Foxwell sat at the small table in the florescent brilliance of the sterile interview room. Clothed in orange scrubs, with the smell of chlorine disinfectant in the air, the bare white concrete block walls were a grim presage of what was to come. Her days of travel on corporate jets and pampered stays in luxury hotels were probably behind her now. She was alone. She had refused her phone call because she knew that whoever she called would connect a dot for someone, somewhere, and it would likely endanger them even more than it would her. With any luck, Francine would realize that something was amiss, but they both knew that the temporary silence was better than leading the enemy to one's home camp.

As she had exited her vehicle, more or less at gunpoint, she had sent one final message to Francine, the single number 5. As with the abort signals used by the team, receipt of a single 5 was an abbreviated way of saying that the operation has been compromised and everyone needed to dump any phones or computers that might have connected them. Thus, whoever forensically examined the phone that the police had seized from her vehicle would find nothing more than a couple of texts and calls to another burn phone. If they got well into the network, they might find that the receiving phone had pinged off multiple towers in the District, Maryland and Virginia, just like five million other phones.

Even though she was handcuffed in front, she could still not relax as they had put her legs in irons to prevent running or kicking. It also prevented her from being able to cross them or shift her weight on the hard, institutional aluminum chairs. Her butt was sore, and she felt filthy. Still, she knew it was all part of the game. She was a graduate of the Army's Level C Survival, Evasion, Resistance and Escape program at Fort Rucker in Alabama and Camp Mackall in North Carolina. Mandatory for pilots and SpecOps personnel, SERE was broken into three sections that prepared soldiers, aviators and contractors to work effectively behind enemy lines. Especially, if captured by a hostile element.

As far as she was concerned, she was already ahead of the game. No one in Wisconsin was going to torture her. She had rights that she could demand whenever she felt the need to demand them. In the meantime though, she had food, a bathroom and reasonably comfortable quarters. They undoubtedly wanted information, and she was the only one who could give them what they wanted, which put her in a bargaining position. Perhaps not as strong a position as she might have preferred, but she still had something to trade.

She had been sitting in the quiet room for almost forty-five minutes before she smiled at the camera that was suspended from the ceiling in the corner. She knew they were watching her. They were looking for body movement, non-verbal cues that she was growing restless and might be more predisposed to talking. This was America. If she had to use the restroom, all she had to do was yell out. If they refused her request, her attorney would simply subpoena the video surveillance records to demonstrate their inhumane and illegal conduct. She knew they were watching, but she did not want to give them what they wanted. They could go fuck themselves.

It was now after one o'clock in the morning and she had become hyper-aware of the sounds of her confinement. She had counted the square ceiling tiles and knew that her room was eight by eight. She sat in the aluminum *suspect* chair and took note of the two other chairs with padded seats and arms on the other side of the table, obviously reserved for the interviewers. She could tell that the seat of her chair was at least two inches lower than the padded seats, designed to make her look or feel shorter than the interrogators. The table was closer to the wall on her side to give her the feeling that she had less space than those on the other side. Yes, it was just a game. She wondered if this type of psychological theatre still worked. She got up and hobbled her way to the other side of the table and sat in one of the padded chairs and used both her feet to kick the other one into the corner.

That was all it took. A minute later, the dark, bald man that she recognized from the beach house came through the door, moved the other padded chair back into the center of the room and sat down.

"Sergeant First Class Davina Foxwell, US Army, retired. Bronze Star with *V* device, Purple Heart with two oakleaf clusters, and the Distinguished Service Cross." Marchand looked at her for a moment before reciting the requirements for the award, which would have appeared on her accompanying citation. "While serving in any capacity with the United States Army, distinguished herself by extraordinary heroism, not justifying the award of a Medal of Honor, while engaged in an action against an enemy of the United States. You must've kicked some fucking ass out there, didn't you?"

She looked at him but remained silent.

He moved his chair a couple of inches closer. "Come on, talk to me for a minute. I was a Marine in Grenada. It wasn't much of a war, but it's all we had. I really appreciate what it took for you to get a DSC. Believe me, they're not going to use your combat experience against you. I'm really curious."

She remained quiet but had not taken her gaze off him.

He shrugged. "Look, I get it. You thought you were working for your country doing all kinds of intrinsically important things. You thought you were a patriot or something, defending the weak, leading the blind, whatever." He paused. "Be honest with yourself. You know you were set up. You and your team have all been set up. You were used by a fucking Washington bureaucrat who wasn't interested in his country, but only in his own rise to power. Not the first time we've seen it. But I have to hand it to him, he really knew how to manipulate; to get people to do things. Just like you. You got people to do things because they thought they were acting on be-half of their country. They were paid by the government, perhaps as contractors, but they were managed by the government, and in some cases even had government-issued credentials."

Stan Marchand got up and walked around behind her chair and pushed it up closer to the table. The metal feet making a screech-ing noise on the tile floor, even though she offered no resistance. "You don't need to push yourself away from us. We're going to ne-gotiate tonight. You and me. I'm not going to read you your rights because this will never go to trial. We're going to come to some sort of agreement that shows how much you love your country, and how your own leaders got you derailed. I'm going to save your ass tonight, and you're going to save ours."

———)((·))(———

Karlsson rolled a bit to his side so that he could retrieve his phone and check the incoming text. "STAND BY – WE MAY HAVE A LIMITED WITHDRAWAL OF SECURITY".

It was from Marchand, and it meant that he felt he was making prog-ress with Davina Foxwell. It was good news as it appeared that Newell had at least one man in front of the house and another in the rear. It would be difficult to take out two different sentries with the rifle. The first shot would alert the entire estate, perhaps most of the county, and drive everyone else into hiding while they waited for the Sheriff to arrive.

He had walked more than a mile to find his spot in the tree line near the top of a gently rolling hill. It was not substantially elevated but gave him a commanding view of most of the estate compound. He had purchased some camouflage mesh material at the gun range during his visit, and while it was not a perfect hide by most accounts, the drapery would offer him substantial cover until daybreak. Unless the security team had a thermal imager, in which case his form would stand out dramatically against the cool backdrop of the woods.

He looked through his range finder and noted that he was two hundred seventy yards from the front door. The side of the house closest to him looked to be about two forty. That was at the end of the house where the main garage was located, and where Newell could be expected to transit if he was coming or going. If one of the security guys was chauffeuring, then they might bring the car around to the front to pick him up, still giving Karlsson a brief window for a shot. Or they would load his ass into a car while it was still in the garage and make a break for the highway, without giving him any kind of shot whatsoever.

The sentry on the front moved around from one corner to the other but was not careful about staying out of the lights. In the low light, at that distance, Karlsson could not be sure, but it looked a lot like his new friend, Rafael. His partner on the back side had much the same routine and was only occasionally visible when he rounded that end of the house. It was three o'clock when he finally got a close enough look at the man on the rear and could see that it was another guy with whom he'd shared a couple of drinks. The military history teacher, Dale Braun.

"What the hell." Karlsson muttered softly. "We warned him."

———————— ‹‹❄›› ————————

Darren Baranowski logged off his laptop and powered down. His research into the illusive Dr. Peter Newell left him with more questions than answers. For one, how did the head of the National Science Foundation emerge as the senior official in charge of a classified project, which was led by the US Space Force? Once that nagging question was answered, the next would be how a three-star general was able to bypass the Chief of Space Force Operations and report directly to a civilian? If that were not the case, then Lieutenant General Nelson Scott's position should have been replaced with his superior or another senior officer of equal rank. Many times, in situations like this, the project was even renamed and reclassified so that there could be no public reference to it later on if something leaked to the media.

It did not take long for the trial lawyer, who had earned his pay in the intelligence field before he ever saw a courtroom, to put it together. The secrecy, the preparations, the cut-outs for communications, all added up to one thing. Newell wasn't working an *op* for the US Government; he was running this for himself. He had built a network and a plan to enrich his own life and then leverage his knowledge to secure something of value from the White House. Maybe NATO or the United Nations. There was no oversight for this. Not from the White House and not from Congress. One scotch-on-the-rocks later, the reality hit him and Baranowski had an epiphany.

Newell used government and academic resources to rush to the front of the line in his search for the illusive ninth planet. He had used his deep knowledge of academic programs around the world to identify the projects that had a specific regionalized search of the cosmos on their list of priorities. He had undoubtedly heard the Sitchin stories of aliens colonizing our planet a half a million years earlier and must have thought he knew how to communicate with them. As far as most people knew, this whole story was all speculation. Even though there were hints of it in the Muslim and Christian texts, even the Mahabharata. The ancient Hindu books. But Newell knew about the Eisenhower deal. He knew about the gold.

Baranowski realized what he had to do. He took one more long taste of the sixteen-year-old single malt and called his brother's cell phone.

"Hey! Is everything okay down there?" His brother was not used to receiving open communications from anyone while on this bleak assignment. Even his brother.

The younger Baranowski recognized that he was taking a chance. "There's been a change in reporting. Scott's dead."

"This is an unsecured line." Tom said quietly as a reminder.

"I know. I need to ask you something and I want to make sure that our friends on the other side of the water understand why we are doing what I want to do."

"Have you been drinking?"

"Of course. From the start of this." He pushed his glass away from him, leaving watery striations on the bamboo table. "The Kuyper Belt is about fifty AU's right now. That means that a radio signal would take about six to seven hours to get there."

"Get where?" Tom was cautiously listening. "Wait. What are you suggesting?"

"I think we've been set up. We've been played. This not a sanctioned project. We've been dumping money and resources into a private operation for General Scott for the past year. It's all a con so that one man could install himself as official ambassador to whoever or whatever is on that planet we're all looking for. He hopes to be earth's official emissary. He's gone completely fucking nuts. The world isn't ready for one-man rule, and that fact alone is going to destroy us even if some alien civilization earnestly wants to work with us."

"We need to send the packet now. We need the Russians to send their packet now as well. I have no idea if the fucking aliens speak English or Russian, or if that autistic kid who produced the musical code, did it in some language that is foreign to all of us. Maybe the autistic kid is an alien. We need to send it now, whether we can see them or not. They're probably out there already and can see us."

"Are you shitting me?" Tom replied.

"No. Send it tonight according to your protocols, and then send the confirmation to Scott."

"But, you said Scott's dead."

"I know. Send it to him anyway, first thing tomorrow. I'll see you soon!"

Baranowski somehow knew that he was on the right track and immediately sent a text to Marco Pozos.

"THINGS HAVE CALMED UP - WALK AWAY NOW".

Baranowski's plan was well intentioned, but it was too late for both the US and the Russians.

Marchand sat close, next to Davina, his legs out in front of him and ankles crossed. His hands were in his lap. He was tired. Probably as exhausted as she had to be, but he would not let it show. He had a job to do, and it all hinged on his ability to persuade her to work with him.

She was finally talking. "So, I give you Newell and his operation, then Francine and I walk?"

"Not totally." He corrected. "You and Francine get to keep the four million that General Scott gave you, but you have to dismantle your network and you have to take the hit for knowing something about the double murder of the two private investigators. And, you know, you'll owe us that one favor."

She looked over the corner of the table. "You want me to say that I was using the PI's to spy on you?"

"Yes. The truth of the matter is that Newell hired some retired FBI type in DC who hired them. Once the surveillance was done, then he would have called you to finish your part of the project. It's not all that complicated, but we want to keep it clean so that Pleasant Prairie's finest can solve their double murder. The retired *Feeb* probably didn't realized that he was being used any more than you did."

"But, if they start checking, they'll see that I wasn't in town when they...uh...shot each other." She commented.

"And that's the beauty of it." Marchand was starting to get giddy. "They can't pin the murder on you because you weren't here. All we need is someone to say they saw it happen. By the time you finish writing your statement, the FBI will be here with a federal warrant to take you off their hands. Your guys that got popped in the attempt on Lenny Hart's wife, are going away. The FBI already has them and there's nothing I can do about that. Jerry's dead and buried, so there's no problem there. You and Francine killed General Scott, but after a review of the evidence, it looked like General Scott was a traitor and a thief and is better off dead, rather than being prosecuted on the evening news. If we tried make a case out of that, the Government would have to be able to demonstrate how a single military officer was able to commandeer an entire satellite network for his own private gain."

"Uh huh." She was still considering her bargaining position.

"Look, Newell is going to have a bad night. If Francine, Rafael and Braun are still there when the shooting starts, you're going to lose them."

"Braun's such a pussy. He really didn't want to do this." She said under her breath.

"They're in or they're out, right now," Marchand handed her the cell phone that the police had confiscated from her car.

"She may not answer. I sent her an abort code." She said, taking the phone.

"I know. But I also know that you have a way of contacting her, even without the burn phone."

—— ((◉)) ——

Karlsson felt along the side of his body for the cell phone, the vibration alone sending an audible shock to his psyche in the cool early morning. "SECURITY WITHDRAWING 0345. ALARM OFF – MAIN COMM LINES DISCONNECTED. HIS CELL PHONE IS ON THE NIGHTSTAND NEXT TO HIS BED. FRONT DOOR WILL BE UNLOCKED".

Karlsson sent back a single "K", for confirmation. It was three forty. Somehow Marchand must have finagled his way into Davina's heart, small as it was, and persuaded her to get Francine to pull the security detail off the sleeping Peter Newell. He was not sure what kind of deal had been put on the table, but whatever it was it saved lives. Maybe even his.

He checked his watch, the black Casio Pathfinder, which had accompanied him on four continents over a period of more than ten years. It was synchronized to the atomic clock in Boulder, Colorado, and could allegedly provide the most accurate time available. It had too many buttons and functions for his personal taste, but it kept damn good time. Thus, when he saw it switch over to 0345 hours, he was not surprised to see the headlights come around the back of the building, and then slow to a stop as Braun and Rafael jumped in.

Francine offered him a parting comment as they quietly drove out of the compound. The driver's window opened about halfway and her left hand emerged with the prominent middle finger pointed in the air in his general direction. Apparently, the deal on the table was not what she would have preferred, but she too saw the futility of combat in this one instance. Newell was going down and she was probably happy that she hadn't been told to do it.

Karlsson quietly rolled over and up onto his knees. He took the camouflage netting and draped it over the rifle, the barrel of which was elevated atop the folding bipod. The fingerprints had been wiped clean on the rifle as well as each round of ammunition, so in the event he didn't make it back up to collect it afterwards, it might be a bit tougher to connect it back to him and the US Government if found by someone else. The nitrile gloves were making his hands sweat, but it was just part of the job.

The truth was that he had kind of grown attached to the ugly piece of steel and wood, but now as he was making his way down the hill towards the house, he could see that there would be little use for a tool intended to hit targets hundreds of yards away. This was going to be close-in work this morning. It wasn't his specialty, but then one accepted the job knowing that there would be disappointments. Dentists didn't get to pick the kind of teeth they drilled, and truck drivers didn't always get the routes they wanted. Sometimes situations just sucked. "Embrace the suck!" He thought to himself as he quietly approached the front door.

He knew from the earlier briefing that there were no pets. Nevertheless, he put his ear to the door to listen for a moment before gently turning the handle and pushing the door open. Inside, the smell of stale cigars still hung in the air. Other than that, there was the smell of new carpeting coming from at least one of the rooms somewhere on the first floor. Even though it was not relevant to his mission, it drew him back to the reality of life. Here was

Newell getting ready to take over the planet, but he still had time to order new carpet.

He had been told that the master bedroom was on the second floor, East end of the house. It would be easy enough to deduce. The stairs were carpeted, and there were enough lamps on the first floor to provide plenty of light.

At the top of the stairs, he paused once more to listen. To smell. To perceive. To feel. The master bedroom door was the only one on the second floor that was closed. There was a good possibility that it was locked as well, but that was the chance he would have to take. As he moved closer, he saw the discarded blue and green autoinjector propped up against the bottom of the door, with the yellow adhesive note attached that read, *He'll be buzzed for about two hours. You're welcome! FD.*

He looked at the label; *DELTA-9/Versed Variant 2.* Karlsson was unfamiliar with the concoction, something that was no-doubt cooked up in a government lab somewhere. The door was not locked. It opened quietly to the luxuriously appointed room, illuminated softly by the lamp on Newell's nightstand. Newell was on his back, propped up on a couple of fluffy pillows, awake but disoriented.

"Come in, come in. Poor yourself a drink." Whatever Francine had given him, the affable guy was fairly chatty. "I hope you have eaten. I'm afraid I haven't much to offer you."

Karlsson opened the drawers on the nightstands but found no weapons. He located Newell's cell phone and moved it to the dresser out of his reach. As an added precaution, he ran his hand under the pillows to make sure there were surprises there either.

Karlsson slid a chair over next to the bed. "That's quite an operation you had, Dr. Newell. I'd be interested in learning more about it."

He offered a sardonic grin, "It is! All paid for by the US taxpayer and carried out under the noses of the very congresses my initiatives either supported or destroyed. It was the most comprehensive intelligence platform ever created. I had people, technology, unlimited funding, all under the perfect cover of education. I was my idea and I saw it to fruition. Father would have been proud." He licked his lips and scratched his nose. "I am curious, how did you get on to us?"

"The FBI tracked the cell phones of some of your players to The Cardigan. Do you mind if I ask how you decided on that place to meet?"

He smiled and yawned, "I own the Cardigan. Well, through a shell corporation. It's one of those places that politicians and power brokers liked to meet. The food and drink were good, and the lighting lends itself to an inviting air of intimacy. The truth is that most of the tables are bugged, there are hidden cameras everywhere, and our wait staff are all highly trained military or intelligence operatives."

Karlsson looked at him. He could not help but feel a sense of wonderment for all the man had accomplished. On the other hand, he was a vile, selfish hedonist who needed to be removed from the system. "Why me? Your team had my name and picture before this event began. What did I do to you that prompted you to arrange for my premature demise?"

He allowed himself a small grin. "Archer Layden."

"The son of the former Vice President?" A chill ran down Karlsson's spine. It was supposed to have been a closely guarded secret. There was no point trying to deny it. "How did you know?"

"Echo Aerospace, the company you were loaned out to, to help track down some counterfeit aviation parts. I'm a member of their board. Layden was shot dead at their training facility, a high-powered rifle shot from a boat in Lake Erie. The timing of the attack combined with your military skills made it an easy guess."

"What was Layden to you?"

"His father and I were roommates at Harvard."

"You roomed with the VP?" Karlsson suddenly understood and had at least found the answer to the question that had been bothering him for several days. "But he lost the election. We uncovered the fraud in the voting systems."

Newell snorted. "You stopped nothing. It wasn't VP Layden's network that was running things. It was mine, and my network remains intact. You will never be able to stop what I have in place."

"Don't be so sure, Doc." Karlsson moved the chair closer to the bed. "You may have a lock on the astronomers and code breakers, but we have something that you don't."

"I doubt that." He was smug but his curiosity got the better of him. "What do you have?"

"Psychics. While your network was busy coming up with ways to communicate with some distant life form through conventional means, we were already speaking with them. Us and the Russians. Probably the Chinese too. What I have learned over the past two weeks is that there are things that I don't understand, but I know that they work. For all your efforts, Doc, all you had to do to talk to them was close your eyes, relax and invite them in. I haven't had any contact personally, but I know some of the people who have. And, from what I hear, those aliens will talk to anyone who wants to talk to them."

He frowned as he tried to force his brain to work through the chemical fog. "What are you talking about?"

"The Tank, The Institute, whatever you want to call them, have been on this full-time for the past week. Lenny Hart, the guy that your team abducted was the first one to find the civilization that had worked on Mars a million years ago, mining gold. Other remote viewers discovered the Eisenhower trade with the gold at Fort Knox. Once they put it together, they started working on cooperation with the Russian team and it did not take long for both sides to make contact. So, even if you had lived, you would not have been in charge of anything."

"I don't believe you." With all of his strength, he pushed himself up on his pillow.

"I didn't believe it either." Karlsson admitted. "But I do know that Francine and Davina have agreed to help us close your network. Every time one of your former myrmidons steps up to take charge of any cooperative effort with visitors from another planet, the ladies will be on standby to shut them down. You lost, Doc."

Karlsson stood and moved the chair back to where he had found it. "Just one other thing, Doc. Are you by any chance left-handed?"

Momentarily confused by the question, he replied with a slight slur, "No, of course not. Why..."

Karlsson stepped forward, shoved the Glock into Newell's right hand and moved the muzzle up in line with his temple before forcing his finger onto the trigger. "Just a small detail. Sleep well."

EPILOGUE

Nerissa and Yasmina stoically listened to the cacophonous noise and sipped their tea in eager anticipation as Hunter warmed up his pipes. It was a familiar tune, originally penned in the late 1800's recalling the flight of Prince Charles Edward Stuart, known then as *Bonnie Prince Charlie*, as he evaded capture after the Battle of Culloden in 1746. Used in numerous television shows and movies in recent years, it was known as *The Skye Boat Song*. It was obvious that Hunter had been practicing as the rhythm of his breathing had improved and the tenor and bass drones were in tune for a change. The legato melody was haunting and inspiring and both mother and grandmother were proud.

"I'm glad to be home." Nerissa said after the impromptu concert. "I hope you didn't worry too much."

"Of course not." Yasmina lied just a little. "I knew you would be fine the second you walked out my door. Of course, it wasn't until they took that two-hundred-fifty-pound linebacker out of here that I was certain that Paul knew you'd be okay. I mean, seriously dear, he didn't fool anyone in those silly nurse scrubs. A stethoscope in one pocket and handcuffs in the other."

Nerissa smiled. "I think they were trying to make him blend in." She said of her mother's temporary bodyguard. "I'm happy you made him feel welcome."

Hunter finished stowing his bagpipes in the case and grinned at them. "What did you think?"

Both women applauded again. "It was sheer perfection!" Nerissa said. "Why don't we load your gear, and I will take everyone to dinner?"

"Best offer I've had all week!" Yasmina said. She reached for her sweater on the back of the chair in the corner of her small living room at *the home*. "He's single, you know."

Nerissa looked at her. "Who's single?"

Yasmina slid one arm in and then the other. "The two-hundred-fifty-pound linebacker."

Neri shook her head. "You never give up." She helped her mom lock up and the three of them walked to Hunter's car together. Halfway to the parking lot she whispered softly, "Mom, you remember Mark Reynolds?"

The name was a jolt from her past. Yasmina had saved the boy's life after an incident at the Institute in California many years earlier, when he was still early in his Marine Corps career. Right after his return from Saigon in 1975, his superiors had recommended him for specialized training with Yasmina and Dr. Kravitz. He had performed well but had become involved in a covert project that had global ramifications and after a near tragic hit-and-run, needed to be hidden. Years later, after a distinguished career in the Marine Corps, he became one of Stan Marchand's golf partners at Gleneagles. "Of course."

"He's in Colorado now." Neri said, remembering that he had been a truly gifted psychic in his own right and had probably saved her life as well.

"Oh?"

"I haven't seen him in several years. Since the…uh…"

"Oh?" Yasmina's mouth turned up in a smile.

"He helped us out on this assignment." They reached the car and she opened her mother's door for her. "The least I can do is buy him dinner, don't you think?"

Yasmina seated herself in the back and reached for her seatbelt with a motherly grin. "I'm surprised it took you so long."

—◈—

Stan Marchand paid the driver and walked up his LimeCoat driveway to his front door and suddenly realized he did not have his keys. As he was about to ring the doorbell the door opened wide to an elated Tricia who had the largest grin he had ever seen. He dropped his suitcase and stepped inside to give her a big hug. After a lengthy kiss and a warm embrace he said, "Wow, what a week! Is that spaghetti I smell?"

"Yeah. I figured you'd be hungry after being out saving the world all that time. You look tired! Do you want to talk about it?" She waited for him to drag his luggage inside and then closed the door behind him.

He sighed. "Not really." He looked into her eyes intently. "I told Paul that I didn't mind doing the occasional view for him, but that I am done with road trips."

"Lot of miles?" She asked as she followed him upstairs.

"Too many. We went from Mexico, back up to Wisconsin, and then finished up near DC. Oh, and Matt Karlsson says to tell you hello."

Karlsson had met his friend Jackie on the same assignment wherein Stan and Tricia had connected. "Matt was on this?"

"Yes." He replied and wondered if that would cause her to grow more concerned. Tricia knew what Matt's military specialty had been. "But everyone is okay, and there's no reason for alarm." He took her in his arms again and began kissing her neck and her ears.

"Stop that! You know what that does to me? I've got spaghetti sauce on the stove." She responded.

Sometime later they sat quietly at the kitchen table enjoying Tricia's special sauce recipe containing just the right amounts of fresh green pepper, onion, and mushrooms. "My mom wants to come for a visit."

He thought for a moment. "Yeah, sure, that's okay." He twirled some of the thin Vermicelli noodles on his fork. "How long is she planning on staying?"

"Just for a few days. Maybe a week. She was thinking about Thanksgiving."

"How much luggage?"

"I don't know. I told her she couldn't bring Dabney."

He recalled the first time he had met Dabney, the tiny French bulldog with bat ears, that he had made fun of. "Good. We don't have a tree for him to hang upside down from. Does she know that we drink, and I play golf a lot?"

"Yes."

"She can stay as long as she wants. Does she want to be here for the wedding?"

"What wedding?" Tricia asked, worried that she'd forgotten about some social event at the club.

"Ours."

She looked at him for a moment to see if he was being sarcastic or was intending the exchange to serve as an official proposal of marriage. "Are you fucking with me?"

"Not at all, young lady! I'm ready, and if you are too, then we should start making some plans."

"But I thought...the...uh...picket fence?"

"I know." He replied. He thought about the lives that he had seen impacted over the previous few days. Lives mis-managed. Lives cut short. He balanced the time of a human life against the generations that would come and go during a fifteen-thousand-year orbit of the sun. "I want you with me and I want us to sail around the sun together. Marry me?"

She moved around the table and sat in his lap. "Of course. Can we get a French Bulldog?"

"No. Our HOA doesn't allow bats."

━━◉━━

Karlsson arrived at the Santa Fe Regional Airport on a United flight via Denver, and was met by Velva in her Blue Ford F-250 crew cab with the white veterinarian box in the bed. The white Caduceus with a *V* superimposed over the staff on the front doors of the cab made him feel that he was home. He was exhausted, as usual, following a major assignment, and often likened the feeling to the adrenaline dump that martial artists experienced in the ring. Adrenaline was a chemical that gave regular humans super-human strength for a few seconds, but at the cost of oxygen and energy. Once the rush was over, they returned to regular human fitness and physiology, with the feeling of being totally drained.

Dr. Capaz handed him his cell phone, which she'd kept charged, and a stack of relevant mail. She knew him well enough to toss the ads and other junk mail.

"I told Jackie you'd been abroad and would be back today. She's coming tomorrow. Says she wants to ride Matilda, the three-year-old chestnut mare that you hardly got to know before taking off to places unknown."

"Do I feel a rebuke coming on?"

"Not from me. It's not my place to tell you how to lead your life. However..."

"Yeah, yeah, yeah. A man my age should start thinking about family responsibilities and understand he's not as young as he used to be."

She glanced at him, keeping one eye on the road. "I'm just busting your chops. You okay?"

"Yeah, I think so."

"You ever going to be able to talk about it?"

Karlsson looked out the window at the dichotomy of a modern city against the backdrop of mountains, unchanged for millennia. "Probably not."

Half an hour later, he was back on his ranch saddling Stoney up for a ride around the adjacent field. They were happy to see each other and spent some quiet moments taking the afternoon air before rejoining Velva and Aaron, who were discussing nothing of significance, over beers on the porch.

In the fading evening light, he opened the newspaper and noticed a small article on page four about the NSF Director committing suicide. The story barely made three paragraphs, with one of those paragraphs focusing on the work of the Foundation. They drank and told stories for two more hours before Aaron wandered off to check the stalls.

"You look peaceful." Velva told him.

"Peaceful? I'm tired." He replied.

"No. I've seen you come back from these things before and you're usually a high-strung basket of nerves. What happened out there? Did you discover yourself? Get closure or something? Find the meaning of life?"

"Naw. Quite the contrary. It's the realization that we are such a tiny component of the universe, and we exist in it for such a short time, cosmologically speaking. The firefly effect, someone called it. Our civilization is like a firefly in the night sky. We blink in for a brief period and then blink out. Sometimes we blink at the same time as other civilizations out there and have that brief instance to strike up a conversation. On the other hand, the light from the stars that we see out there, left their systems hundreds or thousands of years ago and we're just now seeing it. That means that even if we could contact someone from there, their civilization might have died out hundreds of years ago and we won't know it for hundreds of years to come."

Velva raised an eyebrow at him. "Were you on one of those spiritual retreats to Sedona or something?"

Karlsson smiled. "Look at those stars, Velva. Do you think that somewhere out there people are drinking beer on their front porch and watching our silly asses, wondering what we're doing down here?"

"Probably. They would have to have beer if they're that civilized."

As the sun went down in the west, more stars came out in Santa Fe. Karlsson leaned back in his Adirondack chair and took a healthy swig of his beer as he tried to imagine life near each one of them. He thought about a large planet on an inconceivable orbit that would not bring it close enough to earth, to be seen by the naked eye, for another thousand years or so. Right now, it was just something for astronomers to debate. "Maybe one day we'll get there. But it's really good to be home."